ABOUT

Bruce W. Bishop was born and raised in Yarmouth, Nova Scotia, Canada, which is the predominant setting for *Unconventional Daughters*. He received his post-secondary degrees from Saint Mary's University (Halifax) and the Ontario College of Art & Design University (Toronto) and began a freelance writing career in 1997.

His articles and photos have appeared in over 100 print and online publications in Canada, the United States, Great Britain, Australia and Brazil. He was a contributor to several guidebook publishers, including *Fodor's* and *DK Eyewitness Guides*; was principal writer for the *Michelin Green Guide to Atlantic Canada* and authored the *Marco Polo Guide to Muskoka*. He was president of the *Travel Media Association of Canada* between 2000 and 2002.

He now lives in Halifax, Nova Scotia, and is working on a spinoff novel featuring the character of Marc Shehab from *Unconventional Daughters*. The projected publication date is June 2021.

UNCONVENTIONAL DAUGHTERS

by

Bruce W. Bishop

Inspired by a true incident

Published by

Icarus Press Publishing

This is a work of fiction. Names, characters, places, and incidents either are products of the author's imagination or are used fictitiously. Any resemblance to actual persons, living or dead, business establishments, events, or locales is entirely coincidental. Please read the Author's Note for more information.

Unconventional Daughters
Trade Paperback Edition Copyright © 2020 Bruce W. Bishop

Icarus Press Publishing
Fredericton, New Brunswick
Web: www.icaruspress.com
email: info@icaruspress.com

ISBN: 978-1-7774141-1-5 (e-book)
ISBN: 978-1-7774141-2-2 (paperback)

"…'Ah me!' said he, 'what might have been is not what is!'
With which commentary on human life, indicating an experience of it not exclusively his own, he made the best of his way to the end of his journey.

Our Mutual Friend by Charles Dickens, 1864-65

ONE

Bishop Gustav Daniel Björck of the Diocese of Gothenburg sat at his desk in the rectory next door to the Gothenburg Cathedral waiting for his first appointment of the day. His office, which normally smelled musty, had a scent of lemon oil in the air after a thorough dusting and cleaning by the housekeeper.

If there was one part of the job he hated, it was having to process adoptions. He disliked the administration involved, and he knew that some children — through no fault of his own, of course — ended up in circumstances much worse than those they had known.

At the age of 75, he wearied of the daily routine of his spiritual calling. He hoped today might turn out to be one of beneficial closure, and dare he presume, happiness for all involved, including a measure for himself.

He had been briefed that he would be meeting Jacob and Signe Burcharth, a young local couple married the year before, who were hoping to adopt children recently rendered homeless and under the Church's guardianship.

The local orphanage was unfortunately full, and it was up to the Church of Sweden to care for illegitimate or abandoned children. As he looked over the papers of the case spread before him, he reflected on the pitiful circumstances that led to the children being brought to the Cathedral.

The circumstances were horrific.

He heard a gentle tap on the door as the housekeeper ushered in the couple, and she motioned for them to have a seat opposite the Bishop.

As Jacob and Signe settled into the uncomfortable and clunky wooden office chairs, Bishop Björck appraised the couple. The man appeared to be in his early twenties and his wife looked to be about the same age. Where the husband appeared to have a bright countenance, his spouse kept her eyes downcast.

"Reverend Bishop, thank you very much for meeting with us today. My name is Jacob Burcharth, and this is my wife, Signe," Jacob began. The Bishop remained seated; hands clasped before him.

"It is my pleasure, Mr. and Mrs. Burcharth. I understand you are here today to confirm the adoption of the paupers who were recently orphaned due to a terrible occurrence regarding their parents."

"Yes, that's correct, Reverend Bishop," Jacob replied. "My wife and I are planning to emigrate to the United States next year, and we feel that we would like to give the same opportunity to unfortunate local children so they can have a better —", he was stopped in mid-sentence.

"Presumably, you are not able to have children of your own?" inquired the Bishop, looking directly at Signe and expecting an answer from her.

"Umm…that's right," Jacob said. Signe remained motionless and quiet in the seat next to him.

Ignoring Jacob momentarily, Bishop Björck kept his attention on Signe.

"Mrs. Burcharth, the Church of Sweden would not want to separate these children by placing them in different homes. Having more than one child may be considered a formidable task for some women. Do you feel that you can mother them adequately?"

Signe looked up for the first time and addressed the Bishop.

"Yes, Reverend Bishop. With God's will and the help of my hard-working husband, I'm sure we can bring up the children in a safe and loving home," Signe said, and again averted her eyes.

The Bishop sighed. He wished she were a bit more enthused, a bit more maternal in her demeanor, a bit *happy*. He felt she was more resigned to the fact of becoming an immediate parent rather than excited at the prospect.

"Well, all right, then," he concluded. "Since you have the means to support the children, this is not a case of *fattigauktion* — in other words, you are not expecting the Diocese to pay you an amount per month for a year of their care. Am I correct?"

Jacob nodded his assent.

"There are still a considerable number of forms to complete and attend to, and I will also be asking both of you questions separately before the children are released to your care."

Jacob appeared relieved that the first and perhaps biggest hurdle had been cleared.

The Bishop began shuffling the papers before him and read.

"All right, then. We have Martin, age twelve; Elisabet, age five; Collan, age four, and Katarina, the baby, at age three."

Signe looked up, sheer panic crossing her features.

"Oh, no, Reverend Bishop. There were to be the three girls. I, that is, we, did not plan on a fourth child," she said quickly. Turning to her husband, she continued, "Jacob, isn't that right? We had not planned on taking care of four children, surely — ."

Jacob floundered. How could he have missed the fact that there were four children left behind? He looked plaintively at the Bishop.

"I do believe there is a misunderstanding, Reverend Bishop. My wife and I were extremely happy and blessed at the thought of becoming parents to three, but not four, children at the same time. I know that my, uh, our budget does not extend to caring for a fourth child." He paused. "And did you say that the boy is twelve years of age?"

Glancing again at the papers on his desk, the Bishop nodded.

"Yes. There is a seven-year age difference between the boy and his eldest sister."

"Could one not assume that a boy that age might become a very worthy servant, or apprentice, in a decent Gothenburg family, Reverend Bishop?" Jacob asked. "I mean, I was told that a family who bids the lowest amount of money it needs from the parish can be issued a child, especially one who is twelve or older. Surely there are rich Gothenburg families who need extra labor on their estates?"

The Bishop sat back in his chair and smoothed his ample white sideburns. He considered Jacob's query. He had hoped the adoption of all four children would go smoothly, but it was not the first time he had encountered difficulties in the process.

"I must think and pray over this situation," the Diocesan leader said gravely, not conceding to Jacob's correct assumption. "I will notify you when to return for further questioning. Please be aware I am hesitant to take the boy from his siblings, but you do have a valid argument regarding his future welfare. His sisters, though, should be placed with loving adoptive parents as soon as possible."

He stood from behind his desk.

"Thank you for meeting with me, and I will be speaking with you again in the near future."

TWO

Captain Jacob Burcharth – Boston, Massachusetts, Wednesday, June 20, 1883

My dearest parents,

I trust you are both well and healthy since Signe and I left Gothenburg with our precious cargo— the three girls— in what seems to have been a lifetime ago.

On the voyage, Elisabet, Collan and Katarina were perfect angels; adorable at the ages of five, four and three. Having sisters so close in age seems to create a special bond that others may not understand. But I doubt anyone will ever break that bond either.

The sailing across to New York was not as bad as we had anticipated. You know I have had 'sea legs' my whole life, and God spared us any terribly inclement weather which would have made the trip onerous and uncomfortable.

I remember reassuring you that Swedes are very welcome in the United States, and we were! We had no difficulty with immigration authorities upon arrival. Unlike so many Scandinavians who want to go to Minnesota for the free land being offered, I told the officials of my desire to apply for a captain's position and to stay on the eastern coast of this continent.

To that end, we did not stay in New York very long — I believe it was only three days — and then we took the train to Boston where I was told there are many opportunities for trained pilots on the new steamers sailing to Canada.

I am so enormously proud to tell you that I have been offered a position on the S/S Dominion, owned by the Nova Scotia Steamship Company. It is a marvelous vessel that sails between Boston and Yarmouth, Nova Scotia, every Saturday. The crossing is a mere 20 hours and will carry not only cargo, but many visitors from the New England states who are desirous of the cooler temperatures found in

Nova Scotia during the summer months. How delightful that this new country is also a tourist destination!

Signe and the girls are extremely excited about our big adventure, and we will immediately be seeking a place to live in Yarmouth, as the real estate there will be so much more favorably priced than it is in Boston. Signe doesn't mind forsaking city life in Gothenburg for a smaller-town environment. She will begin taking English classes immediately, and I know that the girls will adapt very well to learning a new language.

We have also realized that moving to Canada will offer our family the tale of a lifetime! How many people do you know in Gothenburg who can say they have a son living and working in a country that is younger than the son himself?

I will write again as soon as we are settled in Yarmouth, and I keenly anticipate news from you, as well.

With great affection, I remain,
Your loving son,
Jacob

#

Jacob set his fountain pen on the desk at which he was seated in the lobby of the Parker House Hotel in Boston. He and Signe and the girls were enjoying an overnight stay in the city's largest hotel, and the accommodations were superb.

He finished the letter to his parents. Now would be a good time to have a sherry and a cigar, he thought, before meeting his wife and daughters for dinner in the dining room.

A bartender was on duty in the quiet lobby lounge. Mathieu Robicheau was a chatty young man with a slight French accent. Surprisingly, he was a valuable source of information about Yarmouth. His father, an Acadian woodworker, was living there, and Mathieu had spent a great deal of time in southwestern Nova Scotia.

"I think you and your family will enjoy living in Yarmouth, sir," Mathieu said. "It's quite an up and coming community. The Indians are called Mi' kmaq, and they've been there forever, but the area was settled by Planters from right here in Sandwich, Massachusetts. It was about a hundred years ago that the township of Yarmouth was born."

He noticed Captain Burcharth was listening attentively.

"Where are you from, sir?"

"My family and I are from southern Sweden, young man," Jacob said in his carefully worded English. "I'll be captaining one of the steamers that sails to Yarmouth."

"*Mon Dieu*, that's an impressive job, Captain! You know, my people are French immigrants called Acadians, and we sailed there in the early 1600s *before* the English Planters," Mathieu stated proudly. "We wouldn't pledge allegiance to the French or English crown, so we were expelled — or maybe you say 'deported'? — by the British in 1755. My own family ended up in Louisiana and didn't return until 1767."

Jacob took a puff of his cigar and picked up his glass of sherry, nodding to indicate that Mathieu should continue his story.

Later, in the dining room of the Hotel, Jacob felt re-invigorated by his choice to move his family to Canada after his chat with the bartender, which had almost seemed like a monologue, but a useful one.

He looked with affection at his wife and three daughters. He knew the trip to date had not been easy on Signe, as she much preferred land travel, and now had the added responsibility of three small children.

"Elisabet, stop fidgeting and eat your soup," Signe instructed her eldest daughter. "You see how quiet your baby sister is. You should act more like her."

Elisabet picked up her soupspoon and sullenly sipped more of the vegetable-laden soup.

Katarina, at only two years of age, had only two concerns: hunger and sleep. For now, she was content accepting mouthfuls of sweetened oatmeal. Signe noticed that Collan had finished her soup and sat quietly, anticipating more food to come.

"Signe, dear, I was surprised to learn from that bartender that Yarmouth was named the second largest port of registry for shipbuilding in Canada just four years ago! It appears we'll be living in quite an affluent community."

"But the town sounds like a rather small place, Jacob," Signe commented as she delivered another half-teaspoon of oatmeal to Katarina.

"Oh, I don't know about that, Signe. He said there are a great many Bostonians and New Yorkers who sail to Nova Scotia, especially in the summers, and decent hotels are starting to be built there. That's a darn good idea, you know, since the province sounds like it's becoming a popular tourist destination for Americans."

"That's nice, Jacob," Signe said, and looked at her eldest daughter.

"Elisabet, are you finished your soup? Look — your sister Collan was finished five minutes ago. I'm sure the waiter is ready to serve us the next course. Hurry up now, would you?"

THREE

New York City, New York, Sunday, June 15, 1913

Katarina Burcharth and her sister Collan were excited as they emerged from the train that pulled into Grand Central Station from Boston that morning. Both young women, at the age of thirty-three and thirty-four respectively, chattered like schoolgirls. While dissimilar in looks, they still bore a resemblance to their childhood selves who had sailed with their parents to North America in 1883 from Sweden.

Their father, Jacob, had used his considerable influence as a sea captain to secure passage for both his daughters on a one-way voyage to Kristiania, the capital of Norway. Their eventual destination would be his hometown of Gothenburg where his parents still lived.

He wanted his girls to ensure his parents were able to continue caring for themselves. But he was also hoping that either Katarina or Collan might find a gentleman of means to marry, preferably Swedish, of course. He had watched his three daughters grow into determined young ladies, but in his estimation, it was only Elisabet who shared his traditional belief that marrying a good man led to personal and financial security for any woman. She was currently living in Boston with her British spouse and 12-year-old daughter, Eva.

Jacob's choice of an ocean liner to take his children to Europe was carefully considered. He had been shaken to his core the year before when the Titanic sank, taking close to 1,500 lives. He had felt helpless regarding the recovery efforts. As he was sailing between Yarmouth and Boston when the tragedy occurred, he could not take the time to assist with anything when over 200 of the dead from the famous and ill-fated ocean liner arrived in Halifax.

He decided to book passage for the girls on a ship from the newly established Norwegian American Line christened the S/S Kristianiafjord. Its maiden voyage from the Norwegian capital to New York would be in early June, and he had assumed that by using his influence, he could arrange at least a second-class stateroom for the girls on the liner's return trip to Norway.

Katarina and Collan settled in the backseat of a taxi, their steamer trunk securely fastened. A throng of cabs surrounded them, and seemingly more people than the population of Yarmouth were bustling around the busy 42nd Street terminal.

"Fares are now regulated, ladies," the bespectacled cabbie informed them just before pulling out into the traffic. "I'll have to charge you 50 cents a mile and I reckon that the seaport district is almost five miles from here."

Collan gave Katarina a concerned glance as they were on a strict daily budget.

Katarina winked at her and then turned solemn when she spoke to the driver.

"I completely understand, sir. But you'd not be aware of the benevolent mission my sister and I are embarking upon tomorrow. Indeed, we are taking the cremated remains of some of the unfortunate victims of the Titanic back to their loved ones in Norway," she said. "You see, we've traveled a great distance from Nova Scotia at our own personal expense. Our ship leaves in the morning, and I…".

She gasped slightly, as if overcome with emotion.

The cabbie was fairly new at his job and had not yet become the jaded chauffeur he later personified; one who has heard it all. He rubbed his chin and adjusted his glasses, and then turned to Katarina.

"I guess I could charge you just a small portion of the regular fare. You're kind souls to reunite family members, so to speak." He paused, thoughtful. "You know, it's people like you who are a credit to our country," he said.

"Oh, no, we're from Cana —", Collan began, as Katarina nudged her foot.

"Cannader, Connecticut," Katarina finished, not wanting to lose the discounted rate. "Thank you very much, sir. You are a true gentleman."

The next morning, after a non-eventful night at a guesthouse just around the corner from the South Street Seaport Museum, the two sisters along with hundreds of others were walking on the gangway about to board the S/S Kristianiafjord.

"I do wish we had the time last night to visit the Museum to see the Titanic Memorial Lighthouse that was built earlier this year," Katarina commented.

"Katarina, you would've been struck by a bolt of lightning if you had tried to enter that exhibit," Collan remarked. "I swear, your brazenness shocks me. We could've paid the taxi fare from yesterday. How did you dream up that story about us bringing cremated remains to Norway?"

"Collan, you're a year older than I, but you're so naïve! Why on earth should we pay the full price for a taxi when a little white lie can fix things?"

Collan looked sternly at her sister but remained silent.

As was the norm, Katarina was the image of innocence, decked out in a wide-brimmed hat with peacock feathers, pinned over her low pompadour hairstyle. They had helped one another to dress that morning, each wearing the latest longline corsets as foundations to their new form-fitting and flattering day dresses. Katarina's petite stature, compared to Collan's height, seemed to indicate that she was the younger of the two. She knew this and continued to dress youthfully during their voyage in order to take every advantage of her appearance.

Later, when their steamer trunk was delivered to their first-class cabin, Collan was again noticeably agitated.

"Katarina, I nearly died when you insisted on speaking to the Chief Purser to ask for a cabin upgrade from the second-class tickets Father had bought for us," she said.

"But aren't you happy with this much bigger space?" Katarina pirouetted in the center of the cabin. "It was available, and we didn't have to pay anything extra for it, so I don't understand what your problem is."

"My problem is that you said you were a fashion and society reporter for *The New York Times*, and that you'd be writing about the S/S Kristianiafjord in a very favorable light in an upcoming edition of the paper — *that's* my problem!"

"Collan, it's clearly not *an issue* if the Chief Steward was too stupid to realize he was being duped. Honestly, dear Sister, this cabin was vacant. Either it didn't sell in advance, or its occupants canceled at the last minute." Katarina was steadfast. "It's not like we're *stealing* anything, Collan."

Collan opened their large steamer trunk and began sorting through the accessories in one of its upper drawers.

"Rephrase that, Katarina. You can convince yourself that *you're* not stealing anything. I had nothing to do with this. I'm not like you."

FOUR

Katarina – Aboard the S/S Kristianiafjord – Monday, June 16, 1913

Dear Diary,
I thought that since I am starting a grand adventure, of sorts, I should begin a diary, so I'll be able to remember what happened on my first trip to Europe to meet my grandparents. (Well, at least Father's parents — Mother never talks about her parents, and I don't know if they're even alive and well.) And of course, I must recount here how I met handsome Mr. Carminati, whom I have set my sights on. Yes, I have!

At dinner last night, Collan was distant with me, and for all intent seemed to want to punish me for the white lies I told yesterday. That is so ridiculous! No one was harmed, and I simply wanted to make our voyage a little more comfortable. I just don't understand her sometimes.

This morning, after a fairly decent and typically Norwegian breakfast of marinated herring, cheeses, cold boiled eggs, black bread, and some fruit, Collan retired to the stateroom complaining of fatigue. I'm fairly certain she did not toss and turn all night — at least I didn't hear her having a fitful sleep — so I just have to accept that she continues to be moody with me. I slept as well as one is able in a ship's berth.

There was a mix-up at breakfast with seating arrangements or some such nonsense, so we were asked to dine in the second-class dining saloon instead. I was not pleased after all the trouble I went through to be put in our first-class lodgings, but what can one do?

The second-class saloon has tables of sixteen people each. They are long and narrow with a row of eight individuals on each side sitting opposite one another, as if we were eggs being placed in some kind of oblong container. While it's not uncivilized, the seating is far too close for my comfort. Second class.

I am now sitting in the second-class music room, because apparently the first-class music room is being cleaned due to an emergency. I mean, really! What kind of emergency can happen in a music room, for goodness sake? This is only the ship's second voyage and yet the service is not yet up to par, in my opinion.

A young man of about sixteen is playing "You Made Me Love You" on the piano here —that big hit from last year— and he doesn't even have the sheet music in front of him! I remember those piano lessons I took in Yarmouth before I was eighteen, but can't say I was thrilled about them. Still, if one can play at least a couple of recognizable tunes, it does bode well for a lady's reputation for being cultured.

I noticed a man on the other side of the room when I came in. He was reading a newspaper and was dressed quite well in a dark green sack suit. He appeared to be tall enough to wear this style; I find those baggy suit jackets that extend to mid-thigh should never be attempted by men of a shorter stature. He did smile and nod as I entered and sat down, and I returned his greeting. Perhaps he too was denied entrance to the first-class music room. He looked as if he should be traveling first class, in any event.

Ordinarily, I'm not attracted to swarthy-looking gentlemen as this one appears to be with his striking black hair. I have a morbid fear of, or fascination with, some of these olive-skinned men who sprout unbridled hair in their ears and nostrils. They must surely be from southern European countries...

In fact, he reminded me a little of Antonio Moreno who was in the moving pictures last year with Norma Talmage. A ladies' magazine recently named him the 'King of the Cliffhangers'. I wonder if this gentleman creates suspense when he travels?

Today I wore a beige day dress which I've always liked to wear, as it is accentuated with black piping and goes well with a black clutch I bought in Halifax a couple of years ago.

Anyway, then a waiter arrived asking if I would like a beverage. I ordered tea and overheard the gentleman on the other side of the room do the same. He got up from his chair and approached me.

"Good morning, Miss," he smiled. "Since we are two strangers in a music room being serenaded by a likely piano prodigy, might I introduce myself?"

He had only the hint of an accent, which I couldn't quite place, but he spoke English quite well. And he called me 'miss'.

"Please do," I replied.

"My name is Joseph Carminati, at your service," he said, with the whitest teeth I have seen in years. Presumably, he does not indulge in red wine or coffee.

"I'm Katarina Burcharth, and I'm pleased to meet you, Mr. Carminati. Might I be so bold as to ask if this is a leisure or a business trip to the continent?"

"It's definitely for business," he responded. "I currently live in Kristiania, handling my family's interest in Norway's fishing industry. Unfortunately, I have to make the crossing to New York at least twice a year, but I'm not complaining whatsoever. The pace is pleasant on board, and the maiden trip to America on this ship last week went off without any problems at all."

"I'm happy to hear that, Mr. Carminati. Please sit down and we can enjoy a sip of tea when it arrives. Will Mrs. Carminati be joining you?"

"Oh, I am a bachelor, Miss – or is it Mrs. Burcharth?" he asked, smiling.

Cheeky guy. (I'm having fun telling you this story, dear Diary!)

"There is no Mr. Burcharth, Mr. Carminati," I said, returning his smile.

My, but he was extremely attractive — with not one stray ear or nose hair, I might add!

"Then we are two single lonely travelers about to have tea and a pastry of some kind, and some lively conversation, I hope."

The teenager at the piano, as if on cue, started playing "When Irish Eyes Are Smiling". I was fine with his choice, although I was certain Mr. Carminati had smiling Italian eyes.

Until next time, dear Diary.

FIVE

Aboard the S/S Kristianiafjord – Monday, June 16, 1913

Collan sat in a deck chair on the Promenade Level with a light blanket covering her legs. She was pensive, as was her nature, as she stared over the open Atlantic. She found she wasn't able to concentrate on her book, P.G. Wodehouse's *The Prince and Betty*, since she had re-read the same page several times. She set the novel on her lap.

I prefer to read in private lest others see me, a thirty-four-year-old spinster, indulging in what some might say is romantic fiction. Still, Wodehouse writes beautifully and with such wonderful humor.

Katarina is up to her tricks again. I know she has a decent heart, but I don't understand where her compulsion comes from to tell so many lies. She may say they are 'white lies' or 'untruths', but the fact remains she's engaging in deception all the time. Some day she will stumble in the middle of one of her wild tales and it won't be pleasant when that happens.

After breakfast, an invitation was delivered to our stateroom inviting us to dine at the Captain's table this evening. I fear I'll have to bite my tongue when she begins answering the inevitable questions about her phony career with The New York Times.

I know I'll turn many shades of crimson, and I may indulge in too much wine to relieve my stress of being with her. It takes a great deal of effort to change subjects adroitly when in her company. Sometimes her stories just grow bigger and bigger, and the falsehoods pile up like the cars of a train that have careened off the tracks.

I'm only a year older than Katarina, and yet I remember that she seldom spoke when she was a child. I was the chatterbox and read everything in sight; Elisabet analyzed everything without availing herself of books to try to learn more; and Katarina was simply quiet all the time. She often preferred to play by herself, perhaps getting lost in her own fantasyland.

Collan was convinced that Elisabet didn't really like her as a person, and probably thought of her as being too forthright. She saw so much potential in her older sister, especially because of the valuable experiences she was having by living in a big city like Boston.

When she writes us from there, the news is always negative. She volunteers a lot of her time at the Opera House, but rarely talks about Eva or Nigel to any great extent. I've gathered that poor Nigel practically lives at their store below their apartment; he appears to work so hard. I hope he remains healthy, and I worry about little Eva. I wonder if she's becoming like her Aunt Katarina was when she was small.

Neither Collan nor Katarina had made any future plans as to how long they might stay in Gothenburg with their grandparents. Neither remembered anything from their early childhood years before they left Sweden. Collan vaguely recalled a noisy and busy house, but she knew that childhood memories are not reliable and are often exaggerated, or underwhelming.

Her thoughts drifted to her adolescence in Yarmouth when she first became interested in horses and riding. Her parents had arranged for her to take regular lessons on a farm outside the town in a community called Brooklyn, and she quickly became enamoured with one mare she called 'min vackra häst' — Swedish for 'my beautiful horse'.

It's sometimes hard to believe I started horseback riding fifteen years ago because it's also turned into a skill that keeps me fit, and I love the fresh air. Riding has given me so much respect for horses. If we are to stay in Gothenburg for any length of time, I must find another vackra häst*!*

SIX

Gothenburg, Friday, June 27, 1913

"Oh my God, Collan, I'm feeling a bit like a country bumpkin," Katarina exclaimed as they watched their taxi driver fasten their trunk to the back of his vehicle after they had disembarked from the S/S Kristianiafjord. Collan smiled and looked around her at the city that had been built in 1619 after King Gustavus Adolphus decreed where he wanted Sweden's second largest city to be built.

Gothenburg was thriving in 1913, and yet had also become the main departure point for Swedish emigrants to the United States. Inside the taxi, Collan gave directions to her grandparents' home to the driver, while Katarina glanced at a tourism brochure she had picked up during the voyage.

"Okay," she said to Collan, "there are definitely a few places I want to see as soon as possible. We must go to the Röhsska Museum, which is apparently dedicated to fashion, design, and the applied arts, and, oh! There's the Älvsborg Fortress from the seventeenth century that you can take a boat to, and it's on an island! I'm so glad we made this trip, Collan; I can't wait to go sightseeing."

"But first, we have to meet and greet Father's parents," Collan said. "And I'm sure we're almost there."

When they arrived at their grandparents' modest but immaculate home in Haga, one of the oldest neighbourhoods in Gothenburg, it was Collan who was immediately impressed with its architectural style.

After the welcome embraces and excited smiles all around, her grandfather told her the house was built in the *landshövdingehus* mode: one floor was lined in brick and the rest in wood.

"How fascinating," Katarina exclaimed, almost dismissively. "The home in which Father and Mother raised us was completely constructed in sandstone, and so they will never have to worry about a house fire burning it to the ground!"

Collan rolled her eyes, as Katarina was aware that all Victorian homes built in Yarmouth that they knew of were constructed totally of wood. It bothered her that her sister was deliberately telling a falsehood to their grandparents.

Their grandmother smiled weakly at her two granddaughters; she found their broken Swedish rather hard to fully comprehend. She proceeded into the kitchen to prepare a lunch of pea soup and pancakes with lingonberry jam. She was frail, Collan noted, and moved slowly. She decided to follow and offer help.

"Grandpapa! Can I call you that?" Katarina asked. "Or would you prefer Granddad?"

As he looked at her, he remembered the day Jacob and Signe introduced the girls to him just before they left Sweden in 1883. The children were a handful then, and Katarina, the youngest, while he remembered her as quiet, seemed to have developed a new vibrant personality in the intervening years in Canada.

He scratched at his white beard and answered, "My dear young lady, you can call me whatever you would like. You can even call me by my given name, Olaf, if you wish."

Katarina smiled. "All right then, Grandpapa," she said. "It is so nice of you to offer your hospitality to me and Collan. We are thrilled to finally get to know our grandparents! We have so many questions to ask you and Grandmama."

Olaf offered a wan smile, already beginning to tire of his granddaughter's animated chatter. It was clear that English was her first language, not Swedish. It hadn't been his idea to have them stay indefinitely, but if his own son could not see his parents one last time, the grandchildren would have to do. He just wished he could feel more of a fondness for these women who had never written to him and his wife — ever —from Canada. The bond they should feel with their granddaughters was not apparent, and it occurred to him they might become more like boarders than family members during what could be an exceptionally long visit.

Katarina leaned closer to him, and almost conspiratorially, said, "Grandpapa, I met the most wonderful Italian gentleman on the voyage here. He is from a *very* prominent family in Naples, and they have substantial business ties in Kristiania. I do think I may be a little enamoured with Joseph, and he promised to visit us here in Gothenburg as soon as he can!"

"Well, that's lovely, my dear."

"I rather have my sights set on marrying him, you know," she winked. "Over the last — how many years? — there have simply been no decent marrying prospects in Yarmouth, and I had my choices, believe me." She paused for effect. "No, I decided years ago that I would have to wait for a man of status, of substance. Someone with class...and hopefully, money."

"A man must treat his wife with respect and love, Katarina. Those are the most important things he can give you. But yes, indeed, he should also be able to provide for you."

"Of course, I would certainly expect love and respect from him," she agreed. "But nobility and social status are important, too, don't you think?"

SEVEN

Eva – Aboard the S/S Prince George en route from Boston to Yarmouth, August 1914

Dear Journal,
The sailing is very smooth today, and the sun is shining brightly! I am so enjoying writing in this book; it helps me make sense of the past few years, and here I am now moving to Canada. But it's also good practice to be jotting down my thoughts as often as I can. Someday, I will be a famous journalist! I can feel it in my bones!

I've been thinking of growing up in Boston. It was a fairly good life there, I suppose, until my father died.

I think he really started dying a slow death after that terrible heatwave three years ago. It was finally broken by a really bad thunder and lightning storm on my tenth birthday when "all h. broke loose", as Mama used to say (because a lady never says 'hell' aloud). That heatwave and storm are quite easy to recall.

I was the apple of my father's eye, which was a good thing because Mama was always too busy to do the things mothers and daughters are supposed to do together. She was away from the house all the time, taking part in all kinds of activities which I was told were to help other people, but I always thought she could be helping Father and me at home. I mean, he was working the shop downstairs every single day, and I was mostly alone upstairs in the apartment when I wasn't at school.

Our store was called Carroll's British Sundry Shoppe, and it was on Boylston Street, next to a really nice ladies' wear store that Mama used to talk about and visit all the time. She didn't much care for Father's store because she said she preferred American-made goods. Why would anyone want to buy biscuits or soap from England when the ones made in New York were so much better?

Of course, we weren't real Bostonians, even though I was born there shortly after Mama and Father had moved from Yarmouth, where Mama's family lived. I barely remember a visit we made to see them when I was six or seven.

Father, who was British, had an uncle in Boston who had left him the shop on Boylston Street in his will. Father told me once that when he first arrived in Halifax from London, he took the train to Yarmouth on the Halifax and Yarmouth Railway and continued his trip on the S/S Prince George to Boston.

I used to wonder if it was my father who first fell in love with Mama or if it was the other way around. Now that I think about it, I do think it was Mama who caught his eye in Yarmouth.

Father had said it was 1900 when he met her at a high society event at the Grand Hotel, a newly constructed building that lived up to its name. At the time, she was living at home with my grandparents and her two sisters, my aunts Collan and Katarina.

She told me once that when she was twenty-two, she felt smothered by Yarmouth's small-town lifestyle and wanted to see the world. I think she saw Father as her salvation. Living in Boston sounded exciting, but there was also a possibility of visiting Father's native England sometime as well.

"You've got to do things for yourself," Mama said to me on more than one occasion. "You're just a girl and good things won't come flying into your lap. If you see something you want, Eva, you have to work hard to get it."

I guess I'm rambling a little writing this. My thoughts are rocking with the gentle waves on the Gulf of Maine as we sail toward Nova Scotia.

The day before my tenth birthday, Mama and Father had a really bad fight. To this day, I can remember almost everything they said.

"The weather is never like this back home," Mama had screamed at him. "I hate this city and that damned stupid store you have!"

I remember being surprised she had used a swear word, and I knew that Father had felt helpless as he tried to calm her.

But she was having none of that.

"Nigel, it was 104 degrees on Tuesday," she had shouted. "That's insane. I can't cope with this."

I knew she was already angry with him because he wouldn't buy her one of those new General Electric refrigerators. He had argued saying they cost a thousand dollars — twice what an automobile would cost — and how did she expect him to find the money? Our icebox would have to do.

Father hadn't opened his store for several days during that heatwave. No one was outside shopping unless it was absolutely necessary. The heat was virtually inescapable in the city and everywhere around it.

Father passed just two months ago. I'm still heartbroken. I think it was a combination of stress and worry that led to his fatal heart attack. I felt as if I lost my best friend, and I still have days when I cry a lot. I don't know any of his family over in England so I can't share my grief with them.

Mama sold the store last month and couldn't wait to return to Yarmouth. I guess there wasn't much sense for us to stay in Boston. She needed the money from the sale of the property which of course included our upstairs apartment. We only brought clothes and some trinkets with us on this move.

I've only been to Yarmouth that one time, and I don't think it's a really big town. It's perched at the southwest corner of Nova Scotia, which seems like the end of the earth, but for me, it's a new beginning. Adventure awaits!

#

Eva and her mother, Elisabet, arrived in Yarmouth on Tuesday, August 4, 1914, the same day that the British Empire declared war on the German Empire.

Captain Jacob's gray hair and craggy face weathered by his years at sea were a welcome sight for his daughter and granddaughter when he met them at the wharf where the S/S Prince George had docked.

Elisabet embraced her father for what seemed an eternity in Eva's young mind.

"Father, will you have to return to Sweden because of the war?"

Elisabet was worried and confused about her European heritage. She had never taken much notice of or bothered with world events, but she wondered if Canadians were suspicious of immigrants from

Europe, people like her parents. After all, Canada itself was a recently unified country and firmly entrenched within the British Empire.

The Captain's own anti-war feelings had been influenced by the years he spent in his native country. He knew Sweden had not been actively involved in a war since 1814 and remained neutral in all conflicts.

Without saying anything to his wife or family, he was privately worried that other new immigrants to Canada were already facing a xenophobic backlash, particularly Germans, Austrians, Hungarians, Ukrainians, and anyone from the Balkans.

"No, sweet one," her father replied. "We are Canadian now. I don't think I'll be asked to volunteer to help in this war, at least for now. Your mother and I are here for you and your sisters", and eyeing Eva, said, "and of course this little pumpkin here. Welcome back to Nova Scotia, Eva! Do you even remember your last visit six years ago?"

Eva blushed a thousand shades of red against her blonde hair, which had been tied back in a soft ponytail. Her features were what might be described as classically Scandinavian. She felt embarrassed that she barely remembered her grandfather.

"Come on now, ladies," Jacob smiled, "let's get your luggage in my new car and get home." Beaming, he continued, "What do you think of your father's new means of getting around, Elisabet?"

They stood before his Canadian-made Model T Ford that had arrived from Ontario the previous month.

"Oh, it's lovely, Father," Elisabet commented, and refrained from telling him how many cars were already overrunning the streets of Boston, turning the downtown into smelly and noisy thoroughfares.

Driving along Water Street and to the intersection of Main and Forest Streets, Jacob waited for the streetcar to go clanging by, and then continued east on Forest and turned into a laneway next to his six-bedroom, late Victorian home that he had constructed in 1884. He ordered there be a cupola or 'widow's walk' built on the roof — as a comfort to his wife, Signe, so she would be able to watch for his ship, the S/S Dominion, as it steamed into Yarmouth Harbor after completing its weekly crossing from Boston.

The gaily painted dwelling beckoned a warm welcome to Eva and her mother. They had both tired of the cramped quarters of their

Boylston Street apartment and the summer heat that was an annual expectation.

Eva now equated her former home in Boston with loneliness and the death of her father. She was glad to be in her new home in Yarmouth with her grandparents — although she barely knew them. She looked forward to making friends of her own to dispel the sad memories she left behind.

EIGHT

Yarmouth, Wednesday, February 17, 1915

Elisabet sat by herself in the front parlor of her parents' home where she had been raised. A copy of *Pride and Prejudice* lay on the loveseat next to her, unopened and ignored. The familiarity of the house was comforting, as her mother hadn't changed any furniture in over a decade nor moved anything around. Still, the vague fondness for her childhood home contained a degree of contempt. She had been happy to leave for Boston with Nigel so she could escape the oppressiveness of her parents, and her feeling of not quite belonging with them. And seven months ago, she had made a conscious decision to return.

I'm happy that Eva, who is a very pretty young lady now, has settled into a new school, but that's about all I'm glad about.

The British Empire is still at war, so that means we are too, although the United States is not involved yet. I don't know why, but these things are just too complicated for me. As long as the Bosches don't somehow come climbing onto our Nova Scotian beaches, I feel better not knowing details.

My mother is the same as she has always been: she acts and looks like wallpaper. She carries on every day with this empty look about her, and dresses as if it is an afterthought to do so. You'd think the war had convinced her that drab and dreary had to be her daily attire, and the drearier the better. Maybe having three daughters in rapid succession in 1878, '79 and '80 wore her out. I don't know.

My two sisters remain mysteries to me. Communication has been sparse since they left for Sweden a couple of years ago. The three of us were relatively close enough growing up here in Yarmouth. Occasionally we had our spats which would end up in a screaming match, but generally we got along well.

Collan's bluntness has always been irritating and remains a sore spot. I think she feels superior or something. She's still unmarried and will probably become an old maid.

However, I understand she has fashioned herself to be a rather well-known horsewoman. But I do wonder how long a woman should be gallivanting off to horse shows and such. She's thirty-six now and attends equestrian competitions in Sweden and Denmark. Father tells me she's actually winning some money in these competitions.

Collan is her father's daughter in looks. She has a long pretty face. But her hair has a mind of its own and is stringy rather than curly. It's as black as a raven's feathers. In fact, her hair resembles that of a horse's mane. Poor Collan. Even as an adolescent, I heard her looks referred to as "Horsey" by classmates.

Katarina is so petite, she looks like a young girl, even though she's now thirty-five. I fear she too may become an old maid. Her hair is very reddish in color and quite thick, which must pain her at times to try and keep under control. I wonder if she has changed much — I remember catching her in lies all the time when we were growing up. Nothing major, but irritating, nonetheless.

I like my brunette hair. I think it suits me and my brown eyes. Of the three of us, I got the matching hair and eyes, so I do consider myself quite lucky. Why shouldn't I have some privilege?

Elisabet picked up an envelope on a side table containing an invitation that her father had left for her. He told her that she and Eva were welcome to attend a charitable reception in Halifax on his behalf the following month at The Halifax Commerce Club. It was to raise money for the Canadian and British Red Cross.

Eva will be a pleasant companion. She looks and acts older than her fourteen years. I feel that it was predestined for me to have become a wife and mother. I don't want to give birth ever again, but I can see myself married a second time. Yes, I can. I'm ridiculously young to be a widow.

Father hasn't asked about my finances, but I'm fairly certain Eva and I will be comfortable after receiving the proceeds from the sale of Nigel's store in Boston. That money will not last forever, but I suppose I'm fortunate in that I don't have to work for the time being.

I definitely don't want to spend the rest of my thirties living with my parents. Next week, I'll look into buying a comfortable home in a good part of town for Eva and me. Maybe I'll even look at some homes that are for sale in Halifax when we're there next month. It's not carved in stone that I must stay in Yarmouth.

Halifax, I've been told, has become quite a busy little capital city these days with the war on...the British Royal Navy has chosen it to be its North American base. Father says the harbor there is deep and never freezes, and I suppose in wartime that is an advantage. But in comparison to Boston, I'm sure Halifax is pretty boring and probably like a big sister to Yarmouth.

NINE

Halifax, Saturday, March 20, 1915

It was a dismal and cold evening when Eva and her mother arrived at The Halifax Commerce Club on Water Street for the fundraising event in support of the British Red Cross.

"This place looks very fancy, doesn't it, Mama?" Eva marveled as she surveyed the three and a half story sandstone building. Built by a leading Halifax architect, the Club had opened to private and influential members of Halifax's business community in 1862.

"Yes, it does, dear," Elisabet replied. "But we have to remember why we're here. I will donate some money that your father left us to help all those brave Canadians fighting in Europe right now."

She pulled her coat snugly around her shoulders as she climbed the steps into the building, her daughter trailing behind her.

"I don't want to alarm you, Eva, but your grandfather told me that there's a very real possibility that the Germans could even attack Halifax. I don't know how that's possible, but the Germans want to stop the British naval ships from taking our resources overseas to help the Empire's war effort. So, if we give some of Daddy's money back to England, maybe we'll help things in our own small way."

"I'm sure Father would be happy about that," Eva said, tears welling up in her eyes.

The formidable black door with the brass knocker was opened by a uniformed butler who helped them remove their coats, while a housekeeper took the outer garments away for safekeeping. The foyer boasted a grand staircase, and the butler directed them to a parlor on the right, serviced with double French doors. Within the sumptuously decorated room were two dozen well-heeled Nova Scotians chatting among themselves.

Eva surveyed the elegant room with its superbly dressed citizens. She marveled at the intricately carved floral designs on the heavy walnut and rosewood chairs that dotted the room. A few ladies were daintily holding glasses of sherry while being served canapés by a uniformed waitress.

The massive chandelier was a sight to behold. Its glimmering crystal prisms emitted a soft light which gave the room a warm atmosphere. Lining the four walls of the parlor were dour and ancient looking portraits displayed in heavy ornate frames. To a 14-year-old with limited knowledge of fine art, Eva thought these were not attractive additions to the room.

"Ah, hello ladies," a voice owned by a handsome, stocky man in his mid-twenties wearing a Harris Tweed jacket and an earnest smile greeted them.

"I'm Seamus McMaster, one of the volunteers for the Halifax branch of the Canadian Red Cross. I'm so glad you're here!"

"How do you do, Mr. McMaster?" Elisabet returned his smile, suitably impressed by the younger gentleman. "My name is Elisabet Carroll and this is my daughter, Eva. My father in Yarmouth, Captain Jacob Burcharth, received an invitation to the event tonight, so we are here on his behalf."

"I'm truly delighted, Mrs. Carroll!", Seamus exclaimed, his eyes darting between Elisabet and Eva. "And is Mr. Carroll joining us this evening?"

Eva quickly answered out of nervousness.

"My father is dead," she said. "But it's his money that we'll be donating."

Seamus looked aghast at his unintentional faux pas.

"Oh, my word — I'm terribly sorry. My deep condolences, Mrs. Carroll, and to you, Eva, as well."

"Thank you very much, Mr. McMaster," Elisabet responded, eyes downcast for just a suitable amount of time to signify regret but not overwhelming grief.

"Sadly, yes, my husband died last year in Boston, but we are grateful to be back here in Nova Scotia. I do think that every Maritimer who has been away wants to eventually return, don't you agree?"

Seamus, a little more at ease, nodded.

"Most definitely, Mrs. Carroll. I'm happy you and your daughter have come back home." He smiled once again in such a sincere manner that Elisabet fleetingly thought of asking him if he may be seeking a wife.

The butler returned with a silver tray laden with two glasses of sherry, a lemonade for Eva and three petite serviettes.

Seamus took one of the sherries and the lemonade from the butler, and passing each to Elisabet and Eva, said, "I hope you enjoy these beverages." He then offered each woman a serviette.

Eva shyly thanked Seamus, and Elisabet met his eyes, surprising herself with her boldness. "I know we will, Mr. McMaster. Thank you."

"Please call me Seamus."

"All right, and you can call me Elisabet."

Eva raised her eyes heavenward and then looked away, deciding to inspect the many figurines that were splayed over the tapestry covering the mantle of the fireplace.

"What line of work are you in, uh, Seamus?" Elisabet inquired.

"I'm afraid I'm not quite employed yet, Elisabet; I'm in my final year in the Faculty of Medicine at Dalhousie University."

"Oh, I see. How nice for you," she said. "It's so fitting, then, that you're volunteering for such a worthy cause."

Seamus smiled and then a look of worry crossed his face.

"My goodness," he exclaimed, pulling out a pocket watch and glancing at it. "I'm due to deliver a short speech right now. Please excuse me!"

Seamus turned around and left the parlor momentarily, reappeared, and positioned himself in the far corner of the room.

"Excuse me, ladies and gentlemen — may I have your attention, please?"

The room quieted, and Seamus beamed a broad smile.

"Thank you so much for attending this evening's fundraising event for the British Red Cross. You are true patriots and loyal citizens of the Commonwealth, indeed. I know there are a few of you visiting, or newly arrived from Boston and New York, so I would like to, if I may, tell you a little bit about Halifax's involvement in the war.

"As you know, our lovely capital city could arguably be described as a garrison city that's sadly familiar with world conflicts. Our first European settlers were Britons in 1749, and they were called upon to protect the Kingdom's interests in British North America.

"Since the British Empire declared war a year ago, Halifax has been positioned in the forefront of strategic defense by employing the Royal Canadian Navy to patrol the coastal waters of Nova Scotia. I'm sure you're aware that Halifax is also considered to be an excellent trans-shipment point for troops destined for Overseas Active Service. Did you know we have approximately 3,000 troops in the city right now, and one-third are professional soldiers?

"God forbid that the Germans will ever make their way to the city's outer harbor, but rest assured that militiamen from New Brunswick and Prince Edward Island have very diligently built trenches at positions in the area.

"Finally, your support of the war effort is very much appreciated. And if you could indulge me for one more moment," Seamus said, but was interrupted by a man with a concerned look. The gentleman bore a striking resemblance to Seamus and approached him tentatively with a whispered message.

"Pardon me briefly, ladies and gentlemen. Please carry on," Seamus said, with an apologetic smile, and left the parlor with the man.

"Mama, when do people donate their money?" Eva asked Elisabet.

"Oh, that's not done in an obvious way, Eva" her mother said. "After Seamus, er, Mr. McMaster is finished talking, people will be told to leave their checks with the butler at the door as they're leaving." She paused. "At least that's how we did this kind of thing in Boston."

She craned her neck to get a look at Seamus and the other man in the foyer. Their conversation had become quite animated. Seamus nervously ran his fingers through his thick hair. He returned to the front of the room as the guests fell silent.

"There is no need for alarm, ladies and gentlemen, but I do have some news that certainly brings the current war situation to our own doors," Seamus said. "My brother just told me there was quite a scare this morning just west of here on Lucknow Street. It appears a grave mistake was made by the army battery out on McNab's Island when they tried to stop a steamer from entering the harbor. Two warning shells were fired at the ship, but one skipped off the water and exploded in the city!

"They're still investigating, but so far, there doesn't seem to have been any loss of life nor any serious injuries. However, the roof and probably some bedrooms of a double home on that street have been severely damaged by a 12-pound shell. I'm rather startled by all this, I must admit. It certainly puts this war into perspective when Halifax is so closely affected by events happening an ocean away."

There was a general murmur in the room. Eva had listened intently to Seamus's account. She thought of what a strong man he seemed to be; sensitive but sensible.

"Now, please have another glass of wine or whatever you fancy, and enjoy the rest of your evening! Once again, thank you very much for your financial support."

Eva thought that if human error could trigger such an accident, suddenly Yarmouth might be a much safer haven than Halifax.

TEN

Stockholm, Saturday, October 16, 1915

Joseph Carminati was true to his word and did visit Katarina several times in the ensuing months. Each time he stayed at the venerable Hotel Royal in central Gothenburg which had accommodated guests since 1852. They became a devoted couple in a short period of time, and it wasn't long before he asked Katarina to marry him. The topic of having a family had not yet been broached, but Katarina knew it would be a subject for discussion before too long.

She did not tell Joseph immediately that she had had a hysterectomy in 1901 when she was twenty-one because of heavy bleeding since adolescence during her monthly periods. She still had nightmares about the surgery, but she had been one of the lucky patients who actually survived the ordeal.

Joseph was an industrious sort of man, always looking for new opportunities to meet new business partners, so when a high-ranking Norwegian government official offered him box seats at Stockholm's Opera House, he was happy to accept. The date or the type of performance was irrelevant; he also knew Katarina would be thrilled, and that was equally important to him.

The Swedish Opera House's location, opposite the Kungliga Slottet, the Royal Palace, boasted a striking neoclassical façade and had been renamed at the turn of the century as the Kungliga Teatern — The Royal Theater.

On Saturday morning, Joseph picked up his fiancé and her sister. The three boarded the Western railway line to Stockholm, and about five and a half hours later checked into two rooms at The Grand Hotel Royal.

Joseph felt a slight debt of gratitude to Collan, who had, at times, arranged for outings for her grandparents while he and Katarina enjoyed intimate time at their home in Haga. She would be his future wife, after all, and he had chosen to ignore his Church's rule of avoiding sexual relations before marriage. In any event, Katarina seemed to have no moral or ethical objection to their exuberant private lovemaking.

During intermission that evening, Joseph could not contain his pride as they left the lavish, horseshoe-shaped auditorium at intermission, and proceeded to the Guldfoajén, or Golden Foyer at the top of the grand staircase. With gold stucco on the walls and ceiling, crystal chandeliers, sweeping mirrors, and lavish curtains made from Florentine gold brocade, the Foyer was as impressive as the auditorium.

Katarina was ecstatic. She was wearing one the previous year's so-named war crinoline suits, which featured a bell-shaped skirt and a wide over-skirt. Collan had opted to wear one of the latest fashionable dresses with a hemline that went to mid-calf, frowned upon by traditionalists even in Sweden.

"Joseph, this is what I call *la vie en rose*," Katarina gushed, holding her betrothed's arm. "Look at all these beautiful people and the magnificent surroundings!"

She sipped a glass of Champagne as Collan nodded her assent.

"Yes, Joseph, thank you so much for planning this weekend. It's really special," Collan added.

Noticing what appeared to be a respectful and rather hushed commotion on the other side of the Foyer, she said, "I wonder what that's all about. People seem to be encircling someone. Maybe one of the performers has joined the audience during intermission?"

"No, I think it must be a dignitary of some kind, Collan. I see quite a few rather strong-looking gents on the periphery of the room who look like they may be guarding the individual," Joseph remarked.

Katarina tapped on the rim of her Champagne glass with her gloved hand, signifying to Joseph that it was empty.

"Of course, my dear," he smiled. "I'll be right back." He left for the serving area with Katarina's empty glass and his own.

"Katarina, you could have waited for the server to come back and offer you a glass from his tray," Collan admonished.

"But I wanted to talk to you privately for a moment, Sister-dear," Katarina said. "I do believe that you have caught the eye of that man in the middle of all those others." She stopped, her eyes widening. "And...oh my goodness — they're coming toward us!"

"Excuse me, ladies, but Prince Erik, the Duke of Västmanland, would like to make your acquaintance," said a tall, blond member of the Swedish Armed Forces. Standing next to him was the Prince, twenty-six, pale and thin, but smiling warmly and handsome in all his royal finery.

The army officer immediately noticed the look of unease on the two women before him and repeated his introduction to the Prince in English. Katarina and Collan visibly relaxed.

Their oral and written Swedish was fair to good; Jacob and Signe had spoken the language while their daughters were growing up and they had been taught the basics of reading and writing Swedish. But when they were suddenly introduced to a member of the monarchy, their nervousness was lessened by speaking in English.

"I don't believe I have seen you two ladies here at the Royal Theater before, so I just wanted to personally welcome you. My name is Prince Erik Gustav Ludvig Albert of the House of Bernadotte," the Duke said in his most charming and friendly voice, "but please call me Erik."

Katarina was so shocked by this more-than-welcome interruption, and the Prince's good humor, that she didn't know if she should curtsy, look for a ring to kiss, or simply hold out her hand, which she then saw Collan doing. She followed suit.

Collan curtsied slightly. The Prince took her gloved hand first and lightly kissed it.

"We're delighted to meet you, Your Royal Highness. My name is Collan Burcharth, and this is my sister, Katarina."

"Yes, I am, uh, we are, both, uh, delighted, Your Highness," Katarina said, "and we simply love your country!"

"You are visiting Sweden, then?"

"Yes, from America," Katarina replied.

"Actually, we are visiting from Nova Scotia, Canada," Collan interjected, correcting her sister. "Our parents emigrated there from Gothenburg in 1883."

"That's what I meant, Collan — *North* America," Katarina added, with just a hint of terseness.

"Well, I must say, it was Sweden's loss and Canada's gain, then. I hope you will enjoy your time in the capital. I wish you a lovely evening, ladies. I do hope we may cross paths again," the Prince said, looking directly at Collan.

With that, and a slight bow, he left with his aide. Collan looked at Katarina, and asked, grinning, "What just happened there?"

Joseph approached them carrying two new glasses of Champagne.

"And who were the fellows in uniform just talking to you, hmmm?", he asked Katarina, kissing her on the cheek.

"Only the Duke of Västmanland, Prince Erik!" Katarina giggled. "And he had eyes for Collan, that's for sure!"

Joseph laughed. "Is that right, Collan? Do I hear royal wedding bells ringing?"

Collan felt her face burning, but she was pleased at the attention from Prince Erik.

"You know, he's third in line to the throne, Collan," Joseph informed her. "But the newspapers say he has a medical condition that's kept secret, and lives in his own isolated mansion in Djursholm, just north of the city. You'll never see him in public with King Gustav or the Queen, but he is included in family photographs. I hear, though, that he does enjoy the Opera House every couple of weeks."

"He certainly is very pleasant and friendly for one who is a blue blood," Collan commented.

Katarina playfully swatted her fiancé on the arm.

"Well, aren't you the royal watcher, then?" she joked. "How do you know all these private things about the Swedish royal family?"

A fleeting look of irritation crossed Joseph's face.

"Our company in Napoli has to know many things about Scandinavia, Katarina, and not just Norwegian business."

"Of course, dear," Katarina said quietly.

The lights in the Grand Foyer faded, then illuminated and faded again, signaling that intermission was over.

"I haven't even sipped my second glass of Champagne yet!" Katarina exclaimed, frowning.

Collan reached over and removed the glass from Katarina's hand.

"Here, let me help you with it," she said, swallowing the contents. "Yes, I think I needed that."

ELEVEN

Gothenburg, New Year's Day, 1916

"Joseph, did you remember to tell your secretary yesterday to send a telegraph to Elisabet in Canada today? And it should also wish them all a happy new year , too," Katarina asked her bridegroom. They were just about to get into the luxury limousine made by the Swedish company Scania-Vabis that Joseph had rented to take them to their wedding.

"Yes, I did, my beautiful bride," Joseph replied, giving the driver instructions on where to take them. Both sisters had coincidentally chosen the date of Saturday, January 1, 1916 for their nuptials.

As they settled into the limousine, bundled in woolens and fur outerwear, Joseph reflected how well his family's fishing export business in Italy had continued to do during the war, as his homeland had also declared its neutrality. He and Katarina were about to be married; Gothenburg was growing into an important port city, and he was pleased that his businesss in Sweden had already seen improvement. He was seriously considering the idea that they find a place of their own to live there permanently.

\#

"So, you're getting another father now, it appears, Eva. What do you think of that?" Signe asked her granddaughter.

They were sharing breakfast while the rest of the family was getting ready for the drive to Darlings Lake in Yarmouth County for Elisabet's wedding to Seamus.

Eva frowned slightly at the odd question from her grandmother, who ordinarily did not ask Eva about anything, let alone to voice such a personal appraisal of Seamus.

"Well, I haven't honestly thought of Mama's marriage in those terms, Grandmother. Seamus doesn't seem old enough to be like a father to me, so it's more like he's just my mother's new husband." She paused and continued, "But a new father? No, I wouldn't say so."

As if for emphasis, they both heard the horn of an incoming or outgoing steamship from the harbour, only two blocks away. During the war, the seaport of Yarmouth was thriving. Steamship services serving as a transportation link to the United States continued to stay the course to Boston and New York, providing unfettered employment for many, including Jacob.

"Your mother seemed to become very fond of Seamus McMaster rather quickly, I would say," Signe continued, in an unusually talkative mood. "He does come across as a knowledgeable senior medical resident from Halifax, so I suppose the three of you will be leaving Yarmouth…again, in your mother's case."

"That I don't know, Grandmother. I rather hope not since I'm enjoying school here, and I do like the town. I would think they will go wherever Seamus gets offered a doctor's position, and Yarmouth is booming, so…". The ship's horn blasted once again.

Upstairs in her room, Elisabet was applying her makeup and thinking about the fortunate turn of events with Seamus. They did get along very well, and there was a definite physical attraction between the two, but she also considered that it was important for her impressionable daughter to have a male role model in her life. She felt that Eva often acted like an overly dramatic adolescent and was difficult to discipline at times. Seamus was a perfect candidate for the role of stepfather, so the moment he proposed marriage, she accepted without any reservations.

#

In the meantime, in Gothenburg, Katarina and Joseph were nearing the castle estate where their wedding was to be held. The bridegroom had to do a little extra arm-twisting to secure a private function at Tjolöholm Castle. Located forty kilometers south of Gothenburg, and accessible by train or motorcar, Joseph's father had known the original owners, but they had died a few years previously, ending the family connection that may have made the wedding arrangements easier.

As they drove through the gates of the large property, Joseph told Katarina that the original owners had created the largest horse stud farm in Sweden where they bred and reared renowned thoroughbreds. There was also a driving school. Future coachmen and drivers were taught the skills of the trade.

"Oh, my goodness! Collan will love this place!" Katarina exclaimed, surveying the various buildings, stables, and the Elizabethan-styled castle itself.

"Look over there, Katarina — there's the church, and there's a town hall where the estate's workers can meet. There are even several employee cottages built in the National Romantic style like you see in Denmark, too."

"I am suitably impressed, Joseph," Katarina remarked, wishing she had more than just her sister witnessing her wedding. Surely Tjolöholm could turn the heads of even the most jaded and wealthy of Swedish society.

The current owners, Blanche and her husband, Count Carl Bonde, along with their four sons, lived on the estate after Blanche's mother died in 1906. Tjolöholm was not open to the public, and yet employed a full staff, allowing a few private parties to be held on site.

The Church was bedecked with a few holly and ivy wreaths tied in yellow and blue ribbons but was otherwise formal and austere. Katarina and Joseph adhered to Swedish custom, and walked down the short aisle of the church together, symbolizing that a free man and a free woman were voluntarily uniting in marriage.

After the ceremony, Katarina insisted she thank their hosts personally, and was thrilled to briefly meet Blanche and the Count. She was particularly interested to find out about the Count's background — so much so, that Joseph began to think Katarina was being too intrusive and steered her away from the couple.

Collan was proud of her little sister, and she liked the idea of Joseph as her brother-in-law but couldn't help but wonder how long the marriage might last.

#

As Katarina's quiet wedding reception was winding down, over 3,000 nautical miles away westbound, Elisabet and Seamus were making the final preparations for their own marriage ceremony.

Jacob had wired his good friend Captain Aaron Flint "Rudder" Churchill, to ask if his picturesque summer home, The Anchorage, might be opened for a couple of days in late December and early January for the celebration of the second marriage of his daughter Elisabet.

Overlooking several lakes and the sea, the two-story mansion's Italianate style was exemplified by a rectangular massing, a low-pitched hip roof, bracketed cornices and window crowns, a cupola, and expansive verandas. Jacob had always been impressed by his friend's beautiful home, and he envisioned the wedding ceremony taking place in the main parlor of the mansion, followed by a luncheon in the dining room.

Aaron Churchill, who had turned 66 in 1916, had become extremely wealthy as an inventor, and was owner of The Savannah Steamship Line. Currently, he was living in his mansion in Georgia. As someone who encouraged tourism and enthusiastically promoted his home province of Nova Scotia, he agreed to his friend's idea. He knew that the Halifax, Yarmouth, and Boston newspapers would inevitably run breathless accounts of the 'winter society wedding' at his summer residence.

The Anchorage was vacant in January, so Captain Churchill ensured it was prepared a few days in advance by his property manager for the arrival of the wedding party and guests.

But Captain Churchill was concerned, however. Bad weather could intervene, and the mansion was perched atop a hill; automobiles might have to be parked below to avoid the snow and ice-encrusted road. There was always a chance that guests would have to make their way gingerly up the hill by foot. Nova Scotian weather is unpredictable in all seasons, but particularly in winter. It may be mild, foggy, and breezy one moment with no snow, and the next hour could exhibit a blinding snowstorm coming off the Atlantic.

Jacob was resigned to the fact his own home on Forest Street could not comfortably seat the sixteen guests Elisabet and Seamus had wanted to invite to their nuptials. He also was aware his finances would not allow a fully catered wedding at the Grand Hotel where the majority of Yarmouth's high society events were usually held.

One of Jacob's biggest challenges had been finding a clergyman to marry his daughter, a widow, to a bachelor who was fourteen years younger. It wasn't only the difference in age that local ministers might object to, but the fact that the ceremony was to be held outside of an actual church building.

He remembered meeting a Universalist Minister from Halifax on one of the crossings from Boston to Yarmouth, and with some gentle persuasion by telegram, and the promise of a decent donation to that church, he secured a minister to legally perform the nuptials.

Eva was looking out of one of the windows in the parlor of The Anchorage and watched a small procession of three or four cars drive slowly up the hill toward the mansion. As luck would have it, the roads were clear that day and free from any mounds of snow and ice.

I bet Seamus's widowed mother Monica, and his older brother Thayne, are in one of the cars. They stayed at the Grand Hotel last night after arriving by train from Halifax with the minister. But where is Seamus?

TWELVE

Eva - Darlings Lake, Yarmouth Co., Saturday, January 1, 1916

Dear Journal,
Oh, my goodness, it's late to be writing tonight, but I must chronicle all that has happened today before I forget it all.

I had told Mama several times that I didn't think the Churchill Mansion outside of town was the place to have her wedding to Seamus.

For some reason, Grandfather was quite insistent that her second marriage be at an exclusive venue. I think he hoped this would add import to the marriage. But I think he also wanted to be somewhat of a star in the show, too, showing off his connection to Yarmouth's influential and elite residents. He's turning fifty-seven this year and is getting close to retirement. I'm quite sure he wants to leave behind memories of his prominence and success as an immigrant to Canada.

Aunt Katarina is getting married today, too, over in Gothenburg. Mama says that she is a great storyteller, although I don't know what kinds of stories she means. Maybe fairy tales?

It's too bad that Mama can't attend her sister's wedding, but Aunt Collan will be there. Two daughters in one family becoming brides on the same day is a memorable occasion, but certainly a challenge to any traveler!

The weather gods were smiling and continued to after we arrived at the Churchill Mansion at 10:30 this morning, on time and without incident. The ceremony was scheduled for noon and was presided over by a Universalist minister from a church I'd not heard of before today. I don't think Seamus's mother was too pleased hearing this, as she had probably hoped for a Presbyterian service in a proper church. But Mama didn't want any specific religious "overtones", as she said, to interfere with "her" day.

Mama did *agree to a non-religious song to be sung after the ceremony. We are a seafaring family and the music and words to*

Farewell to Nova Scotia *are haunting to anyone who lives that life.*
With Mama's permission, I asked my friend Polly MacLellan, who has
a lovely voice, if she would sing it. It's one of those tunes that has
really gained popularity since the war started. I can hear Polly now
practicing in the big kitchen of the mansion.

> Farewell to Nova Scotia, the seabound coast
> Let your mountains dark and dreary be
> For when I am far away on the briny ocean tossed
> Will you ever heave a sigh or a wish for me?
> The sun was setting in the west
> The birds were singing on every tree
> All nature seemed inclined for to rest
> But still there was no rest for me

It was a bit damp and chilly in that big house, but the view over
the lake was wonderful in the winter sunshine. Every fireplace was lit
and roaring, so it did get quite toasty in a short time.

Mama wore a lovely bridal dress that has a cream-colored silk
skirt, two soft net over skirts with a cream lace appliqué, and a soft
net bodice with pretty hand knitted lace, shaped into a heart at the
bosom. All over the dress are embroidered roses, which I really liked.
Grandmother, in her less-than-enthusiastic way, helped her get
dressed before the ceremony.

I saw Grandfather chatting to Seamus's brother, Thayne. We
really didn't get a chance to meet him properly that evening at the
Halifax Commerce Club. He seems like a nice man, though, and did
talk to me at the reception after Mama and Seamus were married.

I was startled when Seamus arrived at The Anchorage.

As soon as he saw me, he gave me a very warm and tight embrace
in the foyer, even before I had the chance to help him off with his
overcoat. He then held my face in his hands and said something to the
effect that I would soon be sweet sixteen, and he was so happy to
become a part of my life!

I don't know, but it felt like a really odd gesture coming from him.
I guess I'm happy he'll be a part of my life, too, but he really can't
expect to become my father. No one can replace my real father who I
still miss so much.

THIRTEEN

Eva – Yarmouth, Monday, February 21, 1916

Dear Journal,
Grandmother and Grandfather received a letter today from Aunt Katarina. She wrote that her new husband is an Italian man with "noble" blood, whatever that means. Mama said that just tells us that he comes from a good family, and Aunt Katarina probably will be well taken care of financially. I am happy for her, although I haven't had any opportunity to get to know her. She is twice as old as I am.

(No, she's definitely older than even that, since I am only turning fifteen this year. I wonder if she is too old to have children. That's none of my business, I know, but still…)

It's been over a month since Mama's marriage. Seamus is definitely quite taken with her, even though she's older and he's still a medical student. My grandparents were cordial to Seamus from the first time he visited us after we met him in Halifax. He stayed at the Grand Hotel which is a coincidence, since that is where Mama met Daddy back in 1899. Seamus is always smiling and happy, which is nice to see.

I find my emotions are all over the place these days when it comes to (1) possibly moving, to (2) school, and (3) my friends.

Okay, then, my emotions are all over the place with boys. I wonder if boys have the same intelligence that girls do? To me it makes no logical sense whatsoever why Canadian boys are volunteering to fight in a war over in Europe! And they wait in queues for the privilege of registering! I've seen scores of them leave from our train station to go to Halifax for deployment overseas. I'm at a loss to understand why. Maybe the older I get, the more it might make sense, but everything within me tells me otherwise.

Aunt Collan wrote us at Christmastime before Mama's wedding. She is still in Gothenburg and mentioned that she continues to do well in equestrian competitions both in Sweden and across the water in

Denmark. She lives on her own in my great-grandparents' home since they both died, weeks apart, from a very persistent influenza virus. Grandfather is sad that he could not have been there for them. After all, he hadn't seen his parents in over thirty years since he emigrated to Canada.

It must have taken a lot of courage for him to leave his country and come to this one, which is still so young in comparison to Sweden. Maybe someday I'll be able to see the countries where my Mama and Father were born.

FOURTEEN

Yarmouth, Monday, September 17, 1917

Walking towards the Yarmouth County Academy on Parade Street on her first day of school in Grade Ten, Eva was excited. Not only was she sixteen years old, but she was feeling confident about her future. She had decided that summer that she would study to be a journalist and wanted to attend King's College in Windsor following her high school graduation.

Her mother and Seamus had been married almost two years, and there had been some tense moments at home lately, but it was mostly because they were still living with Grandfather and Grandmother Burcharth.

Signe had been keeping to her bedroom much of the time, and rarely came downstairs for meals, so it was usually Eva who delivered food and beverages to her.

Eva thought about the escalation of the war and wondered if the situation in Europe was affecting her aunts in Sweden. The Americans had finally declared war on Germany in April, bowing to public pressure about the country's neutrality. She had read in one of Grandfather's Boston newspapers that a month after the declaration, 128 Americans were among the almost 1,200 passengers killed when the British owned ocean liner Lusitania was torpedoed by the Germans, just off the coast of Ireland.

She was sad about all the Canadians already killed or maimed in the war since 1914, once again telling herself how senseless it all was. There didn't appear to be an end to the madness which seemed so close, but was an ocean away, simultaneously affecting families on both sides of the Atlantic.

As she got closer to her school, she gazed at the handsome three-story Victorian building topped with a cupola which reminded her of a cupcake atop a frilly decorated square cake. Its semi-circular front door entrance landing was already crowded with excited adolescents re-acquainting themselves after the summer holiday; and the identical balcony above the front doors was equally crammed with young people her age.

Nevertheless, her thoughts drifted to Seamus.

He and Elisabet had become less affectionate with one another over the summer, and Eva didn't understand why. She hadn't heard any loud arguments, and both typically spoke in fond tones to one another; there was none of the 'silent treatment' often witnessed between spouses when quarreling was taking place.

Her mother, at thirty-nine, was an attractive older woman to Seamus' twenty-five years, but the spark that Eva had seen in both their eyes during the wedding on New Year's Day last year had waned.

Eva dismissed the thought that there was any real trouble in her mother's marriage. Perhaps they were just anxious to get out from under her parents' patronage so they could have a home of their own with Eva.

She knew she shouldn't be gazing at Seamus as much as she did when the three were sharing dinners; but she was beginning to feel an attraction to the opposite sex, and the boys at school seemed to be well, so *immature*. Seamus wasn't like them at all.

That morning at breakfast, Elisabet told both her daughter and husband that she had her eye on someday buying a single-family house further up on Parade Street away from the Academy, where there was much more open space and fewer neighbors. This allowed for bigger residences, gardens, and circular driveways.

"I think that's a marvelous idea," Seamus said, putting his hand over Elisabet's. "Do you know of one coming up for sale?"

Elisabet moved her hand away from her husband and became suddenly businesslike.

"I've heard talk of one whose owner is having a difficult time financially," she said. "So, I'll speak to my banker and find out if this is a wise idea to pursue."

"And I would certainly contribute to a down payment, Elisabet, now that I'm working fulltime at the hospital."

"I'd certainly hope so!" Elisabet laughed in a hollow tone. "You are my husband, if not exactly the breadwinner in the family."

Eva watched Seamus's face change from being jovial and encouraging to looking hurt at Elisabet's remark. She felt sorry for him, but then just as quickly thought of her hardworking father and wondered if he had ever seen himself and his family living anywhere but a walk-up apartment on a busy city street.

Elisabet picked up a few breakfast dishes, and before leaving the table, gave Seamus a quick kiss on the cheek.

"But you're a good doctor anyway, Seamus dear," Elisabet quipped.

Seamus didn't look at his wife and wiped his mouth with his napkin before getting up from his seat and abruptly leaving the dining room.

#

Three short months later, the relative peace of Nova Scotia was disrupted, and its population of just under 500,000 was collectively shocked on the morning of December 6.

It was a typically busy wartime day on Halifax harbor with many ships coming and going. History would later show that a failure to follow naval conventions, coupled with tragic miscommunications, added to the ensuing disaster.

The Norwegian ship Imo was en route to New York to receive relief supplies for Belgium. The French munitions ship Mont-Blanc, in the harbor to join a trans-Atlantic convoy, was loaded with benzol, picric acid, TNT, and gun cotton.

The ships collided in the Narrows of the harbor in the northern part of the seaside city. The explosion that occurred was unprecedented in human history. The hull of the Mont-Blanc blasted 984 feet into the sky and the wave of destruction moved to the shorelines and into the city at 3,355 miles an hour. The inferno was at 9,000 degrees Fahrenheit, and the explosion created a tsunami which pulled many unfortunate citizens into the carnage of the harbor.

Almost 2,000 people were killed immediately in the explosion: both civilians and military personnel, but innocents all.

The final tally of the dead which can be related to the explosion was much higher. The total damage to the city was estimated at $30 million, which would be the equivalent of $525 million, one hundred years later.

Money from around the world poured in, from governments as far away and as varied as New Zealand, Singapore, Bermuda, and Jamaica, in small and large amounts; and from organizations such as the British and American Red Cross societies.

The first brave men and women to respond to the disaster were from other parts of Nova Scotia and New Brunswick, as well as from Boston. All were rightly considered to be heroes by every surviving Haligonian.

The Massachusetts Relief Committee sent $750,000; the New York Special Fund, $75,000; and even the Chicago Committee contributed $130,000.

The government of the United States pledged five million dollars to help rebuild the city, but the money was never received. President Woodrow Wilson sent a message of sympathy that was publicized in the Official Bulletin of Washington, D.C., on December 8, 1917. It had arrived at the Nova Scotia Legislature in the form of one long, one-sentence telegram.

#

"I'm not only heartbroken for our fellow Nova Scotians in Halifax," Jacob Burcharth announced to his family in the dining room of his home after everyone in Yarmouth was alerted to the terrible disaster in Halifax, "but for our fellow Scandinavians aboard the Imo. How could that vessel have not been blown apart like the Mont-Blanc? But surely there were no survivors."

Norway and Sweden always had friendly, neighbourly relations, hence Jacob's sorrow. From 1814 to 1905 the two countries had even formed a personal union under one king. They had kept to their own laws except for retaining one foreign service department.

Signe, who was seated with the others at the table and had been her usual quiet self, unexpectedly spoke up, "This doesn't affect my family. I don't know anyone in Halifax."

"Mother, that's hardly the point," Elisabet said, a trifle annoyed. Her mother's behavior had been odd for the past year, since she had been spending most of her time in her bedroom. She had never known her mother to be a chatty woman, but Elisabet was now finding her comments to be either unwelcome or even inappropriate sometimes.

"A bad thing happened to a lot of good people. That's not news," Signe sighed.

"But it's such a horrible tragedy for so many families! Think of the babies and children and people like me who are still in school, and thought their whole lives were ahead of them!" Eva exclaimed, sounding exactly like a typical 16-year-old. "It's so *unfair*."

Elisabet looked at her husband.

"Seamus, will you have to go to the city, or what's left of it, to help out?"

"I have little choice, Elisabet, and I would want to go anyway, and immediately. Our senior doctors will continue working at our hospital here in Yarmouth, but it's the duty of all the younger physicians who can get away to go and help out as much as we can there," Seamus replied.

#

Seamus took the train to Halifax on December 10.

The North Street Station had opened in 1878 and was the second largest built in Canada. It had sustained some damage in the Explosion, but the building and tracks were quickly cleared and repaired, and it re-opened only three days after the gargantuan blast.

Seamus was unsure where he would best serve the survivors of the Explosion. In a telegram, he had told the Canadian Red Cross office that he would do whatever was required of him. He also mentioned that while he had been trained as a general practitioner, he had begun personal studies in ophthalmology, a keen interest.

Over the past summer, he had been procrastinating about broaching the subject with Elisabet. He wanted to further his medical education in that direction. Clearly it would mean a move to Halifax, and he wasn't sure if they could afford the expense.

Granted, they were saving some money by still living with her parents, but Elisabet kept her personal financial status to herself. He had no idea how much she had made from the sale of her late husband's business in Boston.

This had been bothering the young doctor. He knew he was expected to be the sole provider for the family, and he was making a junior physician's salary at the Yarmouth Hospital. But a move of any kind, within Yarmouth by buying their own home, or to Halifax to go back to university, might simply be beyond their means.

When he arrived at the train station in Halifax, the sheer destruction of the north end of the city that surrounded him was overwhelming. It was as if someone had turned off a light switch leaving entire swaths of the city flattened in darkness. And, it was snowing wildly, which only added to the misery.

One in every fifty citizens in Halifax and Dartmouth, the sister city on the other side of the harbor, lost their sight in the explosion. Some were totally blinded, while hundreds more suffered permanent eye damage due to shattered glass and flying debris.

Seamus was quickly put to work working with other doctors and nurses who were tasked with removing glass from patients' eyes, but in 249 cases, enucleations —removal of the entire eye — were performed. That number of unfortunate citizens included sixteen people who lost both of their eyes.

This emergency ophthalmological work went on daily and virtually non-stop until December 19.

Seamus was exhausted, and like so many other volunteers, had not been sleeping or eating properly due to the overall destruction that surrounded him. His heart was heavy. He couldn't count the number of lacerated eyelids he had repaired, nor the amount of pottery shards, nails and mortar that had to be removed from the eyes of the victims of the Explosion. Many had simply been curious onlookers standing near the waterfront, not knowing how huge the blast would be.

He had borne witness to the largest mass blinding of people in his nation's history. Working alongside twelve ophthalmologists and employees from the Halifax School for the Blind, he gained a deep appreciation for the teachers and staff at the institution, which had been in operation since Canada became a country in 1867.

When he returned to Yarmouth on the train just a few days before Christmas, he knew something had fundamentally changed in him. He saw how people's lives could be obliterated in an instant; how someone could watch a sunrise one day, and then never witness another. He made a vow to himself to not take any future day — or even an hour, given to him, for granted. He knew he had to live life to its fullest.

FIFTEEN

Gothenburg, Saturday, July 27, 1918

Martin Karlsson wasn't considered to be a man who was lucky in love, employment, general health, or just about anything else in life. He drifted from one part-time job to another, never staying in one location in Sweden long enough to have established roots anywhere.

Ironically, he had been blessed with classic good looks, and had he bothered enough with his personal appearance, or had the income to enhance those looks, he may have been mistaken for an older version of one of the silent screen's matinee idols that year, Wallace Reid.

But by the time he had turned forty-seven years of age, the years of manual labor, unemployment, and bouts of living on the streets had taken their toll. The only consistent job he had managed to hold on to this year was as a luggage porter at the ocean liner terminal in Gothenburg. He received his pay every two weeks, but that wasn't frequent enough, in his opinion.

One day in early July, while he waited for the steamship Torsten to arrive from London, he idly picked up a newspaper left in the terminal earlier by someone. He was essentially an illiterate man, thanks to having worked on farms since he was about thirteen. He ran away from his adoptive parents at sixteen. Education had never been afforded to the peasantry; there was too much work to do on the homesteads.

He had picked up snippets of English from passengers and crew who arrived and departed Gothenburg, but not enough to have full conversations in the language.

He looked at all the photographs in the newspaper and tried to understand the captions and articles. There were pictures of war, and of government and military officials, crowded hospital wards, and portraits of attractive women and men on the back pages.

As he threw down the paper in disgust, more due to his own sense of self-worth than anything else, he didn't see an inside page separate from the rest which displayed a photo of Collan winning a riding competition the previous weekend.

Martin fell ill less than a week after his last job unloading the luggage of the Torsten. He knew within hours that this was not anything minor.

He was living in a ramshackle boarding house on the edge of the city limits complete with shoddy plumbing, paper-thin walls, and a perpetually irate landlord. He was barely able to get up from bed after hearing someone pounding on his door one hot and humid morning.

"Karlsson! Karlsson! Enough with the coughing! Get yourself to a doctor!"

Martin groaned and opened the door. The landlord.

"I can't do much about it, Holtenius. I don't think I've ever been this sick. I can't afford to see a doctor or go to the hospital."

The landlord scoffed and said, "Ridiculous. You work for the city's port authority. There's a goddam sickness fund waiting for you. Now go — you're making a damn racket here, and I'm getting sick myself just listening to you hack up a lung every ten minutes."

Martin's illiteracy had once again prohibited him from knowing that a small portion of his equally small pay was devoted to dockworkers' union dues.

The next day he was admitted to Sahlgrenska Hospital. He was one of the first Swedes to be diagnosed as having an influenza which came to be known as the 'Spanish' flu. It was an insidious illness that had either started in the USA or China, and then spread to Europe, moving easily among troops that spring.

Martin's middle age and the timing of his sickness curiously helped him. Younger adults had the highest mortality rate with this strain of influenza , and the worst wave had yet to spread throughout Sweden and the rest of the world. His whole body ached. Besides the persistent cough, his body temperature remained high. He vomited repeatedly until there was nothing left in his stomach. Every fibre of his being felt fatigued.

"Mr. Karlsson, I want to tell you how we will treat your illness so you can return to your home and work," an elderly doctor said as he approached Martin who lay supine in a ward of twenty beds, each separated by a cloth curtain of about seven feet in height.

"It doesn't matter," Martin drolly responded, too sick to care.

"Not to worry. Things will be better soon," the physician continued, as if Martin had not spoken at all. "I will give you a drink of cognac and hot tea. Then you'll be given an enema to be followed by camphor injections. Afterwards, you'll be wrapped in your bed linens that nurse will have soaked in cold water. This will induce perspiration, and your recovery will be greatly enhanced with this treatment."

Martin looked at the man through dull eyes. His words meant nothing.

"Now, I can't guarantee that this method will work," the older man said, "so I may inject you with a serum we've used to combat diphtheria." He paused, as if weighing his options. "Then again, a respected colleague of mine finds great success using some of the syphilis drugs, like neosalvarsan and arsenic, for the condition you're in."

The physician laid a hand on Martin's shoulder as if to reassure him.

"And if you begin to have those long coughing fits again, I'll give you another dose of heroin. That will do the trick."

Martin knew nothing of medicines, but he instinctively thought that a variety of remedies to make him better might not help matters at all. He wondered if he would ever leave this hospital alive.

That night, his coughing continually disrupted his sleep, and his dreams always turned to nightmares.

I can hear the girls wailing but they're behind a big, thick door above me. There's a sliver of light coming from the other big door in front of me. I can't breathe; I can't speak; I can't cry; I can't do nothing. The roaring in my head is so loud, now I can't hear. It is so dark except for the tiny amount of light, but I still can't see nothing. I start to scream because an axe blade is slicing into my child prison.

The 'Spanish' flu, so called due to its preponderance in Spain where news coverage of the virus was not censored as it had been in other countries, would kill more people worldwide than the Great War.

Martin survived the pandemic.

When he was released from the hospital, instead of being relieved, the bitterness and anger that had festered since his childhood were reaching a crescendo.

SIXTEEN

Eva – Yarmouth, Monday, September 16, 1918

Dear Journal
I can't believe I'm in Grade Eleven!

I love history and English. Those two subjects remind me every day that I still want to become a journalist. Grandfather doesn't think much of that idea, even though he's not totally opposed to women working in the business world. I wish I had more support from him, though. He doesn't agree with my plan to study at King's College after high school. He says that many newspapers have been failing during the war, and some even have gone out of business, so he doesn't understand why I want to pursue a career in that profession. He thinks I should get a job as a teacher before I get married and have children.

Grandfather's attitude toward women seems so old-fashioned. He sees them ultimately as wives and mothers, but I see an opportunity for women to also be an important voice in society. Studying journalism will hopefully offer me a chance to speak my mind and have my opinions heard and respected.

There is much talk that the war will be over by the end of the year. Wouldn't that be wonderful — a year to be remembered for the end to the Great War! But equally important is that this is the year that most women in Canada were finally given the right to vote. What a fast-moving time I'm living in!

And a weird time, too. Some kind of influenza that started this past spring is going around in Europe right now. The British troops have called it the "Flanders grippe", and it has affected many people, apparently. There is so little news about the sickness; the war has overshadowed everything else in the past four years. I hope the Canadian troops aren't infected with this influenza because they could be contagious when they return home.

Mama misses her sisters who still live in Europe. She doesn't seem to have much in common with Grandmother, but at least that seems to encourage a closer relationship with me. She's always asking me if I've met any nice boys at the Academy, or what books I'm reading. (I'll read anything by Edgar Rice Burroughs!) I'm 99.9% sure that Mama is sincerely interested in my welfare and that makes me feel good.

I am a little worried about her health, though. Even before Seamus received a fellowship after the Explosion to study ophthalmology in Halifax, she didn't seem well.

Yesterday she finally told me about her sleeplessness, her irritation with Grandmother, her aches and pains, hot flushes and sweating, and issues with her cycle. From time to time she is short with me, but I think that's simply due to not feeling well.

Mama turned forty this year, so maybe her body is changing again. I'm going to suggest that she speak to Seamus about how she's feeling in case there might be something seriously wrong.

SEVENTEEN

Gothenburg, Tuesday, October 1, 1918

"I don't understand why the paperwork is taking so long to arrive," Katarina complained to her husband at their home. She watched leaves fall off the maple trees surrounding their house, reminding her of her childhood in Nova Scotia. She wondered if Joseph had thought to hire someone to do some groundskeeping, and she could see that the windows could use a good cleaning, as well.

"There's a war on, the last time I checked, Katarina. You can't expect the mail from Great Britain to Sweden to be either efficient or fast."

"But wasn't the lawyer's fee to buy our titles paid for by your company's solicitor in London?"

"Yes, it was," Joseph replied, sighing. He stopped writing in the ledger on his desk and looked directly at his wife.

"Katarina, this whole charade of maintaining that I'm some kind of nobleman is frankly embarrassing. Yes, my family has history in Naples, but so what? We're not Italian royalty; our family's name has been pronounced Carmignani, Carmignola, Carminati, Carmina, Carmena, and spelled in as many different ways. I'm not comfortable with you or me calling ourselves the Count and Countess."

"But if it's legal to buy a title, Joseph, what harm can it do? It sounds nice and others will treat us differently. We might even get invited to a party or two!"

She stood and walked to the credenza in the dining room. "Will you join me in a glass of *punsch*?" she asked, offering the popular liqueur which was a staple of many households since the Swedish East India Company started importing Batavian arrack from Java in the 18th century.

"Katarina, we haven't had lunch yet, and I still have work to do, dear," Joseph said. "You go ahead, if you wish."

Katarina raised an eyebrow at him to indicate her disapproval, and then poured herself a liqueur glass of the alcohol.

Sensing her growing irritability, Joseph said, "Listen, I promise I won't admit to your friends and relatives that this count and countess thing is more of a lark than anything serious. But please, please, don't ask me to go along with any further — shall we say, unusual? — requests anytime soon."

"Oh, all right, Joseph," Katarina agreed. "For now. But I do want you to send a telegram to that law office in England to find out what the delay is."

She drank the liquor in one swallow and placed the glass on the marble top of the credenza.

Turning to observe him at his desk, she thought, *God, I wish we had a cook and a maid.*

She decided not to say what she was thinking.

Instead, she asked, "Would you like a sandwich for lunch? We have some pumpernickel, gravlax, and there's the last of the pickled herring...".

#

The youthful looking, clean-shaven Dr. Arthur C. Hawkins, Mayor of Halifax, looked visibly concerned as he dictated a letter to be sent to the federal Department of Defense in Ottawa.

Many sailors were returning from their deployments overseas wounded from battle, but some also with a virulent influenza. They were being admitted to the Cogswell Street Military Hospital. Halifax was already sadly lacking in the services of doctors and nurses, thanks to the Great War, and it had been less than a year since the Explosion. The Hospital was already straining with the extra load of patients.

There was a knock on the door, and without waiting for a response, the Public Health Officer for Nova Scotia, Dr. William Hattie, entered the room. The Mayor stopped in mid-sentence and nodded for his secretary to leave the office.

"What is it, Bill?"

"I'm releasing an announcement to the public tomorrow about this influenza, Arthur. We've got to tell Nova Scotians about it, how to recognize it, and how we'll be treating it. I mean, you and I know there are cases across the border in Massachusetts, but the ones here are contained…for now. I think it's only a matter of time — perhaps even a few days before the public might get infected."

The Mayor walked to the window of his office which overlooked the Grand Parade, a military parade square dating back from the first British settlement in Halifax in 1749. At its southern end stood Saint Paul's Church, which the Mayor remembered only too well as being an architectural saviour following the Explosion.

He was not only the Mayor of a city he loved, but a medical doctor and the chief coroner.

Directly after the Explosion, St. Paul's had become an emergency hospital, with its two vestries used to help the wounded. Bodies of the dead had to be stacked on top of one another around the walls of the nave.

Good Lord, haven't we seen enough death in my city already?

"Yes, I have the same fear, Bill. Two seamen died today at the hospital on Lawlor's Island, but the press haven't been told yet. As you know, that's where we're quarantining the crews who might be sick from all the non-military ships. I was just informed an hour ago there are fifteen more people being treated as we speak." He paused. "Bill, I fear we're about to undergo yet another crisis in our city."

"I'm not happy having to agree with you," the Public Health Officer said to his colleague and friend. "What should be our next step?"

"Well, remember last December how valuable the public health authorities from Boston were to us after the Explosion? I think we have to send at least three physicians immediately to that city to see how they're handling this influenza outbreak. We have to minimize casualties in the province, in Halifax —", the Mayor's voice broke for an instant, and he quickly recovered.

"We must do all we can to stop the spread," he finished.

"I'll go to see the Chair of the city's Board of Health right now," Bill Hattie said. "We need him on board immediately. I don't know why this topic wasn't brought up at our first meeting with the Board of Health last Friday. It's not like we didn't know about this virus spreading rapidly. You remember that sudden death we talked about — the young woman in Cape Breton on September first? Then, two weeks later fourteen had died?"

Shaking his head, he left the office. The Mayor was now alone with his thoughts.

Three days later, on Friday, October 4th , sixty-four cases of influenza had been reported in the city. The following Monday, 200 cases and one death had been tallied, and on October 8th , an isolation hospital opened on Morris Street in Halifax. By the following Saturday, there were forty deaths from the flu throughout the province.

All public places, including schools, universities, churches, and theaters were immediately closed. All public gatherings were prohibited. Posters were instantly designed and distributed throughout Nova Scotia, depicting a man holding a handkerchief to his nose and mouth: "Prevent Disease – Careless spitting, coughing, sneezing spread influenza and tuberculosis".

Sydney and Halifax had become targets of the influenza due to the number of returning soldiers, and in Yarmouth, families were also not immune to the virus. It was the deadliest pandemic the world had seen since the bubonic plague of the 14th century.

The influenza had already taken hold in Massachusetts. Due to the constant interaction Yarmouth had with passengers and crew on the steamships from Boston, and people arriving on the Dominion Atlantic Railway from Halifax, the town became a hotspot for the flu.

Eva's concern that the soldiers would return home with that odd contagious "Flanders Grippe" was now stark reality. It would affect her family sooner than she could have imagined.

EIGHTEEN

Gothenburg, 11 November 1918

Dearest Parents, Elisabet, and Eva,

Today is a wonderful day! Germany has admitted defeat in the War! It has been a long time coming, that's for certain. By the time you get this letter, perhaps the world will be returning to normal.

I hope and pray you are all well in Yarmouth; I think of you often and with great fondness. I look forward to the day I meet your doctor husband, Elisabet! I am so glad that dear Eva has a father figure in her life again.

My, so much has happened with my life since we last exchanged letters. I know it is hard for you to picture my wonderful husband, Joseph, but I have been so blessed. (I must remember to post you a photograph of him.) He comes from one of Italy's most noble, celebrated, and historic families. They are fabulously *wealthy and terribly kind.*

Indeed, my parents-in-law have offered to give us one of their many villas outside of Napoli, but I'm not sure if I'd like the oppressive summer heat there. Having been raised in breezy Nova Scotia and now living in Sweden for the past five years, I am quite fond of climates that do not *induce unladylike perspiring!*

I see Collan on a fairly regular basis and in fact I'm going to watch her practice show jumping tomorrow afternoon. (I think that's what it's called.) Joseph and I are remarkably busy, as you might imagine, attending charity balls and supervising work on our new home. It is rather exhausting to be in charge of a household with staff, and I can never keep track of how many people Joseph employs.

Oh yes, Collan! Since Prince Erik caught her eye three years ago, she was invited many, many times to his mansion outside of Stockholm, to the extent that I even said to her that she must guard her good reputation. He is utterly charming, but is rumored to have epilepsy, or some form of mild mental retardation. You know how royalty keeps all its secrets to itself!

I am saving the best news for last.

You can now call me Countess de Carminati! I had NO idea that by marrying Joseph I would become a member of the nobility myself! Isn't it perfectly wonderful! And what an honor to the people of Yarmouth, who can now say they have a Countess mingling amongst them when I visit!

It's an exciting time to be alive! I miss you and look forward to reading all your news.

Affectionately,
Katarina

#

"I thought you looked quite smart out there today riding that big horse," Katarina said to her sister as they sipped coffee at a newly opened horseback riding club on the outskirts of Gothenburg.

"Thank you, Katarina, but I'd say my mare put on a much better show than I did. She did all the work; I just rode her."

"Yes, but that takes skill, and you clearly love this sport. I think you should try out for the Swedish Equestrian Olympic Team!"

Collan sighed, and her voice was tinged with frustration.

"I don't know if that's even a possibility, Katarina. It was only during the last Olympic Games before the War when equestrian competitions were first held, and the next Games in 1920 may not see any change."

"What do you mean by 'change'?"

Collan's eyes widened, as if she were surprised Katarina didn't know.

"It's a *man's* sport, m'dear. When Helen Preece, a brilliant British horsewoman, applied to compete in the 1912 Stockholm Games, the Swedish Olympic Committee rejected her registration. It's bloody ridiculous."

"That's crazy," Katarina said, genuinely shocked. "Women look much more elegant on horses than men…and they're not as heavy!"

"I agree. To add insult to injury, I remember reading at the time when we were still in Nova Scotia, that the president of the International Olympic Committee called her a 'neo-Amazonian'.

Katarina shook her head in dismay.

"Men are threatened by us, Collan — let's face facts."

"I know, Katarina. But now that both Sweden and Canada are allowing women to vote, we have the ability to change things." She paused and looked out to the field where her horse was grazing. "And maybe even the Olympic Games will someday let women compete in horseback riding."

Collan's wait would be a long one. At the Helsinki Games in 1952, women were finally admitted to equestrian competitions.

NINETEEN

Yarmouth, Friday, November 22, 1918

It was official.

The fast spreading influenza was now termed the Spanish Flu and was so named virtually everywhere in the English-speaking world.

The Yarmouth Courier was one of many daily chronicles in the province that ran a hastily composed advertisement for a local product, Minard's Liniment, as a cure-all for the Spanish Flu.

"Spanish Flu claims many victims in Canada and should be guarded against", ran the text for one advertisement. *"Minard's Liniment is a Great Preventative being one of the oldest remedies used…It is an enemy of germs; thousands of bottles used every day. MINARD'S LINIMENT Co., Ltd., Yarmouth, N.S."*

Jacob's home on Forest Street, like hundreds of others in the town, always had at least one bottle of the ammonia-smelling 'Minard's' on hand for the treatment of normal aches and pains, but this time the famous remedy would not be of any help.

Captain Jacob Burcharth, fifty-nine, and his wife Signe, fifty-eight, both born in Sweden, died three days apart from one another on November 18th and 22nd , respectively. The cause of death for both was listed as 'influenza'.

These immigrants who had come to Nova Scotia in 1883 were in sad company. By the end of the final influenza outbreak in early 1920, approximately 2,200 deaths from the Spanish Flu had been reported from all parts of the province — more than the number of people killed in the Halifax Explosion.

Signe had been too ill the week before she died to go to the hospital, so Elisabet and Eva had been taking care of her as best they could.

Wearing handkerchiefs over their faces, they tidied her room, and Eva removed the dishes that had been used for soup and crackers.

Signe had barely eaten anything since the flu had entered her respiratory system and her already mentally depressed condition.

Elisabet hadn't completely come to terms with her father's demise just two days earlier; her emotions were fragile. She was angry at the unfairness of the pandemic, and the fact it had taken her father from her, and would probably cause her mother's death, as well.

Signe grabbed her daughter's wrist as Elisabet was cleaning the night table next to the bed.

"Elisabet, Elisabet," Signe struggled with what little strength she had in her grip and in her voice. "I need you to know that *you're not mine.*"

Elisabet gaped at her severely ill mother as opposing thoughts raced in her mind.

What is she talking about? Has her senility gotten even worse with this flu virus?

"Mother, you're just tired now. Why don't you close your eyes and rest?"

Signe's voice rose slightly, and her eyes widened.

"You and your sisters are not mine. We adopted you three."

Elisabet instinctively let her mother's hand fall back on the bed.

"I never wanted children."

Dear Lord, what is she saying? She's literally on her deathbed, and she's saying that she never wanted Collan, Katarina and me? Maybe she's delusional, or maybe she's talking about someone else, or maybe —

She left the bedroom without responding to Signe. She had never known anger as intense as that which she was feeling.

Until just a few minutes ago, her life had been carefully written in broad cursive strokes with white chalk on a school blackboard. Growing up in Yarmouth, marrying and moving to Boston, having a child, burying a husband, returning to her hometown, re-marrying, and providing care to her aging parents — all were orderly, expected, normal, definitive. It was a life that made sense.

The dying woman lying under a heavy handmade quilt, with every comfort she could have needed before death, had just wiped Elisabet's blackboard clean in one stroke of a brush.

Signe took her last breath minutes later in the bedroom just a few feet away from where a furious Elisabet stood outside the door.

She barely noticed Eva coming up the stairs to stand next to her.

"Mama? Are you all right? You look like you've seen a ghost."

"What? No, no, I'm fine, Eva. Let my mother rest. Let *Signe* rest until the morning."

"Yes, of course. Do you want a cup of tea or something? You really do look pale."

"Yes, that's a good idea," Elisabet said absently as she let Eva guide her toward the staircase and down the stairs.

Later, sipping a cup of hot tea in the dining room, Elisabet stared into the distance, not focusing on anything. Eva looked worried.

"Mama, I know the past few days have been awfully hard on you. First Grandfather passes, and now Grandmother is in a terrible state…"

"You know all about death, Eva. Your father died, too, but he was your *real* father."

Eva gave her mother a quizzical look.

"Well, yes, of course. Do you mean that I'll feel differently when Seamus dies because he is my stepfather?"

Elisabet looked at her daughter with a blank expression.

"Seamus?" she asked, as if a total stranger had been introduced to the conversation. She blinked, stirred her tea, and appeared to return to the present moment.

"We will have a busy Saturday tomorrow, Eva. Off to bed with you now."

TWENTY

Yarmouth, Wednesday, July 14, 1920

"Mama, are you sad that you're selling the family home?" Eva asked Elisabet as they had lunch on the veranda overlooking their neighbor's large rhododendron bushes. Seamus was due to join them shortly.

It was a brilliantly sunny day, and the air was crystal clear with not a cloud in sight. Typical for Yarmouth in mid-summer, the temperature would probably not exceed seventy to seventy-five degrees Fahrenheit.

"Not at all, Eva," Elisabet replied. "It doesn't bother me in the slightest. Once again, it's time for us to move on, and I'm so happy that we'll soon call Broadale our new home by the end of the year. Even if we can't sell your grandfather's house right away, Seamus and I have made enough of a down payment to be able to buy it very soon."

Elisabet was referring to the large home on Parade Street she had particularly admired a few years earlier that included a beautiful ballroom, two spacious parlors, a dining room that could seat eighteen people comfortably, seven bedrooms, three modern baths, and a large, well-equipped kitchen. It had been for sale for several months after the current owner failed to keep up with the mortgage payments and property taxes.

The semi-circular driveway had stone posts at both entrances to tether horses, and there were American Chestnut trees encircling the property which had been planted when the house was built in the late 1870s. They were now fully grown and provided graceful shade in the summers.

Seamus arrived looking dapper in a three-piece summer suit and wearing a boater hat. He put the hat aside on the railing and took a seat next to his wife and stepdaughter, after kissing the cheeks of both women.

"Dear, have some potato salad, and there's cold chicken left for you, too," Elisabet indicated the dishes on the table in front of them.

"Thank you, Elisabet. Lunch looks delicious," Seamus said, as he helped himself to the provisions at hand.

Looking at Eva as he placed his choices on a luncheon plate, he said, "Eva, I haven't had the chance to tell you how sorry I am you won't be going to college this fall."

"Thank you, Seamus. Yes, it was a disappointment, but how could anyone have predicted that King's College would burn to the ground last February? I've been told by the Admissions Office that I'm welcome to enroll once the new college is built in Halifax. I guess it makes more sense to build on the Dalhousie University campus and enjoy the extra facilities there," Eva commented, "although I'm sure the people of Windsor won't be happy to have their historic college relocated."

Seamus nodded in agreement as he poured himself a glass of lemonade.

"Seamus, I hope you haven't seen any more cases of that horrible flu in the city lately," Elisabet said.

"There've been no deaths since the end of April, thank God," Seamus said. "But even with all our precautions, and all the public and medical support we've had since the damned virus landed on our shores almost two years ago, we still had 200 people die between January and April." He paused and twirled his lemonade glass on the tablecloth, looking thoughtful. "Honestly, Elisabet, I thought the pain and destruction after the Explosion was bad, but to see so many families affected by the Spanish Flu all over Nova Scotia has been just as heartbreaking."

"I know, Seamus. And let's not forget the two people who took you into their home here when we got married."

"Well, of course I won't forget Jacob and Signe," Seamus said, a bit irritated. "But I also lost a brother. Thayne was only thirty when the flu took him."

"Yes, I realize that, and I've apologized many times for not going to Halifax with you for his funeral last year."

Eva decided to try to put a stop to an argument that sounded to her as if it had potential to escalate.

"I hope we'll be seeing more of you as the summer moves on, Seamus, and we get ready to move to Broadale," she commented.

Seamus put his knife and fork at the 4:20 position on his plate like a proper gentleman and sat back in his chair.

Wearing a broad smile, he said, "Eva, you'll be seeing so much of me that you'll get sick of having to look at this old mug of mine!"

Eva smiled back at him, knowing she was starting to blush. Elisabet mumbled an 'excuse me' and began clearing the table of the luncheon dishes.

#

Later, in their bedroom, Elisabet and Seamus got ready for bed as if they were two roommates. Polite with one another, the tension was palpable from earlier in the day.

Elisabet emerged from the en suite bath wearing a dressing gown over her nightgown, while Seamus sat upright in bed, shirtless, the top sheet pulled down to his waist. This was his usual signal to show his wife that making love was a desirable expectation.

"Did I mention to you how beautiful you looked at lunch today when I returned from the city?" Seamus asked, winking at his wife. "Just like you do now?"

"Uh, no, you didn't," Elisabet replied, removing her dressing gown, and placing it on a chair next to the bed. "But I hardly feel beautiful lately. Since Jacob and Signe died, I've felt unusually sad and anything *but* beautiful."

She got into the other side of the bed.

"Elisabet, they died over a year ago. We've talked about this before and I told you I think your mother had had severe melancholia for many years before she passed — the words she said to you were nonsense. You have to forget about them."

"They weren't nonsense, Seamus. That night I felt her complete indifference toward my sisters and me. And I've felt that way several times over the years but couldn't understand why. Now I know. Signe may have had melancholia, but she was as clear as glass when she told me that we were adopted, and she hadn't even wanted children."

Elisabet had not referred to her parents as Mother or Father since the night of Signe's revelation.

Seamus sighed.

"I don't know what to say to make you feel better, Elisabet," he said, reaching to embrace her. "Let me show you how beautiful you really are...let's make love and forget all the bad things that have happened..."

"Seamus, no. I'm sorry, I just don't feel like it right now. At all."

She looked directly into his eyes as if he were supposed to read her mind. Seamus put his index finger to her lips.

"It's fine, Elisabet. I understand. I know menopause changes things, but there are some herbal treatments available, like cannabis and medicinal opium. I can get those for you. Just relax now. We're a team, and about to move into a wonderful new home," he said soothingly. "Let's celebrate that."

Elisabet softened and fell into his embrace, and then decided to tell him something that she had kept secret.

"You should know I've written to Collan and told her what Signe said to me that night. I've asked her to check adoption records in Gothenburg for details about us. I need to know if all of what Signe said is true, and who our real parents were. I'm still so angry about this, Seamus."

Seamus studied the ceiling as he caressed his wife's hair.

"You must do what makes sense to you, Elisabet. And Collan and Katarina have a right to know details about their birth parents." He turned her face towards his and kissed her lightly on the lips. "Now, get some sleep."

TWENTY-ONE

Gothenburg, Tuesday, August 17, 1920

Collan continued to live in her grandparents' house in Haga after their deaths. She gingerly held an unopened letter from her sister Elisabet.

She sat by herself at the kitchen table, the late morning sun streaming through the window. She had a cinnamon roll, *kanelbulleshe,* and a strong cup of coffee waiting for her on the table, but she was in no rush. She wished Elisabet were there with her to enjoy this *fika*, that special time over coffee that Swedes enjoyed with friends. It had been quite awhile since the sisters had communicated; she guessed it was probably after the funerals of their mother and father in Yarmouth.

Sipping the hot drink, it occurred to her how infrequent her visits with Katarina had become even though her sister and brother-in-law were still living in Gothenburg. Katarina had continued her attempts to ingratiate herself with the political and social elite of the city, and Collan, who was not at all interested in those people, kept her distance.

She had not told Katarina too much about the relationship she had had with Prince Erik. She definitely did not tell her of the bequest he had left her in his will. She also said nothing about her special friendship with the Prince's primary caregiver, Linnea Nilsson.

The Prince had succumbed to the Spanish Flu, and though he died two years ago, Collan's eyes misted over yet again thinking of him. He once told her that he felt the isolation of living apart from his family was too much to bear, and he had planned to move closer to Stockholm to be near them. It was not meant to be.

After he died at the age of twenty-nine at Drottningholm Palace, Collan had been invited to the funeral, which frankly surprised her as so few had been asked to attend. Neither of his parents were present when he died, and Linnea told her that King Gustav was devastated at losing his third and youngest son even though he had never been particularly close to him.

Katarina, of course, was upset that she had not been invited to the Prince's funeral, and questioned Collan afterwards about who was there, what they wore, and what happened after the service. Collan felt this to be an inappropriate interest in a sad family occasion.

She smiled, though, as she opened the letter from Elisabet. She and her sister were not alike, but basically accepted one another's faults and foibles. She was thankful that her family was staying as connected as they possibly could, considering they lived continents and time zones apart.

Her eyes widened as she read the contents of Elisabet's handwritten note:

Dear Collan,

I hope you're faring well in mind and body and haven't had any health issues of late. We are well here and plan to move into a home on Parade Street this year; you may remember it. It's called Broadale and is located east from the corner of Pleasant Street. Anyway, it became available for sale, and I've always admired the house. Seamus also likes it, so he and Eva and I will be making it our home. (Eva will not be going away to King's College in Windsor this fall as the building was destroyed by fire this past year. It will be rebuilt in Halifax. She hopes to attend next year.)

Of course, once the family home on Forest Street has been sold, you will share in one-third of the net proceeds from the sale. I do hope you will come home for a long visit now that the pandemic seems to have run its course.

Collan, something has been bothering me greatly since the night Mother died. Or, should I say, since Signe died...

Collan broke down in tears as she finished reading the text. She decided to begin an investigation immediately into the local adoption records. But she also decided not to tell Katarina of this bizarre news, at least not at the moment. Katarina would become overly dramatic about the revelation, and Collan wasn't ready to deal with that right now.

Later that day, she discovered how difficult it was to track down adoption records from the early 1880s. However, she did know from stories her father used to tell about emigrating to Canada, that they had arrived in Nova Scotia in 1883.

She also knew that she had been four years of age; Elisabet five, and Katarina only three when they landed in Yarmouth.

Having had no luck inquiring by phone at the Allmänna Barnhusets arkiv, or General Children's Home Archive, Collan was told to start inquiring at the various churches in the city. At the time the girls were supposedly adopted, it was often a local parish that handled the process especially if both parents were deceased. Space in the few orphanages in the area was limited, and the Church of Sweden tried to help by placing abandoned children with interested families who were willing to care for them either temporarily or permanently.

She continued her telephone inquiries and was finally able to secure an appointment the following morning at the office for the Diocese of Gothenburg.

"I'm afraid those are all the details I have about what I know of our family, sir," Collan said to the young deacon sitting across from her in an austere, almost antiseptic office at the Diocesan house. She struggled with not knowing if she should address him as a Reverend, but then assumed he hadn't reached that level of ministry.

Goodness, he's so young looking.

The Assistant to the Archbishop listened to Collan's story very carefully and made notes as she spoke. Of particular interest to him were the full names of her parents, and an approximate date when the adoption may have taken place. Collan also told him about her paternal grandparents who had never left Gothenburg, but she knew nothing of her maternal grandparents.

While the Assistant left the office to search for the parish adoption records, Collan waited and wondered how the discovery of a legal document proving that she and her two sisters were actually born to another set of parents would change their lives.

I always thought it was a bit strange that my sisters and I did not resemble either Mother or Father. And while Elisabet's personality has always been a bit like Mother's, the three of us could quite possibly be the children of different parents.

She looked around the room and randomly noticed that not a speck of dust could be seen on any surfaces.

They must keep really accurate records. Maybe they'll show our birth parents weren't able to keep us for some reason, but maybe they continued to live in this area.

Her mind began to race.

What if our birth parents are alive?

Perhaps we're part of a larger family and we have other sisters and brothers somewhere in the world!

But if there are other siblings, would they want to know about me and my sisters? Maybe they've been searching for their missing siblings, too, and what if they have been feeling as lost and alone as I feel right now?

Later at home, and still reeling from the information she received about their adoption, Collan was overwhelmed by the fact that their birth father, in a fit of rage, had murdered their mother and then killed himself.

And yet, the words that Signe had uttered to Elisabet, "I never wanted children", were weighing more heavily on her mind.

It was at that moment she decided not to tell her sisters about the circumstances of their adoption, that their birth father had committed uxoricide, and that this certainty was blatantly written on the adoption certificate.

She thought it would cause Elisabet less grief if she told her the records contained a note from the Bishop, written at the time, suggesting he thought that Signe may be suffering from a severe melancholia. Collan reasoned that a phony assessment from the Bishop might help Elisabet forgive their adoptive mother's deathbed pronouncement.

She would also not tell either of her sisters that they had a brother, possibly living somewhere in the world, who shared their sad story of their early childhood. Collan's mind needed rest, and she retired to bed.

TWENTY-TWO

Gothenburg, Wednesday, August 18, 1920

On the other side of the city, as Collan was leaving the office of the Diocese of Gothenburg with the startling news about her birth parents, Katarina, by contrast, was giddy with excitement.

The newly named Countess was shaking slightly as she held an official looking letter which had just arrived that morning from the largest orphanage in Sweden, the Allmänna Barnhuset, located in Stockholm.

She and Joseph had been interviewed the previous month as potential adoptive parents, and she had not expected to hear from the General Children's Home so soon, especially since her adoption request had been rather specific.

She had mentioned to Joseph that they were probably fortunate that they could not have a child of their own. Could he even imagine all the physical changes that would happen to her body at age forty during a pregnancy? She had read that it was dangerous for a woman her age to give birth, anyway! But she definitely wanted a baby, because after all, every couple they knew had children. She was sure it was expected for a Count and Countess to have at least one child.

Katarina felt that it was not in her friends' or sisters' best interests to know that she and Joseph were planning to adopt. She had not mentioned her plan to anyone, including Collan, whom she had been avoiding since April. Her sister knew Katarina was not able to have children, but Katarina thought she could fool her friends, so she began to pad her undergarments to give the impression she might be carrying a child.

Oh my, what if the little baby boy is ready to come home right away? I can't just tell our friends that I had a premature birth! What if he's a big baby? I asked for a boy with red hair, like mine. I don't care what color his eyes are, but if they're dark, like Joseph's, that would be a true bonus. I'm so excited!

Two weeks later, Katarina and Joseph brought an infant boy home, and on the train from Stockholm, she worried that she may have to offer a deft explanation should anyone dare to ask. Paolo was a big baby, who had weighed in at ten pounds at birth. He had curly red hair and blue eyes.

But he is our little Count de Carminati — or is that Viscount? And he looks just like me!

TWENTY-THREE

Yarmouth, Wednesday, November 17, 1920

"Mama, that thing is ungodly," Eva commented to her mother when she saw what Seamus had uncovered buried in a crate in the hallway of their new home.

It contained a large polar bear rug, approximately eight feet in length, which would have made any taxidermist proud.

"I truly hope that you're not going to display it anywhere in this house! That poor bear!" she lamented.

Elisabet agreed, thinking that Katarina and her husband had certainly chosen to send a very odd gift as a housewarming present. The crate had taken well over a month to arrive from Sweden, and this 'bear' was not at all what Elisabet had expected. She removed an envelope from the crate and opened it.

"Well then, this is what your Aunt Katarina has to say: 'Dear Elisabet, Eva, and Seamus, I hope you will enjoy this brilliant bear rug and display it proudly in your new home on Parade Street! A confidante to the late President Roosevelt told me at a function at the American Embassy in Stockholm that Teddy had one in his personal study at the White House! I thought it was only fitting you should have one, too, since I am sure you will be receiving many American guests in the future. Seeing the magnificent rug, they will immediately recognize your good taste in décor as similar to their beloved President, and will feel quite at home. When I come to visit, I will plan a big party, and invite all our friends and their visitors from Boston. I'll bet you that a great many Yarmouthians are anxiously waiting to meet a real Countess!'"

Elisabet stopped reading long enough to glance at her husband and daughter, both of whom wore bemused smiles listening to Katarina's braggadocio.

"And she signed off with, 'With great affection, I hope we will see you all soon in Yarmouth. I cannot wait for you to meet Joseph and little Count Paolo! Love, Katarina.'"

Eva groaned.

"Oh, my goodness, is she serious? Is she a real countess, Mama? Wouldn't that mean that her husband is a count? And I suppose he owns property in Italy, too?"

"Eva, your guesses are as good as mine. Your aunt has always loved telling tall tales, to put it mildly. I somehow doubt she's ever met anyone who worked for President Roosevelt, but who knows?"

Seamus picked up the head of the bear which displayed many of its forty-two teeth, including its long, sharp canines. He felt sorry for the animal with the agonized look on its face.

"Don't worry, Eva, I'll find a nice discreet wall and hang the unfortunate creature there," Seamus said. "Maybe in my study, eh? That way you won't have to look at it too often."

"Perhaps you could take Mr. Bear away right now, then, Seamus, thank you very much!" Elisabet directed, in a light tone. She and Seamus had been getting along quite well lately, although there were many days she wondered how long the good will would last.

"Your stepdaughter and I have some furniture re-arranging to do in the main parlor."

Seamus struggled to fold the large, heavy fur rug, and Elisabet and Eva left him to that difficult task.

I want to make Broadale a home where I'll always feel comfortable. I want to choose furnishings that appeal to me in this post-war age, and I don't want any reminders of Victoriana. I certainly don't want our home to appear trendy. Nor does my taste in interior decorating include the display of a polar bear rug! I will not cater to, but will welcome visitors and perhaps host the occasional dinner party. This will be the home of The McMaster family. The Burcharth Family era is over, if it ever really existed...and the only reminders I have of my first marriage are my former married name and the name of Eva's father on her birth certificate.

Eva began to unpack a box of framed photographs, and removed one of Jacob, Signe, Elisabet and her sisters, and placed it carefully on top of the mahogany baby grand piano which occupied a prominent position in the room.

"Uh, Eva dear, no, you can take the photographs away. I think they'll be better displayed elsewhere," Elisabet instructed.

I just want to rid myself of all of them.

"Okay, Mama, I'll put the box of them in the silver cabinet in the dining room for the time being, until you decide where you want them to go."

Eva left the room with the box, and Elisabet evaluated the décor in the parlor. She studied the luxuriously plush chairs, the sparkling crystal lamps, and a few carefully placed wall mirrors in polished wood frames. Yes, the front parlor could be called opulent by current Nova Scotian standards.

She took time to stare at the hand painted murals with bas relief frames that depicted three female figures. She had commissioned a local artist to paint the murals in oil, and her main instruction had been that the visualizations had to be of an anchoress in three milieus.

Elisabet wanted the artist to portray a middle-aged woman withdrawing from secular life to lead a contemplative life. The figure should not be confined to a cell, as was the medieval definition of an anchoress, but should exhibit a solitary strength in expansive locations.

The first mural showed the figure in flowing robes standing on top of the world; in the middle painting she was reclining in a similar, but more lavish dress in what appeared to be a room in a castle with the sea in the background; and in the third, the figure sat wearing a hooded robe, her legs bent, her knees to her breast, outside at dusk in a forest of poplar trees.

Elisabet wasn't sure which of the three murals she preferred. She remembered one morning the previous week watching the artist put the finishing touches on the third mural. He did not detect her physical presence, nor did she realize he was thinking of her at the time.

He understood that his client was challenged with an emptiness in her privileged life. He had noticed her mannerisms, her distractedness, and had felt her desire to put her feelings into something tangible. A new, larger house would not be enough for her. She seemed to have forgotten the many things with which she had already been gifted: good health, comfortable accommodation, food on her table, and people who loved her.

His thoughts wandered as he compared this woman's fortunate situation to his own miserable existence over the past year. He had nearly died with a severe case of the Spanish Flu; he lost his beloved canine companion to old age; and he constantly worried about being able to pay his monthly rent.

He may not have completely understood his client, but he was incredibly grateful for this assignment from Mrs. McMaster.

Elisabet snapped back to reality when Eva re-entered the room.

"Mama, Seamus just asked me if I want to go to the hospital with him. He has to check on a couple of patients, and mentioned a girl of about fourteen who asked to speak with another girl close to her age. I suspect it's a question about female issues that she's nervous talking about with Seamus. She has no siblings, and I guess, no visitors. Do you need me to do anything further here?"

"No, Eva, I'm fine. And you're nineteen years old. You don't have to ask my permission to go anywhere," Elisabet said. "I'll just straighten up a few things here and then do some tidying up in the kitchen."

"All right, Mama, we'll see you soon."

TWENTY-FOUR

Eva – Yarmouth, Monday, December 13, 1920

Dear Journal,
Oh God, I am feeling so guilty. I thought what happened might happen. I know Mama will hate me for the rest of my life. I don't know what to do. Maybe I can just leave for Halifax, or maybe Aunt Katarina will buy passage for me to go and visit her in Sweden. I'm feeling like a complete harlot and yet I can't be blamed one hundred percent — no, maybe I can be. I could have turned away from him.

Seamus and I were returning from the hospital one day last month. It was early afternoon on a Sunday, and Seamus asked me if I wanted to go for a little drive before we returned to Broadale for dinner. I agreed, the weather was lovely, and we weren't in a rush to be anywhere.

He asked me if I'd ever seen the 'Marble Lady', an unusual gravestone at Town Point Cemetery. It sounded interesting, and I'd never go to a cemetery on my own anyway, so I suggested we visit.

We were standing next to a white marble sculpture of a woman reclining in a wheat field. A local doctor had commissioned the artwork after the death of his young wife in the mid–1800s. Seamus said the figure was totally hand carved, and it truly is quite beautiful. It's a real testament to love and heartbreak between two people.

He began to talk about what it was like helping the victims after the Halifax Explosion in 1917, and later, how it felt to witness so many people die from the pandemic.

He said he was afraid of losing any important moments in his life — and I think that's when I knew he was going to kiss me. He did, and God forgive me, but I didn't stop him. I know I haven't really had any male suitors, but his kiss just felt like the most natural thing in the world. I think I have always been attracted to Seamus from a distance, but suddenly that distance between us fell away.

I know it sounds silly and girlish, but it felt as if my feet had been lifted off the ground while he was kissing me. Electricity passed from his mouth to mine and flowed through every vein in my body.

He told me then that he knew he could never have expressed his feelings to me before now, not only because I am nine years younger than him, but more importantly because he is married to my mother. He says he loves her very much. Can he love two women at the same time?

I told him that day that Mother must never know about the kiss. I feel guilty but that first kiss is etched so vividly in my mind, I can almost still feel the tingling. Electrifying! Oh, God, what a cliché from the pictures.

If I had been raised as a regular church-going Christian, I think I'd be damned to hell for what I did. I don't know. I want to tell Mama what's happened, but I am deathly afraid to do so. I think I'll write to Aunt Katarina. I'll have to somehow put a stop to this. It isn't fair to my mother, and it doesn't feel right to me.

I do wonder about Seamus and Mama's personal relationship behind their bedroom door. Of course, that's none of my business, but Seamus (and I) have now created an overly complicated situation for all three of us.

TWENTY-FIVE

Gothenburg, Monday, December 13, 1920

Martin never bothered to look at a calendar because it only reminded him of the fact that he could not read. Nevertheless, he knew today was St. Lucia's Day.

From his perch at Den Törstiga Kråkan — The Thirsty Crow — a bar on the waterfront, he could hear a choir singing somewhere outside the confines of his smoky, badly lit environment.

He looked dully at what had been a full glass of Aquavit in front of him. He needed the numbness found in a few glasses of his favorite liquor, which was similar in taste to vodka, but often had a caraway flavor.

He glanced at the blackboard menu sitting on the counter behind the bar, and assumed that it advertised *glögg*, Sweden's popular mulled wine served with almonds and raisins at this time of year. He hated the stuff.

He was sure the blackboard menu also featured stockfish — boiled ling soaked in lye, and *dopp i grytan* or 'dipping in the pot': old bread that is dipped in ham broth — because both dishes were December favorites in Gothenburg. But right now, all Martin really wanted was more Aquavit.

A younger man, Anders Lindgren, in his early thirties, was sitting at the end of the bar, his valise on the floor. Wearing a business suit, he had just come from an all-day meeting at the Sveriges Riksbank and had to return to Stockholm in the morning. He had been watching Martin since the time he had arrived an hour earlier.

Anders was attracted to older men, and had personally found that since the war ended, many of his gender were more open about their sexuality. Swedish law stated that homosexual acts were prohibited, but this was rarely enforced, so Anders felt comfortable in his decision to approach Martin.

He noted that the older fellow might be anywhere from forty-five to fifty years of age and seemed rough around the edges. But he had that innate handsomeness inherent in some men that no matter when they last shaved, combed their hair, or how they were dressed at any given time, they always looked appealing.

"Hello, mate, can I join you?" Anders asked, sliding on the bar stool next to Martin. "You look like you could use a refill there."

Martin looked at the yellow-haired man next to him who sported a smile beneath his blond moustache, an affectation Martin always regarded as an afterthought with fair skinned Swedes. The moustache was almost invisible, so maybe the guy hadn't even noticed it was growing. *Why bother with one?* But the bottom line was that he didn't care: this was a free drink being offered.

"Yeah, I could sure use another," Martin said, "and Happy St. Lucia's Day."

The bartender overheard the exchange between the two men and poured another shot of Aquavit into Martin's glass. Anders held up his beer stein to indicate to the bartender that he wanted another lager.

"And to you!" Anders said as he offered his hand to shake. "Anders Lindgren."

"I'm Martin Karlsson. Thanks for the drink," Martin said, shaking his hand.

"My pleasure." Anders paused for effect. "You know, you look *awfully* familiar to me, but I can't place you. Did you ever work at the Hotel Royal? Maybe on the front desk?"

"Uh, no, that's never happened, my friend. The waterfront is my backyard. I'm a porter," Martin replied. "You know, carrying luggage around, picking up parcels and boxes, delivering them — that kind of thing. Nothing special."

"But I'd bet that kind of work keeps you in top physical shape, wouldn't you say?" Anders shot back, flirtatiously.

Martin gave him a long look, and then decided to play along.

"Oh, sure, the moving pictures companies are lining up to find out the secrets about my big muscles," Martin said with a rare smile.

Anders laughed.

"Then I'm not wrong!" he said. "But I wasn't kidding before. You really do remind me of someone."

As if struck to the head with a lightning bolt of recognition, he pulled out a newspaper from his valise, and opened it to the society pages.

On one page was a photo of Katarina and Joseph with a caption describing the Count and Countess de Carminati as having been to the theater the night before with other so-called dignitaries.

"Look at this! You could be related to the Countess de Carminati! Truly! The same nose, same eyes," Anders said, passing the newspaper page over to Martin. "And the story says she has red hair, just like yours."

Not wanting to reveal he couldn't read, Martin said, "So who is this Countess and what does that mean, anyway? Is she rich or something, being in the newspaper?"

"Well, I'd think so," Anders stated. "And her husband, the Count, is definitely Italian, judging from his nice dark features. But *she* doesn't look Italian."

Martin scanned the photo again and pretended to read the caption of the photograph.

"It looks like they're having a good time, but I ain't got no royal blood in me, if that's what they are. And I ain't never been to Italy!" Martin scoffed, returning the newspaper to Anders. "I think you owe me a drink for thinking I'm related to someone I'm not!"

At this point, Anders figured he could go far with the rugged potential matinee idol named Martin. It might cost him a few kronor in the long run, but the evening lay ahead of them.

"I suppose I do, good Mr. Karlsson," Anders grinned, signaling for the bartender.

#

Early the next morning in Anders's guestroom at the Hotel Royal, Martin was already half-dressed, his hair dampened and combed, and ready to leave. Anders was awakening with a pounding headache, suffering the effect of the alcohol from the evening before.

He did remember, barely, asking the night desk clerk when they arrived hours earlier if he could switch his room to a twin-bedded room to share with his 'colleague'. He did not need to create any suspicion about having an unexpected male guest with him.

"You're in quite the rush, aren't you?" Anders asked.

"I gotta go to work in an hour, and I already took a bath — hope you don't mind. You must have a real good job to have your own bathroom attached to your bedroom."

Anders smiled weakly.

"Yeah, well, the bank pays my expenses when I have to come to Gothenburg. I'm not rolling in gold, though, believe me."

He looked at Martin closely, and realized his new friend was also clean-shaven compared to his appearance from the previous evening.

"And it looks like you shaved, as well, Mr. Karlsson!" he chuckled. "Now, you're even more dashing than you were yesterday."

"Yeah, I kinda borrowed your straight razor, too."

Standing up from his chair opposite the bed where Anders lay, Martin said, "Hey, you know that newspaper you showed me at the bar last night? You think I could take that with me? I didn't have a chance to read the news yesterday."

"Sure; it's in my valise over on the chest of drawers."

Martin walked across the room to retrieve the newspaper. He wanted to find out more about this countess. He knew where he came from, and it was a million kilometres from wherever that woman came from, but his instinct was telling him something else.

He returned to the bed, leaned over towards Anders, and shook his hand.

"Thanks for the drinks and the bath," Martin said.

Unsurprised at the quick and decidedly unromantic goodbye, Anders said, "You're welcome, Martin. It's been *my* pleasure, that's for sure. How about meeting again the next time I'm in Gothenburg?"

"Yeah, I can see doing that."

"All right, then. Before you go, take one of my calling cards on top of the bureau. Telephone me this coming week. I should know my travel schedule by Wednesday."

Martin saw Anders' business cards in a small leather sheaf next to several fifty öre coins. While he was tempted to pocket the money since his back was turned to Anders, he decided to only take one of the cards.

This guy might be able to help me find my real family.

Slipping the newspaper underneath his arm, he said goodbye to his new friend. He left the room with a noticeable spring in his step, walked down the stairs into the lobby, and out the front doors into the crisp December air.

TWENTY-SIX

Yarmouth, Wednesday, June 15, 1921

The lilacs were almost in full bloom, their scent mingling with the humid air over Parade Street. This was usually an indication that school would soon be over for the year. Yarmouth would typically get a fair amount of rain every June, but the promise of three months of warm weather ahead sustained everyone.

Elisabet was a person who was not easily pleased nor was she terribly patient. Since the task of moving into Broadale and decorating it to her specifications was complete, she felt unsettled and without purpose. She and Seamus had even decided to take separate bedrooms.

It seemed like an inevitable conclusion: she had lost all interest in intimacy with him, or any man, for that matter. Sex was simply not that important to her, so why prolong the charade of sharing a bedroom? She justified her decision further with the excuse that Seamus was working longer hours, and if the hospital rang in the middle of the night, it interrupted sleep for both of them if they were in the same room and in the same bed.

After she had received a reply from Collan last fall confirming their adoptive mother's pronouncement on her deathbed, Elisabet developed a curious detachment from her family.

Well, that's it, then. Now that I know Signe was a very disturbed woman for many years, according to what Collan found out, I can either mourn the fact and feel sorry for what was her lot in life, or I can accept it and move on. I think I'll just accept it. Her malaise was a problem that she never chose to share with her adopted children, so her unhappiness with life was, and is, not my issue.

Elisabet decided it was much easier to see the world in black and white as she moved forward in life; there was no time to search for gray areas or waste time on supposition. Life was what it was, and therefore she would deal with whatever situation was placed in front of her in the future without the useless emotion of worry.

#

Eva didn't know if she appeared different to her mother since her affair with Seamus had begun in March.

After the first kiss she and Seamus shared last December, she weakly attempted on several occasions to sit with Elisabet and confess what had happened. But Seamus discouraged her from doing so, telling her that it was better not to create upset in the household so soon after moving into Broadale.

Eva's guilt only worsened after she and Seamus made love in a linen closet at the hospital. Thinking of that night, she remembered the cloak-and-dagger subterfuge they had to engage in which didn't exactly add to the romanticism of what was her first time. And the location? Hadn't she seen that happen in a second-rate moving picture somewhere?

On that occasion, she told her mother she was staying overnight with a girlfriend from the Academy who lived in Pleasant Valley. When Seamus dropped her off around the corner from Broadale after midnight, she had to find another excuse for Elisabet as to why her evening in Pleasant Valley had been cut short. Seamus, of course, had the excuse of having to work the midnight shift, but Eva felt horrible continually deceiving her mother.

#

On a sunny Wednesday in mid-June, Seamus told Elisabet he was making house calls that afternoon. Eva lied again, telling her mother she was having lunch and doing some shopping on Main Street with her girlfriends.

The two lovers drove to the Cape Forchu lightstation which was built on an island about six miles from town. Since the 1840s, the lightstation with its powerful Fresnel lens had been protecting ships from the rocky shores of southwestern Nova Scotia, guiding them into the entrance of Yarmouth Harbor.

It was accessible via a long wooden breakwater built in 1873. The bridge was used by the lightkeepers and their families, as well as visitors and staff at the Markland Hotel, which had been built in 1904.

Eva and Seamus were not expecting to meet anyone along the way, and if they did run into any acquaintances, what was possibly wrong with a stepfather taking his daughter out for an early summer drive to the ocean?

Seamus parked his car in a cleared area below the lightstation. No one else was around. He carried a blanket, and they both walked gingerly over a hill and onto the many large granite boulders that ran south toward the ocean. It felt as if they were at the end of the world, and Eva swooned a little until Seamus took her hand to help her maneuver among and over the rocks.

They found a sheltered place to sit overlooking the turbulent Atlantic. Seamus laid the blanket on a huge flat stone. They kissed passionately and Eva didn't bother cautioning Seamus when he began to undo the buttons on her blouse. She was feeling a youthful empowerment and confidence, and was head over heels in love with the man. Later, they looked out to the sea and Eva put her head on Seamus's shoulder.

"Seamus, I don't know how much longer I can keep up with the lies. I'm hating myself more and more every day that passes."

"I know, my darling, I'm having a difficult time as well. It eats me up to play such a game with Elisabet. She's a good woman and I do love her, but God help me, I love you more and I think I have since I first laid eyes on you in Halifax in 1915."

"Seamus, you know I was more interested in dolls than in boys back then," Eva jokingly reminded him. "But I'm glad you didn't approach me until I had turned nineteen."

She smiled sweetly at him. "Although, you *could* have made a pass at me when I was eighteen."

"Ah, but that would have only resulted in one more year of turmoil for you — and for me," Seamus suggested. "Where will this relationship go, Eva? I can see spending the rest of my life with you, but I'll be an old man by the time you turn forty."

"No, you won't, Seamus. You're not *that* much older than I am."

"What are you saying, then? You'd give up thoughts of a career and marry me?"

"You know, I was hoping to go to college this fall, if King's does open in Halifax," she replied. "But I haven't heard anything from its admissions office." She playfully hit his arm. "*And* I'd love to have children, and I can't think of a better father-to-be than you!"

Seamus grinned and chuckled.

Eva decided at that moment she had better take a more decisive stance with her first, but very serious relationship. She did love Seamus more than she thought was possible.

"I think we should tell Mama, Seamus. It will be a difficult and messy conversation, but we can handle it. I've felt for months that it's unfair to her, and really to us, to have to hide our feelings for one another."

Seamus said nothing. He took a cigarette case from his jacket, opened it, and offered one to Eva, who declined, and then lit one for himself. Exhaling the smoke, he spoke earnestly, but cautiously.

"I agree, Eva, okay? I don't know what the outcome will be, either, but if we're to have any kind of a future, this secrecy has to stop."

#

That evening after dinner, Seamus and Eva told Elisabet of their affair.

On the way back into town, they discussed how to broach the topic and mutually agreed that full disclosure was the best. They decided each would take a turn explaining how they had grown to love one another over the years, how their relationship had started, and where they hoped it would eventually lead.

Elisabet looked squarely at her daughter and husband after being informed. She hesitated before saying or reacting immediately, and motioned for Seamus to refill her glass of water, which he quickly did.

She carefully considered the consequences of erupting in anger and banishing both of them from the house. Or should she immediately request a divorce? However, both scenarios would not only alienate her from her daughter, but also from Seamus forever. She was still quite fond of her second husband, to the point of wanting to maintain some kind of relationship with him. In her increasing egocentrism, she did want to continue to play a role in their lives.

A third option did not even seem all that unusual to her.

She keenly embraced pragmatism. It may have been losing Nigel in Boston that proved to her she was quite capable of being on her own for the remainder of her life. She *could* be her own best friend and *could* count on herself to make her own decisions. Elisabet did not see this new development as a deterrent to her life plan.

I might not have been wanted as a child, but I refuse at this moment to let that hurt stop me from making choices that benefit me *the most.*

Marrying Seamus five years ago had been the right thing to do; times had changed. Her daughter was in love, and Elisabet wanted Eva to have a happy marriage. But at this moment, it didn't occur to her that her daughter had not planned nor anticipated this situation in which the three of them were now deeply involved.

"You know this is the ultimate betrayal," Elisabet said to Eva, who was looking slightly the worse for wear after the confession. Seamus was mute.

"But I'm not stupid. It was impossible for me not to have noticed the lovesick glances I've seen you give Seamus as far back as our wedding day four years ago."

"Mama, that's not true," Eva responded, unconvincingly.

"You were nearly sixteen then, and almost a woman. He is not your father, thank God for that. But he *is* my husband, and you are basically stealing him away from me." She stopped and played with the napkin ring at her place setting. "And *he* is taking my daughter from me."

Eva looked down at the half-consumed meal before her.

"And Seamus," Elisabet directed her attention to him. "Since we first met at the Halifax Commerce Club in 1915, I saw you had a special fondness for Eva. I don't know why I chose to ignore that fact over the past five years. Perhaps *I* am indeed the fool."

She took a sip of water and continued.

"So, we'll quietly divorce, Seamus. No one need know the details. Both our names are on the deed to this house, and I want you to sign the house over to me. I deserve full ownership of Broadale.

"You can both continue to live here with me, if you so wish, and we can re-arrange our living quarters accordingly. There is obviously more than enough space for you two to have your own large bedroom, and you may even want to have your own parlor upstairs, too. But we *will* share expenses, and you *will not* embarrass me in public with any overt displays of affection. *That I will not tolerate.*

"In two years when you turn twenty-one, Eva, you can marry Seamus. And you *will marry* my daughter, Seamus — that is another condition that I will state in the terms of our divorce. I will not have anyone thinking that my daughter is living with a man in a conjugal way when she is *not* married."

Elisabet sat back in her dining room chair and finished the remaining water in her glass as if it were the finest cognac in the country.

"Elisabet, I'm, I'm almost at a loss for words," Seamus said. "You don't know how much your understanding means to me; means to the both of us."

He paused, and then said, "I know this is awkward. I know this will be the talk of Yarmouth, if and when the news ever gets out. People will not be kind to us."

Eva's eyes were watering. Loving Seamus, and eventually marrying him, would break every social and moral convention of the day. She was well aware of this, and knew it was almost an inevitable result of her love for Seamus.

In 1921, the practice of religion was an important influence in the lives of most people. In the heavily Protestant town of Yarmouth, the Episcopalian and Baptist majority was very conservative in their beliefs. However, the French Acadians, the Irish, and some Scots were inarguably just as staunch in their Roman Catholic faith and traditions. Eva knew the consequences of a life with her mother's husband, divorced or not, unmarried or married to the man, could be dire.

The community's opinion of the family would change. Put simply, it was virtually inconceivable for a woman to marry her stepfather in this small seaport town.

Elisabet, Seamus, and Eva were not prepared.

TWENTY-SEVEN

Collan's Journal Entry - Gothenburg, Thursday, June 15, 1921

I don't think I've ever been happier! It's been a long time since I made an entry in this book, but things seem to be happening so rapidly, it's important that I mustn't forget anything.

Nevertheless, lately I have had moments of concern for my sister Elisabet, wondering how she is faring, now that it has been a year since I told her that Mother/Signe was mentally unbalanced, even if that may not have been true. I don't want her to think that Mother hated us, but it does stand to reason that our birth father may have since he did murder our real mother and left us orphaned.

I still can't fathom what would make him do such a thing unless he was insane — and I don't like to think that my sisters and I are the daughters by blood of a monster like that. I do worry if that tendency can be passed along to his children...

But I'm consciously choosing not to dwell on such matters. And today I'm happy because I just met my nephew Paolo. He's such a sweet little baby, and so quiet, just like I remember Katarina was as a child! He is surprisingly big, and he does have her coloring. She and Joseph are fortunate that the adoption came through that quickly — and to think they were given a boy with red hair!

In typical fashion, Katarina has sworn me to secrecy about the adoption, as if I even know any of her high-society friends to tell! Everything is so dramatic with her.

I am happiest, though, because Linnea has chosen to live with me.

She is my age, forty-two, and both of us fell in love with one another when she was taking care of the Prince. He had continued to invite me for weekly Friday afternoon schnapps or Aquavit, and although it was a bit of journey traveling to see him every week by train, it was well worth the effort. I was also able to develop a very special and caring friendship with Linnea during these occasions.

The three of us had grand times with much laughter and good spirits, literally! He even seemed to encourage the relationship Linnea and I have, particularly after he realized that I could not be more than a friend to him, although I cared for him deeply as a person. He never had a superior attitude or displayed a privileged demeanor.

He died young from all his underlying medical conditions, but he was wise beyond his years. He had a natural empathy for others, and instinctively knew what to say and when to say it.

I watched Linnea care for him — she lovingly doted on him, actually — and always knew that they had a unique friendship that went beyond her professional position as his caregiver.

She told me after he passed that she had revealed to him years before that she had never felt an attraction to men in a romantic way. That's exactly the way I have always felt, too, and apparently, he just smiled, raised an eyebrow, and said to her, "And is that a problem in your daily life?"

No one here in my neighborhood will give it a second thought when they see Linnea move in. We will just be considered two spinsters who are sharing a space to live. People may think she is my hired help because of her previous employment with the Prince, but I will assure her over and over again that that is not the case!

We are both financially secure and I am extraordinarily rich in the love that we have found with one another. I never expected this. They say what we have is against the law, but this makes no sense to me whatsoever. If one of the royal princes of Sweden didn't concern himself about the beautiful relationship Linnea and I have, why should anyone else?

TWENTY-EIGHT

Yarmouth, Thursday, June 15, 1922

The divorce between Seamus McMaster and Elisabet Burcharth-Carroll-McMaster was filed without any fanfare, and the deed to the house was duly changed to Elisabet's sole ownership.

Eva pondered her wedding to Seamus, wondering where and when it would take place. She felt financially dependent on both her mother and Seamus and knew she would capitulate to their wishes on the particulars. She was not naïve enough to assume she would have either a church or a white wedding, and she was sensible enough to know that the wedding would be kept as quiet as possible. However, it would be a proper legal event after which she would be the new Mrs. McMaster.

Elisabet had most things under control for the upcoming wedding ceremony. She rightly assumed that her daughter's marriage to her husband would not be looked on favorably by most, and so one of her first duties was to get two witnesses and an understanding clergyman.

As a telephone was installed at Broadale soon after they had moved in, she had two somewhat lengthy and expensive conversations with the Universalist Minister from Halifax who had married her and Seamus in 1916. He finally agreed, albeit rather grudgingly, to marry her daughter to her now ex-husband and the ceremony took place in the ballroom of Broadale.

\#

In Gothenburg, the relationship between Martin Karlsson and Anders Lindgren from Stockholm developed slowly over six months. Anders was only in Gothenburg once every thirty days on business, but they had met and spent time together on each occasion.

After admitting to Anders that he was illiterate through no fault of his own, Martin's confession further cemented their friendship, due to Anders' understanding and empathetic nature.

Both men were sitting at a café in Haga enjoying strong coffee and cinnamon rolls when Anders asked Martin about his childhood.

"I really don't remember much of anything as a little boy, but I know I was adopted after I turned twelve. I also don't know who my real parents are or were," he said, "and I might have some sisters or brothers, but the couple who adopted me had no other children. I was never around other people my age." He paused and continued, "I guess you could say I'm a loner."

Anders sipped his coffee and asked, "Do you want to try to find your real parents or maybe look for a sister or brother? I might be able to help."

Martin smiled in appreciation, and from his jacket pocket, pulled out the well-worn newspaper page he had kept from his first rendezvous with Anders at the Hotel Royal. He put the newspaper clipping on the table and then retrieved an old, scratched photograph he had kept from his childhood: one that pictured him with three young girls, presumably his siblings.

"And what are these?" Anders asked. "Oh, wait, I see it's that story and picture about the Countess de Carminati. I remember telling you I thought you looked like her."

"Okay, well, the newspaper photograph of the fancy lookin' woman may also be one of the kids in that old photograph, Anders. Do you see which one it could be, if any of them?"

Anders immediately spotted three-year-old Katarina in the photo and matched her with the photo of the Countess.

"Yeah, the littlest child looks like the Countess. She's got a full head of hair and the same nose, for sure. But what are you getting at, Martin?"

"Okay, Anders, look again at me closely and then look at the fancy woman in the newspaper. Look at the boy in the other photograph and the littlest girl."

Anders peered at him as if he hadn't already affectionately studied Martin during their few encounters. Squinting his eyes, and then widening them, Anders saw a direct visual link.

"It's remarkable, Martin. The boy in the photo is definitely you many years ago. The little girl certainly looks like the Countess now," Anders said. "And you haven't lost one ounce of cuteness since you were a boy!"

Uncharacteristically, Martin blushed.

"Stop that! Anders, listen, I want you to read to me what the words are underneath the newspaper photo."

"Umm, okay," Anders agreed, picking up the newspaper page and placing it an inch or two from his eyes, as he was nearsighted.

"The Count and Countess de Carminati, residents of Gothenburg, stepped out on the town last night to take in a play by August Strindberg at the Royal Theater in Stockholm. We hope that the next time they visit the capital, we will be able to see their new son, Viscount Carminati, who no doubt will be raised on a diet of French Champagne and Russian caviar!"

"I *knew* they'd have a kid. So whaddaya think?" Martin asked.

"What do I think about what? You're the boy in the old photograph, but you sure don't look like the Count!"

"I know that. But do you think the Countess and I could be sister and brother?"

"You may well be. In fact, I'd say so."

"Help me reach her, Anders. And I gotta know about the other two girls in that old photograph. I might have two more sisters."

#

On the other side of the city, Katarina had just given Paolo to his nanny for changing and feeding.

Every day, Katarina was exhausted by noon caring for the baby — motherhood did not come instinctively to her — but Joseph had finally agreed to hire a nanny between twelve and eight o'clock to help her with Paolo.

He was spending a great deal of time at his office in Gothenburg since he had closed the one in Kristiania and wasn't traveling between the two cities nearly as frequently.

When he arrived home from work at five o'clock, Katarina greeted him with a kiss and then served him a tumbler of Cinzano on ice after he sat down in their parlor.

"Thank you, sweetheart," he said, "you haven't forgotten one of my favorite drinks on a hot summer's day."

"Did you want some seltzer with that?" she asked.

"And dilute the *gusto delizioso*, Katarina?" He smiled. "No, *grazie*."

She sat next to him on the plush, buttoned-down loveseat.

"I think we should take a trip to Canada to see Elisabet," she said, looking at him intently, gauging for a reaction.

"They've been in their new home for what, almost two years now? I haven't met her yet…and you haven't met her second husband, have you?"

Katarina shook her head no.

"And also, I haven't seen my niece Eva for such a very long time," Katarina said. "She was only a little girl when she and Elisabet returned to Yarmouth after my brother-in-law Nigel died. Indeed, Collan and I left for Sweden *before* they even went back to Nova Scotia."

She looked off into space, as if performing mental arithmetic. "Yes, it's been about 15 years since I last saw Eva. She must be quite a beauty by now."

"You know, sweetheart," Joseph said, sipping his drink. "Maybe we should arrange a small family reunion for you; you should ask Collan to go with you!"

Joseph smiled but failed to add, *So I don't need to go myself to some outpost in that freezing cold country.*

"That's a fabulous idea, Joseph," Katarina said excitedly, "what an entourage we will be!"

"But I'm afraid I can't get away this summer, darling. After shutting down the Norwegian office, the one here is busier than ever. Your sister will be a perfect companion for you and little Paolo. It'll be your return voyage home after all these years."

Katarina looked crestfallen.

"I can't say I'm not disappointed, Joseph. Everyone will expect the Count to travel with the Countess," she moaned, half-smiling. "But I do understand. I just hope Collan will agree to come. We've seen so little of her since we had, or adopted, Paolo."

"If she has any financial worries about the cost of her travel, Katarina," Joseph said, "I'm happy to subsidize her passage to Canada."

"That's sweet of you, Joseph. I think I'll ring her now to see what her thoughts are about taking a trip."

TWENTY-NINE

Sunday, September 10, 1922

Aboard the Scandinavian-American S/S Hellig Olav, one day before arriving in Halifax from Kristiania, Katarina's thoughts returned to her first crossing nine years prior when she and Collan had sailed from New York to the Norwegian capital.

There had been so much world upheaval since then: a war, a pandemic, and the world's largest man-made explosion in her home province of Nova Scotia. She could not have predicted that in 1925, the capital of Norway would once again be called Oslo, so rapidly was the world changing.

From the morning they boarded the Hellig Olav, she was immensely content with their First-Class lodgings, and was thrilled she didn't have to lie to make her way into them.

Collan had offered to pay for Katarina and Paolo's cabin, as well as her own, thanks to a 'little nest egg' from her equestrian winnings.

The excuse was not entirely truthful, but Katarina was blissfully ignorant of the fact that both Collan and Linnea had done very well from the estate of the late Prince Erik, and neither would have to work another day in their lives. Katarina was not the only Burcharth daughter to tell an untruth when it suited her.

Linnea had not been previously introduced to Katarina and Joseph, so Katarina was a bit miffed knowing that her sister's housemate would be accompanying them on this family trip. She was frankly rather surprised that a *non*-family member was coming with her sister. Still, she had decided to keep quiet on the subject since Collan was paying for her transatlantic crossing.

Linnea and Collan were taking Paolo for a stroll on the Promenade Deck, so Katarina enjoyed her solo time in the late morning sun, and drank in her surroundings so she could later impress anyone from Yarmouth who might ask about what her quarters had been like.

Dear God, the baby has been so ornery the whole trip: I deserve this time to myself.

Their staterooms were next door to each other, midship on the saloon deck. Each was of a comfortable size, ventilated, and had washstands, wardrobes, and soft, comfortable sofas. The upper berths could be closed out of sight when not in use.

Katarina had hoped to enjoy the brass beds and silk draperies that she heard were found in the First Class Cabin on one of the other Scandinavian-American ships, but she satisfied herself knowing she could always embellish the description of her stateroom if need be.

That morning, the four of them had breakfast in the First-Class dining room which extended the full width of the ship. Surrounded by walls of polished oak and mahogany, they were given a choice of typical Scandinavian fare, or variations on a North American hot breakfast.

Katarina was relieved that instead of the long tables where they would have to dine with strangers, or commoners, as she had begun appraising others, the First-Class dining room contained smaller group tables. Delicate table accoutrements were utilized, as well as porcelain dishes and teapots, all of which added to the civilized atmosphere that she felt a countess deserved.

While she ruminated on her good fortune in her stateroom, Collan, Linnea and Paolo stopped by the Ladies' Saloon which was located in the Music Saloon.

The two women and the toddler presented a striking and fashionable trio, turning a few heads. Two-year old Paolo was dressed in a miniature navy and white sailor's suit, while Collan wore a khaki riding suit, consisting of an attractive tailored coat in a smart semi-fitted belted style, and perfectly fitting breeches.

That day the fair-haired Linnea had chosen a navy blue, all silk charmeuse 'frock' which hung softly to just below her knees. It was lustrous and simple but was brightened by decorations of unusual embroidery in distinctive panels on the skirt.

Many passengers stopped by to enjoy the Music Saloon. Seating was offered in the middle of the parlor-like area on a circular sofa with buttoned-down upholstery, as well as on smaller loveseats bolted to the walls. Large square rugs with floral motifs covered the floor, and a stained-glass window above the piano delivered muted natural light.

Paolo was more interested in the noise coming from the piano than anything else, but was starting to get rambunctious, so the women brought him into the Library and Writing Room to look for children's picture books.

As they returned to their stateroom to rejoin Paolo with his mother, they walked by several baths, showers, and lavatories as well as the cabin's barber and hair dressing shop. But Collan's thoughts were wandering everywhere, and she had little interest in the ship's amenities.

Should I tell my sisters when we are all in Yarmouth about how much Linnea means to me? Would they understand? Be angry? There are days when I have mixed feelings about myself and my own desires. I can't find anything written anywhere about two women living together as if we were spouses. Why? There must be other women like me and Linnea out there somewhere.

The crossing to Halifax was a full five days in duration, and then the ship would sail to New York City. Collan and her entourage enjoyed the entire upper promenade and the forward part of the saloon promenade deck on the voyage, as these spaces were reserved for the First-Class passengers.

The only drawback they faced was that Paolo was ill most of the time: the little boy had vomited on the first full day of sailing, and remained pale and listless most of the time, except for the brief sojourn to the Music Saloon. While Katarina was not overly concerned, Collan insisted that he see the ship's doctor before they disembarked.

Still, life was leisurely on board the ocean liner, and a post-war giddiness continued to be apparent in the tone and dress of this privileged class.

#

Two days later in Yarmouth, everyone was assembled for dinner in the dining room at Broadale. Elisabet had hired a maid, Mavis Whitman, and a housekeeper and cook, Eliza Rogers, for the duration of her sisters' vacation. Eliza, an African Nova Scotian whose family had been in Yarmouth County for generations, was already attending to Baby Paolo in the bedroom reserved for Katarina on the second floor.

The family and Linnea were all very cordial and proper with one another, but tension was high since neither Collan nor Katarina had met Seamus. They had only found out on their arrival that their brother-in-law was now their nephew-in-law.

There was also the issue of the person unrelated to the family who was seated at the table. Her English was not fluent, so after the polite niceties that followed dinner, Linnea retired for the evening to her own room that Elisabet had designated for her.

Mavis stood by the door of the dining room as an indication she had to clean the table. The family walked together into the main parlor, and Elisabet turned on the electric table lamps.

Seamus brought a bottle of port and a tray with five glasses on it into the room with him.

"Where did you get *that*?" Elisabet asked, gesturing to the bottle. "You know it's illegal to have alcohol now."

"Yes, it is, Elisabet, but I've been saving it since before Prohibition was enacted last year," Seamus said. "And this seems like a perfect time to enjoy it."

There was dead silence around the room as he poured the heavy wine into the glasses.

"And incidentally," he continued as he passed a glass to each of the women, "we do have a supply of similar beverages in the basement. Hopefully, we can have a little party to welcome your sisters back home."

Elisabet chose to ignore Seamus's suggestion and turned to her youngest sister.

"Katarina, I must ask you, whatever in the world possessed you to research how you could become a countess? It just seems so inane and useless! What does your husband think of this? He's not from one of noble families of Italy, is he?"

"Well, Elisabet, I'm glad you asked. Indeed, Joseph's lineage does go way back to one of the presumed first families of Naples, so we felt that he should be afforded his rightful title", Katarina sniffed. "And having a title is neither inane nor useless, I might add," her voice suggesting that the topic was now closed.

Eva did not get the hint.

"That's wonderful, Aunt Katarina! Do you have a place, then, or at the very least, land in Italy that is yours? Do you plan on ever living there?"

"Not really, dear Eva. I mean, deeds to land ownership in Italy are quite complex," Katarina said dismissively. "We are actually quite comfortable in Gothenburg and plan to raise little Viscount Paolo there. You must come visit."

"We would love to do that," Eva said, looking at Seamus for agreement. "In fact, Seamus and I have been thinking of an extended trip to Europe next summer for our honeymoon."

The room fell silent for a moment. Eva had inadvertently introduced the topic that was on everyone's mind: Elisabet's daughter had married her stepfather, and the applecart had most definitely been upset.

Seamus asked, "Would anyone like a little more port?"

The three sisters and Eva all nodded.

Collan was the first to speak, and she chose her words carefully. She knew more about her own and her siblings' parentage than Elisabet did. She also reminded herself that neither of them had told Katarina that the three sisters had been adopted by Jacob and Signe.

"Elisabet, we're so happy to finally be back in Yarmouth where we were, uh, raised. We share so many wonderful childhood memories of growing up here!" Collan said, putting her glass on a side table next to her.

"But I must ask you how the townspeople have reacted to you divorcing Seamus and then allowing Eva to marry him? It's no secret this is a very conservative community."

Elisabet cleared her throat and smiled at Collan.

"Well, Collan, as far as we know, no one in town knows the story," she said, and then noticed the look of surprise on her sister's face.

"The two witnesses at the wedding were from the hospital — Seamus's medical colleagues — so they obviously know of his marriage to Eva. But to our knowledge, no one else in Yarmouth knows. The three of us have been living together at Broadale for almost two years, and even longer on Forest Street, and nothing much has changed, except, uh, for the rooms that we inhabit at Broadale."

"Do you really think the witnesses at the wedding will stay quiet about this? They don't have anything invested in our family's matters, do they?"

"Aunt Collan," Eva started, "we know this must seem rather strange to you and Aunt Katarina. But please know that the three of us agreed on everything. Mama was very understanding about my relationship with Seamus, and felt we deserved to be happily married."

"Oh my God," Katarina said, rolling her eyes. "I'm glad my sister is so incredibly understanding, but Eva, you mustn't be so naïve! When word gets out around Yarmouth, and it will, trust me, I can just hear the outcry now. They'll be saying things like, 'those immoral Swedes, they're heathens' and 'what really goes on in that big house on Parade Street?'"

"That could very well happen, Katarina, but we can't live in fear of what the local people think of us," Seamus stated firmly. "I'm a Haligonian, and I've always felt like an outsider here anyway from the day I moved to Yarmouth after Elisabet and I got married. You get used to knowing you're seen as someone from away."

"And Aunt Katarina, I'm not nervous about the people of Yarmouth finding out about my marriage to Seamus," Eva said. "I really could not care any less what people think. I love Mama, and I love Seamus, and that is that."

Katarina bore the expression of one who has just been strongly corrected and yet wants to show her understanding of the sensitive topic.

"I suppose I'm a little, shall we say, shocked, that the brother-in-law whom I'd never met is now the husband of my niece and not my sister. You must admit it is a rather startling development, hmmm?

"I mean, I'm happy for you, dear Eva, and Seamus, I really am," Katarina continued, in a softer tone. "But I worry for your safety and well-being. I feel Sweden and Denmark are years ahead in their liberal thinking compared to Canada, which is still quite comfortable in its Victorian attitudes."

She sighed and brightened.

"But don't worry, the news that a countess from Sweden is visiting her sister is far more appealing to the locals than some idle gossip that might already be well known to everyone. You don't know how well your secret has been kept, do you?"

Collan had heard enough. She straightened in her chair, and said, "And when they find out the countess only became one by marriage to an Italian who did *not* accompany her on this trip, *that* tidbit should keep the gossip mongers occupied just a *little* bit longer. We all have our secrets, Sister dear."

THIRTY

Stockholm, Wednesday, September 6, 1922

Anders Lindgren sat at his kitchen table with the day's newspaper in front of him as he ate breakfast before bicycling to work.

In the middle of the newspaper was a column devoted to the country's upper-income elite, and a paragraph jumped off the page. Now holding the newspaper much closer to his face, he read:

COUNTESS DE CARMINATI SAILS TO CANADA

The Countess Katarina de Carminati, a resident of Gothenburg, sailed yesterday from Kristiania with her sister, Miss Collan Burcharth, and a companion, Miss Linnea Nilsson, for Halifax, Canada. The two sisters plan to visit their older sister, Mrs. Seamus McMaster who resides in Yarmouth, a town approximately 200 miles south of Halifax, for a two-week stay before they continue their journey to New York City.

Collan Burcharth has been a competitive and award-winning equestrian in Sweden for several years. Linnea Nilsson was one of the principal nurses to HRH Prince Erik, before he died from complications due to the Spanish Flu in 1918.

All three women are well known in Gothenburg's philanthropic community and are sailing on the S/S Hellig Olav. The Countess is a regular patron of the Svenska Röda Korset, the Swedish Red Cross. Misses Burcharth and Nilsson are said to be contributing to a new political and female-oriented journal, Tidevar Vet – The Epoch, *to be published in the new year. It promises to be an influential publication, as it is associated with* Folgelstadgruppen, The Folgelstad Group, . *an association comprised solely of women from Swedish academia.*

Anders raised his eyebrows in surprise. It appeared as if Martin's sisters had all done quite well for themselves. It would now be much easier for Martin to potentially meet with at least two of his siblings. But should he spend the time and energy on Martin's behalf?

Anders was no fool. The man he was involved with claimed to be physically attracted to both men and women, and so far, this arrangement had not caused any division between the two of them. He was beginning to develop real feelings for Martin, but he didn't understand why his lover could not bring himself to kiss him passionately. Martin would turn his head and jokingly say to Anders that kissing was "gettin' too close".

Anders was concerned that he was simply being used by Martin for sexual gratification, and to be a conduit to his long-lost family.

THIRTY-ONE

Gothenburg, Saturday, November 11, 1922

On the fourth anniversary of the Armistice, Martin lay awake in his bed staring at the ceiling. He had had another fitful sleep the night before.

I've looked at that old photo of me and the three girls so many times my eyes have crossed.

Hell, I'm spittin' mad that I didn't get adopted into a good family like they did. Had that happened, I might be a somebody who has money or even a good paying job. I might have learned how to read and write.

But all I got were head slaps and kicks from that bastard Wahlström who offered to accept the lowest amount the church would pay him for taking me on as his 'farm helper'.

Everybody thinks I'm stupid, but I've been told that's what happens to kids no one wants. I was more like that guy's slave. Jesus, I was only twelve years old. I wish I had gotten out from under him sooner than I did.

Finding out about all this family stuff has made me remember most of one of those bad dreams I've been having since I was real small.

I can hear the girls wailing, but they're behind a big, thick door above me. There's a sliver of light coming from another big door in front of me. I can't breathe; I can't speak; I can't cry; I can't do nothing. The roaring in my head has become so loud, now I can't hear.

But now I'm looking through that sliver of light, and I can see there's a man standing over a woman. He is shoving a knife into her chest, over and over and over. Everything is red and black. I start to scream...

I can't explain it, but I now think the man is my father, and the woman he's killing is my mother. The picture is so clear, it's like I was there, hiding behind something. Or in a closet. In a hole.

I need Anders to help me with this. I have to somehow telephone him.

#

A week later, Anders was in Gothenburg again and he met Martin at Den Törstiga Kråkan. Martin had asked him if he could find out if there had been some horrible crime that happened in Gothenburg in the early 1880s.

Martin's eyes had large circles under them as he looked sadly at Anders. Since remembering more fragments of his nightmare, and sleeping little since then, he had convinced himself that he definitely did witness a murder. While not a spiritual man, he hoped it hadn't involved the two people who gave him life, as unfortunate as his life had been.

"It's not a nice tale," Anders reported. "I have a friend who works at *Göteborg-idag,* and he went through the newspaper's archives for me. He did find a major story back in 1882 about a murder-suicide.

"It looks like the article may have been about your birth parents, Martin. It happened in that tiny town just north of here, Fjällbacka. It was a big news story back then probably because it's such a small place, and four children were left orphaned.

"He told me the article said that two bodies were found after a neighbor saw one of the children wandering around outside with no shoes or coat. The dead woman had been stabbed fifteen times and then the man apparently used the knife on himself. The four children were taken to the Diocese of Gothenburg because there was no orphanage in Fjällbacka, and the one here in the city was full.

"It mentioned that the oldest child, an eleven-year old boy, was mute. He didn't say a word when the authorities took him and his sisters to the parish here. They figured he was deaf and dumb. That's all that was recorded at the time."

Martin looked at Anders with a mixture of shock, relief, and resignation. He surely had witnessed his father murder his mother. His conflicting emotions might solve one mystery as to what happened to his birth parents, but he was left with the bigger question of why the terrible crime took place.

Anders looked at him with pity.

"I'm sorry, Martin."

"It's not right I was separated from my sisters," he said bitterly. "They were the only family I had left, and they were taken away by someone else. Someone who didn't want me with them."

"You don't know that for sure, Martin. There could have been many reasons why you weren't adopted by the same family," Anders said. "You don't even know for sure if your three sisters *were* adopted by the *same* parents — maybe they didn't find each other until they were older — maybe even recently."

"I don't bloody care how they all know one another, Anders. I'm not a part of them and I should be. I deserve to be. You saw from that story in September that the *countess* was with her sister and sailing to Canada to see their other sister," he said quickly. "Goddammit, they get to sail across the world, and I probably loaded their bloody luggage onto the ship."

"No, I'm pretty sure that the article stated they had departed from Kristiania," Anders said quietly. He could see Martin's anger escalating. His face had swiftly turned a shade of crimson.

"None of these high society women would ever want to know a man like me, Anders. I feel like a fool for getting you involved with this."

Anders looked into Martin's pleading eyes. He felt sorry for the broken man. Maybe he could somehow arrange a meeting with at least one of his sisters. His position at the bank in Stockholm gave him some influence, at least, when he needed to be in touch with the upper crust of Swedish society.

"Nah — you're not a fool in my eyes whatsoever, Martin. Listen, let me handle this. You'd be surprised what I can find out sometimes. People in my position have learned to be masters of discretion...", Anders said before Martin interrupted him.

"What's discretion?"

"That basically means knowing when to keep quiet and when to speak. I'll see you next month, but don't fret about all this. If meeting one of your sisters is meant to be, it'll happen, okay?"

He squeezed Martin's hand quickly, looking deeply into his eyes, got up from his seat and left the bar.

THIRTY-TWO

Yarmouth, Saturday, September 23, 1922

It wasn't supposed to be a big party, as only eight couples and four single people had been invited, but the 'Welcome home Collan and Katarina' invitation did not receive any regrets from those requested to attend, and it appeared it would be a full house.

It was a warm late-September evening. This was the first social event at Broadale since the McMasters had moved in, and everyone was curious about what the interior of the house looked like. Most were intrigued about the sisters from Sweden as well, whom no one had seen in nine years. Word had gotten around that one of them had married a prince.

As Eva perused all the well-dressed guests in the ballroom, she stopped counting after thirty; she guessed there were about forty people there.

Elisabet had put Linnea in charge of music, which bothered Collan, feeling her partner was being relegated to a servile position. The fair-haired Swede was stationed at her position next to the Victrola.

Eva watched the two women talking as Linnea switched records. They had brought a few new phonograph records with them from abroad as gifts for the family. She admired the Victrola which was a new model with a Queen Anne-style mahogany cabinet with gold trim; the turntable and amplifying horn were tucked away inside for aesthetic reasons. It was a wedding gift from the two doctors and their wives who witnessed her marriage with Seamus; they were definitely on the guest list that evening, and Eva looked forward to seeing them again. She knew they would be discreet.

Wondering where Seamus was in the big room, she recalled the conversation the family had during lunch.

"Everyone, please listen carefully," Elisabet had said. "Tonight, we will obviously keep things quiet about Seamus and Eva; and as I have told you earlier, it is no one else's business but our own. We will pretend that nothing has changed with Seamus and I, and he and Eva are in full agreement."

Eva and Seamus nodded gravely, not entirely happy with the situation, but resigned to the fact.

"Elisabet, don't worry. Remember people are here to meet a countess and her sister who haven't lived in Yarmouth for ages!" Katarina exclaimed, not at all modestly. "Let's face it: nothing much happens at this end of the province. Let them talk about me when I leave!"

She laughed, and barely noticed that no one had joined in.

"Seamus, what about the liquor situation?" Collan asked. She turned to Linnea to translate her question as a referendum about prohibition in Sweden had just been defeated in August.

"Two fruit punches will be served, Collan. One with white rum, and one without. If either of the bowls becomes dry, I've told the so-called bartender where to find more rum in the basement to make more punch if necessary. The alcoholic punch is definitely a much darker pink in color, just so you all know."

Elisabet nodded like a general, and said, "I've hired three persons for this evening. One will be in charge of passing canapés and hors d'oeuvres; I think her name is Claire. She's Eliza's daughter. The second is our maid Mavis's brother, and I believe his name is Charles. He will be manning the table of cold beverages and serving the two different punches. Thirdly, I have one of Eva's old schoolmates babysitting little Paolo upstairs. And of course, Mavis will be helping out all over, wherever she is needed."

"You're as organized as ever, Mama!" Eva said, warmly. She was grateful her mother was taking care of all the details just as she had done for her wedding.

She heard the brass door knocker rap on the front door, breaking her reverie. She automatically started towards it, and then remembered that Mavis was supposed to welcome the guests at the door. She went off in search of Seamus.

The volume of chatter in the room drowned out the Victrola. Eva stood next to Seamus who stood next to Elisabet. To a casual observer, it looked as if Elisabet may have been the mother to the other two: she had a pained expression on her face — whereas Seamus and Eva appeared to be looking for an escape route.

One of the doctors and his wife who had attended Eva's wedding approached Seamus and Eva, who gladly turned towards them. These were people who knew the real situation, and that was a relief to them both. Finally, Eva felt she could enjoy a comfortable moment during the party. Elisabet excused herself and left the ballroom for the kitchen.

Several feet away a small gaggle of women were standing, delicately holding glasses of decidedly non-alcoholic punch.

"And then ohmygoodness," Katarina said breathlessly to the three women surrounding her, "I was absolutely entranced with the gorgeous brass bed in my stateroom. The silk draperies were divine. And the welcome bottle of Dom Perignon! Well, that was lovely, and quite the surprise! The chief steward actually apologized that the cabin was not more in keeping with what a countess would expect! Isn't that sweet?" She took a sip of her rum punch.

"And how did your little boy enjoy the crossing?" one of the women asked her.

"Oh, Viscount Paolo was a perfect little trooper the whole time. I swear, he will be a sea captain one day if he needs the work! He ran up and down the Promenade Deck, with me keeping a close eye on him, of course, and had a wonderful time," Katarina answered.

"But what a shame we won't be able to meet your husband on this trip," another woman commented.

"Yes, but the Count is terribly busy on diplomatic business, always traveling between Gothenburg and Stockholm. I think tomorrow he has an audience with the King. And then he's off to Italy to ready our estate in Naples so we can spend the winter there. The weather is *so* much more agreeable there than Gothenburg is in January!"

She sighed, and took a sip of punch, as if the thought of having to travel to a second home in another country would be exhausting to her. In reality, the only home she and Joseph had was a modest, middle-class house in Gothenburg.

"Ladies, it was so nice to chat with you. Now I must check on my darling child. I will see you again before you leave tonight!"

Katarina smiled, turned, and left the small group in a flourish of cotton and silk pastels that made up her full-length dress. She knew she looked younger than her actual forty-two years. Her plan of standing out in a crowd of conservative frocks was working. She spied Elisabet standing by herself and approached her sibling.

"Dear Sister! You look so glum! Aren't you enjoying the soireé you've planned for us?"

"I'm fine, Katarina, but just a little under the weather these past few days. Nothing serious," she hastened to add. "I hope you're having a good time."

"Oh, indeed I am. But don't you think I should make some kind of speech saying how nice it is to be back in Yarmouth, or something like that? I mean, aren't people expecting the countess to address them?"

"Katarina," Elisabet said thinly, "you are not the queen of Sweden. You received this title, I am assuming, by paying some kind of fee to whomever is able to sell these things. I think it may be best if you managed to keep a low profile. I really don't want the townspeople to be talking about our family any more than they already do."

Katarina paled, not at all happy with the reprimand.

"Maybe you should have thought about that before you allowed your daughter to sleep with your husband," she snapped. "All I'd like to do is bring a little bit of joy to the people of Yarmouth. But what *you've* done only makes the locals speak poorly of us. Don't you see that I'm an asset , and not a liability to this family?"

"I must check on how many trays of hors d'oeuvres are still left," Elisabet said, and quickly left Katarina to ponder her purpose in life.

#

Eva noticed that Seamus was in deep conversation with his medical colleagues, so she thought she would see if the young man working at the beverage table required anything. She did not notice the glazed expression on his face, but he had been pilfering glasses of the rum punch since he had arrived to work that evening.

"Yes, miss, what can I get for you?" he asked Eva as she approached the table.

"Hello there. I'm Eva McMa—Carroll," she quickly recovered her introduction. "I live here. And you are — ?"

"Hullo, Eva. My name is Charles Whitman, but you can call me Chas," he grinned, a little too friendly, Eva thought.

"Yes, well, then, Chas, is there anything you need from the kitchen? More ice? How is the Coca Cola holding up?"

Chas leaned across the table closer to Eva and said, "I don't think I need anything. But do *you* need anything from me?"

Eva was slightly taken aback, but then thought she was making too much of his forwardness.

"No, Chas, I'm fine, thanks. But let me know if you run out of anything."

Chas took a noisy slurp from a china teacup that was placed on a saucer at the end of the table.

"Well, Miss Eva, just remember that if you can't get enough out of that stud over there," he said with a wink, indicating where Seamus stood talking to the doctors, "or if he ain't big enough for you, I can always be available and at your service. You can find me at The Scallop Shell café most nights."

Eva was so shocked at the man's bold and vulgar remark, it didn't occur to her to wonder how he knew she and Seamus were a couple.

Speechless, she turned away and hurried toward the hallway.

He laughed and said, "Hey, I could do your momma and then you. I got lots of time." He took another drink of rum punch from the teacup, having lost count of how many he had consumed.

THIRTY-THREE

Yarmouth, Monday, September 25, 1922

Thirty two years before Eva began to experience what it was like to be shunned in her community, Oscar Wilde, in his novel *The Picture of Dorian Gray*, wrote, "It is perfectly monstrous the way people go about nowadays saying things against one, behind one's back, that are absolutely and entirely true."

In any small town, gossip with a hint of truth can be virulent, especially if one is perceived to be from a privileged family, and particularly if one is not native to the area. And in Nova Scotia, the descendants of Black Loyalists and the indigenous Mi'kmaq had already been living with prejudice and ostracization for a very long time.

Swedes were also *different*, in the eyes of many local citizens. Sweden, while neutral during the Great War, had traded with the enemy. Those people didn't speak the King's English nor Acadian French. They looked like most Anglo Saxons, but would be considered morally suspicious, at the least.

Two days after the welcome home party for her aunts, Eva was still reeling from the comments made by Chas, the bartender. Although not prone to weeping easily, she had been hurt and offended by him, and had to spend some time by herself directly afterwards. After she felt composed, she returned to the party, told Seamus their bartender was drunk, and that he should be removed immediately from the premises.

#

Later in the week while Eva's aunts, Paolo, and her mother took a drive to the beach at Port Maitland, and Seamus was working at the hospital, Eva walked to Main Street with Mavis. Their intent was to buy some fresh meat and fish, but she felt compelled to tell Mavis about her brother's behavior at the welcome home party.

In no particular hurry, they strolled westward on Parade Street towards the harbor and Main Street, passing the Yarmouth Academy, Central School, the Queen Anne Revival-styled Zion Baptist Church, and several handsome late-Victorian homes. Eva felt unnerved about the task before her. Mavis was a good, loyal, family employee; she didn't want her to become upset or feel responsible for her brother's conduct at the party.

"You're awfully quiet today," Mavis commented to Eva.

"Yes, I know, Mavis. I'm sorry about that. It's just that I had an unfortunate encounter with your brother at the party the night before last," Eva responded.

"Oh?" Mavis looked annoyed. "And what did Charles say to you, Miss Eva?" She paused. "Oh, excuse me: *Mrs. McMaster.* I'll have a word with him!"

"No, no, I don't want you to do that. Doctor McMaster asked him to leave the party and paid him for the time he had worked," Eva said. "You see, I think he may have drunk some rum either before the party or during it, and he made a most disagreeable comment to me about my husband and my mother."

She stopped walking and as Mavis did the same, Eva continued, "He clearly knows about my marriage, Mavis. Our family had expressly asked you and Eliza not to talk about my mother's divorce from Doctor McMaster and my marriage to him. It's no one's business other than our own."

"I don't know how he knew!" Mavis said weakly. "But what was the offensive thing he said to you?"

"I shan't repeat it, Mavis, except that it was a very off-color remark that a man should never say to a lady."

"Jesus, Mary and Joseph!" Mavis exclaimed. "Oh, forgive my language, Mrs. McMaster. I'll demand that he apologize to you. I'm terribly sorry."

"I don't want you to do that, Mavis, as it might make matters worse. Please forget about it, and in the future, when we need extra help at Broadale, I hope you have a sister or cousin who can work instead," Eva smiled wanly, not wanting to upset Mavis further.

"You know I think the world of you, Mrs. McMaster. I feel awful about this. I promise I will make it up to you somehow," Mavis said.

A short time later, after they had stopped at the People's Meat & Fish Market on Main Street, they went into the E.J. Vickery Bookseller & Stationer store so Eva could purchase a refill of India ink and a supply of writing paper.

Once inside, they walked past a clerk unpacking a box of goods. Surrounding the two women were displays of souvenirs, postcards, fishing tackle, toys, dolls, and games. A few steps later and they found themselves in an area of the store with shelves of books, magazines attached with clothespins from a line suspended above their heads, and many unopened drawers that contained stationery supplies.

"I wonder where Mr. Vickery is?" Eva mused aloud, looking for the proprietor. Mavis was perusing a small selection of romance novels on the counter.

After several minutes, an elderly man came from the back of the store and stood before them. Unsmiling, he asked, "Can I help you?"

Eva had known Mr. Vickery since 1915 when she was a freshman in high school; he always asked about Elisabeth every time Eva went to the store for any item, large or small.

"Oh, hello, Mr. Vickery! It's so nice to see you again. How are you and Mrs. Vickery?" Eva asked him, ignoring his curt hello.

"We're well, thank you. What would you like today?"

Eva hesitated, nonplussed at his lack of typical friendliness. She decided he was simply having a bad day or wasn't feeling well.

"Yes, please. I'd like a bottle of navy Winsor and Newton ink, and a package of cream-colored writing paper, please. One hundred sheets will be fine," Eva said.

The man turned to the drawers underneath the bookshelves.

"By the way, Mama sends her regards, Mr. Vickery," she added, as he opened two drawers and extracted the bottled ink from one and the paper from another.

"Yes, indeed. That will be fifteen cents, Miss Carroll, or should I address you as the *new* Mrs. McMaster?" he asked, with only the slightest movement of his right eyebrow.

Eva gaped at him. Mavis nudged her to pay for her purchase, and Eva quickly fished for the coins from her small handbag.

Without replying to his question, she gave him the money and muttered a quick thanks. Mavis put the two items into her mesh shopping bag that already contained the paper-wrapped meats and fish bought earlier.

They made a quick exit from the store.

Later that evening, when Elisabet and her sisters had retired for the night, and Paolo had long been put to bed, Eva asked Seamus if they could take their honeymoon sooner than later.

She had already told her new husband what Chas had said to her, and she had to physically stop Seamus from pummeling the disrespectful bartender that night. As they readied themselves for bed, she recounted what had happened in the stationer's store that afternoon.

"Seamus, if old Mr. Vickery already knows about us being married, and if even *he* couldn't keep from scowling at me, I think we can assume that word is out around town. And I guess I'll now be seen as stealing a husband from my own mother," she said, grimacing, as her eyes filled with tears. "I want to get away from here in the spring and go to Europe for our honeymoon. Please try to ask for the time off from the hospital now. Next summer is too long a time to wait."

THIRTY-FOUR

Vienna, Austria, Monday, May 28, 1923

Dear Mama,

Seamus has just gone out to see if there is a letter from you. I am certainly anxious to know how you are getting along. It's nasty to think of you all alone in that big house. I do hope that you still have Mavis (and Eliza?) helping you, and please dear Mama, take care of your dear self and get ready for a good trip to Europe this winter.

This is a great old city! Its beauty is beyond description. Yesterday we visited some of the many big churches here. They are simply gorgeous, and each church has its own particular attraction in the form of wonderful carvings both in wood and stone, and paintings by artists like Rubens, and many of the old masters. Oh! Mama, you would enjoy everything over here. People are so different from Yarmouth people, and things are so cheap, too, compared with the prices in North America.

Seamus just got back with a letter from the Agent in London saying that he is forwarding a letter immediately to us. I hope it is from you. Wherever we go we send the Agent a telegram and he sends us our mail. We are having a fine time here and I am drinking so much beer that when I get home, they won't know me from a typical Austrian.

Your friend Mr. Measan has a large apartment right in the centre of the city where the family lives in winter. Its twenty rooms, including a big reception hall and a billiard room, take up a whole floor of a building. He also has a place in the country where his wife and children spend most their time. We have a beautiful room here now with them, and every day I can practice on their baby grand piano, to review some of those lessons I took at the Academy.

How nice of Mr. Measan to speak so fondly of you and dear daddy and how much he enjoyed spending time with you years ago in Boston. Of course, I was very young then, and I don't remember him at all.

But I am so glad you stayed in touch with him all these years later, so Seamus and I can rekindle the friendship you had with him.

Yesterday we were up on a big mountain where an incredible old castle is, called "Leopoldsburg". It was built in 1101, I think, by the King of Austria, and now contains a café and restaurant. (I might have my dates all wrong in this letter, dear Mama. You know I sometimes get numbers mixed up.) You can't imagine the beauty of the view, though. From a height of 2,000 feet, you can see forever. We took some pictures which I shall send you.

During our time in the city, we have met many interesting people including a famous professor and composer of sacred music by the name of Gober. He is a very funny little man and really quite uninteresting looking. And that reminds me of a couple of nights ago — Mr. Measan's nephew performed in concert and played several compositions by Franz Liszt, which were simply splendid. The audience, chiefly made up of many notable musical and vocal artists of Vienna, was so excited by his talent that they stood and applauded him with their hands and voices.

Mr. Measan has a marvelous voice, and he often delights us in the evenings with operatic vocal numbers. He is visiting here now until October while he sings in the Vienna Imperial Opera House. Then I think he is off to the Metropolitan in New York.

Seamus and I are leaving for Tyrol in the Alps in about a month where Mr. and Mrs. Measan's Alpine house is located. We're going to visit one of the highest elevations in the Alps. I think it is 12,000 feet high, but don't get nervous Mama, because it is quite safe the way we are going. We will mostly travel by train, but I have a pair of Mrs. Measan's boots with big spikes on the soles and I'll also wear one of her leather coats. After all, there may be snow on the ground in July!

We intend to take some lovely pictures of the glaciers and will be sure to send them to you. Everyone here goes up in the mountains — it seems to be the national pastime in summer and winter — and there are really quite good trails to walk up. Seamus & Mr. Measan are going to try to shoot a mountain goat.

How I miss you, Mama. You would enjoy it so much here, I know. Why don't you and Collan buy a house here? Really, Mama, one is considered quite wealthy if they live on 10,000 dollars a year. A fine servant costs about eight dollars a month and three or four thousand dollars buys a mansion. The people here know how to live. You find wonderful little coffee cafes with good cream cakes, fine music, and pleasant, friendly people all over the country.

I know, Mama, that you did not have the opportunity to see all this long ago, but I do like to write you about it. You can show this letter to Mavis and Eliza, if you wish, and tell them I am so rushed I cannot find time to breathe or send them a postcard! There is so much to see, and time is limited. We are going to the capital of Tyrol, Innsbruck, and we may cross the Alps by aeroplane, but I am not particularly fussy about that.

We also want to go to Denmark and then Sweden to say hello to Collan and Katarina. I wonder if the "countess" can accommodate us at her huge estate? Hahaha. We may as well see everything while we're here. It's not so very much dearer if you travel on the trains. (By the way, I am sending a little rubber face beautifier to you, Mama. It is great to massage the face, with and under the neck and chin.)

Now, Mama dear, please don't let yourself get lonely and write to tell me all the news.

Lots of love from us – Eva

P.S. Mama, let me know if there is anything special you would like me to bring home. We are leaving Europe about the 16th of August after Seamus and I spend some time in Edinburgh where he'll be studying. Take good care of yourself, dear Mama, so you will be healthy and well when I get back. Everyone admires the pretty clothes you made me. I have seen nothing better here and when I am all dressed up in my black silk dress, they do some staring, I'll say.

THIRTY-FIVE

Gothenburg, Monday, May 28, 1923

As Eva was sealing the envelope to send Elisabet her letter from Vienna, Katarina was getting dressed in her home, anxious for her day's outing at the new Gothenburg Botanical Garden.

She would not only be meeting the prominent botanist who created the garden, Carl Skottsberg, but she would be interviewed while there by *Göteborg-idag* for a profile on her life as a countess. She thought it was a bit odd that the request for an interview came from a banker in Stockholm, but he did say he had an interest in all things Italian, including the country's noble families. Apparently, he was well acquainted with the newspaper's editor.

She wasn't terribly keen to have to talk about growing up in Nova Scotia, Canada — that seemed far too pedestrian and boring, she thought — so she considered changing her story, and felt that relating a childhood spent in Boston would be much more interesting. Elisabet had certainly written many letters home about the historic American city when she lived there with Nigel and little Eva, so Katarina assumed she could easily spin a tale for the newspaper reporter.

She chose what she felt to be a reasonably regal outfit that day. Her all wool poiret twill suit with a taffeta sash, and a matching brimless cloche hat that fit perfectly on her new fashionable bob cut, seemed very appropriate.

After giving last minute instructions to her babysitter, she telephoned for a taxi since Joseph had taken their car earlier to his office.

Although the Garden had opened in 1919 on the land where a great country estate named Stora Änggården was located, it was four years later that the cultivated areas had opened to the public to help commemorate Gothenburg's 300th anniversary.

Katarina had told the banker that she could only meet with the journalist outside the entrance to the Garden, and only for a maximum of one half an hour, as she had an especially important meeting with Mr. Skottsberg following her interview.

Two men appearing to be in their mid-forties were waiting for her, and she noticed the tall one was not terribly well dressed.

He looks rather dishevelled. Perhaps he's the photographer.

Good heavens! His hair is as red and thick as mine. That's unusual.

Anders introduced himself and gave his position at the bank.

"Countess, I do hope you will forgive me for this slight deception, but I was concerned that you may not agree to meet with us had I been entirely truthful," Anders said.

A flash of annoyance crossed Katarina's face.

"I would like to introduce you to the man with me. His name is Martin Karlsson. Does that name mean anything to you?"

Katarina was completely mystified.

"Well, *no*. Aren't you the writer from *Göteborg-idag*?"

"No, Countess. But *Göteborg-idag* might be more than interested in the story that could unfold from this meeting."

Martin looked uncomfortable, but managed to say, "I am your brother, Countess Mrs. Carminati. I'm fifty-two years old. I work as a porter for the ocean liners that dock here. I'm a good man; we just have never met before." He paused. " You know you were adopted, don't you?"

Katarina listened, but was uncomprehending.

What is this frightful man going on about? Adopted? Who in God's name does he think he is, talking to me like that?

"Gentlemen, I surely don't know what you're talking about," she finally said, flustered. She busied herself searching for a handkerchief from her clutch. "You obviously have contacted the wrong person, but I was under the impression the newspaper wanted to talk to me about my life as a countess. Who are you again? I don't have any brothers — and I most certainly was *not* adopted!"

Anders said, "I'm sure this is all quite surprising, if not shocking, Countess. But we understand you have two sisters, one who lives here, and another in Canada. The, uh, newspaper has information that shows you and your sisters were adopted by a Gothenburg couple who took you to Canada with them in 1883. They did not include your brother, Martin, right here."

Katarina stood motionless and speechless.

They both look so earnest. What is going on? Is this some kind of a ploy to get money out of me? How do they know about Collan and Elisabet?

"This is sheer lunacy. As I have said, you are not speaking to the right person. Don't you think I would know if my sisters and I had been adopted? Good day, gentlemen."

Breathless, and shaking slightly, Katarina went to the office door of the Botanical Garden and rang the bell for someone to rescue her from this madness. The door of the office opened and without saying another word, Katarina quickly went inside.

Her heart was beating rapidly, and she asked the attendant if she could sit down. When he offered her a glass of water, she gladly accepted.

I don't know what to think. What does all this mean?

THIRTY-SIX

Vienna, Tuesday, May 30, 1923

Dear Mama,

I received your dear letter and believe me it was wonderful to read your good jolly letter and know that you are really not lonely.

It has worried me a lot to know that you are all alone, but I know that you are not the kind to sit around and get gloomy. But Mama dear, why do you work so hard in the summertime instead of going out in the good sunshine... Why are you painting the main parlor? It is foolish to do so. How I wish you were here. I miss you so.

I am sending you some snapshots of our whole group. Yesterday we were down in the catacombs where until 200 years ago all the people of Vienna were buried. It is a terribly gruesome place, I can tell you, Mama, with bones and skulls everywhere. We walked over 60,000 or 70,000 skeletons, and here and there were big piles of skulls. Oh! It was an awful place.

We also visited Schönbrunn Palace and it was simply gorgeous! Our room cost an absolute fortune, and had pictures and carvings in it that were over 1,000 years old. It was called the Gobelin Salon, and the tapestries on the walls were from 18th century Brussels. The chairs, also beautifully tapestried, represented the twelve months of the year and the signs of the zodiac. Mama, you would have been as impressed as I was!

It is so hot here today, almost like those summers in Boston.

I am glad Mama dear that you told those Yarmouth women where to get off. I am so disappointed in some of the townspeople and would be happy if you could have a nice home here or in some other jolly place.

We are leaving for Tyrol in two hours, so I shall write again soon. Take good care of your dear self.

With lots of love and kisses,
Eva

THIRTY-SEVEN

Gothenburg, Wednesday, May 30, 1923

Since meeting Anders and Martin at the Botanical Garden two days prior, Katarina had barely slept, or spoken to Joseph — except to assure him she wasn't angry with him — and had asked the babysitter to return the previous day and to come today, also. She needed to know Paolo was being cared for as she continued to reel from the revelations that had been delivered to her.

She didn't know if any of it was true; and she needed to speak to the only ally who might be able to make sense of the situation. She telephoned Collan and was now expecting her to visit.

Katarina dispensed with any opening pleasantries as her sister walked through the door, and blurted out, "Oh, Collan, I am ruined. Ruined! There are two people out there threatening to take a ridiculous story about me, *about us*, to the newspapers!"

She sunk into a chair even before Collan had the chance to say hello and remove her light spring sweater.

Collan wondered what her overly dramatic, prone-to-lying sister was going to say.

"Good Lord, Katarina, what on earth are you talking about?"

Katarina tried to explain to Collan what had happened with the two strangers at the Botanical Garden.

"The city's ruling class will see me as a laughingstock," Katarina said. "To think that you, Elisabet, and I were adopted! Father and Mother must be rolling in their graves as we speak."

Collan sat next to her sister.

"I knew you would eventually find out," Collan said with resignation.

"What are you saying, Collan? That the nonsense these two were spouting actually has merit?" Katarina was silent for a moment, and then the stress of her earlier encounter was evident. She began to cry.

"But we had parents who loved us, we had a normal childhood, we had —"

Collan reached over to embrace her sister.

"Please, Katarina, calm down, and let me tell you what I only found out, uh, three summers ago," Collan revealed, expecting another outburst.

"*Three years ago*, Collan? Dear God, why didn't you tell me? What is our family truly all about, anyway?"

Collan had questions of her own about the mysterious Martin whom Katarina had just met, but for now, she told her sister that yes, Elisabet had written to say they were all adopted. Collan had wanted to know more, and she began an investigation that revealed their parents' horrific murder-suicide, the existence of a fourth child and their subsequent adoption by Jacob and Signe.

She did not tell Katarina what Signe, their adoptive mother, had said on her deathbed to Elisabet. That would be too much information for Katarina to handle at this time.

Collan reminded herself that Elisabet had no knowledge of the murder-suicide, or the existence of their brother.

This is turning into a family nightmare.

"I don't know, I just don't know," Katarina said. "Was this man I met at the Botanical Garden really our brother? I mean, he did have red hair like mine, but I can't imagine us being in the same family! And if he really is our brother, wouldn't he want to know about us?"

"Well, I suppose he clearly does now, since he was there with this banker fellow you mentioned. Until now, I didn't even know if this brother of ours was alive. Tell me everything now of what you remember he said, and please describe him as accurately as you can."

Katarina finally seemed to calm down. She poured two shots of *punsch* into liqueur glasses that were sitting on a silver tray on the credenza. She proceeded to tell her sister her impressions of the man named Martin.

"If he was our brother, Katarina, he would have the family name we had at birth, which was Karlsson, apparently."

"Yes, that's the name the banker used when he introduced him to me," Katarina said, "but really, Collan, it is inconceivable why our true father —I guess one would say 'birth' father? — would kill our real mother. It's just too horrible to even think about."

Katarina drank the *punsch* in one gulp.

"I suggest that you don't tell Joseph any of this right now. I think we should wait to hear from them again, and then let me deal with them," Collan said. "It may not be a bad thing to get to know this man if we really are blood-related."

"I'm a countess, Collan! I bet you that the man is just looking for money," Katarina exclaimed, a fresh round of tears about to return.

Collan tried to hide her annoyance.

"You and I both know you bought your titles, Katarina, and you're not really that wealthy. Joseph wasn't born into nobility anymore than we were. Your titles do not matter. I will deal with this to stop it from getting any more ridiculous," Collan said, acting as the one-year-older-and-wiser sister. "But I do want to meet our brother in person myself to find out what his motivations are."

THIRTY-EIGHT

Yarmouth, Friday, June 15, 1923

Dear Eva,

I so appreciate your letters telling me about your adventures with Seamus in Europe. To think that my little girl at age twenty-two is seeing such marvelous sights and meeting such interesting people.

Yes, Mr. Measan is a lovely man. We had several fascinating discussions when he was in Boston. Incidentally, he was not married at the time, and I met him when I volunteered at the Boston Opera House where he was quite a noteworthy singer. He told me about his Alpine chalet and his home in Vienna, and now you are there enjoying Austria as Mr. Measan knew I might, too, one day.

You do not need to worry about me being lonely, Eva. I am quite busy most of the time. Broadale is so big there is always some little job to do, particularly since there is not a man around. Mavis helps me out, but more with the major cleaning and cooking.

I get myself out for walks now that the tulips, forsythia, and lilacs are in bloom, and I go as far as Frost Park, which is such a pretty spot overlooking the harbor. I have gone once for afternoon tea by myself at the Grand Hotel, but found the staff there acted very cool towards me. I must have waited over twenty minutes to be served, and the dining room was not even busy at the time.

As you have experienced, the townspeople do not approve of our family situation right now, but this will blow over, I expect, when a fresh scandal comes along to occupy their minds. I don't know why they are judgmental; you are married, after all.

I do have some days of extreme weariness, Eva, I have to admit. I hope you know that you have always been a valued child even though you may have thought I was absent for much of the time when you were a little girl. I guess I was just enthusiastic about the opportunity to live in the United States. Boston was so different from Yarmouth — so big and vibrant — I did get caught up in the social side of things, I suppose. It's only when one gets older that you recognize where you have made mistakes in your earlier life.

Your eagerness to please and spunkiness (is that a word, my dear?) have always been such charming characteristics of your personality. I see those traits even more so now in your letters to me.

Indeed, I'm sure those attributes must have also appealed to Seamus, too, do you think, dear? Has he ever told you what made him fall in love with you? He has never told me, although I expect it was partly because I was no longer attractive to him.

I suppose I knew in my heart that when we met in Halifax in March 1915 (yes, I remember the date — I am better at remembering numbers than you are!) that he would become bored with a woman fourteen years his senior. I didn't expect to age as fast as I did, Eva, so be prepared if you have inherited that unfortunate trait from me!

Maybe I should play the record "I Ain't Got Nobody [much and nobody cares for me]" on the Victrola now! Hahaha. But don't worry, dear Eva, I find I can deal with a little sadness from time to time.

I wish I knew what health problems I may have inherited from my real mother. You and I haven't discussed this yet, but I found out that your Grandmother and Grandfather adopted me, and your aunts Collan and Katarina, when we were little girls living in Gothenburg. You may have noticed that your Grandmother was sickly throughout much of her life, so I suppose I should be happy in a way that we were not related by blood after all!

Oh my — yes, we can talk about this when you get home. I am sure you will have questions, and I hope I will be able to tell you more, if you are interested.

Your Grandfather used to tell me tales of his early days in Sweden when he was a young man, so I hope you'll have the opportunity to visit Collan and Katarina on this trip and see Sweden as part of your family history.

Dear Eva, remember that Seamus has an aversion to smoked salmon and herring, so don't order any of that at restaurants. And you probably know by now that he insists on having toothpaste with fluoride ever since they started selling it a few years ago. Whatever you do, don't buy a less expensive brand without it! He will be most annoyed. And you might have noticed he burns from the sun quite easily, so apply olive oil to his skin if you see he is turning pink.

I am happy you are enjoying yourself, Eva. I hope someday to get to Europe before these old bones give up on me. My lumbago has been acting up of late and no matter how much Minard's Liniment I put on my lower back, nothing seems to work.

Love, Mama

THIRTY-NINE

Gothenburg, Friday, June 15, 1923

Collan had asked Katarina for details about everything Martin had said to her, and she also needed to have a physical description of him. It was pure luck that he had blurted out that he was a porter at the dockyards, so Collan was fairly certain she would be able to find him if she looked long and hard enough for a man with red hair.

After a light breakfast she and Linnea left their home in Haga and walked for less than fifteen minutes until they reached the official Port of Gothenburg where the ocean liners docked.

Collan asked Linnea to come along, as a second pair of searching eyes would help. The two women had no secrets from one another which greatly enhanced their relationship.

Linnea was first to notice a tall, lanky, middle aged man with flaming red hair maneuvering steamer trunks and large suitcases off a ship.

"I think that fellow over there could be your brother, Collan," she said, indicating Martin who had stopped several yards away to take a cigarette break.

Collan nodded, and the two approached him.

"Hello! Are you Martin Karlsson?" Collan asked with a smile.

Martin looked at both women and thought to himself that his good looks won out again, even if he felt grimy from working for the past two hours. He smiled in return.

"That's me", he said, "what can I do for you?"

Collan, ever direct, did not hesitate.

"Martin, I am your sister. My name is Collan Burcharth, although that surname means nothing to you, I imagine," she said, "and this is my dear friend, Linnea Nilsson."

Martin dropped the cigarette he had been smoking and forgot to extinguish it with his foot. He simply looked at Collan in amazement.

"But, what? How did you…how did you find me? Now? After all this time?" Then it dawned on him that the Countess must have told her sisters of his encounter with her.

"I don't understand," he said warily. Collan explained the events leading up to their meeting, leaving no doubt that her research into their adoption records had given her proof of their family connection. She gently brought up the deaths of their birth parents, in the event that he didn't know what had happened regarding the murder-suicide.

"Yeah, I know," Martin admitted. "It's awful to think about it. And I guess it explains why I have had bad dreams my whole life. I think I saw him kill her," he continued, eyes downcast.

All three were silent for a moment.

Linnea said, "That had to have been horrible for you, Martin. I am deeply sorry to hear about the parents you and Collan share," she said, touching his hand.

Martin looked at her as if she had appeared out of nowhere.

"Oh, yeah, thanks," he said absently, and turning to Collan, "I am happy to meet you. I met your, er, *our* sister, the Countess, just a few weeks ago."

"Yes, I know, Martin, and because of that, Linnea and I decided to look for you ourselves. But how did you know how to look for Katarina and investigate our family connection?"

Martin explained that he had a friend in Stockholm, a "banker", who first recognized a family resemblance between him and Katarina. "But I just figgered all of you people were too good to even want to know anything about me," he said.

Collan smiled ruefully.

"I'm glad we're finally meeting after so many years apart, Martin, I really am. I wished for so long that I had had a brother while we were growing up in Canada. But you and your friend frightened our sister a great deal last month. More than that, she is still in a state of shock trying to understand what happened with our birth parents," she said. "And sadly, this news also makes us wonder about our *adoptive* parents, too."

"Okay, yeah, I'm sorry I scared the Countess," Martin said, "but you gotta understand that you and your sisters in my eyes won a big prize by getting adopted. All I know is that I wasn't wanted by two sets of parents, not just one."

Collan looked pensive. She was still trying to piece together the many emotions and family history that had come together like a windstorm the night before Signe had died. The fallout started that night with her admission, and poor Elisabet, although shocked by what she was told, was still not privy to all the family secrets. Collan decided she would try to heal her family, and that task would start today.

"Martin, I would like you to come for dinner to our house tonight. We have to start building a relationship. And it's probably best you don't contact Katarina — the Countess — on your own. The three of us can get together later."

The look of relief on Martin's face was evident.

"I would really like that. I won't contact the Countess, but I think my friend Anders, who has a friend who writes for the newspaper, might have already tried to reach her. I hope that was okay."

"My sister tends to crave publicity," Collan said wryly, "so she should be able to decide what to say and what not to say to a journalist."

"Oh, fine, then. So, thank you for inviting me for dinner, Collan. I'm not used to that sort of thing, but I can clean up fairly good when I put my mind to it. What time do you want me there, and where do you live?" he asked, with a feeling of contentment that he had not felt in an exceptionally long time.

FORTY

Edinburgh, Monday, July 30, 1923

Dearest Mama,

First, I must apologize for not writing to you in such a long time. I've thought about you daily, but I have truly no excuse. We're now safely in Edinburgh, but it was such a long journey from Austria to Denmark and then to Sweden. I will tell you as much as I can recall.

It was certainly nice to get your dear letter, and the first thing that greeted me on my birthday was Seamus bringing it to me. How welcome it was. I was very saddened to hear that lumbago had affected your poor back. It is the nasty wet weather we get sometimes in Nova Scotia. You should wear a warm sweater and dry shoes when you're in the conservatory. It's a damp place and not healthy, even with all those plants.

How I wish I were home now, but since Seamus has the chance to learn some new medical procedures, he should take the opportunity. We plan on sailing back on August 17th. Edinburgh is certainly the place to learn; his studies will help Seamus to make good money in the future. But Mama, the North Sea was wild and woolly on the way here (the ship docked in Granton, not that far from Edinburgh) after we left Gothenburg, but we made it.

It has rained every day since we landed in Scotland. Believe me, Mama, Seamus now has a very cranky wife. I am getting really homesick as there is no more excitement to look forward to on our trip, and I am alone for long hours while Seamus is at class. I make him walk with me afterwards, but his little 'pot-belly' is taking a long time to disappear. He loves lamb and vegetables with lots of butter, not to mention good Scotch...and we couldn't be in a better place for that!

It's good to hear all about what you're doing. I enjoy your letters so much and they are written wonderfully well. You have certainly not forgotten how to write. But I'm unhappy you had that experience at the Grand Hotel. I hope there haven't been any more incidents where people have been unkind and rude to you. I feel responsible when I hear that happens.

And Mama, you are not an old woman by any stretch of the imagination. You are beautiful, and don't let your dear self forget that.

Tyrol was an exciting part of our trip but hiking very steep mountainsides is not an adventure I'd like to repeat.

We stayed at Sonnblick for two days (it was d—n high at 10,000 feet!) and on the third day at about seven o'clock, we started to trek downward. Our route this time covered over twenty miles of continual glaciers and we were slathered in grease to keep from burning up. I had a rather scary 'escape' on this route. We were going down a very steep mountain when my foot slipped on a bit of ice and I started, in great style, to slide down on my backside.

Thank God Mr. Measan was ahead of me, and I banged into him, knocking him down and then both of us slipped together for about 100 yards. He finally got his big stick jammed into the snow and stopped our descent.

I was frightened to death and the seat of my pants was completely gone, as was the skin off my arm and hand...but I was safe, so I laughed instead of cried. When the men got over their fright, they soundly scolded me, and for something I couldn't help! But men are men, aren't they?

I've bought a nice pair of Russian boots to go with your Russian black fur coat. It will be stunning for you! Mama, it won't be long before I see you and what nice talks we will have. Is there anything you want from here?

Oh yes, I was going to tell you more about the rest of our trip. When we got to Innsbruck, we took a train to Zurich and boarded another train for an awfully long and tiring ride from there to Copenhagen.

What a lovely city, Mama! I think I liked it even more than Vienna. The Danes seem to be softer in personality than the Austrians we met, and they eat extremely healthy foods. Seamus was missing his rich Austrian pastries and strudel! I absolutely loved Tivoli Gardens and will show you a lot of pictures when I get home.

When we finally arrived in Gothenburg, it was something of a homecoming for me, to see the country where you and all my relations on your side of the family came from. I have much to tell you about the home where Aunt Katarina and Joseph live with Paolo, and where Aunt Collan and Linnea live. I'm happy that Aunt Collan does not have to live by herself. Even though Linnea seems to be a quiet woman, they do get along as if they have known one another forever. (Mama, I don't think Aunt Katarina is as rich as she makes herself out to be. Their home is nice, but not in the least 'palatial' like she would have you think it is! She also said nothing about a home or property in Naples, or even discussed Joseph's family. I fear your sister is a bit of an odd duck, Mama!)

This has been such a wonderful honeymoon for me, and I have you to thank for it, and once again thank you for letting Seamus and I marry. I shan't be a disappointment to you, and I am saving the best news for the last in this letter.

I'm very sure I'm pregnant! You will be a grandmama! I'm thrilled, Mama, and so is Seamus. We will begin looking for a home in Yarmouth for our little family when we return. We want to give you some peace and quiet. I suspect you will not want the imposition of a baby in your life, even if Broadale is a big house!

I am so incredibly happy, Mama, and cannot wait to see you soon. Wear heather for good luck for both of us!

Eva

xxxxx

FORTY-ONE

Yarmouth, Sunday, July 1, 1923

Elisabet was pleased when she was invited to a Dominion Day tea at the home of the widow of Judge James Murray who had been the overseer of the Probate Court in 1898. Mavis and Eliza, who also worked part-time for Mrs. Murray, had told Elisabet what a lovely woman the widow was, and urged her to accept the invitation.

The impressive Regency style home with Gothic influences was located at the corner of Main and Forest Streets. Elisabet had often admired the residence which was built between 1820 and 1825. She had walked by 'Murray Manor' many times as a child since she had been raised in a home a little further east on Forest Street. But for Elisabet, that childhood home did not hold many pleasant memories.

The former office of Judge Murray was located at the front of Murray Manor facing Forest Street and Yarmouth Harbor. Mrs. Murray had left the room untouched since her husband had died twenty-four years prior, but today she allowed the office to be turned into a display space for the Imperial Order of the Daughters of the Empire, also known as the I.O.D.E.

The spoils of war that Yarmouth's sons and husbands had brought back home were placed on her late husband's desk and on the three extra tables that had been brought into the room.

After Elisabet greeted Mrs. Murray and thanked her for the invitation, the widow led Elisabet into the dining room to offer her a cup of tea and a sweet. Elisabet, at forty-five, was one of the youngest women present.

A lady about the same age as Mrs. Murray sat at the end of an oblong table and presided over an elaborate silver tea service. She poured Elisabet a cup of the hot beverage, and then asked if she would like milk and sugar with the tea.

Elisabet demurred, as she had gotten used to having only lemon in her tea during her Boston sojourn, and she didn't see any lemon wedges in sight. She instinctively knew a request for lemon would not be appreciated by the older woman, particularly if the household didn't happen to have any.

Mrs. Murray excused herself to greet a new arrival, and Elisabet decided to look into the late Judge's office to see the exhibits she had been told were there on display. She thought she would be more comfortable in the office, since a quick glance into the parlor showed her that she knew only a few of the women inside, and they were all her adoptive mother's older acquaintances, and not her own.

Two women in their late seventies were chatting in the Judge's office when Elisabet walked in.

"Good afternoon, ladies," she smiled.

"And a happy Dominion Day to you, dear," greeted one with an especially wide-brimmed hat.

"Hello, and happy birthday to our young little country!" the other said, giggling, wearing a cloche that was perched precariously on her mass of white curls which were vainly trying to escape the confines of her hat.

"Yes, it's amazing to think Canada is only a few years older than I am," Elisabet said, attempting to find some enthusiasm for the small talk. She started looking at the items on one of the tables.

Next to a spiked steel helmet known as a *Stahlhelm*, worn by German soldiers, was one lace-up ankle boot, used by many storm troopers, and a visorless cap, known as a *Feldmütze*, which the enlisted men wore. Small place cards helpfully identified most of the items. Alongside the table, on a dressmaker's dummy, a local soldier's badly charred and bloodied uniform was hung.

Elisabet found the display disconcerting, because she immediately thought each of these items as having belonged to a formerly living, breathing young man. Casualties on both sides of any armed conflict were inevitable, but Elisabet had found the Great War to be simply incomprehensible since its inception, and she had chosen to ignore its existence.

The woman with the broad-brimmed hat said, "I don't believe we've formally met. I'm Mrs. Nathaniel Smith, but please call me Beryl, and this is my friend Miss Alice Morris. And you are...?"

"Of course, yes, hello again. I'm, uh, Elisabet Burcharth," Elisabet replied, unsure if she should have used her most recent married name, or her deceased husband's surname.

"Would you be the late Captain Burcharth's daughter, then?" Miss Morris asked.

"Yes, I am the eldest," she said. "I have two younger sisters in Europe."

Miss Morris suddenly became stone faced, while the lesser aware Mrs. Smith continued what was quickly developing into an awkward moment.

"Dear, perhaps we could interest you in a membership to the I.O.D.E.? We're always looking for other women who are 'loyal in everything', which is our motto!"

"Beryl, no," Alice Morris said, *sotto voce.*

"I'm afraid I don't know much about your organization, ladies," Elisabet said, picking up on the unfriendly tone from Alice Morris.

Then, like a lightbulb being turned on underneath Beryl Smith's huge hat, she looked at Elisabet as if seeing her for the first time.

"Oh, my heavens — you're the one who let her daughter marry your own husband! Agh! That's simply disgusting!" She paused to catch her breath before continuing. "Well, Mrs. Whatever-your-name-is-now, immoral women are not welcome into the Order. And I can assume that *your* family is not even from one of the countries of the British Empire!"

Beryl Smith's face was turning as red as the silk roses placed all over the brim of her hat.

Elisabet's eyes widened in anger, her feet rooted to where she stood with teacup and saucer in hand.

"My family's business and its background are absolutely none of your concern, madam," she managed to spit out. "Good day."

She turned and left the room, but heard Alice Morris call out, "Yarmouth *doesn't want* people like you!"

FORTY-TWO

Yarmouth, Wednesday, August 15, 1923

Dear Eva and Seamus,

Since you're due to sail in a couple of days from Scotland to return home, it would be of no use to post this letter, as you'll arrive before being able to receive it overseas. Therefore, I'll save it in the event my thoughts of today might be partially forgotten, and I'll be able to refresh my memory from this letter when you return.

Eva, you have a tremendous responsibility when you become a mother, and if indeed you are pregnant, you cannot do anything about it now.

Seamus, perhaps you wanted a child when you were married to me, but we both decided for different reasons at the time that it was not a good idea.

But I have to wonder if you are now *regretting that we did* not *try anyway?*

Robert Burns once wrote, "The best laid schemes o' mice an' men, Gang aft a-gley", but if we had tried anyway, and had I given birth to a lovely little baby, things would be so much different today, wouldn't they? Eva would have a little sister or brother. You and I might still be husband and wife! Oh my, the mind boggles at what might have been, does it not?

Eva, dear, I'm not meaning to take away any of your joy. To the contrary. Bringing a new life into the world is a mystical thing, but you must really want *to have a child. Perhaps you and Seamus did not exactly plan to have this one?*

Parents treasure their children and protect them forever, even after they have grown into adults. That's when the unique bond between a mother and child becomes even more delicate. The mother should be more diplomatic, more tactful, and more respectful of her child who is now her peer. They'll never be friends, exactly, but they are two adults who are tied to one another by a special bond.

And those parents who decide to adopt children, well, they must *want them more than anything else in the world.*

By the way, I had another very unsettling encounter with two Yarmouth ladies on Dominion Day. I'll tell you all about it when you get home, but be prepared in this town to be smacked with narrow-minded opinions of our personal lives when you least expect it. Incidents like these are tiring and upsetting, and I'm afraid there's nothing we can do about it.

I fear I'm rambling off-course, dear Eva. I don't envy your long journey back home, as I suffered greatly from morning and motion sickness, and if you did inherit that condition from me, more's the pity.

With affection, and have a safe crossing,
Elisabet

FORTY-THREE

Yarmouth, Thursday, August 16, 1923

Elisabet had decided to not visit Vickery's Booksellers and Stationers on Main Street since Eva's unpleasant encounter with the proprietor the previous September.

She had been sending Mavis to the store once weekly to pick up copies of *The Boston Evening Transcript* which she had been subscribing to since moving to Broadale. The newspapers were always recent copies, thanks to the steamers that continued to sail between Boston and Yarmouth twice a week.

While the capital of the Commonwealth of Massachusetts held bittersweet memories for Elisabet, she continued to be interested in the happenings in the city, particularly in the arts and cultural arena.

She sipped a cup of coffee at the dining room table at Broadale with the broadsheet spread out in front of her for easier reading. One headline from the newspaper's society section jumped off the page.

Over the Teacups
with Sally Mae Wilkinson
A COUNTESS FROM BOSTON?

It has come to this columnist's attention from one of our colleagues far across the Atlantic Ocean in Sweden, that the beauteous Countess Katarina de Carminati, 43, who makes her home in that country's second largest city, Gothenburg, is claiming she was born and raised in Boston. Goodness! We didn't know royalty came from Beantown! Didn't we rid ourselves of all that in 1776?

All is not what it appears to be, however. My reporter friend has uncovered contrary information in Sweden that states the Countess, whose maiden name is Katarina Burcharth, was one of three adopted children following a notorious murder-suicide in the southern part of the country in the early 1880s. The couple who adopted the children apparently emigrated to Canada, and not to the U. S. of A.!

Moreover, faithful reader, her husband Joseph, whom she refers to as "the Count", is an Italian entrepreneur with dubious business dealings in his native Naples. Indeed, my colleague at Gothenburg's daily newspaper (its title translates to 'Gothenburg Today') has investigated and reported that "the Count" may not actually hold title to any land in his native country.

Could the Countess Katarina and Count Joseph de Carminati – and even their five-year-old son, little Viscount Paolo – be fraudsters? We are intrigued by this juicy story and want to know more!

Elisabet closed the newspaper as tears began to silently flow down her cheeks.

A murder-suicide? Please God, don't let that be the truth about my real parents. Is Katarina making up stories about them, now, too?

FORTY-FOUR

Gothenburg, Thursday, August 16, 1923

As far as summers were concerned, Katarina felt that this had been one of her worst. Since meeting her estranged brother in May, it seemed the universe was conspiring to make her life miserable. It would not have occurred to her that much of her trouble was of her own making.

In July, a factually accurate article about her life as a countess appeared in *Göteborg-idag*. It was written by a features editor who had received a tip from a fellow writer who knew Anders Lindgren.

Somehow the editor had found that Joseph did not own land or an estate in Italy, and had also uncovered the fact that Katarina and her sisters were not raised in Boston. They had been brought to a small town on the east coast of Canada that no one in Sweden had ever heard of...

Katarina knew her fabricated stories were catching up to her.

The article essentially said she had lied to the writer about her upbringing in Boston; that in fact, she had a ne'er-do-well, petty criminal as a brother; and that the murder of her mother by her father had definitely taken place in 1882.

The article unfortunately did not garner much public sympathy for the immigrant countess; and unbeknownst to her, she had become fodder for derision among the society types of Gothenburg. Following the Great War, tabloid journalism had become popular in the United States, and it was also now becoming well-received by the Swedish population.

Katarina noticed that invitations to charitable events had stopped. The telephone rarely rang. Even the women she had met on the Volunteer Board of Directors at the Botanical Garden had ceased including her in their activities.

She had been feeling a growing disconnect with Joseph, and had to admit noticing a definite lack of interest in intimacy in their marriage. His impatience with her and shortness of temper with Paolo were readily apparent as the summer progressed.

This is not the man I married. Where did that charming Italian go?

FORTY-FIVE

Gothenburg, Friday, August 17, 1923

Martin was pleased with his rare good fortune at having met his sister Collan. Throughout the summer they got together on several occasions, and each time cemented a budding sibling bond.

They decided to go to the Gothenburg Tercentennial Jubilee Exposition since it was only open until the end of September, and it wasn't often one could visit a World's Fair and celebrate the 300th anniversary of their city at the same time.

The most popular section of the Exposition was Liseberg, an existing gardened area Linnea and Collan had visited earlier in May. Collan suggested to Martin they meet in front of the Industrial Art House, one of the many pavilions specially built for the Jubilee.

Later, sharing a pitcher of beer, Martin asked Collan a question which he hoped would not offend her.

"Collan, I really like your friend, Linnea," Martin began.

"She's spoken for," Collan quipped, grinning.

Martin raised an eyebrow, then chuckled.

"Oh, you guessed what I was about to ask you!"

"Well, it was a wild guess, but I thought that since you weren't married, you might be interested in her," Collan said. "She and I have a very special relationship."

"Okay, I do understand that, and you don't have to say much more. You see, I am a bit inclined that way myself, even if the law says we can't be like that," Martin said, taking a swig of his draught.

"Oh, so you *don't* want to date her, then? Well, new brother, that is a relief!" she said, laughing. "And in my experience, I've found the law is often contrary to human nature and against things we can't change, Martin," Collan said. "We're not hurting anyone."

"That's for sure," he said, "and there's one more thing I wanted to ask you about today."

"Sure, go ahead. What is it?"

"Do you and Linnea want to meet my friend Anders the next time he is in Gothenburg?"

Collan smiled warmly. It was nice getting to know her brother and comforting to think they shared a similar same-sex orientation in their romantic attraction for others.

"We would definitely enjoy that, Martin. You haven't been given many chances in life, but maybe meeting Anders will turn out to be a wonderful thing for the both of you."

FORTY-SIX

Eva – Yarmouth, Thursday, August 30, 1923

Dear Journal,
We've been home for several days now, and I've got what everyone
calls a 'summer cold'. My nose is all stuffed up; I'm sneezing non-
stop; and I've used up almost every handkerchief in the house. I'm
pretty much isolating myself, so I don't give the bug to Mama or
Seamus. (Memories of the Spanish Flu, unfortunately.)

Thank God the weather is pleasant, sunny, and warm so I can go
outside into the back yard and sit among the pink, mauve, blue, and
white hydrangeas. They always lift my spirits. I'll be out there today,
writing notes to Aunt Collan and Aunt Katarina to thank them for their
hospitality when Seamus and I visited Gothenburg. I'm glad I got to
know them a little bit better, because on the surface it would not
appear that the three sisters are even related. Each woman is so
different, but I imagine they must have some buried similarities
somewhere.

Mama has been acting differently since we've come back. One
moment she is all smiles and appears happy we're here, and the next
she's practically asking us when we're moving out. Both Seamus and
I would like to stay until the baby is born, at least, so I hope she'll be
fine with that.

She has said little about the tea she was invited to on Dominion
Day, except to mention two women were very rude to her about my
marriage to Seamus. Why are people so judgmental? I didn't know
when Mama married Seamus that things would turn out like this. I'm
almost a mother, for goodness sake, and everything is perfectly
legitimate.

Seamus immediately began working at the hospital again. Our
income has been reduced considerably because of his time off work.
The honeymoon was so expensive, and we're trying to save for a

decent down-payment to buy a house in town. I suspect I'll see little of my hard-working husband from now on!

I'm excited to become a mother, and hope I'll regain whatever respect may have been lost by marrying Seamus. It's curious that I've not heard anything bad said about him since his divorce and marriage to me. I suppose because he's a doctor, he gets some kind of exalted status that prevents gossip.

Dear Journal – only here can I write freely!

I don't want to be absent a lot when the baby is little, like Mama was with me, but I'm fairly sure she didn't do that on purpose. Boston was overwhelming for someone from a small town, and I imagine the excitement of the city was just too much for her to resist.

She closed her journal and put down her pen. She had a fleeting thought that she always gave her mother the benefit of any doubt. Then she remembered writing the letters to Mama on her honeymoon, and having to refrain on a couple of occasions from actually apologizing for marrying Seamus.

If I am feeling some kind of inherent guilt about my marriage, I wonder if Seamus, does, too? He is so hard to read sometimes...

...but Mama gave us her permission to marry. What else could I have done?

FORTY-SEVEN

Haga, Gothenburg, August 30, 1923

Dear Elisabet,

I hope you are well in what I trust and remember is Yarmouth's best month for weather. I also hope Eva and Seamus returned safely, and that the crossing was uneventful. It's always a tiring voyage, but so nice to be home once again.

My dear sister, I know you were upset when I corroborated what Mother told you about us being adopted. I'm afraid there is more to this story, and because I have lost sleep thinking about not being entirely truthful with you, I want to share some additional information.

When I met with the assistant to the Archbishop of Gothenburg three years ago this month, I was told that not only were the three of us adopted, but that we have a brother as well. He was obviously not adopted by Jacob and Signe.

You may have a vague recollection from your early childhood of a little boy around us? Well, his name is Martin, and he is about seven years older than you. I don't know why Mother and Father left him behind, but he sadly had a childhood full of cruelty. His adoptive father treated him most unkindly, and compared with our experience, he was terribly unlucky.

We can assume he was not adopted with us because Mother told you she had never wanted children. Three girls must have seemed more than enough for her to handle as a young woman of 23 at the time.

I've gotten to know Martin in recent months, and he is a handsome, kind, if somewhat wayward man. I'll tell you more about him later when I see you in person on our next trip.

I know that the knowledge of us having a living brother may come as a shock to you since none of us has any memory of him.

I really hate to tell you the further circumstances of our adoption by Mother and Father, or Signe and Jacob, as you refer to them now. Elisabet, they weren't bad people, and you know that. Mother was not a happy woman most of her life, but she did not treat us terribly, did she?

The reason why the three of us (actually, all four of us) were put up for adoption was because our birth father murdered our birth mother. I couldn't find out many details, which are indeed gruesome, and I will not burden you further with that sad story. Poor Martin witnessed the murder, and he told me he has been plagued with nightmares his entire life because of this.

You mustn't feel bad about this information, as terrible as it is. We can't do anything about our past and must live with the consequences of others' actions. We can simply count our blessings.

Think of the lovely home you have now, and the devoted love of a beautiful daughter. You have enjoyed the attention and wedded bliss of two wonderful men — may Nigel R.I.P. — and your health is as good as it can be now that we are all approaching our twilight years.

The last thing I wanted to tell you, dear Sister, is that Katarina and Paolo, as well as myself and Linnea, are thinking seriously about returning home to Nova Scotia.

Katarina can tell you all her reasons for relocating, but suffice to say, Joseph will not be accompanying her. They are amicably going to divorce.

It will be quite an adjustment for Linnea, but I have been teaching her English every day for quite some time now, and she is getting reasonably conversant even if her written English still leaves something to be desired.

She is a very dear companion to me, Elisabet.

The truth is, I miss Yarmouth. I miss Nova Scotia. I particularly miss all of Canada. I do not expect you to house us — I am thinking of building a home just outside the town by the ocean. We will stay at the Grand Hotel in the interim. I love Cape Forchu, but it is not the easiest place to get to in the winter months. I think perhaps Sand Beach or Rockville — or even Chebogue — on the outskirts of Yarmouth, are all nice areas in which to live. Maybe I could purchase a horse! A simple house overlooking the ocean with a small barn and a paddock would be ideal for this gal!

Please don't be upset at what I've told you in this letter, and don't be angry with me for withholding some of this information from you until now. I was only thinking of your welfare, but the burden of keeping quiet about Martin and the circumstances of our adoptions were just too much to bear alone any longer.

With love from your sister,

Collan

FORTY-EIGHT

Yarmouth, Saturday, September 15, 1923

The dampness in the air, and a bank of fog hovering in the harbor made this gray day completely forgettable.

The foghorn at Cape Forchu droned mournfully every few minutes. The only other sound to be heard was the train to Halifax tooting its daily goodbye at the Yarmouth train station. It would stop at many small stations along the Bay of Fundy and in the Annapolis Valley before reaching the city.

Sitting on a stool in the conservatory, Elisabet had just finished reading Collan's letter about the brother they shared, and the other disturbing news about the fate of their birth parents.

I can't be angry, and I can't mourn for people I never knew. Maybe if I were in Europe this would be more real, but I have not stepped foot in Sweden since we left when I was five. Or six. It doesn't matter. The place means nothing to me. It means even less, now, thanks to Collan's detective work. We didn't need to know this information about the parents who bore us. The man was clearly out of his mind; the woman, well, who knows what the hell was so wrong with her that he killed her. And after giving him four children. The bastard.

Just how much information does my family think I need to know? This news comes right after Eva blissfully reported on her pregnancy and after her fabulous honeymoon with my *husband. I was the one to meet him first. I was and am the first woman Seamus fell in love with.*

I mean, this has just gone too far.

Elisabet started grabbing the dead leaves she had snipped from various plants and some wayward weeds, and threw them into a steel pail.

And my stupid little sister, Katarina. She's such a vain creature with a purchased title and dreams of being someone important. She's a scrawny woman with an unrivaled ego who can't construct a sentence together without there being a lie in it. I don't want her here. Who the hell does she think she is to come waltzing back to Yarmouth, a happy divorcée, at that? She thinks men will fall all over her because she's a 'countess'. Men won't notice her unless she's returning with so much money that their heads would spin. And I doubt that is a possibility.

Oh, dear Lord, I am so angry. I wish I believed in you. I wish I could take comfort from some spiritual source that could tell me that I'm understood by others...someone who understands me... someone who could make me understand my foolish mistake in divorcing Seamus so he could marry my daughter. She is all I have, really. She is the only constant in my life. We have been through a lot together, and we need one another.

I fear I made a terrible decision in allowing her to marry my husband.

She picked up the pail and tightened the shawl around her shoulders, about to leave the conservatory. Then she stopped in mid-step, as if someone had tapped her on the arm.

Well, well, well. I wonder if Eva was intimate with Measan in Vienna. After all, she is so young and beautiful, unlike her decrepit old mother whose own husband rejected her.

It wouldn't be a surprise to me if Eva did act like a whore: so like mother, like daughter, again. She stole my husband — why not my lover, too?

Measan was a such a gentle and cultured man. Not at all like Nigel. I wonder what would have happened had Nigel not stopped in Yarmouth en route to Boston. He and I would never have met; I wouldn't have had an affair with Measan; I wouldn't have given birth to Eva.

So, I suppose it was meant to be that Nigel and I met and got married. It wasn't so smart of me to carry on with Measan, but he did keep communicating with me for many years. I think he quite liked me. I recall he even sent me a condolence card when Nigel died.

There have been days when I wondered if Eva might be Measan's child. I never did bother to track the weeks. What difference would it make now, anyway?

And if I hadn't met Nigel, and if he hadn't died, I wouldn't have come back to Yarmouth and met Seamus at a charitable event that Jacob had been asked to attend.

And here we are.

Is that Eva calling from the kitchen telling me that dinner is almost ready? I didn't know she knew how to cook.

FORTY-NINE

Yarmouth, Saturday, September 22, 1923

Seamus was quite pleased with himself.

Ever since his volunteer work with the survivors of the Halifax Explosion, he had developed a dedicated interest in ophthalmology. Although he was not a fully accredited ophthalmologist, he continued to study eye surgery, and had enrolled in countless lectures and seminars, hoping to increase his knowledge of the specialty.

When an article he wrote about the importance of having an ophthalmic surgeon on the battlefield or immediately available after a major urban casualty was published in the *Archives of Ophthalmology*, he was proud that his voice was finally being heard.

Granted, while it was proven that a patient's injured eyes could be salvaged by an expert surgeon, he knew it was unusual for a prestigious ophthalmology journal to accept an article written by a general practitioner.

From childhood, Seamus had always been a confident person. Blessed with good looks and a flawless complexion that women and other men envied, he had always been admired and respected. He had somehow learned at a young age to listen intently to anyone who spoke to him, regardless of their age or intellect, and he knew how to make that person feel as if he or she had just said something profoundly interesting.

Naturally, this trait endeared him to women and men alike. His earnestness, while rehearsed and oftentimes worthy of accolades reserved only for great actors, was largely a conceit. He had always been self-assured with everything except his weakness for rich foods and a regular overindulgence of alcohol. Those habits had been a part of his daily routine since medical school.

He had looked in on Eva that morning, offering her comfort and encouragement as she dealt with the vestiges of a cold along with *hyperemesis gravidarum*. He loved his ability to remember Latin names for medical conditions as common as morning sickness, but he was concerned that her vomiting was continuing into her fifth month. He was anxious to have his first child, but was secretly happy *he* wasn't the one in the partnership giving birth. It remained incomprehensible to Seamus how a human could be put through such an ordeal; he sympathized with Eva in that regard.

In the main parlor, he smoked a cigarette while leafing through one of Elisabet's Boston newspapers. His former wife entered the room, dressed as if she were about to attend a gala afternoon party.

"Seamus! I thought you'd be at the hospital by now," Elisabet said, sliding into a chair next to his.

"I'm starting at five," he said, putting the newspaper on the side table situated between them. "It gives me a bit more time with Eva."

"Yes, poor dear," Elisabet said. "I also felt constantly ill during my pregnancy with her. I guess she takes after her mother."

Seamus looked at her and flashed his most charming smile.

"And clearly that's where she gets her beauty from, as well," he said.

"Oh, Seamus," Elisabet responded, in mock dismissiveness. "But it begs the question: do you miss me at all?"

"You know I do, Elisabet. You were my puppy love, after all," he replied, inclining his body more towards her. "I was just a schoolboy, and you robbed the cradle," he said flirtatiously.

Elisabet giggled.

This is where I want him.

"I do think we should have more of these heart-to-heart conversations, don't you?" she asked. "And I mean that in every possible way, of course."

Like a peacock exhibiting his impressive iridescent feathers, Seamus sat back in his chair and smiled smugly at his former wife.

FIFTY

Halifax, Tuesday, October 30, 1923

TWO STEAMERS IN THURSDAY MORNING
WITH PASSENGERS
Hellig Olav and La Bourdonais
Two Days Late –
Countess de Carminati Landed

The Countess Katarina de Carminati of Sweden arrived in Halifax yesterday morning on the Scandinavian-American liner, Hellig Olav, and then left for Yarmouth where she will visit her sister Mrs. Elisabet McMaster, former wife of Dr. Seamus McMaster, and her niece, Mrs. Eva McMaster. Accompanying the Countess on the voyage was her older sister, Miss Collan Burcharth, and her companion, Miss Linnea Nilsson, all of whom currently reside in Gothenburg.

The Countess, who has sailed across the ocean at least twenty-five times, experienced her first shipwreck with this journey, when the Gustav III scraped along a submerged rock a few hours after leaving Gothenburg, and had to return to that port with two inches of water in her hold.

The rock or ledge the liner encountered was uncharted, and it was believed to have been caused by an upheaval of the seabed in a recent submarine earthquake. Salt water that was found in the freshwater tank led to a further investigation and the discovery of the damage. The Gustav III returned to port, and its passengers boarded the Hellig Olav for the trip to Nova Scotia.

The Hellig Olav reported a very rough crossing and was a day late in her schedule. She landed three cabin and sixty-six third-class passengers and some mail. The steamer then sailed to New York.

Countess de Carminati and Miss Burcharth were in Halifax last year en route to Yarmouth where they had visited their sister. On that occasion, the Countess's son accompanied her. Miss Nilsson also took

part in that visit, which was her first to Canada. ~ Pickford and Black,
agents

FIFTY-ONE

Yarmouth, Saturday, November 3, 1923

"It's so dreary having to transport this huge amount of baggage with me," Katarina complained to no one in particular as she, her sisters, Eva, Seamus, and Linnea were sitting in the main parlor at Broadale after dinner.

"I'd think you'd be grateful to be able to start fresh here in Yarmouth," Elisabet said sarcastically. "I mean, after all, you are without a husband and without your child. Surely your load is lighter."

"Elisabet, that is unnecessarily cruel of you to put it like that," Katarina said, but did not appear at all offended. "I told Joseph that he could have all the furniture from our house. And, given the instability of our marriage, it was best to grant full custody of Paolo to him. It would not have been fair to uproot the child to Canada."

"I don't know why it would have been unfair, Aunt Katarina," Eva said. "He's only three years old and probably would have picked up English easily. You must miss him terribly."

"He *was* a precocious little tyke," Katarina replied. "But my goodness, there is so much to do now to find a decent home in which to live! Fortunately, my Count Joseph provided well for his countess in the settlement!"

She chuckled. Her companions looked ill at ease.

"Eva, how are you feeling, dear?" Collan asked, deflecting attention from Katarina.

"I'm doing quite well now that the morning sickness finally stopped, but I don't know if I could handle ever being pregnant again, Aunt Collan. I dreaded waking up most mornings," Eva said. "But the little miss or master McMaster will hopefully arrive on time at the end of December."

"Maybe you will have the first baby of 1924 in Yarmouth!" Linnea exclaimed, surprising everyone in the room except for Collan.

"You know, I noticed after you arrived that your English has improved significantly since last year, Linnea," Seamus said.

"Thank you very much, Seamus," Linnea said, smiling. "I have had a very good tutor at home."

Collan blushed. Ignoring her partner's compliment, she asked Seamus how things were going at the hospital and if there had been any major problems to date.

"I don't know about major problems, besides our constant lack of nurses, but the good news is that Dalhousie University is finally offering courses in nursing, particularly in the field of public health. And speaking of which, venereal disease is still a huge problem, even five years after the end of the war," Seamus said.

"Seamus, that's hardly post-dinner, polite chit chat, is it?" Elisabet half-jokingly said. "Maybe you'd like to talk about degenerate behavior, too?"

"Oh, Mama, now leave Seamus alone," Eva chided. "He works very hard at the hospital and takes his position very seriously."

Elisabet glared momentarily at her.

"I *know that*, Daughter dear."

Katarina, who had been only half-listening to the conversation, straightened up in her chair, as if an idea had suddenly occurred to her.

"I haven't seen that wonderful polar bear rug I sent you anywhere — oh my goodness — it must have been three years ago! Tell me you've not sold it, Elisabet, please! It's *unbelievably* valuable."

"It's in my study, Katarina. Not to worry. He keeps an eye on me to make sure I mind my Ps and Qs", Seamus said.

In a dry voice, Katarina commented, "And I can see what an amazing job he did."

FIFTY-TWO

Yarmouth, Saturday, December 15, 1923

The Canadian economy shifted after the war ended, and unemployment rates skyrocketed with returning soldiers all seeking work. The Spanish flu pandemic of 1918–19 had also added to the financial woes across the nation.

A brief collapse in markets occurred in 1920 and 1921, but by the time Katarina and Collan were shopping for homes in late 1923, there was substantial fiscal improvement in the country, and it was a good time to buy or sell real estate.

On December 14, Linnea and Collan had finished packing their belongings at the Grand Hotel and were about to take a taxi to their new home. They were having tea in the dining room when Linnea unexpectedly took Collan's hand in hers.

"I just wanted to thank you so much for all the help you've given me in this complicated immigration process to Canada," she said in Swedish to her partner. "It means a lot to me."

Collan was not one to get emotional in public, and replying in Linnea's native language, said, "It means more to me just to have you here and share a life with you, Linnea." On a practical note, she continued, "And remember that your residency papers were expedited because of your knowledge and care for dear Prince Erik. When one comes to this country with experience in handling chronic illnesses like epilepsy, Canada is extremely lucky to have you as a resident."

She paused and smiled. "As am I."

Collan and Linnea's modest farmhouse was in the community of Overton, which was literally across the harbor from the town, hence its name. Collan was pleased she wouldn't have to build a home, and she did get her wish of a water view. A broad expanse of land was included with the house, as well as an attached barn, perfect for owning a horse. She had sorely missed caring for and riding her own horse on a daily basis.

She was aware that her siblings had yet to discuss the circumstances of their adoption and their feelings about the only mother and father they had known. She knew the discussion had to be initiated sooner than later, but she did not want to be its instigator. She worried it would be a heated, emotional debate.

#

Katarina bought a home on Collins Street; the elderly owner had died only recently. She purchased it fully furnished so she wouldn't have to begin shopping for furniture now that the winter weather had arrived. The location was perfect because living next door to her Victorian home were Judge Charles and Mrs. Susan Pelton. Katarina felt it was fitting that that a Countess and a Judge should be neighbors and expected there to be many social occasions they would enjoy together.

#

Eva was expecting her baby to arrive at the end of December, but she hoped he or she might wait until the new year. She wanted a New Year's baby and had continued to drop hints to Seamus that she would be ready to move anytime after the birth. Her instincts as a woman and an expectant mother told her that a rapid move from Broadale and from Elisabet would be most beneficial to her marriage — and would keep her stress levels low.

#

Elisabet was quietly knitting a baby blanket in her bedroom at Broadale but was simmering in her own self-induced resentment to not only Eva, but Seamus, as well. The anger she felt toward him was contradictory and intense; the hurt she felt resulting from Eva's behavior was simply confusing. She second-guessed herself continually, wondering just how much she might have been encouraging their relationship all along.

She acutely remembered giving assent to them to continue their secretive affair as long as they married and avoided any public displays of affection for one another. But she soon realized that the marriage of a daughter to her stepfather was proving to be almost impossible to keep secret.

There are times when I can see why people see this as an unnatural pairing, but really, they are not *blood related whatsoever. I was only thinking that for them to marry was the most sensible thing to do — how can I be faulted for that?*

She was angry at herself because she felt she had acted like some kind of maternal and spousal benefactor to a union which she had never fully understood. She knew what she had to do, almost immediately, to salvage what dignity she had remaining in her life.

I don't understand why things don't make sense to me as much as they used to. And I keep forgetting things that I did just moments ago! I don't think I repeat myself too often when I'm talking, but sometimes Eva gives me very strange looks. Do I talk too *much, or not enough?*

Oh, yes…Seamus. I know what I have to do to keep my dignity.

FIFTY-THREE

Yarmouth, Thursday, December 20, 1923

Eva was miserable.

Her legs, feet and hands were swollen. Her headache was severe and continuous, and Seamus was genuinely concerned. He saw all the signs of toxemia and knew her blood pressure had to be high.

Within two hours, Eva was admitted to the relatively new Yarmouth Hospital on Vancouver Street, which had opened in 1918. Seamus immediately ordered a test using the sphygmomanometer to see the level of her hypertension. He knew she would require bed rest and need to lie on her left side until delivery in order to lower her blood pressure and to increase blood flow to the placenta.

He didn't tell his young wife that her condition could trigger a heart attack; there was no need to overly worry her. Her age, weight, and overall good health were pluses in her favor for a healthy delivery and a full recovery.

Elisabet was going through the motions of decorating Broadale for Christmas. She had instructed Mavis to retrieve a few boxes of ornaments and strings of electric lights from the attic and asked her to acquire a decent Balsam fir that they could erect in the high-ceilinged parlor.

She hadn't employed Eliza much in the past year and a half, but felt she needed her help for the upcoming Christmas celebrations. Mavis told Elisabet that Eliza was working at Mrs. Murray's house that day, and she could reach her there by telephone.

"Hello, Eliza, dear, this is Elisabet McMast, uh, Carroll. I'm sorry to interrupt your work at Mrs. Murray's home, but I am in somewhat of a bind."

"How can I help you, Ma'am?"

"It looks like I'm hosting Christmas Dinner for the family, and I could really use your help cooking the turkey and preparing the dinner."

"Uh, Ma'am, I'm also in charge of a big Christmas dinner for my children and the in-laws, but I guess I can help if I arrive early enough Christmas morning. But you know I can't stay beyond six p.m., Ma'am."

"I suppose I could ask Mavis to serve the dinner. Are you sure you can't stay until seven p.m.?"

"Ma'am, not only do I have to do my own cooking, but you know that colored people aren't allowed north of Forest Street after six p.m., and I live in the south end on Argyle Street."

"But that's ridiculous, Eliza! Whoever made up that stupid law?"

"Well, I don't know , Mrs. McMast —-, uh, Mrs. Carroll. But it's probably the same white man who told some of the shopkeepers to put the 'No Coloreds' signs in their windows."

Eliza heard an audible gasp in response from her part-time employer. Elisabet was at a rare loss for words; she had never noticed those signs in the store windows on Main Street and had no idea that Black people could not venture into the central part of the town after six.

Eliza decided that she would open her employer's mind a little further.

"But Ma'am, you must have noticed that colored people can't sit with you white folks on the main floor at the movie theater, either. We have to sit upstairs in the balcony."

Elisabet coughed and said, "No, Eliza, I didn't know that. I haven't been to see a picture show since I lived in Boston, and I don't remember if the theater there was separated for both, uh, races."

"Well, I'll tell you a secret, Ma'am …the seats in the balcony give a whole lot of a better view of that big movie screen!" She laughed heartily.

"Eliza, can I ask you something?"

"Sure, Mrs. Carroll."

"Where is your family from?"

"Well, I'm from Shelburne, but my husband, he's from Greenville," she said, referring to the Black community in the northern part of Yarmouth County.

"No, I mean, what country did your people come from?"

"Mrs. Carroll," Eliza said, trying to suppress a laugh, "we're from Canada, just like you! My family's been in Nova Scotia since we kept loyal to the Brits around the time of the American Revolution. They brought us up here from slavery in the U.S. and promised land to us, which wasn't all that great, but I've still got relatives in Shelburne County who are direct descendants of those Black Loyalists."

"Well, I had no idea, Eliza. I'm glad you told me."

"It don't make those signs on Main Street go away, Mrs. Carroll, but now you know my people have been here longer than your Swedish parents. Not that it matters a whole bunch, 'cause the Mi'kmaq Indians have been living here longer than anybody else! And they ain't got no special privileges, either!"

Eliza chuckled again, but abruptly stopped. She feared her employer may think she was being rude. When Elisabet didn't respond, Eliza told her she'd be at Broadale at sunrise the following Tuesday, Christmas morning.

"Thank you, dear," Elisabet said, slightly disoriented. She hung up the receiver of the telephone and felt like she had just learned something valuable.

Ten minutes later she had forgotten the whole conversation.

After Seamus was sure that Eva was comfortably settled, and expected to have a good night's sleep, he left the hospital and returned to Broadale. He had called Elisabet to ask if she needed him to pick up anything on his way, so she was expecting him, and greeted him with a martini as soon as he arrived.

After shrugging off his winter coat, hanging it in the hall closet, and removing his galoshes, he gratefully accepted the drink, and followed Elisabet into the parlor.

"We haven't had gin for ages," Seamus commented, knowing that Nova Scotia was still following Prohibition regulations. "Mavis is doing some extra shopping for you, eh?"

Elisabet laughed as she sat on a loveseat in the parlor, careful not to spill her own cocktail.

"Well, she can be resourceful, that's for sure," Elisabet said. "Considering that brother of hers is practically a criminal, heaven only knows where she gets the variety of alcohol she brings to the house. But I found *this* bottle in the basement in the stash of liquor you kept before we divorced."

She appraised her former husband, noticing he looked weary.

"How are you doing, my dear?"

Then, quickly correcting herself, she asked, "And how is *Eva* feeling? I do hope the swelling has gone down, and this event will be nothing terribly serious."

"It can be serious in a small percentage of cases, but we're watching her carefully. Linnea has offered to stop by the hospital with Collan tomorrow morning. I didn't know she had trained as a midwife in Sweden when she was younger. Unlike me, she's quite familiar with the progression of near-term pregnancies, and she'll be a comfort to Eva as she approaches delivery. Of course, I can drive you to the hospital to see her whenever you'd like," Seamus said.

As if distracted, Elisabet said, "Tomorrow is not a good day for me. We're getting close to Christmas, and I have so much work to do before then."

"My oh my," Seamus grinned. "I'd never have guessed you were such a busy bee, because right now it looks as if you're off to a party somewhere."

Elisabet looked down at her silver beaded evening dress and matching shoes and smiled.

"You first seduced me over eight years ago, Seamus — I think you know that I do like an intimate party now and then," she said, sipping her martini.

"And you think I'm seducing you now, do you?"

Elisabet waved her arm, as if saying it didn't matter. "I'd never be so presumptuous to think such a thing!" she said. "But I wouldn't be averse to the idea either."

She looked directly at him, knowing his weakness for flirtation. She also assumed it had been months since he and Eva had been intimate.

Seamus set his drink down on the coffee table in front of the loveseat.

"I would not be much of an ex-husband if I didn't listen to my ex-wife every now and then," Seamus said, reaching over to kiss her.

FIFTY-FOUR

Yarmouth, Wednesday, January 2, 1924

Eva and Seamus decided to name their baby Angus Nigel McMaster, Angus after Seamus's father, and Nigel after Eva's father. The infant did wait until just after midnight on New Year's Day to make his appearance, fulfilling Eva's wish for new beginnings.

Seamus was grateful that his son's birthday would not easily be forgotten.

Christmas Dinner and Boxing Day at Broadale were a familial, pedestrian two days of holiday fare involving unnecessary presents and copious amounts of food and drink. Eliza put together an attractive picnic basket of the rich food for Eva to sample since her hospital stay didn't allow her to enjoy the holiday celebrations at home with her family.

Collan hoped there might be a time when the three sisters would be alone together and could discuss what had happened to their birth parents. When the conversation lagged following brunch on December 26th, Seamus went to his study, and Linnea retired to the parlor to read, Collan closed the doors to the dining room.

"We have to talk," she began. "Katarina, I'm sorry you had to find out all this business of the three of us being adopted from the one brother we never knew."

"It was the beginning of the end for me in Gothenburg, Collan, you know that," Katarina said, playing the victim. "I was a joke in the city once that newspaper story came out and even Joseph's business was affected."

"But you didn't have to agree to have an interview with that journalist," Collan quietly said.

Elisabet looked indignant.

"What's the sense in us even discussing this now? We never knew who our real parents were, and now we find out that our father killed our mother. And the two people who adopted us, probably out of pity, didn't even bother to take our own brother with us? It's no wonder he ended up a petty criminal, and God only knows what else!"

"I think our adoptive parents did want us; or at least Jacob did," Collan said, trying to mollify her sister. "And Martin is actually in a good place now, Elisabet. He has moved to Stockholm and is sharing a flat with a mate of his. I'd love to extend an invitation to him to come to Canada to see us and really get to know you and Katarina. Granted, he is only now learning how to read and write, but it's never too late, is it?"

Elisabet barely heard the news of her brother. Her rant was not finished.

"I should have stayed in Boston. My life, and Eva's, would not be what it is today."

"I wouldn't mind getting to know this brother of ours," Katarina interjected. "Maybe it would be a help to him just knowing he has three sisters who would welcome him. Maybe…"

Collan could feel her own anger rising, but it was not directed toward Martin, Katarina, or her adoptive parents.

Interrupting Katarina, she said to Elisabet, "If you would stop pretending to be the gosh darn victim for just five minutes! You're not seeing the good in your life, and how lucky we all are! You said yourself that there is no sense in us even talking about a sad past that we have no control over. You're right in that regard; it just happened. *It just happened.* But we're all alive and well, and we aren't paupers living on the street as we might have been!"

She paused for a moment to make sure both sisters were listening to her.

"Think of what our lives might have been like if *none* of us had been adopted — or for that matter, if we had been *separated and adopted by three different families*? As much as we may disagree at times, we can at least depend on one another. Count your blessings, Sister, and shut up about a life you *might* have had."

#

Eva's difficult pregnancy would take a long time to forget, and she made a mental note to never intentionally have another child.

Elisabet and Seamus kept their lovemaking quiet and only saw one another late at night after Mavis and Eliza had left for the day. Seamus declined his ex-wife's invitation to share a bed with her overnight, offering the sad excuse that he would feel disloyal to Eva if he did so.

"Elisabet, I'm sorry, but I am Eva's husband. You agreed to allow us to be married, and you and I *are* legally divorced. And now that the baby is here, we have to stop what we're doing. I shouldn't have taken you to bed while Eva has been in the hospital. I don't know what the hell I've been thinking."

Elisabet could barely control her anger.

"Thanks so much for the appraisal, Doctor," she said with bitterness. "I don't know what I've been thinking, either."

She stared at him, not accepting any responsibility for her own actions.

"I could ruin you, you know, Seamus," she said quietly.

"What? What are you talking about?" he asked, getting up from the bed and putting on a dressing gown.

"Never mind. Forget it."

Seamus stood by the bedroom door, about to go to the bedroom he had been sharing with Eva. He wanted the last word but didn't want to totally destroy their relationship.

"Elisabet, we've been acting like two stupid adolescents, but I can't say it hasn't been enjoyable. You know it's time we stopped this," he said. "I've made an offer on a home on William Street across from the Anglican church. Eva and I will be moving there as soon as it's available to us."

"That sounds wonderful for the little McMaster family, Seamus. But don't ring me when you need a babysitter. I plan on being busy for the next while."

FIFTY-FIVE

Yarmouth, 1924 – 1929

From Angus Nigel McMaster's birth on New Year's Day 1924 until the autumn of 1929, life continued on without any major upset for Eva, Seamus, Elisabet, Collan, Linnea and Countess Katarina, who held on to her purchased title as if it were a virtual lifeline. Collan received the occasional letter from Martin in Stockholm, presumably written by Anders, and her brother vowed to visit her in Canada when it was at all financially feasible for both of them to travel overseas.

Elisabet remained somewhat aloof and did not visit Eva and Seamus's new home often. She felt it was up to them to bring her grandson to see her at Broadale.

They were indeed among a fortunate, albeit tiny minority, of Nova Scotians living in the southwestern part of the province who were not overly affected by the economic downturn that followed the Great War.

Katarina had asked Judge Pelton and his wife to drop in for tea at her new home on Collins Street after the levee at the Town Hall on New Year's Day, 1924. She was adroit at handling herself in social situations, but sometimes made the mistake of initiating a conversation that would require her to be overly conversant on topics of which she knew nothing.

"I am so delighted to have you join me today, Judge Pelton, and Mrs. Pelton," Katarina gushed. "You know, it's important for people like us to get to know one another. We must keep little towns like this running!"

"Oh? Are you thinking of entering politics, my dear?" Mrs. Pelton asked, with a hint of mischief in her voice.

The Judge cleared his throat.

"She would be a fool for trying, Susan. Government worked properly during the Great War supporting our steel mills, coal mines and manufacturing plants, but industry has collapsed in Nova Scotia.

Collapsed! If you want to get anything done now, you have to cozy up to all that private money from wealthy Montrealers who are trying to buy up the province."

Katarina listened intently, but not a great deal of what the Judge said made sense to her.

"Of course, federal money from Ottawa will pour into steel and coal , but they're in debt up to their necks with no buyers for their products. No, Countess, I would not recommend that you enter politics at this stage of the game," Judge Pelton decreed.

Katarina's face exhibited her confusion. Had she said she was interested in politics?

"That is simply fascinating, Judge. But no, I hadn't planned on doing anything political. I only just heard that women can now vote in Canada! That's as political as I will get," she said, smiling at Mrs. Pelton.

"You've made a smart decision, then, Countess," Susan Pelton said. "By the way, have you heard on the radio news just how many people are buying everything on credit — especially motor cars? If you ask me, that is living beyond one's means, and it's a recipe for disaster!"

"I so agree you with, Mrs. Pelton," Katarina said. "Why, my sister and I purposely converted the money we had in Sweden to gold, just in case of bad things happening. I don't know exactly if banks can collapse, or whatever, since I don't understand how the banking system works overseas or here — but my sister assures me that was the best thing to do when we decided to return to Canada."

Judge Pelton nodded his agreement and finished the remainder of the tea in his cup. Looking at Katarina, he said, "Well, this has been most pleasant, Countess. Susan and I have another engagement this afternoon, and it is time for us to leave. I hope you will do us the honor of coming for dinner one evening soon. You certainly won't have far to walk."

"That would be wonderful, Judge. I look forward to seeing you both again."

#

In 1925 Elisabet was still financially able to rely on her savings, but soon realized she would have to cut her expenses greatly in order to keep Broadale.

The home was far too large for one individual; she needed a substantial annual income to pay the mortgage and maintain the property. She did receive a small amount of settlement money from Seamus following their divorce, but she was now regretting having been so lenient with him.

Mavis worked only one day a week, so Elisabet busied herself with vegetable gardening, and became a fastidious housekeeper. She finally learned how to cook proper meals and how to preserve fruits and vegetables. And all during this time, her subconscious anger toward Seamus and Eva never wavered.

The new parents were enjoying their home on William Street, and when Angus turned five in 1929, they enrolled him in Grade Primary at Central School.

#

In the summer of '29, Collan and Linnea vacationed in New York for two weeks. In one of Martin's letters, he had written that Anders suggested they look up an acquaintance of his in New York City, Elsie De Wolfe, a well-known interior decorator and actress, and her partner, Elizabeth 'Bessie' Marbury, a literary agent.

A mutual introduction was struck, and a pen pal relationship began among the women, which led to Collan inviting a special guest to visit them in Yarmouth.

#

The only times the ballroom at Broadale had seen any activity during these years was when Katarina decided to host a party for a larger number of eager Yarmouthians than her own home could accommodate.

Word soon spread after she had purchased her Collins Street house that the town now had an officially titled person living full time in the community. It didn't seem to matter that no one remembered knowing her very well before she and her sister had moved away in 1913. They heard that she had lived in exotic Scandinavia for a number of years, and had married into 'royalty'. That was enough information to establish her social identity.

#

As the 1920s wore on, the gossip about the scandalous marriage of Dr. McMaster to his stepdaughter finally subsided. The slow ceasefire came none too soon for Eva whose patience had just about become depleted for wanting to retaliate when she heard someone mutter "whore" or "slut" in her direction.

And so, Eva was given a respite from the comments and rude stares when she returned to shopping on Main Street. After all, everyone wanted an invitation to a party thrown by the Countess de Carminati, and Eva *was* her niece.

FIFTY-SIX

Halifax, Monday, October 28, 1929

"Oh my God, Seamus, be careful!" Eva cried, as her husband turned a corner onto a city street and drove into the left lane of traffic. He righted the car in a split second, and grinned.

"Not to worry, my dear," he said. "My brain will eventually accept that I have to drive on the right side of the road. It's only taken me six years to get used to it."

"You'll give me heart failure if this keeps up, Seamus! Perhaps if you'd drive more often in Yarmouth beyond only going to and from the hospital, you *would* be used to it by now."

"Okay, okay," he replied, pulling into the semi-circular driveway of the new Lord Nelson Hotel on South Park Street. The seven-storey, 200-room hotel had opened the year before and the building's top floor was now also the home of the CHNS radio station — surely a marketing plus for the handsome new property across the street from the Public Gardens.

Not only was Seamus absent-minded when it came to driving, but he was also a notorious procrastinator.

He had continued his sexual relationship with Elisabet, although on a more sporadic basis over the last five years. He couldn't quite fathom why he kept going back to her, or why she welcomed him into her bed, but he was still as strongly attracted to her as he had been when they first met.

In the past week, he had told his ex-wife yet again that they had to stop their covert liaisons; it wasn't fair to Eva and to his five-year-old son to be taking precious time away from them.

In the same breath, he then asked Elisabet to look after Angus while he took Eva to Halifax for a little two-day vacation.

#

"Are you enjoying your first year at school?" Elisabet asked Angus when she picked him up from Central School which was less than a ten-minute walk westbound on Parade Street from Broadale.

"Yes, Grammy," her grandson replied. "It's fun."

"Well, I'm glad to know that, Angus."

They walked slowly along the gravel sidewalk which was littered with maple and chestnut leaves dancing in the breeze. The air was definitely chilly on this late October day.

"And do you like where Grammy lives, in that great big house up the street?"

"Uh-huh. It's big," Angus replied, training his crystal blue eyes on her.

"Then maybe you could come and live with me all the time," she said. "Wouldn't that be nice?"

"Uh, maybe, uh, I dunno."

"I think it's a good idea, Angus. When your Mama comes back with your Daddy in two days, then she's going away *again* for an awfully long time."

Elisabet hadn't rehearsed her motherly pitch to Angus very well and wasn't expecting her grandson to burst into tears.

"But I don't want Mama to go away for a long time," he sobbed.

"Oh, but it won't happen soon, Angus, so don't cry. Here, give Grammy a hug."

"But why does she want to go away?" Angus moved away from his grandmother.

"Well, uh, I'm not sure, but that's what she told me a few days ago," Elisabet struggled with the lie, and reached out for Angus a second time.

"I don't believe you!"

"Maybe I didn't hear her correctly, then, Angus. Let's not worry about it right now."

She squatted and embraced him with both arms and quickly changed the subject.

"I have a great big red apple for you when we get to Grammy's house, okay? It's going to taste so good!"

"Okay, Grammy."

Angus wiped away a solitary tear and said under his breath, "I still don't believe you."

#

"Welcome to The Lord Nelson, Dr. and Mrs. McMaster," the Desk Clerk greeted them with a smile. "How many nights will you be staying with us?"

"Just two, thanks," Seamus answered. "When I called earlier, I asked for one of your deluxe rooms."

Eva smiled and looked around the lobby, admiring the chandeliers, the wrought iron railings, tall wingback lobby chairs, and beautifully carved woodwork. It was the first time she and Seamus had gotten away for pure enjoyment since their honeymoon in Europe when she had become pregnant.

A tall young man came rushing in the front door of the hotel, trying to scribble something in a notepad as he walked, and bumped squarely into Eva who was looking the other way. He knocked into her with enough force that she was thrown off her feet, and she stumbled over the two small suitcases she and Seamus had brought with them.

"Oh, my gosh, I'm so sorry, miss," the young man said, the cap on his head now askew. "Let me help you up."

He reached out to help Eva regain her balance on the marble floor.

"I'm fine, it's all right," she said, feeling a bit foolish for her stumble.

"It was completely my fault," he said, "and I can make it up to you."

Pulling a business card out of his inside jacket pocket, he passed it to her and said, "I'd be glad to give you and your husband a tour of our new radio station on the top floor of the hotel. The views of Halifax from there are amazing."

Eva took his card, glanced at it, and said, "Thank you, uh, Erik. I'm sure my husband and I would like that if we have the time while we're here." She put his card in her purse.

"Hope so!" Erik said, and ran to the elevator.

Seamus hadn't noticed the commotion behind him and was still standing at the front desk.

"I can give you our first-year anniversary rate, Doctor. We opened one year ago this week," the desk clerk said with pride. "Although perhaps you were here last year for the Medical Society of Nova

Scotia convention? It took place at that time, and many attendees
stayed at the Hotel."

"No, this is our first time here," Seamus replied, wishing the clerk
would just get on with giving him their room key.

"All right, then," the young man said. "Your rate for a double
room with a tub bath is eight dollars per night. Is that satisfactory?"

"Yes, indeed, that will be fine."

After being told about the table d'hôte menu for lunch at one
dollar, and dinner for a dollar and fifty-cents in the public dining
room, Seamus and Eva took the modern elevator with the brass
framework to the sixth floor. Their guestroom overlooked the Public
Gardens. To Eva, this was the perfect accommodation for their visit
to the capital city of Nova Scotia.

She kicked off her shoes and threw herself on the bed.

"Oh, my goodness, it is so nice to get away for a couple of days!
Thank you, my darling, for suggesting this. It's just what *my* doctor
ordered," she said, winking at her husband.

"And it is supremely my pleasure, your Ladyship," he said, joining
her on one of the two beds in the room.

"Please no titles, Doctor — they are for my aunt who can't bear to
live without hers!"

"We haven't seen Katarina for quite a while, have we?" Seamus
asked. "I can just imagine the party she'll want to have at Broadale or
at the Grand Hotel once this decade is over and we welcome the '30s."

Eva sidled up closer to Seamus and said, "That won't be for
another couple of months, m'dear. Let's talk about the *right now* and
forget my crazy aunt."

She leaned in to kiss him and he said, "Is this a good time for us?
I mean, I know you don't want to have another baby, and we've been
lucky to date."

"Seamus, we haven't been intimate with one another for a very
long time," Eva said. "And trust me, I know when I have to avoid
intercourse. My cycle is pretty regular."

"I'm glad to hear that, sweetheart…but listen, why don't we go
out and have a little walk in the Gardens across the street while the
sun is still shining?"

Eva replied with a slight frown, but then smiled. She had hoped
that Seamus would make love to her with some spontaneity now that

he would not have to run off to work, and they had no worries about Angus who was safe at home with Elisabet.

"All right then, Dr. McMaster. Let's work up an appetite for dinner and a lovely evening ahead, okay? That's my prescription for you, by the way," she said, pecking him on the lips. She got up from the bed and straightened her dress.

#

The following morning while Seamus was shaving in the bathroom, Eva was in a quandary as to how she might bring up the sensitive subject of their lack of lovemaking the night before.

She was reminded of an expression she had first heard her English teacher use in high school —it was like having an elephant in the room. You could not ignore it; something had to be said to acknowledge the situation.

At twenty-eight years of age, Eva had not been with any other man, but she knew she had to tread carefully with her own husband so as not to hurt his feelings or damage his masculine pride.

"Darling, you've been working so much lately," she started, speaking loud enough for Seamus to hear her through the partially opened bathroom door.

"You must be simply exhausted. Perhaps you should have rested at home instead of taking this trip to Halifax? You could be sleeping late in our own bed rather than driving for over 200 miles and checking into a hotel, as nice as it is," she sighed, glancing around the guestroom.

There was silence, and then, "No, I wanted to come here for you, Eva, and for us to have some well-deserved — and long overdue — time together."

"And I appreciate that, Seamus, I do." Eva paused. It wasn't proper for a lady to vocalize her own sexual desire, and she didn't even know what words she might use to explain how she was feeling.

"It's just that…". She left the sentence hang.

Seamus poked his head outside the doorframe, still with tufts of soap on his neck and face. He absolutely knew what his wife was implying.

"Sweetheart, you have to remember that I am nine years your senior," he said in a halting manner. "Sometimes I just don't have the energy to perform like a stallion."

He turned and went back into the bathroom.

Eva decided the best course of action was to ignore the elephant, and hope for the best.

Good Lord, he's only thirty-seven.

"So, what shall we do today, Seamus? Maybe we could visit the Nova Scotia Museum of Fine Arts? Miss Henderson, my old history teacher, used to rave about the place."

"Whatever you'd like, dear," Seamus called out from the other room.

#

Unfortunately for Eva, the second night of their brief vacation did not fare any better romantically than the first. Seamus awoke early on October 30th, so he dressed and went to the Lobby of the hotel to pick up the day's newspaper.

She awakened to see him intently reading *The Halifax Chronicle*, which proclaimed on its front page:

SELLING FRENZY MAKES NEW DRAMA IN MARKET
Crash Takes $1,000,000 From Halifax Traders

Although the stock market was beyond Eva's interest level, she could not have imagined the impact the crash would have on the whole world. For the next ten years, virtually everyone would suffer through The Great Depression.

They drove back home to Yarmouth that day along Highway 1 through the cool air of the Annapolis Valley to Digby overlooking the Bay of Fundy, and then along the misty French shore which was dotted with small Acadian villages. They finally arrived in Yarmouth; the journey took them seven hours with only one refreshment stop.

They had spoken little, both immersed in their own thoughts.

#

At around the same time they were leaving Halifax, Elisabet was walking Angus to school. She held his hand in one of hers and clutched the lapels of her woolen coat with her other to cover her neck against the damp weather.

"Angus, remember that Mama wants you to come live with Grammy, all right?" she asked him.

"I like where we live now."

Angus didn't seem interested, and he was trying to understand this strange world of older people.

"Your mama doesn't want little children like you in her house which is why she wants you to come live with me," Elisabet said with seriousness. "But I don't want you to tell her I told you that, okay? It'll be our little secret."

Angus nodded in agreement, not knowing why, or to what he was agreeing. He was confused with this strange turn of events but thought it was best to say yes to whatever the big people asked you to do.

FIFTY-SEVEN

Yarmouth, Saturday, November 30, 1929

It would surely be the highlight of the Yarmouth social season.

Katarina had been anxious to throw a party before the calendar page turned to 1930. She wanted the entire town to talk about it, and hope for an invitation. Interestingly, she received the idea from an unlikely source, her sister Collan.

Planning for the big soireé had begun in August after Collan and Linnea returned from New York, both extremely excited after their fast-paced trip. They had met many members of the city's theater community, and even Broadway stars, thanks to their new friends, Elsie and Bessie.

Bessie, who was a theatrical and literary agent, had casually commented to Collan one day, upon finding out she was from Nova Scotia, that she knew a wonderful singer and actor in a vaudeville troupe. Adam Russell happened to be a native of Antigonish, Nova Scotia, and Bessie knew the troupe's manager well.

She told her that he had been one of the original members of the Dumdums Canadian Army Fourth Division Concert Party as a soldier-entertainer during the Great War. The troupe was touring all over North America now, becoming increasingly famous, and Bessie had been most impressed when she and Elsie first saw these men perform in their variety show in New York.

"If I remember correctly, it was in '21 at the Ambassador Theatre. Adam was simply marvelous as 'Penelope'," she informed Collan. "And honestly, even though there are beautiful women in the troupe *now*, he is an amazing female impersonator. The audience loved him!"

Collan had nodded politely and wondered where the conversation was headed.

"So, why don't you drop him a line and say hello? I can put you in touch with the Dumdums' manager. They might be back in your part of the world sometime soon, and you could get tickets to one of their shows. Truly, Collan — I highly recommend the Dumdums, and don't just take it from me — John and Ethel Barrymore *loved* them, too!"

Upon her return to Yarmouth, Collan did write to Adam Russell introducing herself and Linnea, and throwing in Bessie Marbury's name for good measure. She didn't fully expect a reply from this fellow who was supposed to be so famous. She mentioned that he would be welcome to visit them in Yarmouth the next time he happened to be in his home province. She also asked him if the Dumdums would be performing in Halifax because she and her "companion", Linnea, would love to see their show.

When a response came in the mail a few weeks later, Adam Russell wrote that he and three members of the troupe were planning an impromptu visit to Nova Scotia in mid-November for a pre-Christmas vacation. He suggested that he and the "boys" come to Yarmouth to give an abridged performance of their latest production, 'Why Bother?' which had been on tour for the past year.

The moment Collan told Katarina about the suggestion, the Countess immediately took control.

"That is a *stellar* offer, Collan, and of course you are going to take them up on it! Oh, my heavens — this will be an event Yarmouth will talk about for years! And I'll be — I mean, *we'll* be so highly regarded by the Peltons, the Eakins, the McLaughlins, the Richards, the Killams, and all the other important families! They'll know that *we* know such famous people. I'm so excited!"

"Hold your horses, Sister dear. You can't expect the troupe to do this for free, and we would have to provide them with a decent venue where they can perform. And they'll probably need a grand piano, and…" Collan said.

"Of course, that's no problem at all, you know that. Do you think we should have an intimate performance at Elisabet's in the ballroom, or hire the dining room at the Grand Hotel?"

"How about we first see what dates they are thinking about coming here, and take it from there?" Collan asked her sister, resigned to the fact that Katarina was back in full countess mode.

#

Shortly thereafter, the date of November 30th was set, and Elisabet grudgingly agreed to host the performance at Broadale.

Her stipulation was that Katarina and Collan would pay her a rental fee for the ballroom, and allow her to hire staff for the day, evening, and next morning if necessary. The arrangement seemed reasonable to Katarina, and Collan agreed to pay for the Dumdums' accommodations at the Grand Hotel.

Subsequent communication between Adam and Collan promised he did not expect a performance fee; they just needed an upright piano and decent electrical lighting. They had performed in substandard conditions during the War and on the road before becoming almost household names in Canada, so they were used to performing in a wide variety of places and venues.

The invitations were mailed to the elite of Yarmouth society:

Countess Katarina de Carminati,
Miss Collan Burcharth and Mrs. Nigel Carroll
request the honour of your presence for a performance of
"Why Bother?"
by members of the Dumdums Canadian Army Fourth Division
Concert Party
Saturday, November 30, 1929 at Broadale, Parade Street
8:00 p.m. ~ R.S.V.P.
Refreshments to follow

On the day of the performance, shopkeepers mused with their regular clients who among Yarmouth's upper class may have been invited, and who undoubtedly had not.

Elisabet Burcharth-Carroll-McMaster already had a reputation in town for holding a grudge — and wasn't she the one who gave away her daughter to her second husband?

And that divorced countess was probably loony, too, since no man had dared ask for her company since she moved to Yarmouth…and no one really knew the 'bachelor lady' Miss Burcharth who lived in Overton. She was always with another woman when buying provisions in town.

No man would have 'em, obviously.

"They're *all* a queer bunch," Mrs. Nathaniel 'please call me Beryl' Smith said to her friend Miss Alice Morris while having tea at the Grand Hotel that afternoon. In the early 20th century definition of the adjective, the Burcharth family had always been looked upon as odd and eccentric.

"Indeed, they are, Beryl, indeed," Alice agreed, biting into a crustless cucumber sandwich.

"I wouldn't be caught dead in that Sodom and Gomorrah cesspool even if I *had been* invited to this ridiculous show tonight," Beryl sputtered, nearly knocking over a tray of sweets.

"Oh, no, my, nor would I," Alice concurred, but secretly wished she could be a fly on the wall at Broadale to witness a morsel of excitement, something that was perpetually absent from her life.

#

Seamus was helping to unload chairs from a truck sent by the Grand Hotel, as Elisabet was expecting a full house. She watched the activity from the back doors of Broadale and removed a pocket watch from her apron to check the time. She had forgotten the chairs were arriving and didn't remember when the performance was to begin that evening.

Eva was in the kitchen helping Eliza, while Katarina, Linnea and Collan entertained Adam Russell and his fellow performers in the parlor.

Adam, who now was exhibiting a little male middle-aged spread compared to his early days in the troupe, asked Collan where he could go to change into 'Penelope'.

The other three men decided it would be a good time to rehearse the songs that did not require Adam, and excused themselves to the ballroom.

Katarina followed them in case they had need of something.

My, these actors and singers who were brave soldiers have certainly remained handsome. I wonder how they're feeling about a countess being their benefactress.

Katarina was deluding herself, as her rational mind knew they did not need a benefactor at all. This evening was Collan's doing, and the men had generously agreed to perform at no charge as a favor to her.

She half-heartedly listened to the rehearsal numbers, as she wondered how she would introduce the members of the troupe — and herself, of course — before the performance. She stood next to a table on which forty empty Champagne glasses had been placed, and noticed Eva enter the ballroom and walk toward her.

Eva smiled and removed a package of cigarettes from her small handbag and lit one.

"Eva, ladies should not smoke. You look so common, like one of those tramps down on the waterfront."

Katarina was impeccably coiffed that evening and dressed in an Elsa Schiaparelli silk evening gown that was draped with an embroidered and beaded cape. "It's called the Apollo of Versailles," she had bragged earlier to Eva.

"Aunt Katarina, these Sweet Caps are made for independent women," she responded, exhaling a stream of smoke, and vividly thinking of the advertisement portraying the brand she had seen in Maclean's magazine only last week. "And I am an independent woman who has always done what she has wanted. You know that's the truth."

Katarina raised an eyebrow, about to deliver a sarcastic remark, and then decided to change the subject.

"Where's your mother hiding, Eva? Guests will be arriving any moment now."

"I don't know; she was looking frantic the last time I saw her."

Katarina spun around, her beaded cape shimmering. She distractedly inspected the damask tablecloth covering the oval table behind her. Eva had been dismissed by the countess.

Eva confirmed to herself one more time that she didn't really care for her aunt at all.

That woman irritates me so much sometimes.

Where can I put out this darn cigarette? I could have sworn there was a pedestal ashtray on this side of the room.

She found the ashtray and extinguished the cigarette, but her thoughts did not linger on Katarina.

Angus had been acting out of sorts since she and Seamus had returned from Halifax. Her young son ranged from being angry for no apparent reason, to being moody, and then hyperactive. He would cling to Seamus in the brief periods his father was at home from the hospital, while almost studiously avoiding Eva. She made a mental note to discuss his behavior with Seamus, if she could just sit him down long enough to do so.

#

Two hours after the performance by the Dumdums had finished, Collan was thrilled that it was received so enthusiastically by the forty invited guests.

Adam Russell's banter between numbers had endeared him to the room, as he was the only Nova Scotian in the troupe, and he told them how his performing life as 'Penelope' had begun.

"You know, folks," he said, "I enlisted as a private with the Army about fifteen years ago now. My first job was as an ambulance driver in France before I was picked by Captain Mort Planter to join the Dumdums Concert Party as an entertainer." He paused for a beat, stretching out a stockinged leg.

"Do you think it was my long eyelashes, or my great gams that clinched the deal?"

Most of the audience tittered. He winked at them as a few men squirmed in their seats listening to the former soldier's deep voice emerging from a full-figured woman's body. 'Penelope' was a looker, with 'her' bob hairdo and flapper's dress.

"And after I created Penelope, well, everyone seemed to love her, including me," he grinned. "You know, she even received a jewelry gift from the Prince of Wales — I shan't tell you what kind, 'cause that would be revealing a state secret . Penelope has even met Lillian Gish and Mary Pickford when we were performing in Toronto at Massey Hall. Really!"

An audible gasp came from two women in the front row seats who were faithful fans of the moving pictures.

"But it's not all about Penelope," he continued. "I want to give credit to some of the Dumdums who aren't here tonight like our great orchestra leader Arnie Fogg, saxophonist Bud Cassels, and Randolph London, our trumpeter. And these handsome fellows who are joining me here tonight in Yarmouth are just as thrilled as I am to be in your fair town."

The applause shook the ballroom. Katarina got up from her seat in the front row and curtsied to the crowd, as if she had just finished her own balletic performance.

"Oh, boys, boys, boys! And you, too, Penelope! You were all *marvelous* this evening, and we just can't thank you enough for your wonderful entertainment. We are but a modest community at the end of *everything* in Nova Scotia, so we are absolutely thrilled you have chosen to visit and perform in Yarmouth!"

Before she had a chance to continue gushing platitudes, Collan stood up next to Katarina and said, "And I'd also like to thank our sister, Elisabet, for hosting this evening's performance in her lovely home. Elisabet, could you make yourself known and say hello to everyone?"

The crowd and performers waited expectantly for Elisabet, some craning their necks to look for her, but she did not emerge.

She and Seamus were upstairs engaged in furious intercourse on a bed in one of the guest rooms that was seldom used.

#

Elisabet and Seamus left separately from the bedroom and timed each other's re-entry to the party downstairs.

Mavis was bent over and reaching into a linen cupboard in an alcove off the landing of the staircase. In the dim hallway light, she was barely discernable. She was looking for two spare tablecloths that she needed downstairs.

She had long thought that the doctor and his ex-wife continued to be engaged in marital relations, but now she was sure of it as she watched the two of them scurry from the unused bedroom, moments apart. She shook her head in dismay.

Poor Mrs. McMaster. The new *Mrs. McMaster.*

Housekeepers have always been the best purveyors of a family's secrets, yielding immense power should they choose to use it.

Earlier that evening, Mavis had seen Collan and Linnea kiss one another in Seamus's study. She was passing by in the hallway and noticed them through the room's partially opened door.

Those two. I always knew they were perverted.

Mavis felt like she had uncovered a gold mine, or a rat's nest that evening — she wasn't sure which. She had to be circumspect as to how and when to use this new information.

FIFTY-EIGHT

Yarmouth, Saturday, November 30, 1929

Two hours later, all the invited guests had left Broadale, and the three sisters, Eva, Seamus, Linnea, and Adam Russell, still in his 'Penelope' regalia, sat in the main parlor congratulating one another on a hugely successful event.

Adam's fellow performers had decided to go to back to the Grand Hotel to sample the strong rum from Newfoundland that Seamus had given them. He had received it as a gift, but it was not at all to his liking, so he took the opportunity to give it away to more appreciative drinkers.

Collan sat quietly thinking. While they were vacationing in New York City earlier in the year, she and Linnea were impressed with the degree of openness that their friends Elsie de Wolfe and Bessie Marbury enjoyed regarding their personal relationship. Although Elsie had gotten married in 1926 to Sir Charles Mendl, the British Press Attaché in Paris, it was a marriage of convenience for both, since she had been living openly with Bessie in New York since 1892.

Elsie had proudly told Collan that just three years earlier, *The New York Times* had reported that she was "one of the most widely known women in New York social life".

Collan and Linnea had discussed the situation in detail, and felt that if Elsie and Bessie had no qualms about living their lives openly as two women who loved one another, then they, too, should also not have to pretend to be "old maid companions". They also considered the adverse consequences of being open about their lives in their small Canadian town.

I hope I can do this without dissolving into tears, or becoming defensive, or both. I just don't know how my two sisters will react. I'm guessing that Eva and Seamus, being younger, may not understand how big of an issue admitting my love for another woman really is. I must be brave and go ahead with my admission. I know Linnea is behind me and that is truly all that matters.

The few glasses of Champagne that Collan had consumed, combined with the giddiness of an evening well spent, helped her decide that this would be a perfect time with all her family present, to tell them of her true relationship with Linnea.

Katarina looked incredulous; it was as if Collan was telling them she was from another planet.

"Wait, wait, I don't understand," she said. "You two have been carrying on as if you were married to one another all these years?"

Collan and Linnea, holding hands, nodded.

"But that is so…so *unnatural*, Collan. I mean, you're my sister! How could this be?"

"The heart knows what path it must take," Linnea responded to Katarina's outburst. Collan remained silent, but her face was flushed.

Adam/Penelope sat with a bemused expression, listening intently.

He sipped a glass of Champagne, and said to Katarina, "Oh, my darling, your eyes would *cross* at some of the couples I have met in Europe and when I've been on tour in the States. Women loving women and men loving men have been the norm for *aaaa-geesss.* Where have you been?"

"I think you're both an ideal match for one another," Eva said to Collan, smiling. "Maybe we should have a little private wedding-type ceremony for you!"

"Oh, dear God in heaven," Katarina exclaimed. "I've never heard of anything so ridiculous."

"Please, stop, Katarina. You are disrespecting me," Collan said. "We have been through a lot together since we left Canada in 1913. I would hope and expect you to try to be a bit more understanding. You *are* my sister."

Katarina opened her mouth as if to say something further, and then in a rare moment of self-reflection, decided it would be better to remain quiet.

Elisabet, coming across as more generous than usual, said, "As far as I'm concerned, what you two do is no one's business but your own. We've been through a world war, the economy is taking a nosedive…and isn't it almost 1930, for heaven's sake!" She paused for a brief moment. "Or 1931? These are modern times. Look at the changes *I've* made in my life."

Elisabet sipped her Champagne and glanced at Eva and Seamus sitting together.

"I agree with Elisabet," Seamus stated. "Your life is yours to live. I don't think you need to tell everyone in Yarmouth that you are lesbians because many won't understand. But within our family, we cannot and will not judge you."

"Hear, hear," Adam/Penelope said. "Spoken like the intelligent *and* handsome doctor he is, Collan! You couldn't get a better diagnosis."

Katarina got up from her chair, looked at Adam, and said, "Dear, I can give you a ride to the hotel now, if you'd like. And don't forget the luncheon I'm hosting in your honor at my house tomorrow."

"I'll be there with my bells and bangles on, Countess," Adam/Penelope grinned.

"Oh, Mr. Russell, this won't be a *theatrical*-type of get-together," Katarina said. "Just a few noteworthy ladies in town who so admire our veterans."

"Purr-fect! I have an exquisite daytime ensemble I can wear, so don't you worry, Countess."

Katarina looked worried.

FIFTY-NINE

Yarmouth, Monday, December 2, 1929

Snowflakes were falling lightly as Eva walked Angus to school.

When they left the house on William Street, he initially wouldn't take his mother's hand, and Eva attributed that to the boy wanting to look 'grown up'. But by the time they had reached Carleton Street, just a few minutes away from the school, he reached for her hand and Eva gladly took his, happy to see his mood had changed.

"Mama, when are you going away?" he asked.

"What? Sweetheart, I'm not going anywhere," she replied. "Where would I be going?"

Angus looked confused.

"Are you sure?"

"Yes, I'm *sure*, Angus."

He didn't say anything further, but picked up his step, and started skipping on the sidewalk.

"Wait a minute, little man; slow down!" Eva said, laughing.

When they arrived at the doors to Central School, other mothers and their children were saying goodbye to each other, and Eva bent down to kiss her son goodbye.

"Now you have fun today, okay?" She touched the tip of her index finger on his nose.

Angus scurried into the school saying, "Bye, Mama" as the doors closed.

"Excuse me, Mrs. McMaster?" Mavis was standing two feet behind Eva.

Eva turned around, startled to see her mother's housekeeper. She didn't know Mavis had any children who were in this elementary school.

"Why, hello, Mavis! How are you today?"

"Ah, not too bad, Miss Eva," Mavis replied, reverting to her more familiar way of addressing her employer's daughter. "Can I speak with you privately for a moment?"

"But of course. Let's move away from the doors," Eva suggested.

"I don't really know how to tell you this, Miss Eva, but do you remember when I told you that I would somehow make it up to you for the nasty things my brother said to you such a long time ago when you had just married Doctor Seamus?"

Eva recalled the night of the party in 1922 when Mavis' brother had made a crude comment to her, but not so much about the housekeeper's promise after the incident.

"My Lord, I don't know how to say this, but you must know." Mavis faltered for a moment, fidgeting with her hands. "Your mother is, uh, being intimate with Doctor Seamus again," she said, looking away.

"I don't know what you mean, Mavis, I can't —", Eva said, about to use the word 'imagine' until she realized that this could be a distinct possibility.

"And I think it's been happening for some time, Miss Eva," Mavis said, turning a bright shade of red. "I care for you, and I didn't want you to find out in a more, uh, disturbing way."

"But how do you know this for sure?" Eva asked her.

Mavis explained that on several occasions during Eva's bedrest during her pregnancy, the Doctor and her mother were spending hours together in his study with the door closed which was unusual. She had seen him again at Broadale the day before he and Eva left for Halifax in October, and more recently, saw Elisabet and Seamus emerge from the same unused bedroom moments apart, two nights prior, while the Dumdums' performance was taking place in the ballroom.

Eva stared at the older woman she had known for many years.

Fluffy white flakes swirled around the two women as if they were inside a glass snow globe, protected from an outside world of betrayal, lost loyalties, and confusion.

"Thanks, Mavis, uh…thank you for telling me. I won't bring up your name, when, um, if…yes, well, thank you," Eva hurried down the steps to the large schoolyard and walked stiffly to the street, tears stinging her eyes.

SIXTY

Yarmouth, Thursday, December 5, 1929

Elisabet was fairly certain that Mavis had seen her and Seamus leave the bedroom during the Dumdums' performance at Broadale. But she wasn't as sure if Angus might have told his mother that Grammy said that his mommy would be going away for a long time.

Elisabet knew she had to do some mother-daughter reparation. She telephoned Eva and asked her to come by the house for coffee after she had dropped Angus off at school that morning.

Eva was on her guard and armed with the information that Mavis had given her.

"Eva, it's so good to see you on your own. There were so many people at the house on Saturday night, we hardly had time to talk," Elisabet said to her daughter. "It was quite the night, wasn't it?"

"It certainly was, Mama," Eva replied, grateful she could avoid her mother's gaze by sipping on a cup of steaming coffee.

"Dear, I've been meaning to discuss something with you for some time," Elisabet said, choosing her words carefully.

Eva looked at her mother expectantly, wondering if the truth was about to spill out.

"You see, Seamus is not the man that we thought he was. It's fair to say, he is not an honest man."

Eva remained silent as Elisabet continued.

"He has been stealing pharmaceuticals from the hospital dispensary for a very long time now and is selling drugs, like opium and heroin, to some of the crew members on the ships that go to Boston."

"Mama, you must be kidding me, aren't you?" Eva laughed nervously. "That's a very silly thing you are saying!"

Elisabet's expression was anything but one reserved for joking.

"Well, on the wildly unlikely chance it's true, it's a terribly serious accusation you're making."

Elisabet looked at her only child with a pious expression that mixed sadness with resignation. It was a look from someone whose perception of reality appeared to be confused.

"I know, it's been destroying me, Eva. In fact, Seamus is confused and angry at himself for putting his family and his profession at such grave risk. He confessed his misdeeds to me just the other night, privately during the party, and I was simply devastated. I wish I had never brought him into our lives."

"When and where did he tell you this?"

"It was at Broadale when the performance was taking place in the dining room. He asked me to show him where I had stored some of his old suit jackets and trousers that he forgot to bring to your home."

Eva stood silently watching her mother.

Is she lying? She looks like the picture of innocence, but this story of Seamus being a thief seems ludicrous. Is she deflecting my attention away from what she has been up to with my husband?

"Mama, he's the father of my baby and a respected doctor. He can't possibly be a thief who could end up in prison! What will we do if the police find out about this?"

"Leave it with me for now, Eva, and *don't* tell Seamus I've told you. He is embarrassed beyond words and realizes that it is affecting his daily work and his personal relationship with you. He told me he'll stop stealing and selling the drugs, immediately… It's sad, but I have to wonder if he may be using some of them himself."

"Oh my God," Eva cried, her mind now fixated on this potential crisis in her family. "This is a nightmare. How could he do such a thing?"

Elisabet touched the corners of her eyes with a handkerchief as if hidden tears were just waiting to come tumbling down her cheeks.

Eva's mind continued to race at breakneck speed.

What the hell is really going on with my mother and my husband? I don't know what or who to believe; what may or may not be true. Mama has supported me through so much — but how could she betray me and have relations with Seamus again, now that he's married to me?

Is Mavis is making up stories about Mama and Seamus together for some bizarre reason? And why would Seamus have resorted to criminal activity?

"Mama, you *are* feeling all right these days, aren't you?" Eva asked cautiously.

"I've never felt better, Eva. I enjoy having Broadale to myself, as big as it is. It'd be nice if you and Angus would visit me more often, though."

#

Around noon, Eva walked from Broadale to William Street, even though her mother had offered to drive her home. She was dazed, and the chilly December air didn't help to lift the fog that was enveloping her mind.

In the Burcharth family, it was felt that any unpleasantness should be handled with the least amount of fuss.

Therefore, Signe didn't tell Elisabet or her other two daughters that they had been adopted until she was on her deathbed.

Katarina did not tell Joseph that she wanted a divorce until her social status rapidly declined, and she wanted to avoid being known as a common immigrant in Gothenburg society.

Collan did not tell her immediate family that her best friend of many years was also her lover and partner until her confidence was boosted by meeting another lesbian couple in a committed relationship.

Eva did not approach her husband with the news that she knew he was selling drugs illegally because her mother said that *she* would handle the situation.

Mama was so gracious not to disown me when I admitted my love for Seamus.

Mama was the epitome of understanding when she divorced Seamus to allow me to marry him.

But why does none of this feel right?

I won't confront Seamus right away with this ugly story about him stealing from the hospital.

But she wavered.

As a woman, how many times in her life had she been told "don't rock the boat", or, "play the game", "keep still", "play dumb", and "don't make waves"? She wrestled with "keeping quiet" about her husband.

She had to find out the truth.

Eva was not one to take a drink of alcohol on her own. But on this day, when she arrived home, she threw her coat on a chair in the hallway, opened the cellarette, and retrieved a bottle of Seamus's favorite Scotch. She poured the amber liquid into a water glass.

SIXTY-ONE

Yarmouth, Spring & Summer, 1930

The winter of 1929-30 came and went. It was memorable for the fact that Canada and the United States were in the midst of a national economic depression which would not be termed "The Great Depression" until after President Herbert Hoover left office in 1933.

Nova Scotia, however, already had some experience in that regard. There had been high unemployment and low wages since the war had ended twelve years earlier.

Still, the spring of 1930 brought with it high hopes for a new decade of health and prosperity. Everyone assumed the country would not be in the fiscal doldrums for much longer. On a clear day, Yarmouthians could pick up radio programs from WHDH in Gloucester, Massachusetts, and listen to music that reflected American optimism. "On the Sunny Side of the Street" by Ted Lewis and his Orchestra; "Happy Days are Here Again" by Ben Selvin and his Orchestra; and "Puttin' on the Ritz" by Harry Richman were all popular radio favorites.

#

For at least a month, Katarina had been debating if she should make a visit to Boston and New York. She told anyone who would listen that she was "dreadfully bored" with the lack of cultural happenings in Yarmouth.

But instead, she took the Dominion Atlantic Railway to Halifax a couple of times. Her first trip on June 23rd coincided with the much-anticipated opening of The Nova Scotian Hotel, one of the Canadian National Railway's new grand hotels. Typically, a CN train station adjoined these hotels, and that was most appealing for the countess. The train would deliver her directly to her lodgings, and taxi service from its front door could take her anywhere in the city, so she wouldn't need a personal driver.

Before leaving Yarmouth, she telephoned the society editor at *The Halifax Herald* introducing herself as an 'anonymous source' from *The Yarmouth Courier*. She told him that she had heard on good authority that the Countess de Carminati from Sweden would be at the new Nova Scotian Hotel for a couple of days, en route to New York and then to the Far East.

She added the teaser 'Far East' to entice the editor to assign a reporter to interview her; and when that would inevitably happen, Katarina figured it would be easy to make up an imagined trip to the 'Orient'.

#

In the spring and summer of 1930, Elisabet worked laboriously with uncommon dedication in her garden. She had refused to see Seamus even though he attempted to contact her on several occasions. This time Elisabet had the upper hand. She knew her phony story about him stealing drugs did not reach his ears — but it was definitely causing discord in his marriage. Her daughter had confided to her that she and Seamus now slept in separate bedrooms in their home on William Street.

Seamus was ignorant of the machinations of his former wife and unable to understand Eva's continued aloof behavior. He threw himself into working extra shifts at the hospital. He knew he looked exhausted because indeed he was. When he was at home, he would spend a few minutes with Angus, eat, and then go to his bedroom to sleep.

Eva, now confronted with a husband who was effectively absent from their home life, decided to take each day as it was presented, and to hope for the best. Elisabet had told her on several occasions that Seamus was now on the straight and narrow and was working extra hours to make up for the money he had lost by stopping his 'thieving ways'. Eva took Mama at her word, as usual. She was frightened of being the cause of any further tumult.

#

On a sunny Sunday in August, while Katarina was on her second trip to Halifax, Eva took Angus with her and drove to Overton to have a long chat with Collan.

Linnea was delighted to spend time with Angus on her own while Collan and Eva visited in the large, sun filled kitchen overlooking Yarmouth's placid harbor.

"Eva, I hope you haven't let your dream of becoming a journalist die just because you're married and have a son," Collan said to her.

Eva sipped from a frosty glass of iced tea, enjoying her aunt's company.

"My goodness, when Linnea and I would spend weekends in Stockholm, I was impressed to find so many very smart women involved in the newspaper and magazine business. It surely has only gotten better now that we are in a new world and at the start of a brand-new decade!"

"Oh, I haven't forgotten at all, Aunt Collan. I do keep a daily journal just to practice my writing, but honestly, I wouldn't know where to start without having a college degree or diploma."

"Listen, my dear, your mother told me once that the letters you posted to her when you and Seamus were in Europe on your honeymoon were terribly interesting — like reading a magazine article. So, why not write a story about something happening around here and then submit it to *The Yarmouth Courier*? How will an editor know if you are any good if you don't show him something you've written?"

"Oh, my, you've reminded me of how wonderful the honeymoon was…" Eva said with a wistful look in her eyes. "But yes, I suppose I could try submitting a story. I don't know *what* I could write about, though. Yarmouth isn't overly exciting when it comes to daily news."

"Now, now, I don't agree with that at all. What about finding out who the new teachers are at Central School or the Academy this fall, and if there will be any new ones teaching in Port Maitland and Carleton, as well? It may take a couple of phone calls to the superintendent of schools, but an interview with one or more of these new teachers would certainly be of interest to the parents of school age children."

"You know, Aunt Collan, that doesn't sound too difficult at all. I do like talking to people, and I won't need to know a tonne about government, politics, or religion, would I?"

"No, Eva. Just be your friendly intelligent self. And as a parent, you already know the questions to ask a new teacher."

"I appreciate the suggestion. But can I ask you about something else?"

"Sure, dear. What is it?"

"I'm not exactly sure, but have you noticed any unusual changes in my Mama recently? I worry about her."

"What kind of changes, Eva?"

"Nothing I can really pinpoint, but there's some kind of an odd disconnect, as if she is living some kind of alternate life to the rest of us. Does that make any sense?"

Collan sighed. Her sister was the headstrong one in the family and typically did everything in her power to be in control. She suspected that their adoptive mother's admission of not wanting to raise children was still bothering Elisabet. Some people could not let things go.

"I think we all get a bit crankier as time goes on, Eva. Mark it down to getting old," Collan smiled.

"Yes, you're probably right, Aunt Collan," Eva said, unconvinced.

SIXTY-TWO

Dayton, Yarmouth Co., Wednesday, April 15, 1931

By Christmas of 1930, Eva began working mornings at *The Yarmouth Courier* as a part-time reporter. The remuneration was a pittance, but she loved seeing her byline on even the most mundane of news stories.

The following spring, she was thrilled when the managing editor asked her to "get the scoop" on the new hotel that was being built on the shore of Lake Milo in the community of Dayton, about a mile from downtown Yarmouth.

It was constructed to look like a grand château and was owned and built by Canadian Pacific Railway. The company hoped to appeal to the ongoing American tourist clientele sailing to Yarmouth from Boston and New York. A train would pick up the arriving ship passengers on the waterfront and take them directly to the new Lakeside Inn & Cottages which was designed and destined to become a Yarmouth landmark.

Eva secured an interview with the food and beverage manager of the new Inn who agreed to meet with her on the grounds of the property about a month before the grand opening to the public. She was told that he doubled in the role of spokesman for the company.

Marc Shehab, a Haligonian in his early thirties, had gladly accepted the position at Lakeside Inn. Although he had never visited Yarmouth before — like many from the city or elsewhere in the province — he was ready for a challenge, and the free accommodation on site in one of the cottages was a bonus.

His parents had emigrated to Nova Scotia from Lebanon in the mid-1880s and helped forge a small, but closely knit community of retailers and restaurateurs in Halifax over the years. Marc, shorter in stature than many men, knew he was also perceived to be from "eastern Europe" or "Syria" due to his olive complexion, Roman nose, and dark good looks.

None of the prejudicial preconceptions from Anglo-Saxon Nova Scotians bothered him. He had always been tenacious and was a hard worker. A bout with polio as a child left him with his right leg shorter than the left which caused a persistent, but almost imperceptible limp when he walked. It did not affect his work life, and even when he went to Chicago for a year to work in the textile trade, he made enough money to take courses in hotel management at the same time.

He told Eva to meet him by the tennis courts at three o'clock and they would walk around the property, and then tour the interior. Painters and landscapers were everywhere, performing last minute tasks in preparation for the grand opening.

As she parked her car, Eva spied Marc wearing a smart linen suit, talking to one of the gardeners. She had driven Seamus to the hospital that morning, and as was their new routine, he told her not to wait up for him; he would get a ride back home later in the evening.

Marc could not help but be impressed with the pretty and well-dressed blonde woman walking toward him, her hand extended.

"Mister Shehab — my name is Eva McMaster — how do you do?"

"I'm very well, thank you. It's a pleasure to meet you after our brief chat on the telephone, Mrs. McMaster," Marc said, smiling.

"Indeed, it is," Eva said, returning his warm greeting. She already liked this man whose eyes sparkled as he spoke to her.

"Well, let me give you the grand tour of the grounds, and then we'll go inside the Inn so you can see all the wonderful amenities we'll be offering our guests," he said, motioning with a light touch to her arm to follow him.

For the next hour, Eva took notes every few minutes to ensure she didn't miss the details of what the Inn and Cottages offered, and Marc gave her a pamphlet that showed pictures of the other hotels in eastern Canada also owned by Canadian Pacific. The brochure was essentially an advertisement that depicted the extent of CP's commitment to tourism in the Canadian Maritimes.

She caught herself looking at him perhaps a little more often than she should have, but she found his company delightful. He was self-deprecating in a humorous but not self-conscious way.

She typed her brief article the following morning and submitted it to her editor for approval.

NEW HOTEL OPENS NEXT MONTH
Canadian Pacific's latest property nearing completion in Dayton
by Eva McMaster

The Lakeside Inn & Cottages will be open for reservations beginning May 15, 1931, says spokesperson and dining room manager Marc Shehab.

"We are pleased to welcome American visitors and fellow Canadians to Canadian Pacific Railway's' latest addition to its fine portfolio of hotel properties," said Mr. Shehab in an interview with The Yarmouth Courier. Dominion Atlantic Railways, which services the Halifax to Yarmouth route, is a subsidiary of Canadian Pacific.

Located on Lake Milo, just one mile from downtown Yarmouth on Highway 1, the Lakeside Inn & Cottages promises to be a cozy Old-English style hostelry with a main lounge accented by a high-pitched roof and heavy crossbeams that is reminiscent of a baronial hall. There is also a Spanish-inspired Sunroom, and an attractive dining room with many windows through which one can admire the well-kept gardens.

The 68 guestrooms and five cottages are furnished similar to Canadian Pacific's other accommodations in Halifax, Kentville and Digby, all of which are known for their high standards of comfort.

A multitude of activities which are accessible on site or nearby await the guest who has chosen the Inn for leisure purposes.

"We offer tennis, yachting, speedboating, swimming and horseback riding, and can also arrange golfing at the nine-hole course in the south end of Yarmouth," Mr. Shehab explained. "A family may opt to rent one of our cottages but still enjoy all the privileges that the Inn offers, including a meal plan."

An invitation-only opening reception is scheduled for early May to thank the builders and the CP and DAR staff. Local political figures and other special guests are also expected to attend.

#

A couple of weeks later, when the invitation arrived in the post, Katarina opened it immediately, noticing a Yarmouth postmark. She was pleased that it was properly addressed to the Countess Katarina de Carminati.

She sighed and smiled, placing the card carefully on the kitchen table in front of her as steam wafted from her cup of tea.

It's about time. Finally, a party to go to where I can get all dolled up!

You are cordially invited to attend a Cocktail Reception
to celebrate the opening of the newest hotel in the
Canadian Pacific Railway's portfolio
Lakeside Inn & Cottages
Dayton, Yarmouth County, Nova Scotia
Friday, May 8, 1931
5:30 – 7:30 p.m.
Please present this invitation upon arrival. Ample parking is available.

That same morning, Eva also received her invitation to the reception, and showed it to Seamus over breakfast.

"This should be a nice event, Seamus. I hope you'll be able to attend with me."

"What is it? When and where?"

"Remember I wrote that short article for the *Courier* about the new hotel opening in Dayton? Well, we've been invited to a cocktail party to mark the occasion with all the big shots from the Railway company," Eva informed him. "It's next Friday at five-thirty."

Seamus looked uninterested and non-committal as he sipped his black coffee.

"I'm doing nights next week. You know I have to be at the hospital by five every day."

Eva bit her tongue and got up from the kitchen table, picking up the invitation and its envelope at the same time.

"Okay, then, I guess that settles that. I imagine Katarina is being invited. I'll go with her, although her highness won't even notice I'm with her."

Seamus grunted an acknowledgement and concentrated on finishing his coffee.

SIXTY-THREE

Dayton, Yarmouth Co., Friday, May 8, 1931

It was one of those unusual spring days in Nova Scotia that made everyone think summer had arrived early. The informal but highly unusual procession of cars that was seen crossing the small causeway from Highway 1 to the Lakeside Inn & Cottages' impressive grounds was another rarity.

The landscapers had done an exemplary job on the grounds of the Inn, and the lawns were resplendent in beds of daffodils, tulips and other seasonal perennials which impressed the local guests and the visiting dignitaries alike.

Katarina, overdressed for a late afternoon function, walked with a flourish up the steps of the Inn. Eva, looking properly businesslike, trailed a few steps behind her. Jazz music could be heard softly emanating from the grand hall. Opening the large wood and glass front door to greet them was Marc Shehab.

"Mrs. McMaster! How nice of you to come to our little party," Marc grinned the minute he spotted Eva coming up the stairs. "And thank you for the wonderful write-up in the newspaper about Lakeside Inn."

He didn't notice the look of annoyance on Katarina's face because he hadn't acknowledged her before greeting Eva.

"Mr. Shehab, it's wonderful to see you again! I'd like you meet my Aunt Katarina Carmin —, er, the Countess de Carminati."

Katarina held out a gloved hand, expecting Marc to kiss it, but instead he shook it lightly with his own.

"I'm delighted you could also attend, Countess," Marc said, barely redeeming himself in Katarina's eyes.

"Please come inside and we'll take your wraps. I'll direct you into the Grand Hall, and I hope I can entice you with a glass of bubbly?"

That dazzling smile, thought Eva, could move mountains.

What a nice fellow. So sincere.

"Thank you, dear man. Oh, my, this reminds me of the Lake District in northwest England," Katarina commented, looking around the hall. "Have you been, Mr. Shehab?"

Katarina hoped he had not, since she had not been either, but had seen pictures of the area in a book she had purchased in Halifax the previous summer. Marc shook his head no as he took her spring coat and passed it to a young woman working in the cloakroom of the Inn.

"Unfortunately, not, Countess. I trust it is a homey and unpretentious part of England, as is the kind of atmosphere we are aspiring to create?"

"It's simply divine, a divine part of the mother country, Mr. Shehab. Why, I remember when Lady Spinney invited me for tea, and...", Katarina began, essentially speaking in mid-air in case anyone else might be listening. Eva jumped in.

"Mr. Shehab, are you expecting a large crowd today?" Eva asked.

Marc gave Eva a grateful smile; he could see through her aunt's pretense, which was clearly a large part of her character.

"Possibly fifty or so. I hope the speeches from my superiors will be 'short and sweet', as they say. You and the Countess should simply enjoy the surroundings, and perhaps sit out on the veranda for a while, although I know it's a little breezy today. Still, the view over Lake Milo is quite appealing."

"It's a lovely spot, Mr. Shehab, it truly is," Eva said warmly.

"Please, you must call me Marc just as my friends do," he said to her. Katarina didn't miss a beat.

"Now, Mr. Shehab! My niece is a *married* lady and a mother," Katarina said in a half-joking manner, but obviously wanting to assert her familial authority.

Eva shot her aunt a disapproving look.

"Thank you, Marc. We do welcome you to a long and successful stay in our town," Eva said.

Marc signalled a passing waiter who was serving glasses of Champagne on a silver tray.

The waiter sidled up to them, and offered a glass to each, as well as a dainty linen serviette from his other hand.

"Ladies, if you'll excuse me, I must greet some new guests. Please enjoy!" Marc said with a slight bow, leaving Eva and Katarina with their drinks.

"Be careful with that one," Katarina said to her niece, "he's one of those Syrians and you just can't trust them. I don't know why he was hired to manage this new property. Such is the ignorance of this railway company, I guess!"

"Oh, for heaven's sake, Aunt Katarina. He is charming and eminently qualified for the job, and incidentally he is not the general manager. Remember I interviewed him at great length for the newspaper? And as far as being Syrian, I remember when you married Joseph, an Italian, you told me that the Swedes didn't look too kindly on him! But he made you a 'countess', didn't he?"

Katarina's eyes flared slightly upon hearing this — *such impudence!* — but chose not to reply, and instead drank the remainder of her Champagne.

SIXTY-FOUR

Deerfield, Yarmouth Co., Sunday, May 10, 1931

In an effort to bring some feelings of tenderness back into their marriage, Eva thought that on Seamus's first day off in months since the weather continued to be unusually mild, she would make a reservation for lunch at Braemar Lodge.

A drive to the inland community of Deerfield, about ten miles from Yarmouth, would be a perfect getaway for an afternoon. Eva predicted that a day out of town might appeal to Seamus, or so she hoped.

She was still in love with her husband no matter what had transpired, but she continued to need to understand his erratic and seemingly indifferent behavior towards her. She was beginning to think this may be the last chance to save her marriage.

Collan and Linnea were happy to take seven-year old Angus for the day while his parents had their first real chance to be alone together in close to a year. Collan hoped they would take the opportunity to really talk to one another, and she was pleased to facilitate that for her beloved niece.

Located on picturesque Lake Ellenwood, Braemar had been built originally in 1926 as a private resort. There was a large hall with a dining room, a lounge, and a kitchen; and three guest cottages, which soon multiplied to become a total of twelve. Eva's editor at *The Yarmouth Courier* told her that the owner was opening the dining room earlier that year due to the favorable early summer-like weather.

"This looks delicious," Eva said to the waitress, as the young woman delivered two steaming bowls of lobster chowder to their table.

"Oh, 'tis, ma'am," the girl said. "My uncle got the lobster right out of one of his own traps just yesterday. There's so darn many of these creatures! This chowder is some good. My Aunt Marge is the cook here, and you can thank her for the home baked rolls, too."

She smiled at the couple, and after asking them if they wanted anything else at the moment, left their table.

Eva and Seamus said little as they savored the common local dish. Absently buttering a dinner roll, Eva looked out the window to the lakefront and said, "Look, Seamus! Some children are playing in the water already!"

"Bit too cold for an old guy like me," he said, offering a wan smile.

"You're hardly old, and you're as handsome as you were the day I met you!" Eva smiled back.

"Uh, well, these days I've been feeling like something the cat dragged in," Seamus said. "And maybe we should talk about that."

"Yes, we should. You're practically living at the hospital, Seamus. Neither Angus nor I have seen much of you, and I'm worried about your health. Angus really misses spending time with his Papa."

"I know that only too well, Eva, and I'm sorry. I haven't been a good husband or father, and I'm aware that this hasn't just been in the past few weeks. I worry about the Depression, and while there is never the danger of my *not* having work, the patients I've been seeing are simply not healthy overall. The ones without physical issues tend to be deeply melancholic."

Eva knew he was skirting the real issue.

"Seamus, I'm sorry for those people, but even with all that is going on in the world, in *our* little world, you haven't taken any notice of me for an awfully long time. We don't even sleep together in the same room anymore," she said quietly, imploring him for a better explanation.

He sighed and pushed the half-consumed bowl of chowder away from him. He pulled out his cigarettes and offered one to Eva.

"I'll have one later after we finish eating," she said.

Exhaling a plume of smoke, he lightly touched the cigarette to the lip of an ashtray in the center of the table.

"Eva, I have to tell you something before we can continue on," Seamus said, looking directly into her eyes. "When we married ten years ago, and I feel like such a miserable heel telling you this, I don't think I was totally over your mother. I'm afraid I might have acted prematurely — and *immaturely* — in marrying you."

"I see. You'll have to be a little clearer about that," Eva said, withholding her anger.

"It's just that before you and I got serious, your mother wasn't interested in being intimate with me, and I thought she had fallen out of love with me. I was a young med student when she and I first met...", Seamus said haltingly.

"...And you met her *with* me, remember, Seamus?"

"Well, yes, of course I did, but you were just a child then," he replied, and then realized that sounded worse than he meant.

"Aw, you know what I mean, Eva. You were very mature for your age, but technically, still a child. But let me finish, and I swear I'm not trying to make you feel bad here."

"You could have fooled me," Eva said, looking out the window.

He paused, and then continued, saying, "Elisabet was, and God forgive me, probably is, the love of my life. I can't help it. I have never stopped loving her, but that doesn't mean I haven't loved you."

Eva shook her head from side to side, and said sadly, "I'm sorry, but I don't believe that, Seamus. I mean, I can understand that you loved my mother when you first married her, but you can't tell me that the past nine years of our marriage have meant nothing to you."

"I didn't say our marriage hasn't meant anything to me, nor did I say you meant nothing to me. I'm a weak man, Eva, and I am still in love with your mother."

Eva carefully placed her used cutlery on her side plate and looked squarely at Seamus as the waitress came by to collect the dishes on the table. Seamus glanced at her and asked for two cups of coffee.

"No, I'll have tea," Eva said to the waitress, "with milk on the side, thanks."

When the server left, Eva stared at Seamus, knowing she had no choice but to accuse him of being a thief.

Am I looking for revenge?

"You've just verified that you've been sleeping with Mama again. And I've also found out about the drugs you've stolen from the hospital, Seamus, and that sickens me more than what you've told me about my own mother," she said with bitterness. "I'm so disappointed in you, and I pray to the Almighty that Angus never finds this out about his father."

Seamus looked like he had seen a ghost.

"What? What in devil's name are you talking about, Eva? Drugs?"

He stubbed out his cigarette angrily and said, "I have never stolen anything in my life, except for having been accused by your mother of stealing *you* from her. Where on earth did you hear such a ridiculous story?"

Eva looked at him and remained silent for a moment, wondering if she should betray her mother's trust.

"Your ex-wife and my mother told me about it." She folded her arms as she inched her chair away from the table.

Seamus looked as if she had slapped him across the face.

"Elisabet said that?" he asked, his eyes narrowing.

"Shall I repeat myself? Yes, she did. Are you telling me you're *not* stealing anything from the dispensary at the hospital?"

"*Of course* I'm not!" Seamus exclaimed, running his fingers through his curly hair in frustration.

"Then we won't speak of it again, Seamus. Now, what about our marriage since you are supposedly still in love with my mother?"

Seamus's face was a mask of confusion.

"Look, I wanted to explain to you why I've been distant lately, and why there have been times when I've not been home because I have been with Elisabet." He paused, grasping for words before speaking again. "For Angus's sake, should we not continue with our lives as we've been doing? What do you think?"

"What do I think?" Eva raised her eyebrows in surprise. "Carry on as before? I *think* that I gave up going to university ten years ago for you; I *think* that I deserve a man to truly love me and my son, and not pretend at it; I think —"

"I'm sorry, Eva. I really am."

The waitress stopped at their table with the tea and coffee and placed the folded bill in the paper napkin holder, thanking them for their business. She could see that this couple was not in any mood for chitchat. Offering them a hesitant smile, she left them alone.

Fighting back tears, Eva said, "Seamus, I need time to let all this sink in. I don't know what you've told my mother about *your* feelings for her, because now I have to wonder why she hasn't told *me* any of this herself and why she's been betraying me What a damn mess.

"Maybe you *should* move out of the house; I don't know. We can't upset Angus before the school year is finished. Then I guess we'll decide if we should separate. I don't know right now if that's the solution, but I can't trust you anymore, Seamus. I need a husband who isn't sleeping with my mother and who won't be thrown into jail when I least expect it."

Eva scoffed and shook her head at the ridiculousness of the statement she had just uttered.

"Eva, Eva, Eva, believe me. That's an insane story, and I don't know why your mother made it up. Good God, as if I don't have enough on my mind already!"

Seamus looked down at his hands as if they had been caught in a vise. He sighed heavily; a man beaten by his own devices. He pulled out his wallet to pay for their lunch.

As they drove into downtown Yarmouth, Seamus told Eva he had to stop by the hospital to pick up some patient files he needed to study that evening, so he dropped his wife off at their home. He proceeded to go to Broadale.

Arriving at the back door in the late afternoon, he assumed Mavis would be gone for the day, and he could speak privately with Elisabet.

She answered the door to his loud knock, dishcloth in hand.

"If it isn't the prodigal son, or ex-husband. Long time, no see, Seamus," Elisabet smiled tightly, letting him into the kitchen.

"Elisabet, we have to talk. We really do. I know it's been too long since we've seen each other, but I've been thinking about you every single day since we were last together," Seamus admitted, grasping her hands.

"Oh, now, wait just a minute," Elisabet said, removing his hands from hers and draping the dishcloth over the faucet. "You should be thinking about your wife and child every day, not me."

"And I am! I just came from having lunch with her. What in God's name were you thinking when you told her I was stealing drugs from the hospital and selling them?"

"I said nothing of the kind. That's preposterous."

"Of course it is, but she basically accused me of doing so, and when I pressed her, she said that you had told her about it."

"I'll have to have a talk with my daughter, then, Seamus. She is clearly making up stories and for some reason trying to force a wedge between us."

Seamus was beside himself and took a cigarette out of his case and lit it, forgetting to offer one to Elisabet at the same time.

He inhaled deeply and said, "I had to tell Eva how I felt about you. I know that every time we've made love over the past few years I've always said that we had to stop it, and we shouldn't be together like that anymore. But now she knows I've *never* fallen out of love with you. The marriage I have with her is practically a joke."

Elisabet looked at him as if he were an obnoxious relative who would not leave; one who would keep coming back even when told he was not wanted.

"Seamus, I'm shocked and very upset you would treat my daughter like that," she said, her voice rising. "And you have the unmitigated gall to tell me that all this time you have been in love with me? I have had to put up with all the hateful comments, innuendos and outright banishment from Yarmouth society because *I* was the evil, immoral witch who allowed her daughter to sleep with my husband! You've not shared one ounce of the misery I've endured."

She continued, venting all her anger of the past several years.

"I granted you a divorce because you asked for one, and I gave Eva to you because of the deep love I have for my daughter. How dare you come crawling back now that you have made a mess of your marriage to her!"

"Elisabet, darling —", Seamus started.

"No, don't ever call me that again."

"Elisabet, you offered to divorce *me*," he said quietly, "so that there wouldn't be a scandal with Eva and I being together. You even told me then I was stealing her from you, but you must remember, you were not well that year…".

"For crying out loud, Seamus, of course I wasn't. But I wanted the best for you both. I didn't expect you to begin seducing me again when your wife was pregnant! Begging me to sleep with you. And then you continued in the same manner whenever it was convenient for you — and, and, telling me things like, 'no, I can't stay the night', or 'no, Elisabet, I have a spousal duty to Eva'. Flipping heck, Seamus, I'm not some whore you can come back to when you feel like it!"

Seamus's mind was exploding: *hadn't she also been seducing him? Had she not been a very willing partner?*

He tried to embrace her in an apology, but she pushed him away.

"You're not welcome here at Broadale any longer, Seamus. Get out."

She turned and left him in the kitchen alone. He knew better than to follow her and decided he would try to reason with her again tomorrow.

He drove to the Nova Scotia Liquor Commission store, and then to the Grand Hotel, where he booked a room for the night. He called Eva to tell her he had an emergency at the hospital, and he would be home as soon as he was able.

"Seamus, there's so much more that we need to discuss," Eva said, her eyes watering, but relieved he would not see her cry. She had no idea how to salvage her marriage, and wondered if it was worth saving.

"I love you, Seamus."

"I'm sorry, Eva, I've got to go now. We'll talk when I get back from the hospital."

He hung up the phone and thought how desperately he wanted a couple of drinks and to rest. But most of all, he needed some precious time to think.

SIXTY-FIVE

Dayton, Yarmouth Co., Monday, May 11, 1931

Eva called Collan after breakfast before she walked Angus to school.

She invited her to lunch at Lakeside Inn since Marc had given both her and Katarina vouchers for a meal in hopes they would tell their friends that the new facility was open for public dining.

Eva knew it was useless to sit and obsess all day, waiting for Seamus to come home. And even when he did, she wasn't sure she was ready to make any decisions yet about their marriage. Asking for advice from Elisabet was not going to work this time, and Collan was the closest family member who would understand the dilemma now facing her.

Eva tried to push away any random thoughts that she also wanted an excuse to see Marc Shehab again because meeting him could not have happened at a more inappropriate time.

"Do you know what you're going to order?" Collan asked her niece as they looked over the luncheon menu in the bright dining room of the Inn.

"I see the special today is Rappie Pie. I haven't had that in ages," Eva answered, but she was distracted. She hadn't noticed Marc anywhere in the hotel since they arrived.

"You know, that sounds good. I'm glad I finally acquired a taste for it," Collan said. "I remember the first time Mavis made it; it looked like a mound of grey mush on a plate — and wasn't terribly appealing."

"I agree," Eva said, closing the menu. "But if the Acadians can make a savory pie with only potatoes and chicken that looks unappetizing, but happens to be delicious, good for them."

Eva glanced around the almost capacity-sized crowd in the dining room. Yarmouthians were always keen to try out a new eatery, and today at the Inn was no exception.

"Okay, Eva, you didn't ask me to come from Overton to Dayton to chat about food. What's on your mind?"

Eva felt her eyes begin to water, but didn't want to start off a discussion that would make her appear to be an emotionally abused victim in her aunt's eyes.

It didn't occur to her that this is exactly what she was.

She told Collan the whole story, from Angus's odd behavior to Mavis telling her that her mother was having intimate relations again with Seamus, to Elisabet's story that Seamus was stealing and selling opioids from the hospital dispensary.

When she was finished, a waiter came to the table with two glasses of ice water, took their order, and left. This brief respite allowed Collan to gather her thoughts about what she had just learned.

"Eva, hear me out on this one because my viewpoint may be a little different from what you're expecting."

Eva nodded and took a sip of water.

"Let's first look at this accusation that Seamus is stealing and selling drugs. Does that seem like it's in his character to do so?" Collan asked her niece.

"Frankly, no. Over the years, he has always volunteered in medical emergencies. Money has never been a motivator for him," Eva replied.

"Did your mother tell you where she had heard this story?"

"Yes, she did. She said that Seamus told her himself."

Collan furrowed her brows.

"Why would he do that instead of coming to you first? I mean, you're his wife now, and if he wanted to stop his criminal behavior, I would think that he'd confess to you first."

"But Aunt Collan, he told me that he's still in love with Mama," Eva said, tears about to spill. "He clearly feels closer to her. She's the one who apparently hears everything from him."

"But did you believe Seamus when he told you that he's never stolen anything from anyone anywhere?"

"I guess I do; but I'm so confused. Why would Mama lie to me about something like that, Aunt Collan?"

Collan was about to answer when their two luncheon plates of baked Rappie Pie were placed on the table, with side dishes of cranberry sauce and molasses, as was customary in many restaurants in this part of Nova Scotia.

They thanked the waiter, and Collan continued.

"Eva, dear, I don't think your Mama has been terribly well for some time. As you probably know, her change of life came when she was quite young, and that's when her relationship with Seamus began to sour. Later, she didn't take the news about us being adopted very well *at all*. She is my sister and I love her, but even you must have noticed your mother's erratic behavior over the past few years."

Eva thought for a moment and played with the food on her plate, uninterested in it.

"Aunt Collan, it's so humiliating to think that Mama and Seamus have been intimate for the past few years while he's been married to me."

"Eva, I hate to remind you that Seamus has told you how he feels about my sister. He still loves her."

Their conversation was interrupted by Marc Shehab, who approached the table tentatively, not wanting to disturb the women but wanting to greet them briefly. Eva welcomed the interruption.

"Hello, Marc! I wondered if you were at the Inn today," Eva smiled.

"Hi there, Eva!" he said. "I'm glad to see you again."

"Marc, this is my aunt, Collan Burcharth. We've been enjoying today's special; our compliments to the chef. And Aunt Collan, this is Mr. Shehab, the official spokesman for Lakeside Inn. And a wonderful dining room manager, I might add."

Marc shook hands with Collan and the three exchanged small talk about the unseasonably warm weather and the opening of the Inn and Cottages.

"I don't want to take up more of your time, so I'll leave you now. It's been nice to meet you, Mrs. Burcharth," he said.

Instead of correcting his use of 'Mrs.', Collan smiled and said, "Welcome to Yarmouth, Marc. I hope you enjoy your time here."

The waiter came and cleared the dishes, telling Eva and Collan that their Blueberry Grunt dessert and choice of hot beverage as part of the *prix fixe* menu, would be forthcoming.

"This Marc seems like a nice chap," Collan commented. "And he has eyes for you, Eva."

"Don't be silly, Aunt Collan," Eva said, looking away. "A romance is the very last thing on my mind. I love Seamus, I really do. I hope we can come to an understanding, but knowing how he still feels about Mama is something I can't ignore."

#

As Eva and Collan were leaving Lakeside Inn, a front desk clerk at the Grand Hotel was persistently knocking on the door to Seamus's guestroom.

"Dr. McMaster, this is Colin from the Front Desk. Are you there?"

No one from the hotel's morning staff had seen Seamus emerge from his room. Since he had planned on staying for one night only, they wondered why he had not called the front desk to ask for a second night's accommodation after the normal check-out time.

Using a master key to open the door, Colin was taken aback to view a lifeless fully clothed Seamus McMaster slumped over the desk. A nearly empty bottle of Scotch and a drinking glass were the only items on the desk. The curtains were drawn, and the night table lamps were illuminated.

SIXTY-SIX

Yarmouth, Monday, May 18, 1931

Collan, ever the family moderator, took control once Seamus's remains were delivered to the Sweeny Funeral Home on Main Street. Eva was inconsolable. Elisabet assisted by taking care of Angus, and Eva continued to rely on Collan's advice as to what to do next. She asked her aunt to find out if Seamus could be buried at Town Point Cemetery.

Elisabet, nonplussed at hearing of Seamus's death, decided it was best to look stoic and strong for Eva, so that her story of Seamus's phony criminal activity would continue to be cemented in Eva's mind. She picked Angus up at his home on William Street and took him to Broadale for the day and evening. The funeral service was scheduled for noon the following day at Sweeny's.

Collan and Linnea sat in sympathy with Eva.

"Aunt Collan, I need to know if Seamus was taking any drugs himself," she said to her in the living room of her home. "Can they determine that once a person is dead?"

"You know the medical examiner said it was sudden cardiac arrest, Eva," Collan said gently. "It's not a surprise with the stress he was under at the hospital, and you said he was always exhausted when he got home."

"But he was only about to turn forty! Do people die from heart failure at that age? Can I request a full autopsy?"

Linnea said, "I'm not a doctor, Eva, but there might have been a history of heart disease in Seamus's family, too, which wouldn't have helped matters."

"We could ask the medical examiner to see if there were any drugs found in his system, but if that gets out, the whole town will know about it," said Collan.

Eva sighed.

"Well, his mother is gone, and so is his brother, so there will be no one from his family at the funeral service," Eva said. "I'm glad it'll be small and at the funeral home, too. I know some of his colleagues from the hospital will show up. You know, Seamus was not a Presbyterian like his mother had been. He'd probably come back and haunt me if we arranged to have a church funeral."

She laughed once and then started weeping.

"I've physically lost him, but it hurts more to know I had emotionally lost him the day before he died. He wasn't in love with me, and maybe never had been. That's so difficult to accept."

#

In the conservatory at Broadale, Elisabet was showing Angus how to space nasturtium seeds apart when planting them in tiny cardboard containers that would be taken outside after the seedlings had grown.

"I know you're sad, Angus, but your father did the best he could when he was on this earth. He was a very good doctor who helped a lot of people here in Yarmouth, and in Halifax, as well. Did he ever tell you about operating on lots of peoples' eyes after the big explosion in Halifax in 1917?"

"We didn't talk much," Angus said matter-of-factly. "But yeah, he did tell me about that." He stopped planting the seeds and looked at his grandmother.

"Grammy, why did he die *now*? He wasn't an old man like the ones you see on Main Street smoking their pipes and cigars. They look like they're a hundred years old, and they're still here."

"Personally, I think some people die young because they've maybe done some not-so-nice things to other people. If there is a God, he is punishing them for that. Maybe your father hurt some other people more than he helped? We don't know that for sure, do we?"

Angus was perplexed.

"But the soldiers who die, they're not old men, and what bad things have they done so that they have to die young? And they're helping us by fighting the bad guys."

Elisabet put her hands on her grandson's shoulders.

"Maybe they've done some bad things themselves when they were your age, Angus. I don't know, it's quite a mystery in life, isn't it?

Maybe your father would still be here if he had lived a perfectly honest life. But, like I said, he did the best he could," Elisabet intoned, oblivious that her comments to a seven-year-old would be remembered for many years to come.

"Okay, now, let's go cook some hot dogs, and I think I might even have a Coca Cola for you, too. Won't that be fun?"

Angus shrugged and followed his grandmother out of the conservatory.

SIXTY-SEVEN

Yarmouth, Sunday, May 15, 1932

One year later, it was mutually decided that Eva, Angus and Katarina would all move in to Broadale and live with Elisabet. "It's only prudent," Elisabet said, needing her daughter and sister to help pay the expenses for the large residence.

Bankers, accountants, and financial advisors were seeing a slight uptick in the economy, and both Eva and Katarina were advised to try to sell their homes during this positive period. Katarina offered to pay off any remaining debt on Broadale but insisted on having her name on the deed as sole owner. Elisabet complied; she was almost broke, and felt she had little choice in the matter.

In the past year Eva found that Angus was growing into a sullen eight-year-old, and she thought that perhaps boarding school in Windsor might provide him with the masculine, paternal influence that he would be missing at Broadale. But King's School for Boys was for grades six through twelve, and Angus didn't yet qualify.

Seamus's name rarely came up in conversations at Broadale, and Elisabet seemed to actually enjoy the company of the others. Following Seamus's funeral, Eva had to decide whether to have a civil relationship with her mother or find a flat for herself and Angus. She chose to return to Broadale, assuming this would be the best for Angus; but not necessarily for her own comfort.

Everyone had separate bedrooms and Katarina insisted on having her own bath which she paid to have constructed. A grateful contractor and a plumber, eager for a job, finished the new bathroom on the second floor in record time.

Soon after moving in, the women were in the parlor one evening after dinner discussing whether it might be a good idea to have a Dominion Day dinner party on the first of July. Katarina missed entertaining and being entertained, so she promised to take charge of the event.

Eva was about to beg off for the evening when they heard the brass knocker tapping against the front door. She went to answer it and was surprised to see Marc Shehab standing on the steps, hat in hand, and smiling that dazzling smile Eva found so attractive.

"Eva, hello, and forgive me for not calling earlier. I was told only recently that you had moved into your mother's home, and since I haven't seen you since your late husband's funeral, I did want to say hello and ask how you are doing," he said, almost apologetically.

"Oh, heavens, Marc, it's so nice to see you, and please come in," Eva stood back to allow him to come into the hallway. "Let me take your coat and hat."

"Who's at the door, Eva?" Elisabet called out from the parlor.

Eva led Marc into the parlor and introduced him to Elisabet, who shook his hand demurely. Eva nodded to Katarina and reminded him of having met her.

"How could I ever forget the Countess?" he asked rhetorically, and this time, did kiss her outstretched hand, much to her delight.

"Please sit down, Marc. Can I offer you a glass of brandy or port?" Eva asked.

"Thank you very much; I don't mind if I do have a touch of brandy since I've already had dinner," he replied.

Eva went to the cellarette to fix his drink, and Elisabet took a good look at the young man.

"So, Mr. Shehab...."

"Please call me Marc, Mrs. Carroll," he said.

"Well, then, you must call me Elisabet!"

"All right; it's a deal."

"Marc, forgive my curiosity, but where exactly are you from? I mean, you have no accent to speak of, and yet —," Elisabet started.

"I'm from Halifax, actually, Elisabet. And you? Are you a Yarmouth native?"

"No, not specifically. I was born in Sweden and came here as a child. But I *may just as well* be a native," Elisabet answered, slightly flustered. "Actually, what I meant was, what country are you from? Those delightful features of yours look like they may be descended from Egyptian kings!"

Eva rolled her eyes heavenward as she brought the drink to Marc.

"Oh, dear God, Elisabet, please," Katarina said with an exaggerated sigh. "You are really showing how provincial you are, never having lived on the continent and not travelling anywhere except for Boston. It's quite obvious that Marc is Syrian, and —"

"Technically, you're correct, Countess. But my parents, who are Lebanese, came to Halifax from Syria in the 1880s, and have never left. Eva and I found out we were both born the same year, in 1901. So, Elisabet, I'm more of a Canadian than you! Isn't that something?" he asked, grinning. He took a sip of brandy and glanced sideways at Eva. He was happy to see she was quite enjoying his repartee with her mother and her pretentious aunt.

"Isn't it indeed?" Elisabet said thinly.

"Marc, how is business at Lakeside Inn? I'd imagine the Depression is taking its toll on large numbers of leisure travellers from the States," Eva said.

"That's true, Eva," Marc responded. "Luckily, the other hotels in the portfolio help keep Lakeside Inn afloat, though."

"Are you married, dear?" Elisabet asked, with a note of condescension in her voice. She didn't feel an immediate fondness for this man and wondered why he was pursuing Eva.

"Actually, no, I am not," Marc replied.

Rescuing him, Eva said, "Marc, before it gets dark, why don't I show you some of the downstairs rooms at Broadale? You may be interested to see the ballroom and the dining room, in particular."

Marc's relief was apparent.

"I'd be delighted," he said, getting up from his chair and placing his brandy snifter on a coaster on the side table next to him. "Excuse us, ladies."

Katarina gave him a regal nod, and Elisabet simply smiled.

When Marc and Eva were out of earshot, Elisabet looked at her sister, and said, "I don't like him."

"My word! That's basically what I told Eva when we met him last year at the hotel's opening reception. There's something, I don't know, something dark about him, as if he is hiding a big secret," Katarina surmised.

"I'm afraid I don't care enough to even wonder about that," Elisabet said.

SIXTY-EIGHT

Eva – Yarmouth, Thursday, June 15, 1933

Dear Journal,
I recently read a translation of Victor Hugo's Les Misérables, and one line has been in my head every day since then: "Even the darkest night will end, and the sun will rise."
I have to keep believing that.
It's been about a year since Aunt Katarina and I moved back into Broadale. She still is not fond of me, nor I of her, and Mama is somewhere in between the two of us.
I don't understand Mama's moods, which range from staying cloistered in her bedroom for two days at a time, to being extremely happy. We must leave meals outside her door on her dark days, but when she's happy she puts on a nice dress, comes downstairs and joins us for dinner.
I think back to my childhood in Boston, and even though Mama wasn't at home much, I don't harbor any anger or ill will toward her. I am still hurt, though, that she was carrying on with Seamus while he was married to me. There were a few sleepless nights when I actually began to think that some of the local people's gossip about my family could be true. Maybe we're all just immoral "come from away" Europeans, but what does being Swedish have to do with personal morality? I've never lived there and can't speak a word of the language. More's the pity.
I'm proud of my Swedish-English background. I suppose it's unusual I'm an American living in Canada, but even those judgmental townspeople had to have come from somewhere, too.
Angus runs hot and cold, and I understand he misses his father. I do, too, but it's difficult to discipline him when he acts out of sorts since he seems to run to Mama for everything instead of coming to me. When she is 'indisposed', he is even more contrary. It's almost as if at times he has turned against me and the memory of his father.

Marc has been my saving grace this past year; he's the eternal optimist. I swear, nothing seems to make him miserable, whereas I can quickly be negatively affected by those around me. I still try so hard to please Mama; and don't know why. I wonder if this is a flaw in my make-up. I'm giving her my small salary from the newspaper to help with basic expenses here at Broadale. Fortunately, Aunt Katarina pays for repairs and the coal to heat the house, since she basically owns it now. So far, she hasn't been expecting me to pay rent.

Collan and Linnea do come by fairly often, and now that they have quite a garden of herbs, vegetables, and berries, we are provisioned quite well in that regard. They even have a couple of crab apple trees and lots of wild roses on their land, so they make wonderful jellies from the apples and rosehips, and tasty pickles from the cucumbers and onions.

I hesitate to write down the following. I don't want anyone long after I'm gone reading my diary and thinking that I'm a vain woman. But I've wondered why in all the times Marc and I have been together, he hasn't once tried to kiss me. He can be affectionate, surely, but it's almost like having a brother or a close friend...and I'm happy about that since I've lacked both in my life. Maybe he thinks I'm still grieving for Seamus, and he doesn't want to be too forward in case I reject his advances. I don't know.

Nevertheless, Marc has been a breath of fresh air, and I value his friendship tremendously.

Time will tell if a romance develops with him, I suppose. I can see myself married again sometime. But I do think I've become a better writer in the past year, and I want to learn more so I can be a journalist with a proper career, and a decent wage to live on. The Great Depression be damned.

Aunt Collan reminds me from time to time that I don't need anyone in my life to be a happy woman, nor do I need a man to support me. She told me in confidence about the bequest she and Linnea received from a Swedish prince many years ago, so they don't have money worries. If that isn't lucky! I do, however, think of the money Seamus left for me and Angus, and feel grateful for that since Angus is my ultimate responsibility. I want him to be given every opportunity in life. Whatever Mama needs in the future will be taken care of by the family, and I will do my best to help, but that's all.

SIXTY-NINE

Yarmouth, Monday, September 10, 1934

"Are you happy in Grade five?" Eva asked her son in the kitchen of Broadale as he was putting on a light jacket before walking to school. She was washing the breakfast dishes.

"Yeah, I guess so," Angus answered. "Where's my scribblers?"

"You should say, *Where-are-my-scribblers?*, Angus. That sounds better. They're on the pantry shelf where you left them yesterday," Eva replied.

"Mama, can we go away somewhere and not come back?"

Eva stopped her washing, and looked at her ten-year-old who was growing so quickly. This was the first time he had asked her anything of substance in a month.

"Honey, why do you want to go away and not come back? Are any of the kids at school bothering you?"

"No, they're okay," Angus said, "but Grammy is mad all the time, and I think she's mad at me, too."

"We say 'angry', Angus, not 'mad', because 'mad' means 'crazy' or insane," Eva explained, and thought for a second that Angus's appraisal might just be correct. "You and Grammy always seem to me to get along very well. I don't think she's angry with you for any reason."

"I don't know. She tells me sometimes that I'm as bad as my father," Angus said, biting his lip, on the verge of tears. "And that's why he died so young, because he was a bad man."

"Oh, sweetheart, no, that's not true," Eva said, embracing the boy. "I mean, it's not true that your father was bad, and *you're* certainly not, and he died because his heart stopped working, *not* because he did anything bad."

She cupped his face in her hands.

"I don't want you to ever think things like that. Grammy has been feeling poorly of late which is why we don't see her sometimes for a couple of days. When people don't feel well, they sometimes say things they don't mean, okay?"

"Okay, Mama."

"Now hurry off to school, and I'll see you at lunchtime. I'm making a tuna casserole today!"

"Yuck!" Angus exclaimed, and then tried to wink at her, which was a new thing he had been experimenting with for the past week, mostly unsuccessfully. He laughed and ran out the back door of the kitchen.

Almost on instinct, Eva walked to the ballroom, and watched her son run across the yard and onto the semi-circular gravel driveway before reaching the sidewalk alongside Parade Street.

What has Mama been saying to my son? Why tell him Seamus was a bad man? He paid the ultimate punishment for any misdeeds he may have done, so why is she acting like this again? If I confront her, she'll probably deny having said anything like that to Angus.

Katarina continued to sleep late, as she did every morning, so Eva began doing the laundry for the family. The Maytag gas engine wringer washing machine that Katarina had ordered from the T. Eaton & Co. last year was a lifesaver for Eva since she always seemed to be tasked with the role of washerwoman. It was a methodical job, and one that always gave her time to think about the future, or about a story that she had been assigned to write by her editor.

"I couldn't hire help who work as hard as you," Elisabet said jauntily as she walked into the kitchen. She was dressed as if she were about to teach a class of students, looking at once studious but approachable.

"Good morning, Mama," Eva said, kissing her mother lightly on the cheek. "I'm glad to see you up and about today."

"Oh, you know, things to do and people to see, as everyone says," Elisabet said, filling the kettle with water to boil.

"Oh? Where's that, then?"

"I have to go to the hospital to speak to the administrator. He telephoned me to say that they are naming an Eye Clinic after Seamus. One of his patients donated money to the hospital in his memory."

Eva stopped wringing some of their clothes and stared at her mother.

"Why is this the first time I'm hearing of this, Mama?"

"Dear, he only called me yesterday, and you were at the newspaper office."

Eva decided to tread lightly on the issue because she also wanted to ask her mother about why she had been describing Seamus as a 'bad man' to Angus.

"I see," Eva said. "And don't you think it might be more appropriate for me to talk to the hospital administrator since I am Seamus's widow?"

A cloud fell over Elisabet's face.

"Now you listen to me, Eva. Seamus was my husband, and I stupidly agreed to divorce him so he could marry you. I sacrificed my happiness and my life for you, and if anyone is to take the credit for the hard work that Seamus did for his patients, it will be me, not you," Elisabet said with an edge.

Eva was taken aback; she did not know what to say.

"And another thing to remember, dear," her mother continued, "the administrator knows that Seamus was stealing and selling drugs, and it is up to me to convince him that was only a brief aberration in Seamus's poor life, which he admitted and regretted before he died."

"But Mama, I'm —", Eva started.

"No, never mind, Eva. Please drive me there now; I mustn't be late for my appointment."

#

When Eva returned home after dropping Elisabet off, she was still angry at her mother's behavior, and she had yet to discover why she had been maligning Seamus to Angus.

It was almost noon, and forgetting about the casserole she was to make, she started preparing a plate of cold cuts and salad for Angus's lunch for when he arrived home from school.

The phone rang, startling Eva. She immediately thought it might be the hospital administrator asking her to join the meeting with her mother after all.

"Hi kiddo, how're you doin' today?" It was Marc's friendly voice on the other end of the telephone line.

"Hi, Marc. Gee, it's nice to hear a chipper voice right now," Eva replied.

"Oh, you know me, Doll. Remember it was Oscar Wilde who wrote that we are all in the gutter, but some of us are looking at the stars! That'd be yours truly!"

Eva smiled into the receiver and said, "You sure do look at the stars, Marc. That's why I like you so."

"That's good then, Eva, because we will literally be looking at the stars early next week. How would you like to meet Amelia Earhart in person?"

SEVENTY

The census taken in 1931 for the Acadian village of Wedgeport was 1,294 which almost ensured that every resident would personally know everyone else in this close-knit community. It had been first settled in 1767 by returning Acadians who had been expelled to the Boston area by the ruling British.

Bluefin tuna had always been attracted to this outpost on the Atlantic Ocean. For decades, if not centuries, it was due to the abundance of feed in the sea for them. A highly regarded fish around the world, the three species of Bluefin cannot be bred in captivity, so the danger of overfishing and diminishing their numbers had always been a real one.

Sometimes called *giant* Bluefin due to their size and weight, rod and reel tuna fishing was popular in Wedgeport in the early 1930s. This tiny part of Canada was considered to be the 'historic sport tuna fishing capital of the world'.

Celebrities and politicians took note of this unique sport fishing opportunity and came to try their luck. Notable figures during the Depression years who visited included Babe Ruth, President Franklin Roosevelt, American singer Kate Smith, Ernest Hemingway, heiress and socialite Ethel du Pont, author Zane Grey, and aviatrix Amelia Earhart. They and other wealthier individuals were among the many who sought the reward of capturing a Bluefin off the coast of Nova Scotia.

Amelia Earhart, the first woman to fly solo across the Atlantic Ocean in 1932, made a quiet visit for two weeks to the area with her sister. They stayed with fellow American friends in the nearby District of Argyle.

Marc inadvertently heard of Earhart's secret visit when two of his affluent and regular American clients at Lakeside Inn told him of her trip. It did not take much sleuthing to find out when she would be visiting the wharf at Wedgeport to talk to Captain Evée LeBlanc who was renowned as one of three local fishermen who had started harpooning tuna a decade earlier.

The affable Captain LeBlanc was the first fishing boat captain people looked for when seeking to experience the excitement of tuna fishing. All his day trips used his personal boat, *The Judge*.

"I'm really excited," Eva said breathlessly to Marc as they drove to Wedgeport. "Are you quite sure she'll be there this afternoon?"

Marc, in the driver's seat and happy to be away from the Inn for a few hours, smiled and said in a mock British accent, "My dear lady, all of my best sources have told me thus, and you may get the scoop of your journalistic career!"

"Oh, Marc, do you really think so?" Eva asked, hopeful. "Who, by the way, are your sources?"

"Ah, I don't believe I am required to divulge that, Miss Nosy Reporter, but I don't mind telling you that Suzette, who makes all of our salads at the Inn, just happens to be dating one of Captain LeBlanc's sons, and…" he revealed.

"…And she is undoubtedly your hotel's biggest tattletale!" Eva finished the sentence for him.

"She is, *indubitably*, Miss Nosy Reporter, she is!" Marc laughed as he picked up speed on the narrow road leading from the community of Arcadia to Wedgeport.

#

A short time later, Marc parked his 1930 Plymouth convertible coupe several yards away from the buzz of activity on the wharf, which was presumably due to Miss Earhart's visit, Eva thought. About a dozen people were crowded around Captain LeBlanc's fishing boat.

I may even be able to get a photograph of her!

Eva had instructed Marc to look nonchalant as they sauntered over to the activity. She asked him to keep her Kodak box camera hidden in a satchel she normally used when shopping. She knew that Miss Earhart was quite shy and unused to her massive celebrity of the past few years, so she did not want to come across as an annoying member of the press.

When they arrived, it appeared that the famous aviation pioneer was saying goodbye to Captain LeBlanc. She and her sister were shaking hands with him, and then they slowly walked to a nearby four-door sedan. Eva was happy to see no one was following them.

"Miss Earhart, excuse me, please!" Eva cried, hoping to grab the woman's attention for even a brief comment.

Amelia Earhart stopped and looked at the blonde woman who was walking rapidly toward her with a man about her age directly behind her, carefully carrying a canvas satchel.

The two women exchanged pleasantries and then spoke for a few minutes. They shook hands, and Eva surprised herself by motioning for Marc to take a photograph of the two of them. Miss Earhart, who would disappear from the sky on an ill-fated flight just three years later at the age of thirty-nine, said goodbye to Eva and Marc with a smile and a wave from her car.

The Yarmouth Courier carried the story the following day:

FAMOUS FEMALE FLYER LANDS IN YARMOUTH
Amelia Earhart on two-week private vacation
by Eva McMaster

A visit to Nova Scotia by Miss Amelia Earhart, famous flyer, has been confirmed when she was interviewed by the Yarmouth Courier and admitted her identity, pleading that she was traveling incognito. She did not wish undue publicity to disrupt her visit to Yarmouth.

Miss Earhart did divulge her interest in tuna fishing. She hoped there would soon be an opportunity to try the challenging sport with her sister, guided by an unnamed tuna fishing captain in Wedgeport. She is currently vacationing in the area. Her place of accommodation in Yarmouth County at a private summer residence owned by a United States citizen has not been released, but is reputed to be in the Municipality of the District of Argyle.

According to information secured by the press, she will be sailing soon for New York from the Eastern Dock in Yarmouth, but an exact date has not been confirmed.

SEVENTY-ONE

Yarmouth, Thursday, September 20, 1934

"Marc, thank you again for such a wonderful opportunity," Eva said over the phone to her friend, reminding him to look for a copy of yesterday's Courier so he could read her brief article which was indeed a scoop, although a brief one.

"My pleasure, Eva. It was fun to get away for a little while and exciting, too, I must admit," Marc said.

"You know, I tried to figure out how to write that *maybe* she was staying at Lakeside Inn & Cottages, but you know I have a hard time fibbing!"

Marc laughed, saying, "My, you are an intriguing woman. I appreciate the thought, but we probably wouldn't have wanted a bunch of her fans tromping all over our gardens, in any case. By the way, Eva, are you free for dinner Saturday night?"

"I most certainly am, Mr. Hotelier!" Eva said.

They arranged to meet, and Eva hung up the phone and walked into the dining room for breakfast.

"I can't believe you met Amelia Earhart and didn't even tell your own aunt," Katarina wailed as Eva entered the room. "She and I would have gotten along like a house on fire, I'm sure of it."

"First of all, good morning to you, Aunt Katarina," Eva said. "What brings you out of bed and featuring your adorable self at eight o'clock in the morning?"

Katarina ignored Eva's sarcastic question and pressed on, saying, "I think I met the pilot she flew across the Atlantic with. I believe it was in Stockholm, back in '28, four years before her solo flight. Oh my — we would have had a wonderful time talking about him."

Eva studied her toast and jam, trying to hide her disbelief.

"Aunt Katarina, I barely had two minutes to talk to the woman. So even if you had come along with Marc and me, you wouldn't have been able to talk to her. Trust me on that," Eva said with finality.

Katarina harrumphed and buttered a slice of toast.

"Mama, when are we gonna fly to New York?" Angus asked his mother, his mouth full of porridge.

"Honey, don't talk with your mouth full," Eva said. "Don't you worry, someday soon we'll *sail* to New York, and you can see King Kong!"

Eva remembered that Angus had been fascinated with seeing photos from the movie which had been released to rave reviews the year before. It had not yet made its way to the movie theater in Yarmouth.

Elisabet poked her head in the dining room with a stern look on her face.

"Eva, could you come in the kitchen with me for a minute?"

Eva followed her, knowing full well they hadn't finished their talk from two days ago.

"For your information, the hospital wants you and your son to be present when it dedicates its optometry clinic in Seamus's memory," Elisabet said, as if this were an obnoxious duty that no one would want.

Eva was surprised hearing this news in light of the manner in which her mother had spoken of the dedication a mere forty-eight hours previously.

"Oh, my, well, isn't that nice that, uh, *Angus*, will witness his father being honored like that," she said.

"I'll be there, too," Elisabet stated flatly.

SEVENTY-TWO

Yarmouth, Saturday, September 22, 1934

"Eva, when I asked you to dinner, I didn't think it would be at my place of work that I see far too much of, already," Marc said to Eva as he held out her chair at a quiet table in the dining room of Lakeside Inn. "My assistant manager is ill, so I have to work this weekend."

"Don't be silly, Marc! It's a real treat for me to spend time with you, but also to escape from my mother and my aunt for an evening. Their idea of fun is to devour the society pages of *The Boston Herald American* these days. Mama now has a subscription to it. Then my aunt claims she's met half of the famous people mentioned in the stories. It's very tiresome, believe me."

"I'm glad you're not upset that we're not dining elsewhere, like the Grand Hotel, because —", Marc began.

"Excuse me for interrupting, Marc, but that's not a place I want to see anytime soon. The memory of Seamus dying there alone is still pretty vivid," Eva said.

"Oh, of course, how thoughtless of me to bring it up. I was doing some reading on the Hotel this past week to see if I could pick up any tips on guest service that may be lacking here. The most glowing report I found at the library was from a 1911 issue of *The Busy East of Canada* magazine from New Brunswick. So, it wasn't exactly a timely review."

"Oh? What did it say?" Eva asked. "Now you've piqued my writer's curiosity."

"Well, the writer of the story called his article 'The Best Hotel in the Maritime Provinces', and he said that American visitors would find a, quote, 'rare and delightful climate', unquote, and that people who had hay fever are, and I'm again quoting him, 'absolutely immune in Yarmouth'."

Marc paused to take a breath and smiled as he continued.

"Can you imagine, Eva? My allergies have *not* disappeared since I moved here! Then the fellow wrote about the town's water supply which comes from Lake George, eighteen miles from the hotel, and flows in by gravitation. He said the water was particularly superior because it was absolutely free from typhoid germs. But you know what the funny thing is? He forgot to write *anything* about the Grand Hotel in any detail — his story was more like a climate and water report!"

"So, I assume you didn't learn about any hospitality secrets or special recipes from the Grand, is that right?" Eva asked, smiling.

"No, I'm afraid not, but that's all right," Marc said. "The standards of CP Hotels are pretty high and probably above those at that hotel, anyway."

The waiter appeared at their table with a bottle of Sauvignon Blanc, showed the label to Marc, opened it, and poured about an ounce for him to try before confirming his choice. Marc nodded to the waiter to go ahead and pour for Eva.

They toasted to the fine autumnal evening ahead of them, and knowing Eva was fond of seafood, Marc told her he had pre-ordered Lobster Newberg for her.

"Wonderful, thank you," Eva said.

"So how are you doing these days, Eva? I mean, *really* doing. Are you happy with your living arrangements and such?"

Eva sighed and said, "My goodness, we are so fortunate during this Depression compared to so many. I can't really complain about anything, and just think of the wonderful dinner I'm about to have with one of my favorite people." She took a sip of wine, and hoped she wasn't being too flirtatious.

"And you're one of my favorite people in Yarmouth, too," Marc said, flashing one of his bright smiles at her and raising his wine glass a second time in a toast.

"You know, Marc, you've not talked about any old girlfriends or a wife you may have left behind in the big, bad city! Surely, there's a trail of broken hearts in Halifax," Eva kidded.

Marc's expression turned from being frivolous to one more serious.

"That's a very long and possibly boring story, and I don't know if I'm ready to get into it right now," Marc said.

"Oh, gosh, I don't mean to pry, I was just having you on, Marc. Please don't take offense," Eva said with a worried look.

"None taken, my dear," he said, back to his jocular self. "I do feel close to you, and perhaps the next time we meet I'll tell you a little more about my life in Halifax before I decided to conquer this bustling seaport." He chuckled.

"I'd like that, Marc, I really would. Good friends are hard to come by, and I'd like you to be around for an awfully long time."

SEVENTY-THREE

Yarmouth, Monday, October 15, 1934

There was only a small number of invited guests and hospital staff on hand for the opening of the Yarmouth Hospital's new, but modest, optometry clinic, named with a plate on the door: *The Dr. Seamus McMaster Eye Clinic.*

"This is definitely *not* a terribly exciting celebration," the overdressed Countess Katarina de Carminati whispered to her sister, Elisabet, as she looked around the hallway outside the clinic. Collan, overhearing her loud whisper, frowned at her. Elisabet looked disinterested.

Eva stood nearby with Angus. Alvin O'Brien, a rotund man with tiny oval eyeglasses, approached Eva and asked if he could have a word before the formalities were to begin. Eva smiled her assent and asked Angus to take a seat on one of the hallway chairs and read the book he had brought with him, a new *Hardy Boys* mystery, while she spoke briefly to the hospital's chief administrative officer.

"Mr. O'Brien, this is such a wonderful occasion, and I thank the Board of Directors for its tribute to Seamus's memory. I can't tell you how much we appreciate it."

But Eva still had a lingering doubt that there may have been a grain of truth in her mother's story about Seamus stealing hospital pharmaceuticals.

"All things considered," Eva said quietly, and tried not to look embarrassed.

The older man seemed confused by Eva's remark, and said, "Oh, my dear Mrs. McMaster, Seamus was well liked here by all his colleagues, as well as the staff. He worked so hard for the hospital and the whole community, it's the very least we could do."

"I guess I mean that sometimes he may have had a tendency to not, uh, follow, hospital procedures," she continued vaguely, looking for a reaction from the CAO.

"Why, Mrs. McMaster, I'm sure I don't know what you mean! I always found Seamus to be one of the most honorable and professional doctors we had on staff. Perhaps he was joking with you one day saying he took a sandwich from the cafeteria and forgot to pay for it, or..." Mr. O'Brien said, clearly confused.

Eva laughed nervously.

"Oh, yes, Mr. O'Brien, that's exactly it, I'm sure. He was a notorious procrastinator and could be a little scatterbrained sometimes. You know how busy some doctors get!" Her voice trailed off as she realized her mother had definitely concocted the tale about Seamus stealing and selling drugs.

Mr. O'Brien smiled and explained to Eva how the proceedings would take place, and she nodded in all the appropriate places. "One more thing, Mrs. McMaster. I'd like you meet the benevolent person who donated the money to fund this memorial clinic."

"Of course," Eva said, as he motioned for a woman to approach them. She was dressed in black and about the same age as Elisabet.

Eva immediately noticed how red the woman's eyes were, as if she had severe allergies or had just been crying.

"It's lovely to meet you after such a long time," the woman said. "My name is Morag MacDonnell. Seamus, uh, your late husband, operated on *my* late husband's eyes after the Explosion in Halifax in '17. My condolences on your loss."

"My sympathy to you, as well, Mrs. MacDonnell. And I'm also grateful for your most generous donation to the Hospital in Seamus's name."

"Oh yes, the dear man," she sniffled, on the verge of tears. "He was a very generous, very kind soul." Morag MacDonnell fished for a handkerchief from her purse, excused herself and walked swiftly down the corridor.

Surprised at the encounter, Eva looked at Alvin O'Brien.

"Mrs. MacDonnell must still be grieving the loss of her husband," O'Brien said, "although he died several years ago in Halifax. Occasions like this one can be quite emotional for some people."

"Yes, you could say that," Eva said.

Knowing it would never be verified, Eva instinctively felt that Seamus may have had an affair with Morag MacDonnell when he was married to Elisabet.

Maybe it was here, or maybe it was during his frequent trips to Halifax years ago...

Her naïve heart was slowly but inevitably becoming stronger and more educated with life's continuing lessons.

SEVENTY-FOUR

Port Maitland Beach, Yarmouth Co., Saturday, October 20, 1934

Marc picked up the phone in his office at Lakeside Inn and asked the hotel operator to connect him with the number for Broadale. It was a brilliant day with a little wind, but with a true autumnal feel. The temperature was in the upper forties.

"It may be the last good day weather-wise to take a long walk on the beach before it gets too cold to do so, Eva. Can I pick you up?" Marc asked. "I haven't been to Port Maitland since I arrived in Yarmouth."

Angus was showing his Aunt Katarina how to play checkers, and Elisabet was nowhere to be found in the house, so Eva jumped at the chance for some time away from Broadale with Marc.

Since the dedication of the new eye clinic at the hospital, Eva wondered how she would deal with the series of lies her mother had been telling her. She typically avoided conflict, but she desperately needed to know if her mother had lied to her out of malice, anger, or something else.

Could Mama be losing her faculties?

#

The drive to Port Maitland along Route 1 was a little over thirteen miles from Broadale, and both Marc and Eva enjoyed the rolling farmland and the trees still resplendent in their fall coats of red, yellow, and orange.

As they drove past Darlings Lake and the Churchill Mansion, Eva was about to tell Marc that the imposing white residence had been where her mother and Seamus had married, but then thought better of it. That piece of history was better left buried, she thought.

They were soon in the tiny village of Port Maitland, a community of a few hundred souls, mostly of English origin and with strong

Baptist leanings. They turned off the main road and followed another that led westward to the public wharf where several fishing boats were anchored at low tide. Marc parked his coupe next to the only other car there. After taking a light blanket from the trunk in case the wind picked up off the water, they made their way to the beach, which stretched for over half a mile.

The beach at low tide looked liked one giant field of shiny wet flat cement, with nary a rock, driftwood, or bit of scrub brush on it. One had to squint to see the line of surf in the distance. Its breaking water created a low whooshing sound and their noses tingled at the intake of the cold salty air. It would be several hours before the expanse would be flooded once again by the high tide of the Atlantic Ocean.

"You can almost taste the air, can't you?" Eva asked, inhaling deeply. "I was too young when we lived in Boston to have known the difference between city air and seacoast air. I really appreciate it now."

"Me too, Eva. Although my cottage is right on Lake Milo, one can't compare what it's like to be by the ocean and to be lakeside. And even when I left Halifax to spend a year in Chicago, I so missed smelling the Nova Scotian sea air. Lake Michigan can't hold a candle to the Atlantic."

"Oh? I thought you might have been in the Great War, since you seem to be more worldly than other men I've met," Eva said.

"I did volunteer, but my bad leg, thanks to the polio I had as a child, prevented me from being accepted. I ended up in Chicago to help my uncle in his textile business instead."

"Isn't it called the Windy City, and aren't there lots of gangsters there?"

Marc laughed, picked up a small flat rock, and threw it ahead of them, attempting to make the rock skip over the hardened sand.

"Not so much when I was there; Prohibition and Al Capone and the 'boys' came along in 1920, and I had returned to Halifax by then," he explained. "It's a crazy, lively city, but in fact, I really loved my time there."

"Really, Marc? Were there many other Lebanese families? A larger number than the community in Halifax?"

Two seagulls cawed above them, swooping low, and the couple looked up instinctively.

"Yes, there were. Many emigrated to the Chicago area around the same time my parents came to Canada. In fact, my father's brother was on the same ship with them when they left Beirut, but he wanted to sell his textiles — mostly table coverings — at the World's Columbian Exposition in Chicago in 1893. He went south to the U.S., and did pretty well for himself, and that's how I got my job in his company in 1918."

"You were a kid!" Eva exclaimed.

"You're right; I was just seventeen, and I had to grow up pretty quickly, but I'm glad I did go."

They continued walking quietly for a few minutes in the brilliant sunlight, both enjoying its warmth on their faces.

"Did you meet a girl in Chicago while you were there…maybe your first girlfriend?"

Eva grinned and punched him playfully on the arm. Marc chuckled, but seemed to be weighing how to answer her question.

"Oh, Eva, Eva…I don't know if you're ready for a long story that I'd have to ask you to keep to yourself. You have enough on your mind right now as it is."

Eva stopped walking for a moment and looked directly at her companion.

"Marc, of course you can trust me. We've been each other's confidante for some time now, wouldn't you agree?"

"Yeah, you're right, we've shared a lot." He paused and thought of how to expose an integral part of himself that he had to keep secret.

"I don't want you to ever forget this, Eva. I think women are ultimately the stronger of both sexes; they have to be, in order to continue populating the earth! But look at me: I did not decide that I would be born Lebanese and be raised as a Christian; I did not choose to have polio over other childhood diseases; I did not decide to only grow as tall as five feet, six inches! And, I didn't choose my brown eyes."

Eva looked at him but could not understand what he was trying to tell her. He shuffled his feet and appeared to be extremely uncomfortable.

"Well, yes, I agree that there are many things in our own lives that we have no control over," she said.

"Ah, skip it for now. I'm doing a lousy job talking about myself, aren't I? Let's just enjoy the afternoon, okay?" he asked.

"Okay. I'm probably not the most attentive listener at the moment anyway, Marc, as I'm trying to straighten out my family situation. But I do want you to know that I'm here for you, and you can always count on my support. You're not sick with an incurable illness, are you?"

Marc shook his head. "Nah, I'm fine."

"You're a dear friend, and I don't want that ever to change," Eva said, hugging him. She didn't notice his eyes were brimming with tears.

SEVENTY-FIVE

Yarmouth, Saturday, October 20, 1934

Before Marc picked up Eva for their visit to Port Maitland Beach, Elisabet left Broadale via the kitchen door and walked for five minutes eastbound on Parade Street until she reached Mountain Cemetery.

She didn't know what led her to the 11-acre, non-denominational burial ground that afternoon. It featured a stone chapel that was built and dedicated to its donor three years after she had bought Broadale in 1920, but she had never ventured into the graveyard to take a closer look at the structure. She decided that would be her excuse if anyone asked why she left Broadale that afternoon.

During the walk she encountered no one, and there were no vehicles driving along the street. The silence was overpowering; there was barely a breeze, and Elisabet felt completely at ease.

The door to the chapel was open, and she sat in the last pew closest to the door. Light streamed through the stained glass and hand painted windows. The only person she was thinking of was her first husband, Nigel. She closed her eyes, and in her mind, Sunday, July 26, 1914 vividly returned.

She was staring emotionless at Nigel from across the shop as she removed tins of shortbread from a shelf to dust the weathered items. Wiping each, she then returned the tins to their appointed display space.

I doubt he has sold one box of these godawful things this summer.

He was humming an indecipherable tune, while he unpacked a crate of teacups and saucers emblazoned with the images of King George V and Queen Mary.

She glanced at the china he was unpacking.

More junk that Bostonians won't buy.

"We're getting a bit of a respite from the heat today, aren't we, my dear?"

Perspiration had collected on his forehead.

A lone fan attached to the ceiling slowly circulated. It moved the still, hot air around, providing no comfort whatsoever.

"Nigel, it's 84 degrees outside and probably about 94 in the store right now," she said. "That's not really a respite. I just hope that Eva is cooling off a bit with her friends at the YWCA gymnasium today."

"Yes, one can hope," he said, more interested in making sure the cups and saucers were not nicked or cracked as he removed them gingerly from the straw packing.

"I'm missing Nova Scotia terribly, Nigel. Can you shut the store for a week so the three of us can sail to Yarmouth? We haven't been in about seven years."

"That would be an impossibility, my dear. I can't afford to close the store in the middle of the summer. We need every customer we can get right now. Sales are down, and I thought you knew that."

Nigel tried to sound stern, but it only sounded like a mild rebuke.

"And besides, you do get to see your father occasionally when he has shore leave here."

"Occasionally is once in a blue moon." She considered her options. "How about if I go with Eva, then, and you can stay here?"

He stopped unpacking, took off his reading glasses, and gave her a petulant look.

"Elisabet, I think I provide very well for you and Eva. I have not once argued with you about your volunteer work with the Boston Opera, where you seem to spend an inordinate amount of time. But did it ever occur to you that perhaps I would like to have you here at the store a little more often, to help out, and to let me have a couple of hours off now and then during the week?"

"And what do you think I am doing in this insufferable heat right now, Nigel? I am helping you now."

He sighed. His face had turned a ghastly shade of gray. He pulled a handkerchief from his pocket and wiped the beads of sweat above his eyebrows.

"As I have said many times, and every summer to you, Elisabet, if I were able to play God, I would take the heat away from the city simply so you could be happy. But I am not God and I cannot do that. Please, for all that is good and holy, stop whinging about the weather."

She threw the damp rag in her hand on a countertop.

"All right, Nigel, I will stop whining, which is how I pronounce the word. But you know what? From today on, you won't have any more help from me. I don't care what happens to this store. You order items from jolly ol' England without having any idea what Bostonians really want to buy. Have you forgotten that the Americans won the War of Independence? Those stupid King George teacups will collect dust and rot here for the next fifty years. I can't believe you..."

She stopped speaking. He had placed his hand on his chest and was having trouble breathing.

"What's the matter with you?" she asked, annoyed. She picked up an upright desk chair and brought it over to where he was leaning against a display counter.

"Here, sit," she said, and guided him into the seat. It was at that moment she realized he was in serious medical distress. She didn't know the difference between a heart attack and cardiac arrest, but assumed he was in the throes of one or the other. She looked at him as if he were a laboratory rat, and waited for instructions from a teacher who would never materialize.

She did not panic and watched his agony with dispassion. Her thoughts were sluggish but clear.

I'll probably never have to spend another hot summer in Boston for the rest of my life.

In approximately five minutes Nigel Godfrey Carroll, originally from Southampton, England, died at the age of forty-two.

She picked up the receiver of the candlestick telephone that he had only purchased a month earlier for the store and prepared to act like a grief stricken wife.

SEVENTY-SIX

Yarmouth, Saturday, October 20, 1934

"Where's your niece?" Elisabet asked Katarina as she walked into the parlor following her visit to Mountain Cemetery.

"She's gone to the beach with her Syrian friend," Katarina replied with disdain. "Can you imagine? And it's almost the end of October."

Elisabet picked up a copy of *Maclean's* that had been left on the coffee table, and idly leafed through it.

"What about the boy?"

"Angus? I think he's next door with the MacNeil kids."

Elisabet made a non-committal grunt and continued randomly flipping the pages of the periodical.

"You seem to be in an odd mood," Katarina commented. "What's going on in your noggin these days?"

Elisabet returned the magazine to the coffee table, leaned back, folded her hands, and looked at Katarina as if she hadn't seen her for a long time.

"Do you know that I *loathe* you, Katarina?"

Katarina's eyes widened, and then assuming her sister was making a joke, protested in mock horror.

"Oh no! Did I forget to polish the silver this month? It was my turn, wasn't it? The job completely slipped my feeble little mind!"

Elisabet granted her a half-smile.

"I'm quite serious, Katarina. I have for quite awhile now. You sent Seamus and me a ridiculous polar bear carcass as a housewarming gift. You bought an honorific title to add some fake prestige to your sad little life in Sweden and then you couldn't get that right, either. So you got rid of that Italian husband of yours, not to mention the child you adopted, and came back here as if you were a long-lost queen returning to her throne. No one in this town likes you, Katarina, and they laugh at you behind your back."

Katarina was completely shocked, having no idea from where Elisabet's vitriol was coming.

"And I mustn't forget that when I was at *my* wit's end, grieving the loss of my husband — that's Seamus, not Nigel — you swooped in and made me sign the deed to Broadale over to you. You're a callous bitch, Katarina."

Katarina finally regained her composure and straightened her back, ready to counter her sister's accusations.

"I saved you, Elisabet. *Saved* you. You almost lost Broadale. You might recall we're in an economic Depression right now? You had *nothing*, not a penny to keep this place going. You're damn lucky that I still have enough money to keep Broadale in operation, not to mention keeping you, and Eva, *and* your grandson — or is it stepson? — in the home I thought you loved."

"You're delusional, Katarina," Elisabet said. "Seamus and I have enough money to hold on to this house. It was our dream home and it still is."

Katarina was incredulous. Could Elisabet hear what she was saying? She was spouting nonsense, talking as if Seamus were still alive, and they were still married to one another.

"I don't know what kind of pill you've taken today, Elisabet, or maybe you're suffering from a severe lack of sleep, but I can't talk to you any further right now without blowing up. You seem to forget that you appalled your sisters and this whole town by allowing your daughter to carry on and then marry your husband. What on earth were you thinking? Oh, and by the way, Seamus is dead!"

Katarina angrily jumped up from the loveseat where she was sitting and left the parlor.

Elisabet was unperturbed. In her mind, the past was co-existing quite well with the present. She looked at the murals she had commissioned for the room, and felt somewhat at peace, but her persistent anger at everything and everybody who had wronged her was never far from the surface of her consciousness.

She went into the kitchen and glanced at the clock hanging above the refrigerator.

I can't believe how long it took to convince Nigel to buy a refrigerator for us. No, not Nigel. It was Seamus, yes, that's right,

Seamus. I wonder if he'll make it home for lunch today. Maybe I can pan fry some haddock for him. He likes that.

The back door opened, and Angus bounded in and jumped on a stool by the sink.

"What's for lunch, Grammy?"

Elisabet looked at him blankly, as if she couldn't quite remember how he fit into her universe.

"Well, hello, young man! I was just thinking of making some fried fish for lunch because if your father makes it home from the store, he really likes that. Is that good for you, too?"

"But Grammy, Daddy is dead, and he worked at the hospital."

Elisabet blinked in rapid succession.

"Yes, of course, dear. Sometimes your Mama forgets," she said vaguely.

"You're my Grammy, not my Mama! Geeeeeez," Angus drawled, and left the kitchen.

#

Katarina was in the study with the door closed, speaking on the telephone. The polar bear rug, hanging on one wall and dominating the room, appeared to eavesdrop on her conversation.

"I tell you, Collan, she is in such a state accusing me of all manner of ridiculous things. And ungrateful! I've got half a mind to tell her she can move out anytime she wishes, and — "

She paused and listened for a moment, and said, "No! I'm *not* making this up or telling fibs! Collan, she said she loathed me — *loathed* me!"

Another minute went by as Katarina's older sister spoke.

"Yes, okay, then. Don't let on I told you all this because she'll surely fly into a rage. I'll see you soon. Goodbye."

Katarina hung up the telephone and stared into space. She tried to decide whether to go to her bedroom, stay in the study, or leave the house entirely and go for a walk. Collan wouldn't arrive for an hour, and she didn't want another run-in with Elisabet.

#

Collan put the receiver back on the telephone. She thought about how she had probably been witnessing her older sister gradually decline mentally over the past few years, but she couldn't pinpoint when it had begun.

Her mind drifted back to the Dumdums' performance in 1929, and how Elisabet had openly acted as if she and Seamus were still a couple. Eva had seemed to be a bit player on their stage, rather than Seamus's current wife and the mother of their son.

She finished washing the breakfast dishes that she had started before the telephone rang and then went in search of her partner.

She found Linnea in their vegetable garden harvesting the last of their bounty for the season and told her she was going to Broadale to see her sisters.

In this late October air, the deciduous trees on Vancouver Street were rapidly becoming denuded. Collan's car drove slowly down the hill as dead leaves from chestnut, maple, and oak trees fluttered in its wake. She anticipated the drama that was to undoubtedly unfold when she arrived at Broadale. She dreaded a prolonged argument with Elisabet.

#

Returning from their beach walk, Eva and Marc drove past Lakeside Inn on Lake Milo and arrived at Broadale just a few minutes after Collan.

Collan had parked her car on the semi-circular driveway and ascended the steps to the front door. She knocked twice using the brass door knocker, and as she was expected, opened the front door and went inside.

Lying at the foot of the staircase, her eyes gazing to the heavens, was Katarina's dead body, a pool of blood forming underneath her head.

SEVENTY-SEVEN

Yarmouth, Tuesday, October 30, 1934

Countess Katarina de Carminati

Funeral services for Countess Katarina de Carminati were from St. Paul's Anglican Church Monday morning at 9:00 o'clock. The service was a Requiem Communion with the Rector, Rev. A. Elliott, the celebrant. He was assisted by Rev. Gordon T. Ferris as Epistoler. Lieutenant Ernest Cleveland was at the organ and during Communion played "Dies Irae". The Russian Anthem for the Departed was rendered by the organist during Ablutions. Committal services were from the Mortuary Chapel, Mountain Cemetery. The bearers were vestrymen of the Church, A.H. Morris, I.L. Putter, F.H. Judge, and S.C. Rideout.

Countess de Carminati was well known in Yarmouth where she returned in 1923 after many years abroad in Sweden. She resided at her estate on Parade Street.

She is survived by an only son, Paolo de Carminati, of Gothenburg, Sweden who was unable to attend the funeral services. There are two sisters living: Mrs. N. Carroll, Yarmouth, and Miss C. Burcharth, Overton, as well as one niece, Mrs. S. McMaster, also of Yarmouth.

She was predeceased by her parents, Captain Jacob, and Mrs. Signe Burcharth. Born in Gothenburg, Sweden, she emigrated to Yarmouth in 1883 as a child with her parents and siblings.

She was involved with several prestigious charitable organizations in Sweden and was decorated on more than one occasion by the King of Sweden for her dedicated work of a humanitarian nature. This selfless commitment had been one of her finest contributions to her native country and to the city of Gothenburg.

#

"Eva, did you write Katarina's obituary?" Elisabet asked her daughter during lunch at Broadale a week after Katarina's unexpected fall down the main staircase.

"No, Mama; I understand Aunt Katarina's lawyer gave my editor most of the information, except for the funerary details, obviously, which I passed along. But Katarina had written the rest of it herself," Eva explained.

"It *is* a bit overdone in parts," commented Collan. "To my knowledge, she did not receive any medals from the King. Also, I was completely unaware that she had begun attending services at St. Paul's Church."

"I don't believe she did while living here at Broadale," Eva said, "but she must have started going after she bought her house on Collins Street."

"Well, I'm sorry she passed at the fairly young age of — what was she, Collan — fifty?" Elisabet asked, without any interest in the answer.

"She was fifty-four, Elisabet, and I agree. Katarina was extremely healthy and should have had a long life ahead of her," Collan answered, her eyes carefully watching her older sister's emotions.

"But she was, oh, so clumsy! I wonder what she needed in her bedroom so badly in the middle of the day that she was even upstairs," Elisabet said.

Eva heard the telephone ring in the study, and she excused herself from the dining table to answer it.

Returning a few minutes later, she said to her mother and aunt, "That was Katarina's lawyer. He'd like us to go to his office for the reading of the will at two o'clock."

Elisabet became energized.

"All right, ladies, let's get these dishes cleared away and do our duty," she said. "Eva, don't forget that Angus will be out of school and home about three-fifteen, so you must be back here by then."

"Yes, Mama, I'm quite aware of that," Eva said, surprised that her mother had not only remembered her grandson's name, but where he was on that day. It was perhaps the most coherent comment Elisabet had made in recent weeks.

#

Collan decided to return to Broadale with Elisabet and Eva after their meeting with the estate lawyer, as she knew her sister would be in a state of fear, frustration or hurt, or a combination of all three.

Eva didn't bother to ask her mother or Collan, but she poured three glasses of dry sherry and served the others in the parlor before taking a glass for herself.

"What in heaven's name am I supposed to do now?" Elisabet asked no one in particular. "She left Broadale to her son in Sweden — who has never even been to Canada — and is not of legal age. I am homeless, pure and simple."

"If you are, so am I and so is your grandson, Mama," Eva corrected her.

"She did this on purpose. She could never stand me and always had to make herself look better than me," Elisabet said, ignoring Eva's comment.

"Elisabet, listen to what you're saying. Katarina did not *plan* to die last week, but she was smart enough to have a will made up when she bought Broadale from you. She simply wanted to leave something to her son," Collan said.

"The son she *abandoned*, Collan! You know how selfish she was!"

The three fell silent.

Eva murmured, "Mama, don't speak ill of the dead."

Collan said, "I agree, Eva. Look, Elisabet, the lawyer has to get in touch with Joseph and let him know the details of the will. I would imagine that you, Eva, and Angus can stay on here indefinitely. It's not as if the child is going to leave his school in Sweden and come to Canada to force you out of a house he inherited from a mother he probably doesn't remember very well, if at all. He was only three when she left Sweden and returned to Yarmouth."

Eva heard the back door in the kitchen open and close, signaling her son was home from school. Finally, she would have a bit of reprieve from her mother's incessant negativity.

SEVENTY-EIGHT

Overton, Yarmouth Co., Monday, December 24, 1934

"You know, I'm glad your family is coming here for Christmas tomorrow," Linnea said to Collan, "because Angus can sure use a change of pace from that big old house in town."

She put a final decoration on their Balsam fir tree and stood back admiring the bedecked evergreen.

"That's for sure," Collan said. "And now, my darling girl, here is the big reveal!" She plugged in the electrical string of lights connected to the tree, and it came to life in the picture window of their home.

"I am so happy here, Collan, and so glad to be with you," Linnea said tenderly. "We are very fortunate women."

They embraced, but Linnea sensed a slight reticence from her partner.

"What's troubling you, Collan?"

Collan took Linnea's hand and sat with her on the overstuffed chesterfield.

"I wish I knew more about how my sister's brain was working, Linnea. I mean, Elisabet has always been rather self-centered, and that is something one can put up with in a family member, but my heart is telling me that she might also be a dangerous person."

"Why do you say that?"

"Because on the day that I found Katarina dead at Broadale, you may remember that she had called me just an hour earlier saying that she and Elisabet had gotten into quite a row. Over the years, I'd gotten complacent about how Katarina either exaggerated or even lied about things, but that phone call was different. She actually sounded frightened."

"Like she was physically scared of Elisabet?"

"I think so. And afterwards, Elisabet showed absolutely no regret that the last conversation she had with Katarina was contentious. I'm not saying she was *happy* that she died, but she seemed so detached from it all — and even blamed Katarina for her own clumsiness in falling down the stairs."

Linnea traced her index finger over the top of Collan's hand.

"I'm so sorry for your loss, Collan. Katarina was one of the liveliest people I had ever met, and I miss her being around. She was a bit larger than life, wasn't she?"

Collan smiled sadly at her partner.

"I'm not normally a religious person, Linnea, as you know, but I pray Elisabet never lifts a finger against Eva or Angus. I could never forgive her for that."

#

Christmas morning arrived at the same time as a fog bank descended over Yarmouth County. It would not be a white Christmas, but one that was so densely gray, cars were driving at a snail's pace; locals described the weather condition like 'trying to see through pea soup'.

Angus, at age ten, was beyond believing in Santa Claus, so Christmas Day did not hold a great deal of significance for him. He enjoyed being out of school for a few days, but wasn't happy there was a lack of snow as this reduced his outdoor playing options. Angus McMaster was a serious child in an adult world. He was having regular upsetting dreams after his grand aunt had tragically died.

That day, back in October, Angus and his buddy, David MacNeil, had been playing catch in the expansive backyard at Broadale when David complained of being hungry. Angus remembered 'Aunt' Katarina had made a batch of delicious *Pepparkakor* ginger cookies the day before but had forbidden Angus to eat more than two at a time. He knew there were some left, so he figured he could simply slip into the kitchen via the back door, quietly grab a few of the cookies from the tin, and quickly dash out again.

He knew his plan was only going to work if his grandmother or grand aunt were not in the kitchen.

He was successful in getting into the house undetected, and as he was stuffing several of the biscuits into his pockets, he heard his grandmother and Katarina yelling at each other, but the angry voices were not coming from any room on the main floor. In fact, it sounded like the commotion was coming from the landing at the top of the staircase.

Then, all became silent except for a brief shriek, followed by a series of muffled thudding noises. He stood transfixed in the kitchen. At that moment, the boy decided it was better not be discovered, with or without cookies in his pockets, and he ran out the back door.

#

Eva attributed Angus's unnatural quiet demeanor lately to his having to process another death in the family. She felt he had never quite gotten over his father's unexpected demise three years earlier, and now another adult he had loved was no longer a part of his life.

She was still perturbed about her mother's web of deceit but feared asking certain questions in the event the answers might reveal something she didn't really want to know.

Collan had invited Marc for Christmas Day dinner since he didn't have any relatives in Yarmouth with whom to share the holiday celebration. She, Linnea, and Eva all looked forward to seeing him, knowing he would provide some much-needed levity.

After Elisabet and Eva had exchanged small gifts at Broadale, and Angus was playing with some new toys he had been given, the mother and daughter lingered in the dining room having another cup of tea after breakfast.

"When are you two going to move out?" Elisabet asked Eva, apropos to nothing they had been discussing.

"Move out? Move out of Broadale? I haven't given it much thought, Mama, since we haven't heard from Katarina's ex-husband yet about what they might do with the house."

Elisabet placed her cup carefully on its saucer and looked directly at her daughter.

"It's likely he will put Broadale up for sale. Why would an Italian and his son who don't even speak English want to come to this hellhole?"

"Mama, don't say that. You've always loved Yarmouth. It's a beautiful part of Canada, and you can't presume to know what Joseph is thinking," Eva said.

"Will you buy it if he puts it up for sale?" her mother asked.

"Gosh, well, as I said, I haven't thought of this at all, Mama," Eva replied, "and if he does want to sell it, it's likely I can't afford it."

"Do you mean to sit here and tell me that you didn't get a lot of money from your husband's — my former husband's — life insurance?"

Eva stiffened against the back of her chair.

"There was some money, yes, which will help provide for Angus's future now that he doesn't have a father," Eva said, "but honestly, I hadn't thought of buying real estate with the money left to us."

"I deserve half of that money," Elisabet stated.

"Mama," Eva started, "I'll do all in my power to see that you never want for food and shelter, but you can't seriously expect me to give you half of the money allotted for my son's, and my, future."

Elisabet took a deep breath, as if she were about to dive underwater and needed enough oxygen to safely survive the ordeal.

"This discussion is not yet over," she said, getting up quickly from her seat at the dining table, and left the room.

Eva took her own deep breath and sighed.

An hour later, after washing and drying the breakfast dishes, Eva tapped on the door to her mother's bedroom.

"Mama, don't forget Collan wants us at her house around three since the Christmas dinner will be earlier this year," Eva said.

"I'm not feeling well. I'm not going," Elisabet responded from the other side of the door.

Eva briefly thought of trying to persuade her mother to attend the dinner, and then re-considered.

"I'm sorry to hear that. I'll check on you when we get home this evening. Merry Christmas, Mama," Eva said.

The response was dead silence.

SEVENTY-NINE

Yarmouth, Friday, March 15, 1935

During the first three months of 1935, the residents of the Yarmouth area quickly tired of coping with the extremes of the weather. The daily temperature did not exceed nineteen degrees Fahrenheit except for the week of March 15th when it jumped to between thirty-three and thirty-four degrees. But it was a brutal time: everything that was expected to freeze stayed frozen. There were fishing vessels trapped in ice all over the province, and more than an average number of people were being treated for frostbite in the Yarmouth Hospital.

Eva couldn't help but compare Broadale to a big, cold barn during this time. Fortunately, the house was equipped with a coal-burning furnace. It was located in the basement near the outside southern wall so that coal could be fed directly through a window to a storage bin, but even that convenience did not compensate for the inadequacy of the furnace to heat the big house.

Angus liked watching the coal delivery man when he arrived. He paid close attention to how the man pulled out the chute, secured it to his truck with adequate supports, and then carefully pushed it into the basement window. The flow of coal from the truck into the basement always made Angus laugh, which was a rare emotion to see coming from the boy that winter.

There was one grate in the floor directly above the furnace which provided heat to the main living area, and another on the second floor to capture the rising heat. But in a house the size of Broadale, the high-ceilinged hallways and large rooms, including the dining room and ballroom, were cold and drafty in winter. The family closed the door to any room they weren't using to try and conserve the heat.

Elisabet announced she would be moving her bedroom into the study on the main floor, and promptly hired two local men to remove the polar bear rug and take her bed and dresser downstairs. Eva wasn't sure if she was having difficulty climbing the stairs to the second floor, or if she simply found the upstairs too cold. Whatever the reason, Eva didn't question her reasoning as the two women kept their conversations to a minimum these days.

Eva asked for additional hours at the newspaper office, which she was given, but she still always managed to pick up Angus from school in inclement weather. She was particularly concerned about him being home alone because he told her on more than one occasion that his Grammy was still acting "weird".

After Katarina's death, Eva took on the responsibility of paying the bills for Broadale, and she did so willingly. She had long chats with Marc about how difficult it was to do all the chores for the big house especially during these harsh winter months, but she tried not to complain too often.

Now that Angus was eleven, she enlisted his help whenever it was appropriate. She wanted him to know how to shovel coal from the big bin into a bucket so he could pass it to her, and in turn she would feed the furnace. He was too young to light the fire, she felt, or to stoke the hard fuel, but he was a strong boy and needed to learn how to do certain important household chores.

Then there was the additional job of banking the furnace at night which she had to do each evening before going to bed. She would close the vents, limiting the amount of air available for combustion, and then she cover the burning coal with a layer of new coal.

Angus also watched his mother sift the coal to salvage any that was unburned and then she would place the burnt ashes into containers or bags. The bagged ashes then went to the trash, while ashes in containers would be saved to cover the outdoor steps when they were slippery from the snow and ice. Eva thought that her son would be able to help with this task next winter.

Marc offered to ask one of the maintenance men working at the Inn to help her out, but Eva felt she had to do the work. The uncertainty of her part-time job, and the modest amount of money left from Seamus's life insurance did not allow her to think of hiring any outside help.

#

"Mama, I'm leaving for work now, and I'll drive Angus to school," Eva called toward the partially open door to the study where her mother had retreated after breakfast. "He's outside now brushing the snow off the car. Do you need anything?"

"All right," Elisabet responded. "Goodbye."

Eva shrugged her shoulders and left the house via the kitchen door.

Elisabet looked around her bed sitting room, but in her mind, she was in the small apartment she had shared with Nigel in Boston. She was unhappy that as usual Nigel was not there and that maybe he had taken the baby to the shop downstairs.

Fine. I'll go to the Opera House, and maybe that lovely singer Mr. Measan will be there. At least he pays attention to me and always compliments me on the frocks I wear.

She went to her closet, and ignoring the dresses on hangers, pulled out a steamer trunk which she had used when she returned to Yarmouth in 1914. She was losing touch with place and time, but she knew her best frocks had been put into this trunk. With her mind convinced it was twenty years earlier, she pulled out a white tea dress with puffy sleeves, a narrow waist and full, flared skirt.

This is perfect to wear today. I'm glad I have a plan because otherwise I will be so bored here in this miserable apartment. On days like this, I miss my parents in Yarmouth.

Elisabet Burcharth-Carroll-McMaster checked her makeup in the bathroom mirror before leaving Broadale through the front door. She looked quite striking in her summer outfit, the white dress blending with snow-covered steps and driveway.

She was happy she remembered to take a parasol with her because the sun could get very intense here in Boston and she did not want her face to get burned. The parasol was also handy to use as a cane so she could steady herself on the slippery steps.

#

About a half an hour later, at Central School, Miss Remington was teaching her Grade 5 class about composition writing when she noticed Angus McMaster intently gazing out of one of the classroom windows.

He seemed to be transfixed by something as the young teacher approached him.

"Angus, what's so interesting out there in the snow that you can't pay attention to what I'm teaching?"

"Miss, I think my Grammy is outside, and she looks like she's lost," he replied.

The teacher looked out the window to see an older woman in the schoolyard dressed in Edwardian-style summer clothing. She was staring off into space across the street, and then turned her body in the opposite direction. She slipped and fell to the snow-covered ground.

"Oh my God," Miss Remington said, dashing towards the door of the classroom. "Children, remain at your desks and continue writing your stories. I'll be right back."

#

Angus was able to identify his grandmother, and Elisabet was admitted to Yarmouth Hospital suffering from exposure and extreme confusion. Eva was notified, and she rushed to check on her mother's condition.

EIGHTY

Yarmouth, Monday, April 1, 1935

"Aunt Collan, I'm afraid of leaving Mama alone now," Eva said over the telephone. "I mean, she's never had a spell like that, and she doesn't even remember it happening!"

"Linnea and I can give you a hand, Eva; don't worry. But I know how obstinate your mother is, and she wouldn't want you babysitting her at Broadale all the time, anyway. Really, dear, you can't quit your job at the newspaper now that you're getting many more interesting assignments," Collan said.

"I'd be very grateful, Aunt Collan," Eva said. "She hasn't been too bad this past week. Thank heavens she didn't get frostbite that day. It was quite mild out with that warm front that moved in briefly two weeks ago. The doctor said that if the temperature had been below freezing, she *would* surely have had frostbite because she'd been out wandering around in summer clothing for about forty minutes."

"When should I come over? I have an appointment at the bank tomorrow at nine a.m., so I could be there by ten," Collan said.

"That sounds wonderful, thanks. I leave here with Angus at eight forty-five. Mama's been sleeping later since that episode in the snow, and she'll only be alone for a little over an hour until you arrive at ten."

"Remember to keep the back door unlocked," Collan said.

"Yes, I will, for sure. Thanks again, Aunt Collan."

They ended their conversation, leaving Collan worried about her older sister who was only fifty-seven years old. She wondered if many people became senile at that age. She regretted not knowing of any health concerns she and her sisters might have inherited from their birth parents.

Sometimes, Collan had grim thoughts that one of them would end up psychopathic like their father — or equally as bad, flat out insane.

#

The following morning Elisabet awoke just after nine, and felt her surroundings were eerily quiet. She wondered if it was some kind of holiday because there were no street noises to be heard, and Boylston Street was always busy.

She put on a dressing gown and slippers, left her bed sitting room, and walked down the hall to the very chilly and damp ballroom, instinctively knowing there would be windows there offering a view of the street.

She opened one panel of the heavy curtains and peered out, rather surprised at the lack of horse-drawn carriages, but pleased to see some pedestrians on the sidewalks.

I'm late doing the laundry and I have to wash my undergarments. I might as well wash Nigel's at the same time.

She walked back to her room, picked up the clothing she wanted to wash, and took it into the kitchen. She ran the water into a basin and scrubbed the clothing with a bar of Sunlight soap. After rinsing the items and wringing them out to the best of her strength, she descended the stairs into the basement so she could hang the garments to dry on a clothesline that Nigel had installed for her.

Wanting some fresh air from the outside to help dry her clothing, she opened one of the basement windows on the east side of the building.

As she was coming up the basement stairs to the kitchen, she heard a knock on the back door. She opened it, looked directly into the woman's face, and scowled.

"Mother, what are you doing here?"

Collan hesitated, and a wave of alarm washed over her.

"Elisabet, it's me, Collan, your sister," she smiled, and attempted to take one of Elisabet's hands in hers.

Drawing back from her, Elisabet was stone faced. The circuits in her brain were beginning to slowly connect.

"Oh, hello, Collan," she said. "How are you today? How is the weather outside?"

Collan entered the kitchen, closing the door behind her. She sensed her sister had no idea who had come to visit. She was simply going through automatic pleasantries and repeating her name because

Collan had introduced herself. She wondered how long it might take Elisabet to come out of her confused state.

"I think April may be coming in like a lamb," Collan said, "since March was such a lion. Gosh, I can never remember how that saying goes." She chuckled.

Elisabet smiled, copying Collan's light banter.

"You're in your dressing gown. Have you had breakfast yet?" Collan asked.

The question acted like a light switch in Elisabet's head, and she was brought into the present. She glanced down to see what she was wearing.

"Collan! Good to see you. I haven't had breakfast yet. Do you want to join me? Where is Linnea?"

"Linnea is at our home in Overton, Elisabet. How are you today?"

"I'm fine, I suppose. I'm happy that I haven't had the flu or a cold all winter. You know, Collan, I've been thinking of putting Broadale up for sale this year. It's really too big for just one person."

Collan wrestled with how to comment on this illusion.

"Elisabet, you must have forgotten that Broadale is now owned by Katarina's son in Sweden. You don't own it any longer," Collan said gently.

Elisabet looked at her sister as if she had lost her mind, and her anger rose as she spoke.

"Don't be ridiculous, Collan. Why would Katarina's son own my house?"

Collan again tried to take her sister's hand in her own.

"It must have slipped your mind, Elisabet. Katarina died last fall. She owned Broadale and left it to her son in her will."

"You're mistaken, Collan. I've never heard anything more ridiculous in my life. Katarina isn't dead! She lives here now and drives me batty most of the time with her delusions of being someone famous."

Collan had recently read in one of the Boston papers about the discovery of an illness called Alzheimer's Disease. The name was first used in medical circles in 1910, but was still not widely known twenty-five years later. Elisabet's behavior certainly seemed to indicate that there was something seriously wrong with her ability to remember and think coherently. She wondered if her sister were being affected by this malady and instinctively knew it would be best to go along with whatever she was saying so as not to upset her.

"Oh yes, silly me," Collan said. "Never mind what I said. I haven't had a good strong cup of coffee yet to wake me up. Why don't we fix something for breakfast then, Elisabet?"

"All right, yes, stay for breakfast, Collan. I'm going to go wash my face, get dressed and put a little lipstick on. Do you know where everything is?"

Collan waved her sister away, saying, "Of course I do. I'll see you in a few minutes."

#

Collan remained at Broadale for the remainder of the day until Eva returned with Angus after school. The two sisters had prepared dinner for the evening, and Collan set aside two takeaway plates for her and Linnea. Before leaving, she asked Eva to join her in the kitchen, and told Elisabet that she'd be back in a moment using the excuse that Eva was giving her a recipe.

"Her confusion comes and goes, Eva. We can be talking in the present for a full half an hour, and then it will be like a light dimming; and then she looks very confused and upset," Collan informed her niece. "I found that if I kept her mind on pleasant things, her mood visibly improved. We even played some old Victrola records from when she was your age."

"I've noticed that, too. I'm going to stop correcting her when she says things that are clearly wrong because she just gets angry with me," Eva said. "I must admit, it's hard not to tell her what's true and real; and even harder to have to agree with every crazy thing she says."

"I know. Try not to worry. I'll be back around nine thirty tomorrow morning with Linnea. I'll leave her here with your mother while I do the grocery shopping," Collan said.

"You are a lifesaver, Aunt Collan!"

EIGHTY-ONE

Yarmouth, Wednesday, April 3, 1935

At nine o'clock the coal truck drove to the back of Broadale and stopped at the basement window closest to the furnace, and the driver began his monthly delivery. Every homeowner knew that coal delivery day was not the time to be in the basement as coal dust settled on everything, blackening surfaces, and making breathing difficult.

Elisabet was awakened by the noise coming from the truck and the coal landing in the large bin in the basement. She rose from the bed in a near panic; the noise wasn't familiar to her that morning.

A story that Seamus had told her long ago about an errant military shell landing on top of a Halifax residential home in March 1915 became her reality. She was convinced the Germans were now invading Nova Scotia, and they were digging into the basement of her home.

They want to tunnel their way into Broadale. Dear God in heaven, I know I have never prayed to you, but please stop them now; stop them from invading my home. My parents are elderly, and my husband is a doctor, working at the hospital. I am all alone. Please take pity on me, dear God.

One half hour later, after calling out her name numerous times, Collan and Linnea found a shaking and near hysterical Elisabet crouched on the floor behind the closed door of her bed sitting room closet.

#

Collan calmed Elisabet and managed to get her back into bed, reassuring her that the Germans had left, because they had found a better place to build a tunnel.

"Listen, Elisabet — there's no more noise; they've gone. Isn't that a good thing?"

Her sister was visibly less upset and closed her eyes.

Linnea was in the kitchen making toast and jam, and a hot cup of tea to serve to Elisabet. Collan telephoned Eva. The women knew in their hearts that Elisabet now required medical attention. Her behavior was getting more and more extreme and beyond their ability to cope with it.

EIGHTY-TWO

Yarmouth, Thursday, April 4, 1935

Eva's morning ritual was to awaken Angus in his room after she had washed and dressed, and be first in the kitchen to make breakfast, ensuring her mother could help herself to a serving of the same after she had awakened at a later time.

When Eva came downstairs and saw the lights on in the kitchen, her guard was up. She approached the room tentatively and was somewhat relieved to see Elisabet in regular day wear, putting a kettle of water on the stove to boil.

"Good morning, Mama," she said, "you're looking well today. Are you feeling better?"

"Why shouldn't I be well, Eva? I'm fine, except for one thing."

It was at that instant that Eva noticed her mother's underwear, dry but covered in coal dust, laid out on the kitchen table like exhibits in a museum about to be catalogued and then displayed.

Elisabet looked triumphantly at her daughter.

"You don't think I can't see how you're trying to make life more difficult for me in my own home, do you? Look at my clothing. It's filthy. You ordered a delivery of coal purposely knowing I had washed my undergarments, didn't you?"

"Mama, the coal comes on the third day of each month, first thing in the morning. You have been living here long enough to know that! Did you forget? You were quite upset by the noise yesterday," Eva replied, as diplomatically as she could. "Maybe you hand washed your clothes the day before yesterday and left them hanging in the basement, so they got covered in coal dust from yesterday's delivery."

"I did no such thing! You and Katarina are trying to drive me crazy!"

Realizing she couldn't win in a losing battle, Eva's mind raced to find a topic that would get her mother's mind in a different place.

"You know, Mama, you've never told me much about your volunteer work at the Boston Opera House years ago. Was it fun? You must have met some interesting people..." Eva prompted.

Her words did have the desired effect on Elisabet who proceeded to tell her details about the opera company and the building itself.

"And Alfred was an amazing lover," Elisabet said, "I'll never forget him."

Hearing her mother's admission, Eva dropped one of the eggs she was about to put into a pot of boiling water on the stove.

So, she did have an affair with Mr. Measan. Her mind is allowing her to divulge this to me; she doesn't remember Seamus and I stayed with him and his family in Austria in 1923. Or does she remember?

As Eva cleaned the shattered egg off the floor, Elisabet continued reminiscing.

"He was right there when I needed him. I had this sourpuss of an English husband, you know, who never left the stupid store he owned. All he did was work. Alfred and I had some wonderful, very amorous times in Boston. I distinctly remember a party in Cambridge at the home of one of the Harvard music professors, and —"

Eva was sobbing. Her heart was breaking for her deceased father and yet she was grateful he wasn't alive to hear about his wife's indiscretion.

"Oh, Mavis, my dear, I didn't mean to upset you. I forgot you Catholics are dead set against any extra-marital dalliances whatsoever, aren't you?"

Eva recovered long enough to pour a cup of tea for Elisabet, and attended to the stove, turning away from her. She heard Angus coming down the front staircase to the main floor and decided to continue to play the charade of being her mother's housekeeper who hadn't worked at Broadale for at least three years.

"Would you like a soft-boiled egg and some toast, Mrs. McMaster? I'll bring it to your bedroom."

I don't know how to do this. I don't know how to do this. I have to telephone Aunt Collan as soon as I get Mama to go and eat in her room. I don't want my son to see her like this anymore.

\#

Linnea opened the front door of her home in Overton, and the postman gave her a familiar looking yellow envelope, a telegram. She brought it into the kitchen and gave it to Collan who had just gotten off the telephone with Eva.

Western Union
PA313 24 NT = FT01X NJ 17 04APR35
Miss Collan Burcharth
Grove Rd Overton Yarmouth Co NS Canada
JOSEPH PAOLO MARGARETA ARRIVING 05 APRIL HALIFAX STOP ARRIVING IN YARMOUTH 06 APRIL VIA TRAIN STOP ACCOMMODATION ARRANGED GRAND HOTEL STOP

Collan sighed as she folded the announcement and put it back in its envelope.

Looking at Linnea, she said, "My sister has gone mad, and we're about to have company. My former brother-in-law, his wife, and son are on their way here from Europe, and they couldn't have chosen to visit at a worse time. It looks like you'll be speaking a lot of your native language in the next few days, my love."

#

After calling her office to ask for the day off to take care of Elisabet, Eva telephoned Dr. Ben Talmage, one of Seamus's friends who had attended their wedding. Talmage, soft spoken and approximately the same age as Eva, was the only psychiatrist serving Yarmouth, Digby, and Shelburne counties, and even though he was a busy specialist, he agreed to see Elisabet at Broadale on his way home that day.

Eva told him over the telephone — once she knew her mother was preoccupied with her sewing — that Elisabet's spells would range from not knowing what year she was in; to periods of paranoia when she thought other people were planning to attack her; to not recognizing the people closest to her.

And, most curious and sad to her, Elisabet's guileless admission in describing a sexual affair she had as a young married woman and mother.

When he arrived at Broadale, Eva introduced Dr. Talmage to Elisabet as a professional friend of her husband since today Elisabet believed she was still married to Seamus, and that he was in Halifax helping victims of the 1917 Explosion.

"Mama, Dr. Talmage treats people who have been having difficulty remembering things, so he was kind enough to drop by today to say hello," Eva said, downplaying the intent of the medical visit.

"It's so nice to meet you, Dr. Talmage. You know, I have been a little forgetful lately, and dear me, maybe a little confused at times! But I am so pleased to have a visit from such a handsome man."

Smiling provocatively at him, and in a quieter tone, she said, "Please excuse my maid, by the way; I have no idea why she calls me 'Mama'!"

The doctor smiled sympathetically and began asking Elisabet a series of questions, to test her short-term memory. He chatted with her casually, drawing out her answers regarding the date and time of the year, exactly where she was currently living, and who held the office of Prime Minister of Canada. Eva watched and listened to her mother fail miserably at the task.

Dr. Talmage told Elisabet he would be back again the following day and gave her a shot of an opium derivative to help her relax and have a long night's sleep.

Standing on the landing of Broadale's front steps, he was about to tell Eva what he thought the best course of treatment for her mother would be when Collan pulled up in her car and approached them. Eva introduced the doctor.

"Thank you so much for seeing my sister today," Collan said.

"You're welcome, Miss Burcharth. Both of you should know that Elisabet is suffering from acute anxiety which comes and goes in waves, as you both have observed, but it's unpredictable. Sadly, this condition does tend to get progressively worse. I don't think at this point, though, that she's a candidate for the asylum in Halifax."

Both Eva and Collan froze at the mention of an asylum. The word suggested permanence and hopelessness.

"After I see her again tomorrow, I should be able to make a more complete diagnosis. At the present time, there are two methods of treatment that can be used for this condition that are known to have a measure of success."

"What are they, Doctor?" Eva asked.

"I think that sleep therapy, also known as prolonged narcosis, may be effective in your mother's case, Eva. I would administer injections that would allow her to sleep for one to two weeks at a time; and perhaps even longer, should her spells gain in frequency and strength."

Collan looked skeptical at this course of treatment and asked about the other option available.

"It's electroconvulsive therapy. The psychiatric community sees this remedy as being quite successful in a number of cases. In layman's terms, the illness is literally shocked out of the patient's brain."

"I'd think that's something that my sister would have to have done in Halifax or Boston, is that right?"

"Yes. I'm hearing wonderful things coming out of the United States this year. There's a new operation called a lobotomy. Hypothetically, if your sister were to be violent and dangerous, Miss Burcharth, this type of surgery would be ideal since it removes the part of the brain that rules emotions and thoughts, and leaves the patient with his or her intelligence intact, feeling serene and anxiety-free!"

"Yes, I'd imagine that to be remarkable, Doctor, but Mama isn't a threat to any of us. Herself, perhaps, but she is not a dangerous woman," Eva said.

She glanced at her aunt, expecting her to nod in agreement, but Collan remained expressionless.

"When I come by tomorrow, I'll bring some information on sleep therapy, and you'll be able to read how we'll keep the patient clean during the prolonged narcosis. Your mother will have to be admitted to the hospital, of course. In between injections, she'll become slightly conscious, which gives the nurses enough time to pick her up to be put on a commode, and to be washed. Naturally, we'll change the bedding when necessary."

Eva understood the gravity of her mother's illness.

"She'll be fed fluids before each injection and at intervals when possible," he concluded.

"My, oh my, there's much to think about," Eva said to the doctor. "Thank you again, and we'll see you tomorrow at the same time?"

"Yes, that's correct. Good evening, ladies," Dr. Talmage replied, as he walked down the steps to his parked car.

Collan placed her hand on Eva's shoulder as they watched the psychiatrist drive away.

"I'm afraid, my dear, that there's yet another issue we have to deal with."

Eva looked worriedly at her aunt.

"The heir to Broadale, his father, and presumably his stepmother, are arriving in Yarmouth the day after tomorrow. You and Angus and your mother might be served with an eviction notice."

EIGHTY-THREE

Yarmouth, Friday, April 5, 1935

Eva greatly reduced her hours at work to be with her mother during the day. She realized that she had to be prepared for any kind of behavior at any time from Elisabet.

After breakfast when they were both sitting in the parlor and Angus had left for school, things seemed relatively normal, at least for the time being.

"You haven't told me yet when you'll give me my share of Seamus's life insurance money," Elisabet said to her daughter.

"Oh, Mama, isn't it enough that you are being taken care of here with your food and accommodation? You don't need money for anything, and if there's something you'd like to buy, I'm happy to get it for you," Eva said.

Elisabet was silent and made a production of opening the morning newspaper.

"Besides , as I told you, the money is intended to help me provide for Angus's future," Eva continued.

"That's your son," Elisabet said, putting the newspaper on her lap.

"And your grandson," Eva smiled, hoping her mother would get into a lighter mood. She was happy that Elisabet seemingly knew what was happening in the present.

Maybe Mama's anxiety is manageable if it just comes and goes in short spurts. I think I could handle that. But this horrible feeling of not knowing when she might go off again...

"Oh, and Mama, you will have another little visitor soon. You'll be seeing Katarina's son again for the first time in thirteen years! He was here with his mother when he was two; remember that? But this time his father, Joseph, will be with him. Joseph has never been to Canada," Eva said.

"I thought Katarina divorced him and abandoned her son," Elisabet said. "Why on earth would they come to visit her now? Where is she, anyway, this morning?"

And we're back to the starting line. If I tell her Katarina died and left the house to Paolo, that will start another round of accusations, and just further the stress for the two of us. It's time to change the subject again.

"I guess you'll have to ask him that question, Mama. Listen, why don't we play a game of Eights? You know, that new card game we learned a couple of years ago?"

"Eva, you can't fool me. You've stolen my husband and now you're stealing every cent I have from under me. You'll probably even cheat at the card game."

Elisabet's malfunctioning brain considered her next line of attack.

"I don't know how you turned into a whore and a thief. Your poor father is probably rolling around in his grave right now. I thought we brought you up to be better than that," Elisabet said, with no obvious venom, but as if she were reciting from a pre-written script. The scene in the room was playing out almost professionally, and Elisabet knew her lines to perfection.

Eva thought she was beyond being shocked by her mother until now.

Years of deferring to her wishes, years of feeling guilty about her relationship with Seamus, years of instinctively knowing that Seamus had not gotten over his love for her mother, and then recently finding out that Elisabet had been cheating on her father pushed Eva to her breaking point.

She saw herself lunging across the parlor at her mother, pushing her to the floor, and then covering her head with a large brocade cushion, and pressing down as hard as she could to extinguish every living breath from her body. She felt her heart beating so strongly she thought it would jump out of her chest.

And that noise! What was that noise? It's loud and repetitive.

Oh my God...someone is tapping the brass knocker on the front door of the house.

Eva rose unsteadily to her feet and walked to the front door as Elisabet calmly picked up the newspaper and started reading the front page.

Marc was at the door and Eva fell into his arms in relief, crying.

"Eva! What's wrong?" Marc asked. "I've tried calling you, but your line has been busy more than once. I was getting worried."

She led him back outside to the landing at the top of the steps.

"Oh, Marc, you're such a sight for sore eyes. You couldn't have arrived at a better time," Eva sobbed. "I'm having a really rough time with my mother's crazy mood swings. She's being mean and horrible, and I know she's sick with some kind of anxiety illness, but there's only so much —"

"Hey, now, take it easy," Marc said. "Is your aunt coming over today?"

"Yes, she should be here soon because Doctor Talmage from the hospital will be returning today, as well."

Eva told him the details of what the psychiatrist had told her and Collan, and the prolonged sleep treatment that seemed inevitable to start at the hospital.

"Oh my gosh, that's quite enough to be dealing with at the best of times, Eva. I'm so sorry you're having this upset," Marc said, pulling her into him for another embrace.

When Eva pulled away from him, grateful for his warmth and empathy, she said, attempting a smile, "And my late aunt's ex-husband is arriving tomorrow with his new wife and his son who now owns Broadale! We may be out of house and home, too!"

"Good God in heaven!"

"I know; it's all nuts, isn't it? Marc, I can't leave Mama alone for any length of time. Heaven only knows what she may do in there. I have to get back in the house," Eva said.

"How about I come in with you until Collan arrives? Do you think your mother will remember meeting me?"

"I guess we'll find out. Thank you for doing this. I could use a break from the madness right now."

When Eva and Marc entered the house and walked into the parlor, Eva hoped her mother would not remember Marc and she could re-introduce him and steer them into talking about any number of non-family and non-controversial subjects.

Instead, Elisabet took one look at Marc and said, "What's he doing here? Aren't you that Syrian who wants to sleep with my daughter?"

She haughtily stood up from her seat, and taking the newspaper with her, left the room for her own bed sitting room.

"Gosh! She thinks she knows me that well!" Marc whispered to Eva, providing her with a needed but smothered giggle. "Let me take you out for dinner after your mother is settled in the hospital, okay? You need a relaxing night out, Eva."

EIGHTY-FOUR

Yarmouth, Saturday, April 6, 1935

Eva awoke with a feeling of hope and peacefulness that she had not experienced in an awfully long while.

She was still amazed that admitting Mama to the hospital the day before had been free of any drama as Elisabet believed she was going to a hotel for a rest. Collan paid for a private room for her sister, and the transition had been flawless.

"Now you be good, Housekeeper," Elisabet had said to Eva when she got into Dr. Talmage's car. Eva ignored the slight but noticed that her mother truly didn't know her from Mavis and didn't even know Mavis's name anymore. "I expect my house to be perfectly spotless when I get back from the resort. And maybe that colored cook can prepare some of my favorite dishes, too. I won't be away for very long."

Both Eva and Collan were reassured by Dr. Talmage that Elisabet was in safe hands and would be monitored closely for the initial twelve days of treatment.

"Ladies, remember that I've diagnosed Elisabet with psychoneurosis, or anxiety. I don't believe she has melancholia, schizophrenia or is manic. Nor do I believe she has paraphrenia, even though your mother is getting older. So, I hope the treatments will give her some relief from the distress she's been feeling lately."

While Angus was at school, Eva prepared for her dinner guests that evening. Collan offered to pick up Joseph, his wife, and his son at the train station, and get them settled at the Grand Hotel. After a brief rest, they would all arrive at Broadale together.

#

Champlain was the name of an adult tabby cat who lived in Eva's neighborhood. An overweight feline, he was true to his moniker and explored every inch of his available territory. When he saw a partially opened basement window at Broadale, he squeezed himself into the eight-inch wide space , perched for a moment on the inside ledge, and then jumped down onto the cement floor.

Once inside, Champlain was curious to know what he might find in the many nooks and crannies. He managed to stick his head into some very cramped spaces, instinctively hunting for mice or any other mammals smaller than himself. He jumped up on a worktable adjacent to the opened window and knocked over a kerosene lantern placed there to be used when there was no electrical light available.

The lantern fell onto a stack of old newspapers. Its glass chimney shattered, and the liquid contents of the glass receptacle began to spill onto the newsprint.

Champlain was startled and quickly jumped up from the table to the window ledge, wiggled his way out of the narrow opening, and returned to his adventures in the outdoors.

#

"My, your command of English is enviably flawless, Margareta," Linnea commented in Swedish to Joseph's second wife as the newly arrived visitors sat down to dinner at Broadale.

Paolo, a tall boy of fifteen, still with the striking red hair that Katarina had been so pleased to see he had as a baby, had grown into a spoiled young man. After she had left for Canada twelve years earlier, Joseph had tried to compensate Paolo for the divorce by giving him whatever he desired. Now he had inherited a seven-bedroom home in southwestern Nova Scotia to add to his arsenal of toys.

"But what about *my* English, Linnea," Paolo said proudly. "I have been studying it since I was a young lad, and now I am almost a man."

"You do very well at it, too, Paolo," Linnea admitted.

"Joseph, I know you and Katarina spoke English a great deal at home in Gothenburg, so perhaps for Eva's benefit, we can all speak English during dinner tonight," Collan suggested.

"That is perfectly fine with me," Joseph said, "and I know my wife and son feel the same. By the way, Eva, it is most kind of you to have us for dinner on such short notice."

"You're welcome, Joseph, and it's my pleasure. As my aunt and Linnea will attest, the past few days have been a little more than hectic, but my mother is now resting comfortably in the hospital."

"Yes, we were sorry to hear she was ill," Margareta said, tossing her wavy auburn hair behind her. "Do you think this is the time to talk about Paolo's inheritance of this house?"

A little taken aback, Eva managed a smile.

Paolo said, "Of course I do not remember being here when I was only two years old. Maybe I cried too much and that is why my mother abandoned us!"

He chuckled, but no one joined in.

"It's quite a large place and would be perfect for me and my mates as a summer vacation home, don't you think, Father?"

Collan glanced at Eva, and looking at Paolo, said, "You're quite a risk taker, young man! You can clearly see how much work goes into the upkeep of a home the size of Broadale. But that would certainly keep you and your friends busy all next summer! In fact, the house has been needing a decent paint job for a few years now."

"Son, you can't presume your friends will be able to come all the way to Canada next summer. Even I cannot leave my job for more than two weeks…", Joseph said.

"Now, Joseph, we haven't even discussed this amongst ourselves, but there is a chance I could accompany Paolo to Nova Scotia next year," Margareta said.

Eva was beginning to feel that the ground was being swept from under her feet. Things were happening so fast, and it appeared there was no regard given to her living situation, and that of Angus and her mother. She looked directly at Paolo who was only four years older than her own son.

"Excuse me a moment, but not only did your mother's — and my aunt's — death come as a sad shock to all of us, but this home has been in my family for the past fifteen years. While I don't argue the fact that your mother had every right to leave the house to you, Paolo, she certainly did not expect to die when she did. This was her home, too. So, I hope you'll all respect what I've just said, and at the very least let me know when my son and I are expected to move out, or if we'll be allowed to rent the house indefinitely," Eva said.

Paolo seemed at a loss for words, so his father spoke for him.

"We have no intention of putting you and your son out on the street, Eva, but before we leave Yarmouth in the next couple of weeks, I will tell you what decision my family has reached about the property. Will that be satisfactory to you?"

"Yes, Joseph. Thank you," Eva said. "Now, shall we retire to the parlor for a glass of port and maybe some lemonade for the boys?"

"I want to go back to the hotel now, Father," Paolo said, with a definite edge in his voice.

Joseph considered his son's wish.

"All right, Paolo," Joseph said, and then looked at Eva apologetically. "Thank you again for a lovely evening, but we are a bit tired from our journey. I'm sure you understand."

"Oh yes, we do understand, Joseph," Collan remarked. "It is exhausting enough to sail across the Atlantic, but then having to take a train for another two hundred miles to reach Yarmouth is terribly tiresome." She shook her head in resignation.

#

Later, after the guests had left, and Angus had gone to bed, Collan, Eva and Linnea sat in the parlor with their glasses of port, grateful for the time the three could spend in relative peace.

"I saw right through you, Aunt Collan! You were brilliant, painting a picture for Paolo of him having to do a lot of work on the property next summer — and then reminding them all what a long trip it is from Sweden to get here," Eva grinned.

"Skål!" Linnea said, lifting her glass for the other women to toast with her.

"Skål!" Eva and Collan repeated, confirming their solidarity on the subject.

"Seriously, though, I wonder what they'll decide to do with Broadale. If they choose to move in next year, I'll sell every darn piece of furniture, every lamp and knickknack before they do! The will said nothing about a *furnished* house, did it, Aunt Collan?"

"No, indeed it didn't, Eva, and while I'm not a lawyer, if I had seen 'house and contents thereof' in the will, I wouldn't have been very pleased with my late sister's judgment."

"You know, it's so sad that your mother has no idea what is going on, Eva, but I suspect this ordeal would be even worse if she did," Linnea said.

Collan took Linnea's hand and smiled warmly at her understanding of the situation.

"That is true, Linnea. Sometimes I think that when a mind tends to live in the past, it shows 'Where ignorance is bliss, 'tis folly to be wise'," Eva said. "That's by the poet Thomas Gray from 1742, and for some reason, the quotation and the date have stuck in my mind since memorizing it when I was in my last year of school."

Collan nodded and said, "If Elisabet were lucky enough to be thinking clearly, knowing these people might move into Broadale would probably push her into the sad state she's in right now anyway."

EIGHTY-FIVE

Yarmouth, Sunday, April 7, 1935

It had been four years since Seamus's sudden death at the Grand Hotel, so it was Eva who suggested she and Marc dine there when he asked her where she would like to go for an evening out. She felt she was now in a different frame of mind — a much more positive one — so she dropped Angus off at Collan and Linnea's home for dinner and joined Marc in the dining room at the hotel shortly thereafter.

"The Grand" as locals called the establishment, still retained much of its Victorian, turn-of-the-century charm forty-one years after its opening.

The dining room was not overly formal. The chairs were Duncan Phyfe style, decorative yet functional, and not suited for an overly long repast, but were comfortable enough. The hardwood floor glistened, and two large mirrored buffets were placed against one wall. The dining tables were set for four or six people, seating about sixty in total. The place settings on the handsome tables invited family gatherings and visiting business clientele to enjoy the ambience, and the dozen electrified chandeliers imbued the room with a soft warmth during dinner service.

Marc pulled a chair out for Eva to be seated, and she admired how crisp and clean the starched tablecloths and napkins were.

She noticed Joseph, Margareta and Paolo seated on the other side of the room, so she smiled and waved at them, but made no attempt to approach.

They can say hello to us on their way out; it looks like they're on their dessert course. I don't owe them anything else now, and it's so nice not to have to cook for anybody tonight!

She thanked Marc for holding out the chair for her.

"It's hard to believe I've been in Yarmouth for four years," Marc said after they had ordered their main courses of Digby scallops au gratin and mashed potatoes.

"Really? Has it been that long? So much has happened since you arrived, Marc, and you've certainly put your personal stamp on Lakeside Inn. They're lucky to have you here!"

Marc looked a little embarrassed for a moment, but then brightened.

"And opportunities are awaiting me, Eva. I've been offered a job at The Nova Scotian Hotel in Halifax. From what I can tell, the Personnel Director from that hotel stayed at Lakeside Inn for a weekend this past winter, unbeknownst to me. I guess he liked what I've done with the management of the dining room and the menu there. The offer is called a 'lateral job move', but it's a much bigger hotel, and the salary is better! And, as you know, my parents are there in the city."

Eva found it hard to contain her surprise at the news.

The whirlwind hasn't stopped moving yet. What next could happen?

"Oh, Marc, I'm incredibly happy for you, but sad you'll be leaving! We've done so much together in the last few years; I'm sure tongues were wagging that Eva McMaster was spinning a web for the handsome hotel manager at Lakeside Inn!"

"Aw, let them all talk, Eva," Marc grinned, "I've had worse things said about me before, that's for sure."

"I shall miss you, my friend," Eva said, taking his hand for a long moment.

Marc felt a lump in his throat and cleared it.

"It just means that you and Angus will have to come and visit me regularly and meet my Lebanese family. I know my mother would love to teach you how to make kibbeh, kafta, and tabbouleh, which just happen to be my three favorite dishes."

"Hmmm…I think I can manage that, and summer vacation for Angus is just two months away. I could even visit *The Halifax Herald*'s offices and offer to be their Yarmouth correspondent! What do you think, Mr. Hotelier?"

"I think they would hire any journalist in a heartbeat who can claim she has met and already interviewed Amelia Earhart, that's what I think!"

#

Charles "Chas" Whitman, the delinquent brother of Elisabet's former housekeeper, Mavis, had been in and out of jail for various minor offenses since the night he worked the beverage table at the party thrown in honour of Katarina and Collan in 1922.

I remember Mavis telling me back then that the daughter of the old bat who hired me had married her mother's second husband. Christ, that weird family thought they was too hoity-toity for words, not wanting anyone in town to know about it. What a joke. The daughter was nothing more than a slut like all them rich bitches.

He had been released from the town jail on Main Street just a week before — yet again — but this time, he was flat, busted broke.

He stood across the street from Broadale, smoking a cigarette and looking carefully at all the doors and windows of the large home.

I dunno, but the place looks pretty easy to break into. I watched the old bat leave the house a couple of days ago with a couple of suitcases. Tonight, the daughter took her kid out more than an hour ago. I don't want no one home when I get in there. It's gettin' dark, but that basement window just needs a push, it looks like, and I'll be in.

Okay, so I remember where the ballroom is, and the doctor's study was right next door to it. Heard the doc dropped dead a few years ago, so he ain't around. That's what he gets for diddlin' with the mother and the daughter at the same time. They done wore him out!

There's gotta be some cash in that big desk of his. I heard these Europeen types don't like banks, so they gotta keep their cash at home, right? Shit, and I remember where the jerk said he kept his stash of rum and gin in the basement. Maybe I can score some of that good stuff, too. I can friggin' well do this job in fifteen minutes, tops.

#

Eva and Marc had finished their entrées and the table was being cleared when Joseph, his wife, and son stopped to greet them. Marc stood up, and Eva remained seated.

"There you are! Hello, Joseph. This is my friend Marc Shehab. Marc, this is Joseph Carminati and his wife Margareta, and their son Paolo. They're visiting the Yarmouth area for a couple of weeks," Eva said.

Hands were shaken, and Paolo looked like he wanted to bolt from the room.

"I'm going upstairs, Father. A pleasure meeting you," he said to Marc, not meaning a word , and quickly left.

Eva acquiesced to her own good manners and invited the couple to sit at their table and chat as she and Marc awaited dessert.

"Thank you, we will," Margareta said with a slight lilt in her accented English.

"How have you been enjoying Yarmouth so far?" Marc asked them, quickly morphing into his hospitality persona. "Maybe we can give you some tips on where to sight-see?"

"That would be nice. We find the area pleasant enough, yes, but a little on the cool side," Margareta said. "We drove to Cap du Forchu today to see the light station."

"It felt like we were at the tip of Canada," Joseph added. "A scenic spot, as you know. And nothing like my native Napoli!"

The Italian businessman, Margareta, and Marc chatted about their homelands, and Eva felt a little left out of the conversation, but was just as relieved not to have to play hostess that evening. She nodded and smiled throughout their talk and felt content for the time being. Surely this family would not take Broadale away from them, at least not immediately. If they would just let her rent the house until she found a smaller home for herself and Angus, and possibly Mama, she would be grateful.

#

Chas Whitman continued to keep a close eye on the property. As darkness fell, he walked across the street to the home, pushed in the hinged basement window he had noticed was ajar, and squeezed his relatively small frame inside. He slid over the ledge and onto the basement floor.

He remembered where the staircase to the upstairs was located. Lighting the first of several matches to find his way, he climbed the stairs and entered the kitchen. He stopped and listened for any activity, but all was quiet except for a grandfather clock in the main hallway signaling the time. The sound helped guide him to the study. The last remaining slivers of twilight allowed him to recognize large shapes, so he avoided bumping into the furniture.

Once inside the study, he thought he had chosen the wrong room. Lighting another couple of matches, he couldn't see the biggest fixture he remembered: the polar bear rug. Turning to his right, he could discern a double-sized bed.

Damn! Where the hell is the doc's desk that was here? Am I in the wrong goddam room?

Lighting another match, he saw a rectangular piece of furniture in the far corner. Seamus's mahogany desk had been moved up against one wall instead of it being the centerpiece in the room.

He walked quickly towards it and started rifling through the drawers, looking for anything of value. He noticed a lone pewter candlestick on the top of the desk with a taper in it, and eagerly lit the candle so he could better see the interiors of the drawers.

Papers, papers, papers. Notebooks. Fountain pens, bottles of ink, a dish of paper clips, pencils...where was the damn money?

The last and deepest drawer provided his only income from the burglary: a coffee tin full of change — pennies, nickels, dimes, and quarters — that Elisabet and Eva had been contributing to for over a year.

He knew his time was getting short, and he wanted to grab at least one bottle of rum from the doc's stash in the basement, so he took the lit candle and the coffee tin with him, and gingerly moved his way through the house and down the stairs into the basement.

Once there, he found the worktable that he remembered had a large wooden box underneath containing the bottles of liquor from the Prohibition years. He convinced himself that this family would only have used the rum and gin for big parties, and since booze was legal again, there would most likely be some of the hooch left behind. He placed the candle on the end of the table, directly above where the box was situated.

Chas was having a difficult time opening the lid of the box, due to years of neglect and coal dust caking the edges of the lid. He tugged at it, and then crouched down to give it a stronger pull, banging his shoulder on the edge of the table in the process.

The candle fell over onto the kerosene-soaked newspapers, causing a small explosion that immediately lit the pile. Chas was startled , and as he fell backwards, he lost his footing, and hit his head on the concrete floor, and lost consciousness.

Flames spread rapidly throughout the basement, and soon the majestic wooden home, only seventy-four years old in 1935, was burning out of control.

#

The Yarmouth Fire Department had been serving the town well since 1867. It owned a '33 Chev Bickle fire engine, which had the capacity to pump 900 gallons of water per minute from a fire hydrant. This was still not enough waterpower for the volunteer firefighters to contain the huge blaze.

Eva was just about to get into her car at The Grand to pick up Angus from Collan's home when the fire engine went speeding past her on Main Street and turned onto Parade Street.

I hope the fire isn't a serious one, she thought, as she noticed a steady stream of other cars begin to turn onto the same street.

Oh, my goodness. What if it's the old Yarmouth Academy where I went to school, or Angus's Central School?

She got into her car and drove to Overton. When she arrived, Collan, Linnea and Angus came rushing out of the house.

Collan embraced her niece.

"Oh, thank God you didn't go home first," Collan said with tears in her eyes. Angus threw his arms around his mother's waist.

"What? What's the matter?" Eva questioned, frantically looking at them.

"Broadale is on fire, Eva, I'm so sorry," Collan managed to say. "I just received a telephone call from the Chief of Police asking if I knew where you, Elisabet and Angus were. They had immediately phoned Broadale when neighbours reported seeing flames in the basement. They were frightened one or more of our family were in the house when the fire broke out."

"I have to sit down. Oh my God. I can't believe this is happening! Angus, take your Mama's hand," she said as the four hurried back into Collan's home.

EIGHTY-SIX

Yarmouth, Monday and Tuesday, April 8 - 9, 1935

Collan and Eva stared at the smoldering embers, remnants of what was once one of Yarmouth's finest Victorian residences. Eva was wearing the same clothing she had worn the evening before. None of her personal belongings could be salvaged from the rubble.

She didn't weep over the loss of the house; she was pragmatic and grateful that she, Angus and Elisabet weren't at home when the fire occurred. So far, the Fire Department had not determined the cause of the inferno, but its ferocity had destroyed the family's home and all of their possessions.

She appreciated that Collan had insisted she and Angus stay with her and Linnea in Overton for the foreseeable future. Until Eva could go shopping, Linnea offered to loan her some clothing as they were about the same size.

And thankfully, the family who lived next door to Collan had a son a year older than Angus, and the mother had already dropped off some clothing for him.

In less than twenty-four hours, Eva had gone from thinking she might have to move out of Broadale, to now not having a choice in the matter.

"Aunt Collan, could you please call Joseph at The Grand for me, and tell him what has happened? My goodness, they've come all this way and now their son has only inherited a piece of land. I don't even know if Mama or Katarina had kept up payments on house insurance. I've never come across any documents."

"Of course, I'll call, Eva. Come on, let's drive back to Overton. There isn't anything you want to search for, is there?"

Eva sighed.

"No, I don't think so. It's awfully sad to see this grand place reduced to ash, but we're alive. I'm glad Mama may never know or understand what has happened to her beloved Broadale."

#

When Joseph was informed of the news about Broadale's destruction, he was secretly pleased. This would mean he and Paolo would not be arguing about his son's future visits to Nova Scotia. There was now no reason to spend the time and money undertaking long voyages here. He felt no real kinship for the area and decided to immediately put the plot of land up for sale once the debris had been cleaned up and removed. He also planned to find out if the house had been insured. He was content to make these decisions as his son was a minor and would not have any input in the matter.

#

Marc called Eva at Collan's home repeatedly once he had heard the news of the fire, offering Eva and Angus the use of one of the cottages at Lakeside Inn even though he would only be there himself for another three to four weeks. Eva politely declined his offer, but thanked him for his generosity and vowed to see him before he moved back to Halifax.

#

The last phone call Eva made was to Dr. Talmage's office to make an appointment with him to discuss Elisabet's course of treatment. She also wanted to see her mother for herself even if Elisabet would be sound asleep during the visit.

#

"Asleep and comfortable, I hope?" Eva asked Dr. Talmage the next morning as she stood in the doorway of Elisabet's room at the hospital.

"As comfortable as one can be in that state, Eva. She's been lucky so far to not have any poisonous side effects of the Somnifaine that some patients do suffer from," he replied.

"Such as…?"

"Well, unfortunately, there is a range of issues, but her blood pressure has remained steady; there is no kidney infection; she's not feverish and isn't sweating excessively. One thing that we do monitor at all times is her breathing, to make sure that she hasn't developed a lung infection, like pneumonia."

"Doctor Talmage, I may have asked you this before, but there is so much going on right now, and we've just lost our house to a fire, that my mind is fairly muddled. But, honestly, what are the chances that my mother's mental state will have improved once she's awake after twelve days of being asleep?"

"I heard about the house fire, Eva, and I'm sorry for your loss. It's stressful for you to have to deal with that while having a parent in the hospital," he said. "We've found that in patients like Elisabet who have a psychoneurosis that almost fifty per cent don't undergo a change in their behavior, but twenty per cent showed a marked improvement which is often permanent."

"And the other thirty per cent of cases?"

"I've read in the journals that ten per cent of anxiety-ridden patients have a slight improvement which is maintained, and another twenty per cent relapse soon after treatment."

Eva sighed.

"Her chances of recovery aren't that great, are they, Doctor?"

"Only time will tell, Eva. We'll watch her behavior closely after these first twelve days of narcosis. I'll consult with my colleagues in Halifax and we'll decide if the treatment should be continued for a longer period."

He cleared his throat and appeared to be reticent about continuing the conversation.

"I hate to bring this up, Eva, but the longer your mother is in the hospital, the more expensive this will be for you. She obviously doesn't have a home to go back to, and so the only other option you have would be to commit her to the Nova Scotia Hospital in Dartmouth. When your mother was of sound mind, she'd have been more familiar with its old name, the Mount Hope Lunatic Asylum."

Eva took a long look at her mother. Apart from the natural placement of her arms at her sides above the bedcovers, to a casual observer she could have been dead.

"Once again, Doctor, there's a great deal to think about, and I'll talk with my aunt about this. Let's presume my mother's behavior remains unchanged after treatment. Would she be a safety risk to herself or others if she were to live with her sister?"

Eva was flooded with guilt at the thought that Collan would want to, or feel a duty to, take in her older sister as a permanent houseguest. But if she were to do so, Eva vowed she would do everything she could to get a better-paying job to assist her aunt with the additional expense of having Elisabet live with her and Linnea. She knew she could never share a home with her mother again.

Where will Angus and I live?

She fought to keep her emotions in check in front of the doctor.

"It's difficult to determine that, Eva. My personal psychiatric view is that when a patient has an underlying mental condition, like melancholia, the condition may only be exacerbated with increasing anxiety. Living with her sister may do just that. For example, someone who may be schizophrenic or be exhibiting psychopathic tendencies might become dangerous if his or her anxiety does not improve."

Eva listened carefully, and thought of her father, whom she was desperately missing under the circumstances. She felt transported back to her childhood in Boston and struggled with memories of her thirteen-year-old self who had felt abandoned when her father died so unexpectedly.

Now what do I do?

EIGHTY-SEVEN

Yarmouth, Wednesday, April 10, 1935

The Great Depression was still affecting every facet of life in Canada. Local governments could not afford to financially help the unemployed. The average family in Nova Scotia only received nineteen dollars a month in assistance.

Eva was nervous as she approached *The Yarmouth Courier*'s editor, Basil Doyle, a weary but highly intelligent newsman of seventy-five. She knew the paper's advertising revenues had dropped dramatically in the past six years, but Basil was never one to complain or seem overly worried that his paper wouldn't survive.

He had telephoned her the day before to make sure his story on the fire that destroyed Broadale was factually accurate. He would not have assigned the story to her as the shock of her home's destruction was literally too painful for her, and she would not have been able to write objectively about what had happened.

"Basil, I would like to increase my work hours here, and I can do as much overtime as you want me to," she said.

He looked at her with sympathetic eyes.

"Eva, I'm so sorry you and your son are facing this hardship right now. And I understand your mother is in the hospital, too, so this is clearly not an easy time for you," he said.

Eva explained to him that because her mother's fate was unknown — that she may never recover from her mental illness, and the only option might be to institutionalize her — she didn't know which way to turn to increase her income.

"You know, I was very fortunate in my younger days to have been given this building and basically inherit the newspaper business from my father," Basil said. "And let's just say there has always been a bit of a cushion to fall back on. But unfortunately, I can't increase your hours as I've already done so. I've had to let two of my full-time reporters go, and they sell me individual stories now as freelance writers."

Eva was starting to panic. This was not the outcome she had expected.

"But I do have an idea. James Campbell, the executive editor of the *Halifax Daily Bugle*, owes me a favor from many years ago. The Bugle is owned by one of the wealthiest families in the Maritimes, so it can withstand big drops in advertising dollars," Basil explained.

"That surreptitious visit by Amelia Earhart to Yarmouth for two weeks last September frustrated my friend at the Bugle , because he wanted to get the scoop on why she was here and who hosted her visit. To this day, you're the only reporter in the province who was able to meet her in person, and I proudly told my friend this. Of course, I sent him a copy of the Courier the day after your story ran."

Eva warmed slightly to the compliment and wondered where the conversation was headed.

"It was such a short piece, Basil, and hardly indicative of what I can write."

"I know that, Eva. But do you know what he said? He said, 'Basil, that's the kind of reporter I want working at the Bugle; a real crackerjack who will go out and find the stories about noteworthy people visiting and living in Nova Scotia'."

Basil paused and smiled at his reporter who had impressed a city newspaper editor from afar.

"I think it's time for me to give James a call, Eva. Would you consider moving to Halifax?"

#

Later that day, when Eva, Angus, Collan and Linnea sat down for dinner at Collan's home, Eva was anxious to tell them about her excellent chance at getting a reporter's job – full time — at a daily newspaper in Halifax.

As dishes of food were being passed around the table, Collan said, "Eva, I've been thinking about what Dr. Talmage told you regarding my sister's prognosis. Elisabet is my only remaining sibling, besides Martin, of course, who I might never lay eyes on again unless he does visit sometime in the future. I feel like I should take her in when she leaves the hospital. But what is worrying me is you and Angus finding a decent place to rent in Yarmouth. I am happy to help you financially with a loan, and..."

"And I don't think that'll be necessary, Aunt Collan, but you're a sweetheart for not only suggesting Mama stay here, but also for offering to help me, as well. You see, I'm being considered for a job at the *Halifax Daily Bugle*! In fact, the phone call from my editor to his editor friend in the city has already been made."

Linnea and Collan exclaimed their congratulations, and Angus joined in, jumping off his chair and throwing his arms around his mother's neck.

"Mama, are we moving to *Halliefax*?" he asked, eyes wide. To an eleven-year-old child who had never been out of his hometown, this was a life changing event.

"I think we might do just that," Eva smiled and kissed her son on his cheek. "Now, eat your dinner. We're not moving tonight!" she laughed.

EIGHTY-EIGHT

Yarmouth, Thursday, April 11, 1935

When Eva spoke with Basil the first thing in the morning, she found out he had been speaking with James Campbell, his friend at the Bugle the night before. Campbell wanted Eva to telephone him immediately so he could go over the job contract with her, and explain the terms of employment, particulars about salary, and a starting date.

She was beside herself with excitement and felt a compulsion to visit Seamus's gravesite at Town Point Cemetery — the place where he had kissed her for the first time and where she had wanted him to be laid to rest.

It was a glorious spring day in Yarmouth County. Eva brought Angus with her before dropping him off at school. She knew it could be a long time before her son would again visit his father's grave. Facing the Tusket River, they walked the length of the cemetery and stopped to admire the sculpture of the Marble Lady.

The spring peepers were out in full force at Town Point, and Eva felt that the chorus of small chirping frogs were singing a tribute to a new life for her and Angus. Snowdrops and a few fledgling crocuses were appearing all over the perfectly manicured plots. New beginnings were evident everywhere.

As she expected, Angus was fascinated by the reclining marble woman. Smiling in affection, she touched the head of the statue and motioned for Angus to move on.

As they approached Seamus's gravesite, she wanted to believe that he had been in love with her once, for perhaps four years, from 1920 to the time Angus was born in '24. She chose at that moment to forgive Seamus's shortcomings and tried to understand his lifelong love for her mother. Fate had not been kind to either of them: he was gone forever, and Elisabet might never again live in the present. Health and happiness were not guaranteed for anybody.

She brushed away some dead leaves that had collected around Seamus's headstone.

"Angus, I don't want you to ever forget your father. He loved you, and he was a good and caring doctor who helped many people when they were sick or injured. That's important to remember."

"I know, Mama." Angus looked up at his mother. She seemed older to him lately, and he recognized that the events of the past several years, although not totally understandable to an eleven-year-old, had given his mother a personal maturity and the confidence to change their lives. Squinting in the sunlight, he asked, "So when are we going to move to *Halliefax*?"

Eva laughed and tousled her son's curly hair.

"First you'll have to learn how to pronounce the city's name. It's 'Hal-i-fax', Angus. And right after my Little Man finishes this school year, we'll be off in just a couple of short months on our big adventure. It'll be great fun!"

THE END

The purchase of this e-book or paperback *greatly* supports my personal livelihood. If you enjoyed reading
Unconventional Daughters
please consider writing a short review to spread the word to fellow bibliophiles.Click the link to your Amazon supplier.

Thank you very much for your support,
and I look forward to reading your comments!

Canada: https://www.amazon.ca/review/create-review?&asin=B08N5NKQTQ

USA: https://www.amazon.com/review/create-review?&asin=B08N5NKQTQ

United Kingdom: https://www.amazon.co.uk/review/create-review?&asin=B08N5NKQTQ

Germany: https://www.amazon.de/review/create-review?&asin=B08N5NKQTQ

Italy: https://www.amazon.it/review/create-review?&asin=B08N5NKQTQ

Japan: https://www.amazon.jp/review/create-review?&asin=B08N5NKQTQ

Australia: https://www.amazon.com.au/review/create-review?&asin=B08N5NKQTQ

Please join my mailing list and I'll send you the free e-book,

'Armchair Traveling for Wannabe Wanderers'

– a PDF compilation of some of my favorite travel articles since 1998 –

Go to http://www.brucebishopauthor.com

Follow me on Facebook:
http://www.facebook.com/bbishop.writer
On Twitter:
http://www.twitter.com/Bruce_W_Bishop
On Instagram:
http://www.instagram.com/bruceinhali

DEDICATION

To my parents, Camilla & Bill Bishop,
who always encouraged me to pursue my dreams.

ACKNOWLEDGEMENTS

I am indebted to author and publisher *Jamie Campbell*, and principal
editor *Maureen Bishop Freeman* for spending a great deal of time
helping me find my way with the production of this novel.
I'm also grateful to the 'early believers': Greg Bishop, Pauline Cann, Jude
Carson, Pamela Delaney, Judy Eberspaecher, Vernon O'Reilly-Ramesar,
Carol Stief, and Deborah Tobin.
Thanks also to Anita Bain, Alice Robbins, archivist Lisette Gaudet and
author Sharon Robart-Johnson.

AUTHOR'S NOTE

When I was a teenager living in Yarmouth, N.S., I acquired four handwritten letters from 1927 that were written by a young lady in Nova Scotia on her honeymoon in Europe. She had married her stepfather. They piqued my interest enough that I kept them, and it wasn't until the COVID-19 lockdown in March 2020 that I decided a story could be written around this odd marriage (and I had the time to do so!), almost 100 years after it had happened.

All the characters and events portrayed in this book are fictitious or are used fictitiously. Apart from well-known historical figures, any similarity to real persons, living or dead, is purely coincidental and not intended by the author. The real historical figures' actions in the book are obviously fictitious, including any dialogue. (Although Amelia Earhart really did visit Wedgeport, N.S. for sport tuna fishing in the 1930s!)

Canada

Major historical events such as the Halifax Explosion and the Spanish Flu did occur on the dates provided in the novel, and statistics regarding the same have been verified. There was an actual incident in March 1915 when two warning shells were fired from the army battery on McNab's Island in an attempt to stop a steamer from entering the harbor.

The Lord Nelson Hotel and *The Nova Scotian Hotel* in Halifax exist and are open, the former under the same name, and the latter as the *Westin Nova Scotian*. The Halifax Commerce Club does *not* exist, but the historic Saint Paul's Church does exist.

The original *Grand Hotel* in Yarmouth was demolished in the 1960s, was re-built, and is now known as the *Rodd Grand*.

Lakeside Inn and Cottages operated as a Canadian Pacific Railway hotel for many years, but was sold in 1960, and re-opened as a nursing home, *Villa St-Joseph du Lac*.

The Markland Hotel on Cape Forchu opened in 1904, but closed in 1925 due to lack of business following the Great War.

Braemar Lodge in Yarmouth County no longer exists, and the area is private property.

The Anchorage, Captain Aaron Churchill's summer home, still stands, and is privately owned. *Murray Manor* in Yarmouth also exists, and at the time of publication, was for sale.

The original *Cape Forchu Lightstation* outside of Yarmouth was demolished, and re-built in the early 1960s. The community of Overton is real as are *Town Point Cemetery,* the 'Marble Lady', and *Mountain Cemetery*.

Port Maitland Beach is a Nova Scotia Provincial Park and continues to be a popular summertime destination.

"Broadale" is fictitious, as is St. Paul's Anglican Church in Yarmouth.

The "Dumdums Canadian Army Fourth Division Concert Party" was inspired by *The Dumbells Concert Party* that became, after the Armistice, a leading Canadian vaudeville troupe. It was formed in 1917 near Vimy Ridge, France by ten members of the Canadian army's Third Division, including one serviceman from Pugwash, Nova Scotia.

Outside of Canada

Two historic hotels mentioned in the novel (*Hotel Royal* in Gothenburg and *The Grand Hotel Royal* in Stockholm) continue to welcome guests over a century after they were first opened.

Tjoloholm Castle near Gothenburg, also referred to as a manor house, was built between 1898 and 1904, and currently offers hotel rooms and food and beverage facilities.

The waterfront pub in Gothenburg, *Den Törstiga Kråkan* (The Thirsty Crow) is fictitious.

Today's *Royal Swedish Opera House* was named *Kungliga Teatern* (The Royal Theatre) at the turn of the 20th century, and would have been so named in 1915.

The Boston Opera House was an opera house located on Huntington Avenue that opened in 1909 as the home of the *Boston Opera Company*. It was demolished in 1958 after years of disuse.

The Parker House Hotel in downtown Boston has been open since 1855 and is now the *Omni Parker House.*

The names of the ocean liners that crossed the Atlantic that are mentioned in the book were actual passenger vessels that sailed between Europe and North America (as were the steamships sailing between Yarmouth and Boston).

In 1911, two Swedish automotive companies were merged to create *Scania-Vabis*, which today is known as *Scania AB.*

The names of newspapers from Sweden, Nova Scotia and Boston are either fictitious, real (but have ceased publication), or are still in operation.

Allmänna Barnhuset (the Public or General Children's Home), was Sweden's largest orphanage. It was founded 1633 in Stockholm and remained active until 1922.

#

At the time of this writing, thirty countries around the world (of 206 sovereign states), including Canada, Sweden, and the United States, recognize same-sex marriage.

Manufactured by Amazon.ca
Bolton, ON